THE 13th LETTER

The Mesdames and Messieurs of Mayhem

The 13th Letter

by the *Mesdames and Messieurs of Mayhem*

CARRICK
PUBLISHING

Project manager: M.H. Callway,
Editor: Donna Carrick
Cover Art and Design: Sara Carrick

Paperback Edition 2024
ISBN 13: 978-1-77242-197-2

Praise for In the Key of 13

"Sometimes I rooted for the murderer and sometimes cringed at the deed–but loved this book."

~Reader review, M.M. Bishop

Praise for Thirteen

"A book full of great stories that make you sorry when it's finished."

~Reader review, Marg

"A great collection of "crime" fiction that has what one expects with strong characterizations, inventive and clever endings—plus real, emotionally complex situations…"

~Reader review, Doncan Armstrong

Contents

In memory of:

Author Rosemary Aubert,
wife, sister, friend, author, mentor, teacher.
With love and deepest respect.

FOREWORD

Welcome Readers!

M, the thirteenth letter of the alphabet. It begins so many wicked words: malice, Machiavelli, malfeasance, and *murder*. But M does have its lighter side. It also heads up mischief, melody, misadventure—even madcap! And, of course, the ***M**esdames and **M**essieurs of **M**ayhem.*

And so we embraced "M", the thirteenth letter of the alphabet, as the theme for our sixth anthology. After all, thirteen is our lucky number! Our 22 authors have let loose their wild imaginations to create their deviously crafted tales, using "M" or literally, a thirteenth letter, as their inspiration. Most of our stories are light-hearted to counter our troubled times, but fair warning: a few shade into noir.

We hope you enjoy all the stories and remember: *M is for Mesdames, Messieurs, mystery…and murder!*

On a sadder note, earlier this year, Rosemary Aubert, one of our founding members, passed away after a lengthy illness. She wasn't always a crime writer. She began her writing journey as an accomplished poet, but to earn a living, she turned to the romance genre, working as an editor for many years and later publishing several novels of her own. Always up for a challenge, she drew on her Italian heritage to write her first crime story, "The Midnight Boat to Palermo." It won the Crime Writers of Canada Award for Best Short Story—and a leading crime fiction author was born!

Rosemary went on to create the popular award-winning series of *Ellis Portal* thrillers. She became a sought-after speaker and beloved teacher of creative writing; many of her students went on to be published and to win awards themselves. Incredibly generous, she remained unfailingly supportive of her fellow authors and a true warrior against life's adversities. We miss her terribly and in honor and friendship, we dedicate *The 13th Letter* to her memory.

M. H. Callway
Co-founder of the Mesdames and Messieurs of Mayhem

THE MIDNIGHT BOAT TO PALERMO

By Rosemary Aubert

What I loved most about meeting the midnight boat was not the motion of the waves, though I often thought the movement of the sea made it easier to sleep than the stillness of my bed. Nor was it the moonlight that I loved, for I was afraid of moonlight and am to this day. Many of the women in our self-help group speak of their fear of moonlight. Sometimes they connect it to abusive fathers or to their general terror of night. I loved my father, and he never abused me in the way some of these women have been abused. But like them, talking now about my youth, I have stirred up a memory that I had buried long ago—forty years, in fact. I have suddenly understood that my father was murdered. I have suddenly remembered that I was there when he was killed. I have suddenly realized the name of his killer.

What I loved most about the midnight boat to Palermo was the silence. For my world, both then and now, has been a very noisy one. When I first came to this country, though I could not speak the language, I knew already that I spoke too loudly. How else could it be? There were, after all, seven of us, and we lived in a tiny hut on the shore of the inlet. We didn't call it an inlet, of course. That's a word I learned much later—in a writing class sponsored by the government. But an inlet it was, a little indentation in the rocks of the shore of Sicily. And when you spoke, if you were to be heard at all, you had to shout not only above the sound of all the brothers and sisters, not only above the arguing of my parents, but above the sound of the sea. That's what we called it. Not an inlet, the sea.

Like most of the people of our village, we were not rich. But we had plenty to eat and good clothes to wear, even though the Second World War had been over for only a few years. Twice a year, my mother would go to Rome and buy me and my sisters dresses, blouses with lace, shoes to wear to church on Sunday. Looking back on it now, it amazes me that we never questioned such extravagance. Nor did I question my mother's attitude about these trips. For weeks before, she'd be so sweet to us, so kind. Instead of her usual severity, she'd be almost gay. Though she said she hated to leave us, it was hard to ignore her happiness, just as when she returned, it was hard to ignore how angry she seemed to be for weeks. My mother, I thought then, was an unpredictable woman. But now I see, after all these years, she was far more predictable than I could have imagined.

When my mother was home, which was most of the time, she was a good mother. She sewed, she cleaned, and she made a tomato sauce that was famous in our little village. To this day, I can see her standing at the stove preparing it. She would start by heating a huge black iron pan and carefully dripping onto its hot surface a thin dribble of the purest olive oil. Then she would take a bud of garlic and, carefully separating out each clove, would peel it with her slow, strong hands. When the heated oil had turned the garlic as golden as itself, she would add pieces of beef. This meat, too, would soon turn a golden color, filling our little house with its aroma. When the meat was done, she would add the tomato paste. It has been more than forty years since I have seen these things, but I remember as if I were standing there now how she would go to a little pantry off our kitchen, a place that was always cold, no matter the time of year, and from one of its shelves, would take an earthenware crock of tomato paste. This paste had been dried in the sun by her own grandmother, and it was almost black. Of course, I used to think it looked like poison. Yet even then I understood that the tomato paste made the sauce rich and thick and gave it such a deep flavor that it seemed to have been cooked forever. However, when she added this ingredient, my mother had to be very careful. If she added too much, or if she didn't cook it until it, too, was almost golden, the sauce would be bitter—a failure. After the tomato paste, the only other ingredient she added was fresh tomatoes. And one other thing—the secret. When the sauce had cooked for two hours, my mother would add a little cupful of sugar. It was my job to bring her the sugar from a cupboard across the kitchen, and I would sneak a taste for myself before I got to her side. When she caught me doing this, she would laugh.

Thursday was the day she made sauce. And Thursday was the night that it was my father's turn to meet the midnight boat to Palermo. I always thought that my father died on a Friday, but now I understand that was too simple a way to look at things. He was found dead on a Friday. He was killed on Thursday—the Thursday we, he and I, like always, were supposed to meet the Palermo boat but didn't.

My father, and all the other men in the village, worked in the sugar factory. Being only eight years old, I thought the factory had been there forever. Now I see that was wrong. It could only have been set up after the war, when I was two or three. When I was little, though, the sugar factory was one of the centers of my life. Though my own children seemed to spend all their time in school when they were eight years old, I certainly did not. There was only one teacher, an old woman whose son had gone away and never come back and who could speak of little else, even when she was supposed to be teaching us math or the history of the rulers of Sicily. It was easy to slip out of school—or not to go at all, which was what I often did. The minute I was free, I headed for the factory.

Now it is very important for me to explain that I did not go to the factory to eat the sugar. The mysterious thing about the factory was that nobody was ever allowed to eat the sugar there. Zi Antonio had forbidden it. Anyone who so much as tasted the tiniest bit would have to leave their work—forever. Zi Antonio was the mayor of our little village, though that word—mayor—is another that we never used, that I never even learned until I came here. My father told me that Zi Antonio said it was bad business to eat your own product, that that was how people lost money, that it showed a lack of respect.

I had another way of looking at it, and it was one of the reasons that I visited the sugar factory so often. In order for this to make sense, I have to describe how the sugar factory looked. Though now that I finally know what I'm *really* describing, I must admit that this might not at all have been how the factory was—just how it looked to me when I was eight years old.

Unlike any other building in our village, the factory was built of some clean, smooth material—concrete, I'd say. And it had no windows. The only way you could see inside was if you stood by the wide rear door, which I often did.

The roof of the factory was covered in pipes, sticking up toward the sky. Sometimes steam shot up from them like a volcano. When this happened, it scared me and I ran away. But I always came back.

The only times I ever stayed away for long were the few times that Zi Antonio, himself, chased me. He hardly ever came to the sugar factory, though he seemed to be everywhere else in town, including our house. As I recall, the first time he caught me, I was merely wandering about the factory yard. Out there were piles and piles of barrels just like the ones we got when we met the Palermo boat. He caught me completely by surprise. I was leaning over a row of barrels, thumping them, the way I'd seen my mother thump an eggplant to see if it was ripe. I'd just about decided that the barrels were empty, when I heard a shout close behind me. I jumped a mile. Zi Antonio towered over me like the picture of the ogre in the storybook my cousin Teresa had sent me from America. I started to cry.

Now I have to say about Zi Antonio that he always treated me and my brothers and sisters very well. "No, no, no," he said simply and shooed me away.

The second time he caught me, I was doing the same thing. The barrels seemed empty that time, too. The third time Zi Antonio said that if I continued to play there, my father would lose his job.

What I was really trying to figure out was whether the sugar in the factory was poison and whether something the men did to it made it not be poison anymore, so that when it left the factory we could eat it.

Everybody knew that Zi Antonio was the boss of the factory. We knew also that he was a special friend of the old woman who was our teacher. We knew, too, that Zi Antonio was somehow in charge of the parish church, though we assumed that must only be when the priest wasn't praying or doing holy things. Zi Antonio, for instance, was in charge of charity—being a very generous man. He was also always present at funerals, consoling the mother and the widow.

Zi Antonio was also a special friend of my mother. It was because of him, I always thought, that she took such care every Thursday when she made the sauce, for he was always our dinner guest on that night.

It was regular as the clock. All afternoon my mother would cook the sauce while my father worked at the factory. Zi Antonio would arrive. My father, being a quiet man, would say very little at the table, but Zi Antonio was funny, and his jokes kept us in stitches.

I ate faster than the others because I had to get ready to go with my father to meet the Palermo boat. I packed us a lunch. I got our sweaters and blankets. And I filled the lantern we needed to signal the big boat and let the sailors see what they were doing when they lowered the barrels into our boat.

Once in a while, a wind would arise, or the open boat would be slashed by rain, but my trust in my father was absolute. I see now that what I was doing with him was the most dangerous thing I've ever done, but I felt safer then than I have ever felt since.

I would ask him to tell me his stories of the sea, and he always did. He knew about pirates, about explorers, about the sacred missionaries of the Church.

As we pulled away from the beach behind the sugar factory, the sun would be low over the water. I would lie against the pile of blankets as my father rowed slowly away from the village. As the last thing to fade from sight—the chimneys of the sugar factory—slipped away, the rocking of the boat would start to get to me. I would doze off. Often, the next thing I knew, I would be lying on the boat bottom staring straight up toward the stars.

Nothing in my life since has ever equaled the peace of those voyages. It seemed we drifted out there for hours. In the silence of the night, I asked my father what was in the barrels that we took from the Palermo ship into our own. He smiled and said that it was a syrup from far away, that it was needed in order to make sugar. Sugar cane? I asked him. But his eyes were trained on the water, and he didn't answer.

I also asked him why nobody at the sugar factory could eat the sugar. This was a trick question. I knew, as all children do, that sometimes if you ask a question over and over again, the answer that has always been the same answer, can slip into a different answer—the truth. But he said, as he always did, that it was bad business, that it showed a lack of respect and that all the sugar in the factory belonged to Zi Antonio.

He said that Zi Antonio was the boss of the sugar factory but that he, too, had his own bosses and no matter how you lived your life, there was always somebody who had the power to tell you what to do. I didn't know what he was talking about.

I asked him why we had to wait so long. This he had explained again and again. He said that the boat to Palermo had left a country called Turkey, that when a ship was at sea, the wind could speed it or slow it, that the waves could be so high that the boat had twice as far to go—up one side, down the other. I laughed at his joke and, huddled in my warm sweater, settled back to enjoy the sandwiches I had made for us.

Often, when the boat did come, I'd be asleep, and sometimes I only woke up when I heard the shouts and saw the barrels being lowered down. Then I would fall asleep again and not wake up until our little boat reached the shore. I would crawl out onto the sand and wait there as my father rolled the barrels up into the yard of the factory. Then, he would take my hand and lead me along the path that went to our house. We'd tiptoe in, and he would tuck me into bed. Usually, I was fast asleep before my door even closed, my sisters breathing silently beside me.

My memory of those nights is so vivid and complete that I remember every detail of the night that was different—the night my father was killed.

For some time before that, the arguing of my parents had been often and loud. They'd always argued, but never so much or so violently. One Thursday, my father came home from work in the middle of the afternoon. He looked different—angry and even scared. He told my mother that the sugar factory was about to close. Then, he started to drink wine. Usually, he had a little wine with his supper, but this day, he started drinking in the afternoon, which I had never seen before.

As always, my mother was cooking the sauce for supper. Despite the troubles of my father and the fact that she was fighting with him, her hands were sure as she dropped the meat into the sizzling oil. When he realized that she was making Thursday dinner as if nothing had happened at the sugar factory, he started to yell at her. How could she have Zi Antonio for dinner when he was about to ruin them all? She said Zi Antonio had nothing to do with whether the factory stayed open or closed. I had no idea what any of this meant. I was waiting for my mother to add sugar to the sauce. My father grew more and more angry. Then he stormed out of the kitchen. I ran after him, but he slammed out of the house. When I went back to the kitchen, I saw that my mother had the little cup of sugar resting on the cupboard. I stepped up, stuck out my finger and reached up to coat it with sugar. To my amazement, my mother slapped my hand so hard that I hit it on the edge of the cupboard and cut it. She didn't even offer to help me. She told me to get out, to wash it off, and to come right back. I did everything she said. A little later, my father came back and went into my parents' room, where he remained.

Zi Antonio did come for supper that night, but there were no jokes. He wasn't even hungry. All we ate was salad, cheese and bread. He and my mother whispered as we all sat at the table. I thought they were whispering to keep from waking my father who had fallen asleep after drinking all that wine. I kept waiting for my father to wake up, for us to go out to the boat. But every time I tried to get up from the table, my mother told me to sit down.

After a long time, my father did wake up, but I knew it was too late for us to go out. It was already dark. My mother now seemed a lot less angry than she'd been. She had even put aside some sauce for my father, and she cooked him macaroni and ladled the sauce onto it. He, too, must have been over his anger, because I could see how hungry he was. He ate it all. Then he went back into the room he shared with my mother, stretched out across the bed and fell back to sleep.

I was heartbroken. All day I'd thought about our trip out to the Palermo boat, and now, clearly, we weren't going. I went to bed myself.

But I had a hard time sleeping. In the middle of the night, I got up to ask my parents if I could get in bed with them until I fell asleep. I crept down the hall. Their door was open, and I looked in. They were lying side by side. A broad ray of moonlight fell straight across my father's face. He had told me again and again that it was bad luck to sleep in the moonlight. Here he was, sound asleep, completely unprotected from the moon. But even more disturbing was the sight of my mother. The moonlight fell on her face, too. She was not asleep. Her eyes were wide open, staring straight up and full of tears that fell down her face, sparkling like diamonds in the pale light.

I knew then that she was sorry they had fought. I knew, too, that their room was no place for me. I went back to my own room and fell asleep.

Things happened very fast after that. The next day, my father couldn't wake up. The doctor came. Then the priest. He was dead before either got there. They said it was the shock of knowing that the factory was going to close. They said he must always have had a weak heart. They said it was such a shame—a man in his thirties with five children….

Zi Antonio saved us. He told my mother that he would look after us all. He said that his bosses had decided to send him to Canada. He said we could all go with him. My mother wore black clothes all the way to Canada. We had stopped in Rome to get them.

After we got to the new country, our lives settled down. It was strange at first to have Zi Antonio with us every day, instead of one day a week. It was strange to have a father—he and my mother soon married—who worked in an office every day instead of a factory. And it was strange to live in a real city instead of a village. But there were so many good things—the school, the museum, the parks, the friends. Before long, I forgot about Sicily. I never, of course, forgot about my father. But it hurt to think of him dying at such a young age. He had been my friend. Now I had other friends. And after a while, I hardly thought about him at all.

Zi Antonio offered to send me to university, but I was rebellious. When I left school, I, like my father, went to work in a factory. It was clean work. If you paid attention and worked quickly, you could make good money. I started at the machines, sewing pajamas. I soon moved up to hand-stitching dresses, and then, I became one of the senior women. At the time I left, I had been making the finest wedding gowns, beading lace that cost five hundred dollars per meter.

After many years, the orders started to fall off because of the dresses from China. One by one the women had to be let go. Finally, there were only four of us left—the wedding women. Every day for two years, I had gone in thinking it would be my last day, and one day it was. The boss was crying. She didn't even have the money to give us a settlement. The last thing she did was pay the wages she owed us. That was it.

Except for the counsellor. The boss gave a little speech about how the government had provided counselling for us all. We could learn to write resumes. We could explore retraining. We could learn creative writing—to get in touch with our inner selves, she said.

What could my resume say? That I had been sewing for thirty years? For what could I retrain? And I had already taken a writing course from the government.

The only program left was "Looking into Ourselves." So it was this workshop that I signed up for, this workshop in which I discovered the secret I had been keeping from my "inner self" all my life.

It happened so simply and so suddenly. I went to the community center where the workshop was to be held. At first everyone was nervous and embarrassed. But it was all women and pretty soon we started to chat. As the weeks went by, I started to feel comfortable talking to the women in the group, who ranged in age from a little younger than me to a little older.

One night, there were some young women there—all sitting together and so pretty, the way my mother was the day she left our village to come to Canada with my stepfather.

One of these girls told us that she went to a different group every night in order to never have to spend an evening alone. The silence was total as she told us in a shaky voice that she had been a drug addict.

Now of course, for women my age, to have a granddaughter on drugs is the ultimate terror. I had even gone to a lecture once about all the different drugs and the history of where they came from, sponsored by the police.

The girl spoke only a little—laughing and crying as she told us about herself. What she said was that the first time she ever saw heroin, it looked just like sugar. That it sparkled and she had put out her finger and taken a little and tasted it, expecting it to be sweet, but it was bitter. And that should have told her all she needed to know.

I saw it then. I saw the whole thing. I saw my father lifting up his arms to receive the barrels of opium from Turkey—just like the police told us about. I saw the factory with its frightening pipes and its strange white product that no one was allowed to eat. I saw Zi Antonio with his fine suits, with the respect, the fear of everyone in our village. And I saw my mother slipping a silk blouse out of a shiny paper bag from Rome.

I picked up my coat and my purse and I walked out of the center and all the way home.

But even then, I had only figured out part of it. It took me until far into the night before I realized what Zi Antonio and my mother were doing every Thursday night. And then, most cruelly of all, I remembered my mother's sharp anger the day I watched her put the secret ingredient into her famous sauce. The day I reached out my finger to taste the sugar as I had done so many times before.

I was sick the next day. All day I dreamed about my childhood. By the time my husband came home, I could no longer tell what was a dream and what was reality.

Perhaps next week, I'll return to the group. I'll tell them I'm still depressed about losing my job, that I feel tired all the time, that I'm afraid a woman my age can never find work again. But I'll never speak about my mother. To whom would I tell her story and why? From the day we came to Canada, we lived a law-abiding life. We went to school, then we worked, then we married and sent our own children to school. Zi Antonio died, and so did my mother. My children have never much wanted to know about the old country.

No, I am the only one remaining who knows the secret of Zi Antonio and my mother. The night I looked in and saw my father so very still that the moonlight on his face could not wake him, I took this secret to myself, without even knowing. Now, because of a few troubled words, I do know. But the secret stays with me. It floats in my mind, detached from all else, the way our little boat floated—a small speck on the waters that lapped the shore of our tiny village, spilled onward toward the bay of Palermo, crossed the Mediterranean, then slipped out to the real sea.

The 13th Letter

M

The End

About the Author

After a successful career as an internationally published romance writer, Rosemary Aubert turned to the world of crime, graduating with a Certificate of Criminology from the University of Toronto and publishing the six-volume award-winning, Ellis Portal mystery series. Rosemary also worked in the real world of crime. She was a security officer at the United States Consulate. She ran the office of a half-way house for men leaving the federal prison system. She served as a Community Relations director assisting women coming out of the prison system. And for ten years, she was a bailiff in the criminal courts.

These experiences introduced Rosemary to a wide variety of people—innocent and guilty, dangerous and safe. These denizens of the real world of crime inspired the characters that inhabit "The Midnight Boat to Palermo."

Born in Niagara Falls, New York, Rosemary has long made her home in Toronto, where she has worked as a university instructor, an editor and a bookstore clerk and of course—a writer.

This book is dedicated to the memory of our dear friend, mentor and inspiration, author Rosemary Aubert.

M IS FOR MOOLAH

By Melodie Campbell

A phone was ringing. Damn, it was loud. How was a person supposed to sleep when …?

Crap! I forced my groggy brain to listen for the ring tone. Not my fiancé Pete. He was *My Guy*. Not my Uncle Vince. That would be *The Godfather* theme, for obvious reasons.

I listened more carefully. *The Pink Panther*. That would be Nico. I reached for the phone on the bedside table, then clicked it on.

"It's not even nine," I grumbled. "On a Sunday!"

"Have you heard about Uncle Tony, Gina?"

"Which one?" I said, with no sarcasm intended, surprisingly. There's a well-known saying that you're not really Italian unless you have at least two uncles named Tony. We have three, and a cousin.

"Bova, silly. Great Uncle Bova. He gets out this morning."

"Huh?" I'm never good before my starter coffee.

"Hospital, not Sing-Sing. They're letting him go home from Emerg. Didn't you hear?"

"Hear what?"

"Yesterday. Actually, late Friday after midnight. Poor bugger got up to pee, thought he heard something and fell down the stairs. Bonked himself on the head."

He was already bonkers, I nearly said. But my guardian angel caught me in time. Which surprised me, because she's been missing in action for a while.

"Poor Uncle Tony!" I said instead. No, I hadn't heard. I'd been on a day trip to Niagara Falls with Pete, and as far away from family as I could get. One whole blissful day away without getting in touch.

"Aunt Alma called a few minutes ago. She just got Tony home and discovered his house had been ransacked overnight. She wants us there. Pick you up in an hour." Nico clicked off.

Aunt Alma. Oh, brother. Or rather, Oh, sister. I actually felt sorry for Tony, having a sister like her. Hell, I'd feel sorry for Satan.

I moaned and sat up. That's when I remembered that Pete wouldn't have been calling me anyway. This was because he was on the other side of the bed.

"Who was that?" His voice was thick and groggy.

"Nico," I said, pulling myself out of bed. "We have to get up. Things have happened."

"When have they not?" he groaned.

***

Nico was long and lean, with bleached blond hair and a curious habit of dressing in wild parrot colors. Which is to say, he was unique. Coincidentally, he was my favorite cousin.

Nico had been the family B&E expert for as long as I can remember. But recently, he'd gotten hooked on interior decorating. A little while back, we actually caught him breaking into people's homes just to rearrange their furniture. I convinced him this was not a good hobby, and he recently hung up his Lone Rearranger night activities to become a legitimate staging consultant for the real estate trade. More on that in another book.

We go way back… approximately 32 years back, as we were born in the same year to sisters. I was a few weeks older and probably none the wiser. Nico has gotten me out of more than one jam. Needless to say, I have a lot of time for the goof.

We piled into Nico's VW Beetle and were on our way across town. Nico drove in the manner I had come to expect…like there was a posse of turtles after us. I try not to get frustrated.

"Here's what I don't get," Pete said from the back seat. The *whole* back seat. As a former NFL quarterback, he was a big guy and had to sit crossways to fit. "What did this poor fellow have that was worth stealing?"

It was a reasonable question. Tony Bova was in his 80s. He lived in a low-rent area of Hamilton, also known as The Hammer. Our skyline includes steel plants. We consider smog a condiment.

The house was older than he was. People who live in run-down houses usually don't have a lot of jewelry and expensive electronics to steal. To boot, he was widely known as a cheapskate. So why burgle his house?

"That's obvious. Money," said Nico. "He was a bookie. It's a cash business. You remember, don't you, Gina?"

"Right," I said. Nice, that my brain was finally working. "And he didn't trust banks." This was probably because the family had a habit of robbing them.

Nico nodded beside me and shifted gears. "Remember how he used to keep his moolah in a shoe box, and dole us out a buck or two when we kids visited?"

"Buck? I remember a quarter." The guy was an utter skinflint.

"True," said Nico.

Oops. Did I say that last bit out loud?

"I used to accuse Mario of picking my pockets when we were kids. But now that I think of it," Nico shifted again, "it only happened at Uncle Tony's. Sonovabitch."

I grunted in agreement. You had to be a twisted type of no-good weasel to steal from family. Not to mention, it might be a mortal sin.

There was no need to do so, either. The man made a good living, peddling odds. My uncle was uncommonly good at it, a whiz at calculations on the fly. And as he was allergic to spending the proceeds…

"He must have a lot of shoe boxes by now," I said thoughtfully.

We arrived at the Victorian clapboard house to find Aunt Alma standing in the foyer with something menacing in her hand.

It's hard to miss Aunt Alma. She stands about four foot nine and has a similar diameter. I have a lot of aunts. She isn't one of my favorites. Suffice it to say, if there's something that needs improving, Alma will point it out.

"Look at this place!" she said, gesturing at the mess in the parlor. "They trashed it! Cupboards opened and emptied. Cushions upturned. Books—all those lovely books thrown onto the floor. And the kitchen! What they did to the kitchen! Canisters dumped over. You can't walk in there without trailing flour and sugar and Gawd knows what else. It's criminal! It's BEYOND criminal!" Which made all the difference, because being merely criminal was hardly an indictment in this family.

Alma was just getting started. I have to say, she had a point. You could hardly tell what the place might have looked like before the trashing. In the past, Nico had tried to describe it, playing with décor styles like "Early student housing" or "Depression chic." But all that was lost now.

Alma waved a butcher knife at the three of us. Nico and I backed up quietly.

"Bastards!" She gave a long, heartfelt sob. "Tracking flour all over the place. Not even bothering to take off their shoes! Where were they born—in a barn? There should be a special ring of hell for all men. Careless, thoughtless, the lot of you." She spit the words through her teeth.

"Men?" said Pete. "How do you know—?"

"OF COURSE IT'S MEN!" she yelled at his face. "No woman would ever be so reckless! Because who's going to clean it up, do ya think? WHO? Some snot-faced punk, that couldn't even cook his own breakfast? Not bloody likely. Animals, they are! Worse than animals."

"Maybe they were in a hurry?" Nico ventured.

"And maybe I should cut off their tails with a carving knife!" Alma threatened. "And by tails, I mean something else! When I catch the punks who did this…"

She left it unsaid, which was probably just as well. The two men I arrived with were engaged in panic breathing.

I figured it was time to change the mood. "You can put the knife down now," I suggested.

Alma stared at the thing in her hand, then plunked it down on the small hall table with a shrug.

Well, thank God for that. We didn't need another crime added to the mix.

"Where's Uncle Tony?" I asked cheerfully.

Her breathing calmed down at that. "He's in the bedroom. Didn't break any arms or legs, falling down the stairs. Just got banged and bruised, and smucked his noggin. The doctors worried about concussion; that's why they kept him in."

"So good to hear he wasn't badly hurt." I tried to sound sympathetic.

"Luckily, I had one of those adjustable beds delivered here late last night." She clucked in satisfaction. "His old mattress was disgusting, lumpy, and probably flea infested. But would he do anything about it? No way, the old cheapskate, so I had to take over, like I always do. I called in a few favors, and here we are. It pays to know people." She sounded triumphant.

Yes, I understood that she was acting in her younger brother's best interests. Still, the poor guy had been stuck in hospital. She took an unnatural glee in being able to manage his affairs when he couldn't do anything to stop her. Man, I don't like women who get all smug and controlling.

I pointed to the stairs, and she nodded. We all tromped up the steep wooden steps, in a procession. Tony wouldn't part with good cash for carpet runners, of course.

The bedroom was straight in front of us, on the other side of the small landing, which explained how they were able to get the new bed up there. No turns. I entered first.

With the top of the bed sloping up, Great Uncle Tony looked a mite wee and scrawny. Ancient, even. I actually felt sorry for the poor bugger.

I went to stand right beside him. "I'm so glad you weren't badly hurt falling down those nasty stairs, Uncle Tony. And no broken bones. I mean, what are the chances?"

"Three to one," came a mumble from the bed. He opened one eye and grabbed my arm. His voice was raspy and weak. At first, I couldn't make out the words, but he repeated them, and it sounded like, "Bed. Where's bed?"

"You're already in bed, Uncle Tony." I tried to say it soothingly. No question, his head had been whacked. Poor guy was all mixed up.

The grip on my arm was surprisingly strong. "No! The old—" He mumbled a few more words that I couldn't understand.

I turned to my cousin. "Nico, can you make out what he's trying to say?"

Nico came to my side and Tony released his grip on my arm. I moved out of the way. Both scrawny hands reached up to pull Nico down toward him. The voice that came out was almost painful to listen to, raspy whispers gasping for air.

When Nico came up, he turned to Aunt Alma. "He wants to know where the old mattress is."

"That old thing!" she said dismissively. "It was a health hazard. I told Mario to take it to the dump this very morning. He should be back soon."

Mario was another cousin, about my age and short on brains. I didn't have a good history with Mario.

"But does Tony appreciate it?" Aunt Alma continued. "No, not him. All this work I do to keep him safe, and he doesn't appreciate a thing. I don't know why I bother. I—"

Weird sounds were coming from the bed. Choking, growling, I don't know quite what to call it. But what I can report is that Uncle Tony's face had gone a scary shade of claret.

And that's when I figured it out.

"Oh no!" I cried. "The mattress. They got the shoe box, but they didn't know about the mattress!"

"Didn't know what?" said Aunt Alma.

I looked around at the blank faces. And then I turned to Uncle Tony who appeared to be having what might best be described as a…conniption.

"You told Mario to take the mattress away!" I said to Alma. "Eye-yi-yi-yi-yi!" I spun around in a circle holding my head.

"Truly, I don't understand you, Gina," said Alma. "It was a lumpy old thing—"

And then the impossible happened. Uncle Tony, who could barely roll over, stood right up in the bed and launched himself at her.

"Interfering old poop!" he yelled.

Everyone screamed as brother and sister hit the floor in one muddle of bedclothes, aprons, flailing arms and blue language.

"He's gone mad!" cried Alma, scrambling to her feet and making for the stairs. Then Tony—old Uncle Tony who couldn't spell the word spry, let alone demonstrate it—was off the floor like an Olympic athlete and hot on her tail.

We followed them out to the landing. Alma had reached the bottom step when the 'thing' happened. Maybe it was the way his pajama leg hung loosely over the front of his foot. Maybe it was just that the post-mattress revelation adrenalin rush had petered out.

Whoops! Down the stairs Tony tumbled—no wait, it was more like a toddle—for the second time in three days, hitting every step neatly on the way down. It was like watching a slow-motion movie reel.

"Just like Tim Conway on the Carol Burnett show," Pete admired.

He rolled leisurely to the bottom—truly, it was painstaking. Pregnant sloths have been known to travel faster. And then…silence. Even Alma had stopped caterwauling. I raced down the stairs, with the others following me.

Great Uncle Tony lay in soft heap, a fetal position, with his eyes closed. I crept closer and peered down. No limbs appeared to be bent in awkward positions. It was almost as if he were sleeping peacefully.

"Is he dead?" Nico was right behind me, with his fingers in front of his face, peering between them.

Pete, who was accustomed to players being knocked out on the field, stooped down to do the wrist test. "Nope. Still beating."

"Someone call an ambulance," said Alma half-heartedly.

Nobody reached for their cell.

"What about the police?" said Pete.

"NO!" yelled Nico and Alma in unison.

Man, it was loud in here. I needed to think. So I sat on the bottom step and fell into a world of my own. Mumbling went on around me, but I blocked it out. I sat there for several moments, assembling the jigsaw puzzle pieces in my mind, until a voice cut through the fog.

"So, you're saying Tony was hiding money in the mattress?" Pete said to me.

I shrugged my shoulders. "That's what I figure. When the shoe box got filled, he'd make a slit in the side of the mattress, stuff in the dough, and sew it up. Hence the lumps. Then he'd start over again with the shoe box."

Someone whimpered. I think it was Tony. I poked him with the toe of my shoe, in sympathy.

"Wait a minute. That's it! Holy cannoli," I said, slapping my palm to my forehead. "It has to be family."

"What has to be family?" Nico appeared to be shivering.

"The thieves who broke in last night." I shot to my feet. "Who outside the family would know that Uncle Tony didn't use banks? And who but family would know that he fell down the stairs?" I used my arms for punctuation. "The thieves who tore up this place figured the moolah would be in the house somewhere. Years and years of savings. It wasn't a coincidence. They took advantage of last night, because the family grapevine spilled about Tony being in hospital and they assumed the coast would be clear."

"But who would rob a poor old man?" said Pete, my dear, innocent fiancé. Did I mention, I love him to pieces?

"What are you talking about? He was a mean old sonovabitch! Oops." Nico put a hand up to cover his mouth.

"Always was a selfish bastard," said his own sister.

How's that for a recommendation? I thought.

Someone, probably Tony, grunted. I'm pretty sure he opened one eye.

"'Course he doesn't do the bookie thing anymore. He's retired," I explained to Pete, then paused. "Isn't he?"

Nico, who is more connected than I am, shifted uncomfortably. "Sort of," he said. "Of course, he likes to keep his hand in, giving odds for everything that happens in this burg. Like who is going to get hit next…what marriage is going to blow up. You know the drill, Gina. And they still use the business as a front. To launder money."

I turned and stared. "Now that doesn't make any sense at all. Bookmaking is illegal. How do you launder money through an illegal business??"

"That's the genius of it all, Gina," Nico enthused. "No one would ever suspect."

Pete made a sound like an asthmatic donkey. I threw up my arms in surrender. This family was friggin' nuts.

"You ask too many questions, Gina." Aunt Alma shook her wobbly round head. "It isn't good for your stress levels."

"What questions?" The voice attached to the body at the front door was familiar to me. It was familiar to all of us. Mario stood on the threshold, looking his usual dopey, cherubic self.

I darted forward and grabbed both his arms. "Where did you put the mattress?" I pleaded into his face.

Mario smiled, like he was chuffed that he knew how to answer that one. "Me and Luca took it to the dump."

"Well, you gotta UN-take it, you nincompoop! It has Uncle Tony's life savings in it!" I stepped back and swatted him one on the arm.

"It does?" Mario's cute, moronic face twisted. "Aw, sweet bugger balls! *That's* where it all is? We didn't even think of that." He looked at Alma and Nico. Then he looked at me, and out popped a tiny, "Oops."

"You?" hissed Aunt Alma. "YOU'RE responsible for this unholy mess of a house? YOU were the thief who broke in?" Her chubby hands went to fists.

"Sonovabitch!" said Nico, outraged. "You'd steal from your own…actually, wait a minute. This has a certain poetic justice to it."

Me, I had a different take. "I'm gonna kill him," I muttered. Well, somebody had to.

"Hold on, Gina," Pete grabbed both my arms to hold me back.

"No, I'M GONNA KILL HIM!" Alma repeated.

With blinding speed, Mario was out the door and down the steps like a squirrel at a dog convention.

"You may have to wait in line, Gina," said Nico, peering out the doorway. "Aunt Alma is gaining fast. In fact, I have to think—"

"Seven to one, to win!" mumbled the bookmaker from the floor.

The 13th Letter
M
The End

IF YOU SHOULD FALL

By Donna Carrick

Marlene had not intended to spend her life managing a sugarbush. In fact, her earliest memories were of planning her escape. She'd head to the city and break free of the drudgery, toil, and borderline poverty to which her parents had dedicated their lives.

She was going to be an *Actress*. With a capital A. She had aspirations. Maybe even pretensions.

And she might have made it, too. She had the looks, everyone said so. She was smart, top of her class in most subjects. Able to think on her feet.

Then she fell in love with Jim MacDougall, the son of a nearby maple farmer.

And the die was cast.

Truthfully, Marlene didn't mind giving up her childhood dream. It was a fair trade, forty-plus years married to the kindest, most honest man she'd ever met. Sharing a home, children, and the work to which each of them had been born. They were good at it. A success, even, in these later years, after the decades of grueling struggle that marked the beginning of their marriage.

And they'd built a life together, one of which they could be proud.

Time is no friend, neither to men nor to women. But it had been forgiving to Marlene and Jim. It had granted them their health, a valuable commodity as they neared retirement.

Time had also given them three loving children. The eldest, Gracie, was now nearly 40 herself, a wife and mother to three teens.

Marlene hoped that she and Jim had instilled in their children the tools required to build their own happiness.

Love, she knew, has nothing to do with glamorous goals or grandiose gestures. True love can be found in the minutiae of daily life. The hamburger made the way he likes it. The shower head he repairs for her, even though he's perfectly happy to use the bathtub. The way he offers his arm when the stairs are icy. Knowing he will always be there to pick her up if she should fall.

These are the lessons Marlene hoped her children would employ in matters of love.

Of course, as is often the case, neither Gracie nor the boys wanted to follow in the family business. Farming was too hard, and in these parts, winter was an annual sluggish, almost funereal march through the calendar.

She couldn't blame the kids. She, too, had wanted a different life once upon a time. She could understand the yearning for flight, to break free of the often-brutal landscape of the near north.

This time of year, though, brimming with the promise of spring, the countryside was anything but brutal. A heady perfume, the fragrance of life itself, permeated the still-cool air.

Sweet. Welcoming. Genial. The scent of renewal.

Marlene loved the way her kitchen window faced the southeast meadow, and the MacDougall's prized sugarbush beyond.

The still-naked maple branches surged with energy, nursing buds that were invisible, except for the slightest variegation of color where leaves would soon unfurl.

She turned to her stovetop, lifting lids and stirring the sticky mass, the last few quarts of this year's harvest. The final batches were always kept for their personal use: gifts for friends, for family far and wide, as well as two or three bottles for their own cupboard.

Jim had long since disappeared into the bush, making sure all the taps and buckets were gently removed. It was important to allow the trees to heal themselves fully every season. These were decent producers, almost 200 acres with little other than sugar maple, mature trees and saplings growing together the way nature intended.

She and Jim had worked through the past week, boiling sap down to its precious gold in huge evaporators, sterilizing the beautifully embossed bottles. J & M MacDougall, known throughout the county as one of the finest mom-and-pop producers of pure Canadian maple syrup. It would go to market in the coming weeks, kicking off the season in late April, with the popular Maple Syrup Festival in their local town.

It wasn't easy to make a living in the sugarbush. Many tappers lost money year after year. Only those willing to suffer the work past tree disease, poor weather and sapling immaturity ever reached the point where some badly needed dollars came their way. After all, this was Ontario, not Quebec, where powerful, efficient corporations had taken over a swath of the production.

Still, Marlene and Jim had been lucky. Marlene's family, the Fords, were one of the earliest sugarbush tappers in the county. They learned from their Native neighbors how, and more importantly when, to tap, boil, prepare and preserve the golden syrup.

Jim's family were newer to the trade, having settled in Simcoe County a mere 80 years ago. But his people were long-time farmers with a keen eye toward good land. They knew the bush they bought, in fact this very 200 acres where Jim and Marlene had raised their children and still lived, was a strong, healthy and mature lot.

This was to be their last season. They had decided, after discussing all options with Gracie and the boys, near the end of last season. As they usually were in all life-changing decisions, they were on the same page. Marlene and Jim were ready to sell. Retire. They would go out at the top of their game.

They found a buyer for the acreage, the equipment and the family name, and signed the deal, confident they'd negotiated the best possible price. Better to sell on the tail end of a lucrative season. The sugarbush could be a notoriously fickle provider.

Jim shared her mixed feelings. They'd been lucky throughout the decades. They'd made their plans, and for the most part, God had not laughed at them. Things had worked out for the best, even when roadblocks and challenges had risen.

They would move into a cozy house in town, with a hospital nearby and access to groceries. It was the right decision. There was no reason to think God would laugh at their retirement plans.

They were strong and independent now, but in a few years?

Who could be sure?

Leaving the only home they'd ever shared was going to be difficult. No doubt about it.

Discombobulating.

Marlene knew their love for each other would help smooth the transition.

As her own mother had so often asserted, life wasn't for sissies.

"Shoo, shoo," she said, scolding the curious marmalade tomcat who'd hopped onto the counter. He was a good-natured fellow, and a darn useful mouser for a male. One ear had been chewed up in an encounter with a stubborn raccoon, but he was otherwise in fine form. "Get on down now, Bill. There's nothing for you up here."

Mason, one of their two shepherds—well, part shepherd, truth be told, and part Heinz—rousted himself from the edge of the kitchen and came to investigate his water bowl. He and Max would soon need to go out.

Only these final batches of syrup, the ones for personal use, were boiled down in Marlene's country-style kitchen. The thick liquid was at a delicate stage. If left too long on the heat, it would crystalize and be unsuitable for bottling. Max and Mason would have to wait. She'd be able to turn down the burner in a minute, she figured. Then she'd tromp out onto the mucky snow and check on Jim while the dogs did their business.

She peeked through the window once again. It was lunchtime, and Jim should be back any minute, wanting a sandwich.

He appeared on the edge of the bush, glancing toward the window. He probably couldn't see her in the bright sunshine, but he waved anyway as he always did, and she waved back, smiling at this small, shared gesture of love. Then he made his way toward the "shed", a modern, tall and long building to the right of the main house, just out of sight of the window.

Marlene wondered why Jim was stopping by the shed. They'd prepared the last of the harvest for market yesterday, the labeled and embossed bottles all neatly and securely packed into their boxes, and stacked onto pallets for easy loading onto trucks that would arrive in early April.

Most of the harvest would be shipped to distribution centers throughout North America. A dozen cases would be held back, saved for nearby supermarkets and for the local festival.

There was no risk of wild animals breaching the shed. It had been built ten years earlier, with a view to safeguarding the product and its flamboyant packaging. Suppliers didn't want boxes that were dirty or damaged in any way. The building was temperature-controlled, hygienic, and surpassed all government codes.

Jim must have forgotten something in the shed yesterday.

Marlene gave the three pots another stir, covered them and turned the heat down low. It wouldn't do to let the syrup cool before filling the sterile bottles.

"Come on, boys," she said, wiping her hands. Max and Mason were getting on in years. Still, they didn't have to be told twice. They hopped to their feet and led the way to the side door. Marlene pulled her warm jacket and knitted scarf from the closet.

As she was zipping her coat, she thought she heard Jim's voice. Was that a shout? Pulling on her boots, she hurried to open the door. Jim must have fallen.

The dogs raced past, nearly knocking her off her feet, barreling toward the shed. She shut the door, preserving the warmth of her kitchen—it was still cold out, after all, even though the relatively warmer temperatures had allowed for a terrific harvest.

Her boots threatened to stick in the snow-covered mud, and she trudged as quickly as possible toward the shed. From her vantage point, all seemed in order, but she couldn't see the main shipping doors, or the long far side of the building.

"Jim," she called, "is everything all right?"

A shot rang out, Jim's rifle, from the sound of it, though why he'd have it with him she could not have guessed. Had he encountered a bear?

Another shot, higher pitched and almost deafening. The dogs barked wildly, prancing and pacing on the far side of the shed.

Jim must have heard a noise at the shed and gone to investigate.

She rounded the building and spied him, her husband, fallen onto a bank of snow.

The dogs reached him first, on high alert, seeming to guard the pile of winter garments heaped between them.

"Jim!" Marlene ran to where her husband of 40 years lay, fresh blood sullying the clean white mound.

"Get back to the house," he whispered. "Call for help."

"Put your arm around my neck. Quickly."

"No," he said. "I can't do it. Get help."

Marlene looked up in time to see a man of indeterminate age pointing a handgun at her. Turning slightly, he shot Mason, catching the dog's back right paw.

Mason yelped and Max went berserk, chasing the man.

Another shot, and the intruder disappeared around the shed.

"Come on," she said. "I've got you."

But Jim didn't answer, was unconscious, and she wasn't strong enough to lift him without his help.

Marlene grabbed Jim's rifle with one hand and patted her pocket with the other. Damn. She'd left her phone on the kitchen counter. She'd have to head back to the house.

She whistled for the boys. Mason followed her, limping and splattering blood, toward the house. "Max!" she hollered, and the dog reluctantly gave up his howling and hurried after her.

Once back inside, she bolted the doors and secured the windows. Although, it would be easy enough to break a window if anyone really wanted in.

Next, she checked that there were still rounds in Jim's hunting rifle. Yup, four rounds remained. She grabbed her phone from the counter and dialed.

"This is 9-1-1. What's your emergency?" the operator said.

"I'm at Sugarbush Grove, number 1705 Concession 3 just northwest of Maplewood. My husband Jim MacDougall has been shot. There's at least one intruder outside our house. I think Jim's still alive. I couldn't move him and he's losing blood."

"Stay on the line, Ma'am. That way we can track your call. What's your name? Is the victim breathing?"

"This is Marlene MacDougall." Marlene reached into the high cupboard beside the sink and pulled out two more cartridges. She stuck them into her pants pockets. This would give her 10 rounds, in addition to the four still in the rifle.

"My husband, Jim, is 70 years old. He needs help. I'm taking something out to bandage him now."

Setting the phone back on the counter, she reached for the cotton curtains over the sink. She used her kitchen scissors to cut them into strips and stuffed the makeshift bandages into her left pocket.

She noticed a warm, dark stain on her coat. She must have leaned into Jim's blood when she bent over him. Her husband needed her. She had to hurry.

"Mrs. MacDougall, are you safe at the moment?"

"I'm in the main house. I've locked the doors. My two dogs are with me. One's been shot in the leg. I'll tend to him as soon as I look after Jim."

"We're sending help now."

"I won't hang up, but I'm putting my phone in my pocket. I have to get out there and help Jim." Marlene was aware that she was speaking in a high-pitched, rapid voice. She hoped the operator could make out what she was saying.

"Okay, Mrs. MacDougall, I understand. Please do not engage the intruder. You can speak to me if you need to. I'll be able to hear you with your phone in your pocket."

Peering through the kitchen window, Marlene strained for the best view. Still, she could not see the shed.

Mason was curled and whimpering at the edge of the kitchen, his paw a bloody mess, but Max followed her to the door. She paused a moment, unsure whether Max would be a help, but decided it would be foolish to leave a good dog behind during what was likely to be a fight.

"Come on, boy. Let's go help Pop."

Max seemed to sense the moment called for silence. He barked once, but a look from Marlene shut him up, and he trod silently beside her as she made her way to the far side of the shed.

What did this guy want? she wondered. They weren't rich, didn't live ostentatiously, in a way that would entice potential robbers.

She recalled a news story from a few years back: a couple of hapless thieves had stolen a load of maple syrup from a sugarbush farmer, killing him and his son and injuring a worker before making off with an entire harvest.

The damn fools had, of course, been caught trying to ship the load stateside for sale.

"Stay," she ordered Max, and he sat beside his fallen master. Marlene dropped to her knees, but it was clear Jim was gone. He wasn't breathing. She felt his neck for a pulse, but it was too late. She'd taken too long in the house.

A sob escaped her, but she stifled it. The intruder could be in hearing range. He might even be watching her now, from the sugarbush. She scanned the edge of the forest but could not discern any hint of movement from within the naked trees.

She reached into her pocket for her phone, careful not to disconnect the call. "My husband's dead," she said softly, holding back tears. "The intruder is still here…somewhere."

"I hear you," the operator said. "Remember, do not engage the intruder. Can you get back to the house?"

"I'll try. I'm putting the phone back in my pocket now."

"We're about ten minutes away, Mrs. MacDougall. Try to get to the house, and don't attract attention."

Marlene signaled to Max to *Stay*. Jim's rifle under her arm, she crept to the corner of the shed. She heard their voices before she could see them.

"She looked straight at me," the first man said. Peering around the corner, she saw two men. The smaller, the shooter, still held his gun in his hand. In truth, she could not have identified him. His black toque was pulled low against the cold, and his parka was the style worn by men of every age in these parts. It was one of those that caused a bulge in the midriff, so you couldn't tell whether the wearer was slender or had a paunch. To make matters worse, he wore a thick dark plaid scarf, which covered his chin and made it hard to decipher his features.

"What do you want to do?" his partner asked. He was taller, a bear of a man in a great brown coat designed for outdoor living, a brown hunting cap pulled over his ears. Even without a scarf, the bulky coat and hat hid his face such that she could only just make out a long hooked nose and the edge of a black mustache.

The burly man appeared irritated, hoisting boxes and heaving them into the truck. He seemed to be hauling the lion's share of boxes, his friend moving more slowly.

"We have to do her," the gunman said. "She saw me full on."

"She's likely called the cops by now. Let's get this show on the road."

Marlene pulled back, gesturing to remind Max to stay still.

The boxes had been stacked on pallets, so anyone with half a brain would have saved themselves a ton of work by bringing along a forklift to move the product. But these idiots were moving the boxes one by one. At this rate, it would take them half an hour to load enough syrup to fill the truck.

The 9-1-1 operator had said help was ten minutes away, but Marlene knew in these parts emergency services could take much longer. It all depended on whether the OPP had a unit in the area, or whether they'd have to send one in from Midland or Collingwood.

Ambulance service was often faster, but in a potentially violent situation, they'd hold back for the police to arrive first.

So, she could be waiting 10 minutes, or 20, or even 30, for help. Meanwhile, two armed men were planning to kill her.

If she engaged them, she could be killed. Max would attack the men if she gave the signal, but they might shoot him as well.

They'll search for me in the house. Marlene glanced around, considering her options.

Moving her hand to signal Max to heel, she made her way stealthily to the edge of the bush. The early March trees would not offer much camouflage, but they would provide limited cover, and the maneuver would buy time. Especially since the killers wouldn't expect her to be in the bush.

"This is taking too long. I'll deal with the old woman while you finish up."

His friend grunted, no doubt used to being saddled with the bulk of any physical labor.

Marlene could make out the open end of the truck from where she and Max crouched behind one of the older maples. The syrup was being loaded faster than she'd expected, the thief heaving boxes at an accelerated rate.

"Get back here quick," he said, "or I'll leave without you. Cops'll be here soon." He loaded another box. "This was supposed to be easy."

"I'll be right back. Wait for me."

Marlene watched as he disappeared behind the shed. A moment later, he reappeared, slogging through the muddy snow in running shoes. He cursed, his shoes threatening to sink with every step.

He tried the side door, but she'd turned the lock when she and Max shut it behind them.

He wrapped his gloved hands around his eyes and looked through the kitchen window. Then he made his way around to the front door, where she could no longer watch him.

His friend was almost finished loading boxes. In a moment, they could be on their way, if his partner gave up on trying to find her.

The thought of them escaping did not sit well with Marlene.

"How far away?" she asked the operator, keeping her voice low. Sound would carry this time of year, in the crisp late-winter air, and with no leaves to absorb it.

"Just ten minutes," the operator said.

"You said that fifteen minutes ago." Marlene wasn't being cross, just trying to get an estimate of how long it would be till help arrived.

"Are you in a safe place?"

"For now. I'm in the woods. I have my husband's rifle. There are two of them, both armed, I think." In truth, she hadn't seen a gun on the bigger man, but it stood to reason they would both be armed. Then, almost as an afterthought, she added, "They're planning to kill me. I saw them, and they know it, and one of them is in the house now, looking for me."

"Stay hidden, Mrs. MacDougall."

Just then, the smaller man reappeared at the side door. His movement startled Max, who began to bark and run back and forth at the edge of the woods. The commotion drew attention, and the gunman spotted Marlene.

She dropped her phone back into her pocket. A country girl since birth, she knew better than most how to train a rifle. But normally, when hunting, you took aim at a still deer. The little man was a poor target, moving fast and frenetically toward her and aiming his handgun.

It was now or never. She got him in her sights and pulled the trigger.

He went down. She didn't have time to check his status, whether he was dead or merely wounded. Down was down. His partner would have heard the shot.

Sure enough, the big man stuck his head around the corner of the shed, pointing his gun first at Max, then spotting Marlene where she crouched behind the maple.

"Put your gun down, lady," he shouted. "I don't want to hurt you."

She didn't answer. It would be pointless to banter with him and would diminish any advantage she might have. If he came toward her, she would shoot him, plain and simple.

She dared to glance back toward the house. Jim's killer was no longer where she'd left him. So, only wounded after all.

That was a problem.

Now she couldn't see either man. The loading doors of the shed were hidden from her view. If she approached, she risked being killed.

Meanwhile, Max was going nuts. She couldn't calm him down, would have to let him bark himself hoarse.

Carefully, keeping a close watch on the shed, she moved from tree to tree, trying to gain a vantage point where she could see the loading doors. She had to know if both men were still gunning for her, or whether they'd holed up inside the shed, or the truck.

It would make more sense for them to get into the truck. Then they'd have a chance of making off before the OPP arrived.

Without even thinking of it, she trained the rifle on the front tire.

BAM!

The tire deflated.

Knowing these large trucks had multiple wheels, she next took aim at the second cab tire.

BAM!

It went down, effectively rendering the truck immobile.

"Goddammit!" the little guy shouted, appearing at the passenger side of the truck.

His partner slid across the cab seat and jumped to the ground, aiming his weapon at Marlene from behind the cab.

Meanwhile, his wounded friend had limped behind the truck and was now pointing the business end of his gun at her.

Unable to control himself, Max went wild, racing toward the petite man. Before he could react, Max got hold of his jacket and sunk his teeth, pulling him to the ground and out from behind the truck.

Marlene took aim, but was afraid of hitting Max, so did not immediately fire.

The bigger man saw an opportunity to fire on Marlene and gave up his cover, causing Max to leap toward him.

BAM!

Marlene took the clear shot, and Jim's killer went down. This time, she suspected it would be for the count.

"Get off me, you fucker!" The big man was protected from Max's teeth by the bulk of his coat, but confronted with the dog's frenzy, he could not get off a clean shot. He ran for the cover of the shed, Max refusing to let go of his parka.

Finally, he delivered a blow to Max's head. The dog fell to the ground, momentarily dazed and unable to resume his attack.

BAM!

"Dammit," Marlene muttered. "Just a leg shot." She took aim, but Max once again got in the way.

For a frozen second, Max danced out of the line of fire. It was just her and the man, both leveling their weapons, in an instant of certain death for one of them. Her entire life had come down to this moment.

She took the shot.

***

Voices floated in and out of her consciousness. OPP, paramedics—Marlene had no idea who was speaking, or what they were saying. She tried to focus, but the world was out of her grasp. She allowed herself to fade beyond the reach of a painful reality.

"Three dead males. One elderly woman, critical condition, shot in the abdomen. Two injured dogs. Send veterinarian assistance."

Marlene was blissfully unaware of the extent of her injury, as the ambulance sprinted over the snowy country roads at top speed. Her unconscious mind took her backward in time, to the early days with Jim. To the years before financial success, before children.

As the siren wailed and the medics tended to her wound, she was blessed with the most exquisite of dreams. It was just the two of them, she and Jim, young once again. Loving each other throughout every daily task, every plan. Lifting each other from every fall.

The essence of love passing between them in the air they breathed, in the food they shared. In their quiet moments resting by the fireplace, or at work tending to taps on their beloved maple trees.

Love binding them, as they toiled together every spring, boiling down the sweet richness of their lives.

Guiding them as they planned for their future together.

A future worthy of aspiration.

Somewhere deep in her fever dream, woven into the howl of the siren and the voices that spoke so urgently above her, Marlene heard a strange sound.

It grew in volume from a hum to a roar, until it reverberated in her ears and could no longer be denied.

God had chosen this moment to laugh.

The 13th Letter

M

The End

THE LIFTED LETTER:

A Gloria Gamm Gambit

By J.E. Barnard

One hand clinging to the polished dark banister, Gloria Gamm peered down the dauntingly high staircase. In the vast hall below, black-tie waiters scuttled to and fro, hauling trays. Bruisers in too-small tuxes stood by to open doors for them, spilling laughter and light across the grooves worn into the stone floor by centuries of feet.

Centuries? Long Island had been forest only a hundred years ago. The castle was making her nervy. Or maybe it was the risk involved in Alfie's plan. If it went awry, they'd both earn a one-way trip out to the cold, dark Atlantic on their host's yacht. The floor grooves were probably fake, another of Monty's attempts to make his barrels of dosh look like Old Money, instead of so fresh they still reeked of bootleg whisky.

Alfred Harrington the Fourth's arm slid around her waist. His voice enveloped her in fumes of illicit gin. "Hey, doll-baby! Cute a-you to wait for me."

She wafted the booze away with one hand and removed his fingers with the other. "You snag this party frock and you're replacing it, Alfie."

"Did I buy this one?" He leaned precariously to peer down her spangled V-front, his blond waves shifting to reveal the motley yellow and purple around his left eye. A souvenir from one of the tuxedoed bruisers below.

"You? Hah! I borrowed my entire wardrobe from the costume mistress over at the Palladium, and she'll have my guts for garters if they don't come back intact. So paws off,

Alf. You ain't got the dough to cover my expenses. And if Monty gets wise...."

His sideways smile slipped. "You'd never tell him?!"

"No, but...."

The proposition had seemed simple enough when Alfie pitched it to her, on his knees in the dressing room she shared with a dozen other kickers.

"Gloria, kitten. Just convince him you're my angelic cousin from Dullsville and say you'll plead for Daddy-O to cough up the dough I owe him. I'll introduce you to my pal Sammy when he rolls in from Hollywood next month. He can take you far, far from the third row of the Follies."

Now that she was here, in Monty's weekend lair, she had big doubts. Any man who could afford a pre-aged stone floor might not be swayed by her back-row footlights glam.

"We ain't in the music hall no more, Alf. A little glitz, a little kiss, won't mean a swizz against all Monty's ritz. He could buy a dozen like me two dozen times over."

Alfie straightened up. "Chaps like that can't tell old money from new. Or off-the-rack rayon from a Coco Chanel original. Paste on your dancin' face. It's time to mingle and swill."

The huge salon blazed white and gold, from walls to spindly golden furniture to the frames around paintings of ladies in fluffy old gowns and puffy white wigs. Even the ceiling was gilded. The guests' diamante headbands and beaded frocks shimmered under three massive electric chandeliers. Men in sports coats snagged glasses from trays circulated by the black-tie waiters. Monty in his white tux was the ringmaster of all this glitz, standing before a massive marble fireplace—white with golden veins. Wouldn't the flames and soot spoil all its shiny smoothness?

No fire tonight anyway, with a sultry breeze drifting in through tall glass doors from the ocean beyond. Yes, the actual ocean, at the bottom of Monty's lawn. She'd seen it from her bedroom balcony. A bedroom, bath, and balcony all to herself, a suite bigger than the whole apartment she shared with three other dancers in the Big Apple.

Alfie tugged her forward, his hand clammy on her bare wrist. "Monty! Great party as usual. Can I introduce you to my cousin Gloria?"

Monty lifted Gloria's hand onto his meaty forearm. "I seen you lookin' at my ceiling, honey. Ain't it pretty? I bought the whole room from this old English lord. Paid him a packet to get it taken down and shipped over here. Bought lotsa other stuff too. All genuine antiquities. Betcha went to one-a them finishing schools, am I right? Girl like you is sure to appreciate the goods. Grab a glass and I'll take you on a tour.

"Wally," he bellowed. Guests jumped. Booze sloshed. "Bring Miss Gloria some champagne. The good stuff."

Looked like Monty was buying the gag.

As a waiter scurried over with a white-swathed bottle, Alfie gave her a wink of approval. He drifted away, following the throng outside, where strings of naked light bulbs led to open-sided pavilions. Scandal-sheet Johnnies snapped pictures of the attendees. Somewhere out there a jazz band struck up. Monty patted her hand as a sweating glass of bubbly appeared on a tray in front of her.

"Follow us," he told the waiter. "And keep the little lady lubricated."

"Oh, Monty," she giggled, shimmying her shoulders to make her frock sparkle, "you'll get me tipsy."

"You're safe with me, Miss Gloria. Uncle Monty keeps the wolves away." The same line a million older men had told her since she grew knockers. She batted her eyelashes instead of rolling her eyeballs.

The large room next door had dark wood bookshelves on two walls, more big glass doors on a third and, on her left, dark wood paneling dotted with small pictures that glittered almost as brightly as her borrowed party frock. She peered closer but Monty pulled her along the nearest shelves.

"Now this here's my library, see? Bought every book from this falling-down wreck they called a manor house over in Cornwall. You ever been to England? Cornwall's that bit stuck out on the bottom corner. Got a map on the desk here. I'll show you."

And show he did, item by item around the large room.

Out on the lawn, the jazz band played on. Folks danced under the pavilion and darted laughing through the ornamental bushes, drank and laughed and flirted. The moon tracked across the dark water. In the wood-paneled library, Monty pointed Gloria from one shelf to another, then to trinkets under glass. She disguised a yawn by rubbing imaginary champagne bubbles out of her nose. They hadn't done the whole library yet. Who knew how many more rooms filled with treasures she'd have to pretend to know something about, before he'd let her get a word in about Alf?

At last they reached the far door. A bruiser in a tux opened it. But Gloria wasn't stepping even one room further from the lights and crowds with a man old enough to be her 'uncle.' A girl only had her reputation, after all, and if she had to sell hers, it wouldn't be for a cheap promise from a boozehound like Alfie. She'd save it up for Hollywood. She cast her eyes over her shoulder, searching the library for an inoffensive reason to stall.

Oh, those smaller pictures that glittered! She dashed back to the paneled wall and stared up as if dazzled. Which, after the first glance, she was.

"Wait! Tell me about these letters!"

"Goils," Monty muttered, but he followed. "Anything with gold on, hey? You know I told you how I bought all these books from a falling-down mansion in Cornwall?"

"You never bought these there too?"

Her wide-eyed appreciation didn't have to be faked. Large capital letters took up most of each framed page, followed by rows of spiky, indecipherable printing. Each page was decorated with painted vines or ribbons, some with animal heads and birds, simple repeating patterns or complicated interwoven ones. Some had people standing or seated, wearing long robes and hats or hoods. Monks she recognized by their bald heads and brown robes, but other clothing was done in bright blues and reds, greens and yellows, white spotted with black and black splotched with white that was likely supposed to be fur. But what really glittered were the lines of gold: they edged the animals, burnished the letters, glowed along robes. Every picture was so dainty, so pretty, that she moved along the rows utterly entranced.

Until Monty's coarse voice intruded again.

"Illuminated letters they're called, on account of all the shiny gold. Every single page cut out of books older than the Queen of England's castle. Framed I don't know when, but who cares? They didn't make glass fronts for pictures that smooth and clear in them olden days, am I right?"

"They are divine." Gloria reached the end of the row and started back.

Her host stood square in her way, pointing. "This letter M, here? That's for Monty. I'm getting it made just like this on flags to fly all along my drive. That'll tell folks for sure what a classy guy lives here."

"Class all the way," she murmured, admiring the curlicued capital G. She wouldn't make a flag of her initial. She'd have a brooch made of gold, set with precious gems in all the colors of this painted one.

As she glided past Monty, he snatched her arm. She stopped instantly and braced her feet in case he tried to pull her in. Where were all the waiters? The door-bruisers? They'd all vanished. No doubt Monty had signaled them to disappear and she, swayed by the golden letters, hadn't noticed. That would teach her to get distracted.

"Monty," she said sweetly, meeting his eyes without a hint of flirtation. "A girl doesn't like being grabbed like a tennis racquet."

"Oh." He looked down at his hand, blinked, and quickly tucked it behind his back like a schoolboy. "Uh, sorry, Miss Gloria. I forgot myself. You are a classy dame, that's true, and Uncle Monty is on best manners tonight. But you like my little letters and all my other treasures, and I thought, maybe…."

"You thought," said a sultry voice from across the room. "I know what you thought, even if Miss Finishing School's too naïve to guess."

Gloria spun away just in time to avoid a champagne bottle that had probably been aimed at her head. It bounced off an armchair cushion, skidded along the floor, and executed a half-turn near her feet. A final froth sputtered from its neck as Monty stuttered, "C-Carlotta!"

If Gloria had been a naïve finishing school debutante like Alfie's real cousins, she wouldn't have recognized that name, or the woman who strode through the tall glass doors, her scarlet evening gown swinging and her dark curls tossing like flags in a gale. Diamonds flashed at her wrists and throat, but they were no match for the fire in her eyes.

Carlotta Crane, noted nightclub singer and Monty's current mistress.

Rumor backstage at the Follies was that Monty bought up every loose diamond in New York City to lure Carlotta away from Diamond Jim Daley. When Jim confronted the new couple at the Central Park Casino Club. Monty's bruisers beat him bloody right there on the dance floor, while the band played on and the samba troupe kept right on stamping and swaying around the mayhem. While Diamond Jim vanished from his usual haunts to heal his bruises and plot revenge, Gloria's fellow kickers debated the choreography in case anyone started a rumble on their stage.

Carlotta, the cause of all that kerfuffle, stalked across Monty's library. One scarlet fingernail circled toward his face.

"Don't you Carlotta me, you cheap hood! You're looking for a classy dame with a family name to move in and make you some blueblood babies. But you ain't getting rid of me that easy, pal."

Gloria oozed away. Two steps more and she'd be out the door she'd entered by. One step…Her tush thumped up against a hard body. A bruiser about to grab her?

Alfie's gin-soaked breath filled her ear. "Get thee behind me, like a good little hoofer."

She pivoted past him and out the door just as something crashed. Glass showered down from the door frame. Alfie shook a few sparkling shards off his jacket and held out his elbow to Gloria.

"Just one of those things," he murmured and led her toward the roaring outdoor party she'd almost forgotten. Fireworks soared from the yacht dock to burst in white stars high above. They'd barely set foot on the lawn when a flashbulb blinded Gloria. She flung up her hand too late, while green dots revolved in her eyes. Alfie laughed.

"Good one, Jimbo!"

"Who's the luscious lady, Alfie?" leered the photographer. "You sure go through 'em."

Alf wrapped his arm around Gloria's borrowed dress. "Ain't she a peach?"

The camera flashed again.

As the green spots swirled anew, Gloria said, "Oh, sir, please don't print those! If my mama finds out Cousin Alfie took me to a party here, she'll make his daddy banish him to some strictly tee-total state where he'll dry up and blow away. And she'll do worse to me."

"Cousin, hey?" The newshound lowered his camera. "Tell ya what, for a sawbuck I'll work some darkroom magic and put another doll's face instead of yours."

Gloria shook her head. "My mama chose this dress for me special. Please, sir. Don't let it get into the papers."

"What it's worth to ya, Mr. Harrington, to keep yourself safely among the gin joints?"

When Alfie hesitated, Gloria leaned close to whisper, "Want someone to recognize my picture and tell Monty I'm not your cousin at all?"

He jumped. Pulling out a billfold, he peeled a bill and passed it over. "Not a peep, Jimbo?"

"You betcha, boss." The newshound freed one hand from his camera, folded the bill into it, and flicked his hat brim with his index finger. "Nice to meet you, miss."

"What if Monty knows I'm not your cousin?" she'd asked.

"He's got no entrée into our circles," Alf had assured her. "I've got fifteen aunts, all married off and most moved away. To track down all my cousins and get their pictures he'd have to send guys to every city in the Midwest to read their Society pages. And none of Monty's guys can read that well."

She could only hope that was true, or they'd both be in the soup. Er, the ocean.

Dawn found Gloria shimmying down from her bedroom balcony in her borrowed wardrobe's beach trousers and her most flexible rubber-soled shoes. She'd tried going along the corridor to the main stairs, past Carlotta Crane's double-doored suite which, rumor had it, connected internally with Monty's suite further along. But a mean old woman waved a knitting needle menacingly and swore at her. Carlotta's personal maid wasn't going to allow her anywhere near Monty's suite. Not that Gloria was headed there anyway. She just wanted to store up some innocent conversational gambits about the statuary she could barely make out over a hedge beyond the swimming pool. So she crept hand by foot down the niches and curlicues around her personal porch's columns. Soon she was balancing on the carved stone railing of the terrace below, one arm around the column and the other hand shielding her eyes to survey the mansion's outdoor features.

The white-topped party pavilions were straight ahead, the grass around them littered with bottles, napkins, a scattering of sleeping drunks—at least, she was assuming they slept—and what seemed to be filmy feminine underthings. Waiters in shirtsleeves were collecting glasses and folding up chairs. Clearly she'd missed a wild time by retreating to her room the instant Carlotta reached the dance floor.

The far right-hand lawn was flat and bare, with not so much as a statue to talk about. The statuary she'd glimpsed from higher up wasn't visible from here, but she knew where to go: past the hedge beyond the pool. Leaping down, she set off.

She found the pool area decorated by more sleepers in chaises and one in the shallows, his evening wear merging with the black-and-white tilework like a kind of camouflage. His necktie was undone, his collar too, and his head rested on black-clad arms folded over the pool's top step. If he hadn't managed to slip in and drown by now, he was probably safe until he woke on his own, so she left him there and followed the hedge until a break appeared. Eagerly she turned in, only to find her way blocked by a metal gate that reached her eye level. Its wrought iron scrollwork was so ornate she could barely make out a warped letter M in its midst. A fail for Monty's grand plan, there. Maybe he was having a new gate made to match his illuminated M flags. If not, she could suggest it, and earn his approval before she hit him up with her plea for Alfie's loan extension.

The gate didn't budge when she rattled the latch. Locked. Probably to keep the drunken barbarians away from his imported marble figures. The hordes had been kept out of the house too, once the party really got going.

Ah well, a little gate wouldn't stop a game girl like her. She stuck toes into the bottom curlicue of the M and a hand onto the upstroke, hoisted herself, found another foothold and another handhold, and soon was scrambling down the other side to the smoothly raked pea-gravel below. She was in!

Along the tall hedge she strode, turning left, then right, into a wide courtyard where the hedges suddenly shrunk to her knees. And here, at last, were statues: draped women pouring invisible water from urns, an archer aiming his bow out to the sea, a nude god with impressive goat horns and hooves. He had reed pipes in his hand. She'd seen his likeness in more than one theater lobby. He was the god Pan, sacred, some uncle had informed her, to musicians and traveling troupes. One more tidbit to feed to Monty, if he ever let her wedge a word into his endless bragging.

She'd just spotted a gleam of what might be gold through a taller hedge on the far side when…

"Ahem!"

She jumped, executing a three-point spin in mid-air to see, not Monty or his bruisers, but a weedy stranger in a natty blue blazer and yachting cap. At his wrinkled neck was a jaunty anchor-strewn cravat, yet his pinched face was too pale to belong to any sailor she'd ever met.

"Young lady," he said sternly, "you are trespassing."

"No, sir. I'm weekending here with my pa—cousin Alfie."

"I think," he said, raising one eyebrow all the way into his cap, "that I would recall inviting weekend guests. Especially unaccompanied young ladies."

"Monty invited me. Us."

The pale face mottled instantly. "Monty? That cockroach? That…bootlegger! Is it not enough that you degenerate inebriates keep me awake night after night with lights and shrieks and what passes for music? I am contaminated by mere proximity to that debauchery. Jenkins, call the police! Jenkins!"

"Oh, dear," Gloria exclaimed. Getting herself arrested would seriously hamper her odds of helping Alfie. "Have I strayed off Monty's property? I am so very sorry, sir. Your beautiful statues lured me. The god Pan with his pipes…such a delightful piece. I'll go at once."

"Hmm." The purple blotches receded. "I was unaware that Monty was acquainted with anyone who understood art."

Gloria gave him her best head-tilted smile, a little shy, the one most uncles enjoyed. "Not as much as I would like to, sir," she said plaintively. "There's been no one to explain it all to me, you see. That archer. I was wondering if it was…" She trailed off and, like clockwork, his voice filled in.

"The young god Apollo. You'll have noticed, of course, that he's aiming at the rising sun." The pale face brightened. "A little conceit of mine, most effective during these earliest days of summer, before the sun shifts further north. I have Artemis, with her bow, on my other lawn, set to line up with the autumn equinox. Would you care to see her?"

She beamed up at the old string bean and tucked her hand into his offered elbow.

"I would adore to."

He beamed back. "Nelson D. Hammsworthy the Third, at your service, my dear."

"Gloria," she replied. "Visiting my cousin, Alfred Harrington the Fourth, down in the Big Apple."

"Ah, the Harringtons," said Nelson D. as he led her around another tall hedge into another courtyard filled with statues. "Old Alfred—that would be the grandfather of your cousin—was a dear friend. But I suppose you're from the female line and not a direct descendent, or I'd have heard of you. Alfred was very proud of his granddaughters, but not a one that didn't have a face like the back side of a barn door. Very flat, all of them. Not like you with that delightful tilt to your nose."

She'd have bet good dollars it wasn't their flat noses the old goat found unappealing. But she only shrugged her shoulders, shaking loose his gaze from the neckline of her borrowed blouse, and pointed to the nearest piece of carved stone.

Twenty minutes later, after duly admiring the statue of Artemis and a half-dozen other blank-eyed figures, Gloria gazed with some bewilderment at a golden pig on a plinth as big as a horse-drawn hearse. The rising sun struck sparks on its back. Looking over her shoulder, she lined up the second-floor balconies on Monty's massive house. Yes, this was the gleam she'd spied from her balcony.

"Um, is it an idol, like the, uh, Golden Calf?"

"Golden Calf!" Nelson D let out a snicker like a cartoon horse. "Oh, you delightful girl. I'll remember that. It's the symbol of my house. The Hammsworthy icon! We made our fortune shipping livestock, you see, back when the railways were new. Of course, we expanded beyond that humble start, but this was my father's little way of reminding people that, be their beginnings ever so humble, they too might rise to our stature after a few generations of putting their shoulders to the wheel of commerce."

Not that any humble folk would ever see the golden pig, hidden as it was from the street and even the neighboring estates, visible only to passing yachts. Gloria smiled and said it was lovely, and then added that she must be getting back as Alfie, er, Alfred would be wondering where she'd got to.

"Bring him for tea this afternoon," said Nelson D. genially as he steered her back across his statuary gardens. They were heading for an overgrown gate, far lower and less ornate than the one she'd climbed to get in, but he hustled her to the left, along the tall hedge that separated his estate from Monty's. "It wouldn't do for me to invite you indoors on your own, without a relative to chaperone you. But I've got some lovely old paintings from European masters I'm sure you'll find utterly delightful."

Another hour of listening to an old man drone on about his purchases. Oh, goody. But maybe…

"I don't suppose you have any illuminated letters, do you?" She ran her hand along the spring-green leaves, giving him what she hoped was a winsome side-eye. "I've got a pash for those. Monty has a whole alphabet on his library wall and they're just the bee's knees."

"Does he now?" A foxy expression passed over the pale old face, so fast it left only a ghost of itself behind. Nelson D. beamed down at her once more. "My gate is based on an illuminated letter from a collection kept at our home in the south of France."

"Really?" She'd glimpsed several monogrammed gates from Alfie's roadster, and a few turreted roofs too, but she'd been mostly concerned with not losing her borrowed hat to his driving.

"I kid you not, er, kiddo." One liver-spotted hand waved at the familiar gate in the hedge.

"Oh," she said, as the awkward M she'd deciphered on the other side revealed itself to be a perfectly understandable H from this one. "H for Hammsworthy?"

"Precisely. You'll see it on our front gates as well, if you're out driving past."

"I'll look for it special," she assured him. "Monty is going to get flags made with his illuminated M, and maybe gates too." She was going to suggest that as the next step to class up his estate. It was well short of promising to marry him, but even if she'd been a girl with a pedigree, there was only so far she'd go for an amiable mooch like Alf.

She almost didn't notice Nelson D's foxy expression returning, so swiftly did it come and go. What was he plotting?

"Now you run along," he said, "and ask Alfred to bring you for tea around three. Come by the front gate, so you needn't trouble yourself climbing over."

Oops! "You saw me?"

"Indeed. Most athletic you were about it. Not at all what I expected of Monty's degenerate guests, and now, of course, I see why. A good education, a healthy upbringing, lots of fresh air and sports at your school, I don't doubt." He opened the gate for her and tipped his hat as she scooted through. "*A bientot*, my dear."

Breakfast was underway on Monty's terrace when she arrived. All the houseguests currently conscious groped for their coffee cups and pretended to listen to their host. Carlotta, lounging ornamentally at his side, speared Gloria with a deadly glare. Whatever Gloria asked of Monty, his mistress was sure to oppose. How to keep the jealous singer from wrecking her and Alfie's plan?

"I've been taking my morning constitutional," Gloria said with an airy wave. "I'll be right back when I've changed." Then she skedaddled into the castle, across the worn stone hall, and, since there were no waiters to see her, up the stairs three at a time. Which of her borrowed frocks would be suitable for both brunch here and tea next door?

As she came out of her personal bathroom, her nose freshly powdered and lips lined discreetly with Debutante Pink, she paused to peer out at Nelson D.'s grounds. Now that she knew the layout, she could easily pinpoint the Apollo and Artemis statues by their bows. The golden porker's back gleamed, too. Monty's pool, this side of the dividing hedge, sparkled blue, empty, and inviting as a gardener skimmed stray petals off its surface, but the lawn surrounding it looked more bare than before. This place really needed some statues to slay the party palace atmosphere.

Aha! If the suggestion of statues came from Carlotta, Monty could class up his joint and Carlotta might see the value of having an ally instead of a rival. Gloria scribbled a note on gold-embossed letterhead from the spindly writing desk. On her way down, she slipped the folded page between Carlotta's double doors and went on her way with a tapping two-step. All she had to do was survive breakfast.

But Carlotta didn't go upstairs all morning. Leaving Monty to his business's demands, she led the guests to the pool and casually shed her frock to reveal a sleek bathing costume beneath. No swimming for her, though. She was still sunning when waiters arrived to set up tables for a poolside lunch. Monty appeared soon after, but didn't stop talking, eating, and waving a cigar around long enough for Gloria to make her pitch about monogrammed gates, let alone Alfie's loan extension. When he started making plans for their afternoon, she had to interrupt.

"I am so sorry, Monty, but I promised Uncle Alfred I'd have tea with his old pal today. He wouldn't have let me come all this way with Alf otherwise. Isn't that right, Alf?"

Alfie's bleary eyes met hers over his coffee cup. "Sounds like my pop, all right. Him and his stuffy old pals. Can I have a nap first, so I don't snore into my Lapsang?"

"Oh, sure. Tea's not until three." She beamed at Monty. "If you don't mind, I'll spend that time in the library admiring your treasures. By myself."

Carlotta's eyebrows went up.

Monty said brusquely, "Youse'll be back for dinner?"

"We wouldn't miss it."

As Gloria strolled away to the library's tall glass doors, eager to admire the illuminated letters by daylight, the black-tie waiters were already swarming over the brunch table. She was almost sure she recognized a couple from Monty's city clubs, and another vaguely familiar one was pottering about by the pool. Thankfully, they showed no signs of recognizing a Follies girl behind her Debutante Pink lipstick. A girl brought up like Alfie's cousin wouldn't notice the staff, so she pretended they weren't there even when one dashed over to open and close the library's glass door for her.

Alf was more awake by the time they were sauntering down Monty's drive. "You're one smart cookie, Glo, pretending to know someone else up here. Really selling your alias. Soon's we're far enough from the house, I'll hail a cab to take us to the yacht club for a cocktail, hey? This dog needs more hair on his chest."

She rolled her eyes. "No, you won't neither. What if somebody told Monty we were at the yacht club? We're going right next door." She pointed to Nelson D.'s monogrammed gates. "Right there. So, start thinking up which of your mother's sisters I belong to. Someone who's married and far away. Old Nelson D. is sure to want details."

He whistled through his teeth. "I don't even wanna know how you convinced that old fossil to invite us, but you've got a big future in deception."

"In acting, don't you mean? Mention it to your old pal in the new moving picture industry."

A wizened butler let them in. "The master was called to the telephone," he told them with a wheeze as he led them down a long hall hung with stuffy-looking Hammsworthies. "He will be with you shortly."

The room in which he left them was crammed with over-stuffed sofas amid tables dotted with porcelain knickknacks and photographs in silver frames. The tea table was set for three, its stands loaded with sandwich slivers, strawberry tarts, and any number of other tasty treats. Gloria was sure it would be a violation of upscale etiquette to sample the wares before their host arrived, but oh, how she yearned to. Between waiting for Monty to pause for a breath and her fear of using the wrong fork, she'd hardly eaten a bite all day.

"Tell me some things to talk about," she whispered to Alfie. "Things your real cousins would know."

He cast a knowing eye around the room. "Tea service is Wedgwood. English. Probably belonged to his mother since, as far as I recall, he's never married. Those dancing shepherdess figurines are Meissen, the cherubs on the mantle are Dresden. I'm not sure what chintz pattern this is covering the chairs and curtains, but it's a lot like my Aunt Dottie's morning room in Denver. That enough to get you going?"

Gloria grinned. She'd won over Nelson D. this morning with a lot less.

But Nelson D., when he finally appeared, didn't ask about her mother or talk about his artworks. He barely pretended interest in her gambits about the tabletop figurines. Even though he was perfectly polite, his glances at his wristwatch came more and more frequently until even Alfie took the hint. Setting down his third tart half-eaten, he reminded 'Cousin Gloria' that they must get back for the tour of their host's yacht.

"Oh, you mustn't miss that," said Nelson D., rising at once. He showed them out himself, not bothering to ring for his antique butler.

"Well, shucks," said Gloria, holding her cute little straw hat against the whoosh from his closing front door. "He was much nicer this morning."

Alfie pulled her along the drive. "That's not the only odd thing," he said. "Wearing black tie with his yachting jacket? It's just not done!"

"Maybe he wanted to see if I'd show up with you, to be sure I was who I said I was."

As soon as they set foot on Monty's worn stone hall floor, Nelson D.'s behavior lost their attention. Tuxedoed goons seized Alf and marched him toward the gold and white drawing room. Gloria hurried after, utterly ignored as the men stopped before the marble fireplace, where Monty was alternately waving and gnawing on a fat cigar.

"You good time Charlie," he snarled. "Think you can get back at old Monty by stealing his treasures? You got one chance to cough it up or you got a one-way ticket to the deep blue sea."

Alf went paler than his linen jacket. "I've stolen nothing, Monty, honest. I don't even know what's missing!"

Gloria scanned the room for a clue. Almost at once her eyes fixed on a break in the middle row of illuminated letters. The 'M' was missing.

Carlotta Crane, coiled on an armchair, pointed one scarlet fingernail at Gloria. "There's your thief! Search her!"

Monty's bruisers flexed their huge fists, eyeing Gloria. Monty took his cigar from his lips. Alf murmured something that sounded like a prayer. Gloria put a hand to her lips.

"Not your lovely letter M? But how? It was right there an hour ago."

Monty glowered. "You sure about that?"

"Of course." She turned worried eyes on him. "And I am not carrying a handbag or anything large enough to conceal that frame, so don't you think of blaming me. Or Alf either. It wouldn't fit into his jacket pocket. Ask any of those waiters who were buzzing around outside. We didn't carry anything out of here with us."

Monty glared at the staff gathered down by the glass doors. They quailed as his eye passed over them. One or two bravely nodded, and someone muttered, "Their hands were empty, boss." After chewing the end completely off his cigar, Monty spat it onto the carpet.

"It's gotta be Diamond Jim," he growled, "gettin' his own back over Carlotta. How'd one o' his goons sneak in here in full daylight?"

He waved a hand. The bruisers released Alf. He and Gloria retreated silently to the hall, where another goon eyed them from beside the front door. He didn't approach, only swapped his toothpick from one side of his mouth to the other. If they tried to leave, he'd probably stop them.

"Alf," she murmured, "take me upstairs. We gotta talk."

In her bedroom Alfie paced. "We gotta scatter, doll. He'll throw us both off his boat if we stay."

"Not as long as he thinks we're both Harringtons," Gloria said. "He knows how much heat your father could bring down."

"That didn't stop him getting me socked in the eye!"

"You said yourself that anyone else who owed him that much woulda been hanging by his thumbs in the basement. Park your boots and help me think." He lit a cigarette, offered her one. She shook her head. "How would this Diamond Jim know which one, out of all Monty's European treasures, would hurt him the most to steal?"

"He wouldn't." Alf slumped into a chair. "Even I couldn't pick a single letter out of the alphabet. There're a dozen smaller items in that room alone that are worth more."

"Then why that one, and only that one? Could Carlotta have taken it to frame me and put Monty off me for good?" Gloria looked around for any sign of disarranged drawers or cushions. "She could have hidden it in here the instant we left."

Alf leaped up, pitching his smoke out the nearest window. "We'd better search this room before she convinces him to come looking."

A quarter-hour later, he replaced the last cushion on her little sofa as she closed her last drawer. Either the M wasn't here, or Carlotta was more devious than any diva in history.

"Now what?" he appealed to her. "We sneak out and run for the city?"

"And then where? All the way to Europe?"

"California?" he offered hopefully.

"We can't run forever, Alf." Gloria turned slowly on the spot, revolving the day in her mind. Somewhere there had to be a clue as to who took the *M*, and how, and why. Had Monty told any other guests about his plans for that *M*?

And then she knew.

"That fink!"

Alf looked up from the carpet. "Who?"

"Nelson D. That's who!" Gloria glared out at the pool. "He was right out there after lunch, waiting for us to leave for his tea party. I thought he looked familiar from one of Monty's clubs in the city. But it was Nelson D. all right. He sneaked over wearing his black tie like a waiter. Prob'ly carried a tray right in through the glass doors to the library and out again, with the framed letter under a napkin. Since we were already at his house, he didn't have time to completely change clothes, so he just threw on his yachting jacket and figured we wouldn't notice. But you did, Alfie. You spotted that black tie right away!"

"I did, didn't I? I'll be a hero!" Alf didn't look chuffed for long, though. "If we tell Monty who has it, he'll want to send his goons over to get it back. Carlotta will try to stop him, since she wants to be accepted by these toffee-nosed mansion-dwellers. But if Nelson D. gets even his cravat ruffled, he's sure to tell everyone at the yacht club how he was accused and mauled by that upstart even though he was at tea with you and me when the theft happened. Then Pops will want to know who you are, and if that gets back to Monty..." He flung himself onto her bed and threw his arm over his eyes. "We're doomed."

"Ain't you ever had a problem your Daddy's money couldn't solve? Out in the real world, we don't give up so easy. Only..." she tapped her Debutante Pink lips with one finger. "Will this really make us heroes, or will Monty drop us overboard because we know too much?"

"As long as he never finds out you're not my cousin, he'll be happy." Alfie peered from under his elbow. "In fact, if we get that letter back without violence, Carlotta will love us both. And she can make Monty mind his manners. She might even insist on him rewarding us."

"Izzat so?" Gloria gazed out at the distant golden gleam of the pig. There had to be a way to get Nelson D. to give back that M. What did he value as much as Monty cherished that letter?

The Saturday night jazz was hot and the gin was flowing freely when Gloria gathered her little crew at the far end of the pool, where the last light string lost the fight against the dark.

"Shush now," she said, tossing her borrowed feather boa over her shoulder, "and follow me. We gotta be ready when the fireworks start."

"Ready, chief," said Jimbo, hoisting his camera bag over his shoulder.

"You sure you can erase our faces outta this charade and make a print by breakfast tomorrow?"

"For what you're paying, doll, I could turn you into Theda Bara and him into Napoleon."

"Ready," said Alf, clutching a champagne bottle in one hand and dangling a pair of glasses from the other. "Although I still think we need more ladies' knickers."

Gloria batted his cheek with the end of her boa. "You go around asking for knickers, someone's gonna get curious and follow us. Then the jig will be up for sure." She hooked Alf's yachting jacket off a towel stand and led the way along the hedge toward the smaller gate, buried deep in shadow.

Twenty minutes later, the fireworks began. With all those starbursts flaring across the sky and reflecting off the moonlit ocean, who was to notice, or care, about a handful of flashes closer to the ground, half hidden by hedges and statues?

Sunday breakfast started a bit later, but Gloria didn't bother going for an early-morning constitutional. She applied her Debutante Pink lipstick, gave a last tug to the flowered frock the wardrobe mistress had assured her was suitable for Sundays on Long Island, and hurried down to the terrace to pick a seat where she could see the pool and, beyond it, the hedge hiding Nelson D.'s gate.

Alf slouched out a few minutes later, taking a seat beside her. He accepted a cup of coffee from a black-tie waiter and guzzled it down, signaled for a refill and lit a ciggie. Then he tapped his lighter on the glass-topped table, over and over. Click, click, click.

"Stop it, Alf," Gloria murmured. "Nerves will give the game away."

He glared, but pocketed the lighter.

Other guests ambled out, got settled. Eventually, Monty and Carlotta appeared. This time the singer's gaze lingered on Gloria with speculation rather than rage. She'd had time to think about the statues. Good. Gloria gave her a small smile and got one twitch of the lips back.

Monty was still grousing about his missing letter when Nelson D. appeared through the hedge, one hand clutching a white-wrapped parcel. Alf jerked like a startled goat. Gloria slapped at his neck. As everyone stared, she said, "A terrible big insect. I hope your neck won't swell and cut off your breathing, Alfie."

Thus, Nelson D. was climbing the terrace steps, his long face purple with exertion and ire, before Monty noticed him. The cigar waved.

"Welcome, neighbor. Pull up a chair. Bring 'im a coffee, someone."

"I wouldn't sit down in this den of iniquity for a million dollars in gold-plated stocks." Nelson D slapped a large photographic print down on the table by Monty and threw a crumpled page of gold-embossed notepaper on top. "I don't know how you created this, this…*farce*, but you win. Here is your blasted letter M back. If that photo gets into a single newspaper anywhere in America, I will sue you all the way to the Supreme Court."

Placing his square, flat parcel on Monty's plate, he spun on his heel and strode back the way he came.

Monty ignored the photograph in favor of unwrapping his precious illuminated letter. Carlotta snatched the crumpled note and read it aloud, projecting to be heard the length of the table.

"Bring back the letter M or this photo appears in all the Sunday papers."

She spun the photo for a closer look, laughed, and held it up for the rest. Gloria looked too, as if she didn't already know what she'd see.

There was Nelson D.'s iconic golden pig in pride of place, wearing a feather boa, with a flapper draped over it, her bobbed hair hanging down to hide her face. Below her slumped what looked very much like Nelson D. himself, in his yachting jacket, his back against the pig's plinth. In one hand he held a champagne glass at a precarious angle. The other hand rested on a pair of filmy knickers easily visible against his dark trousers. As the image passed hand to hand, Carlotta gave Monty a nudge.

"No business at breakfast, but you gotta thank them that got him to return it, honey, before things hadda get nasty."

"What? Who…?" Monty looked up, bewildered. Carlotta handed him the note. The photo made its way back to him.

"It's our notepaper." She raised eyes filled with sly amusement. "Now which of our guests was wearing a frock like that one last night?"

Monty frowned. "I don't know. Why would I know? You think I look at goils' dresses?"

"No, sweetie," said his mistress, her luscious lips smirking with suppressed laughter. "But I do, and I can tell you that it's Miss Gloria and her cousin Alf in that picture, all tricked out to look like Nelson D. and some floozie. Don't take offense, Miss Gloria. I can see you're a real class act."

Monty frowned at the photo again. His beady eyes shifted between Gloria there and Gloria at his breakfast table. "It was you done this?"

"Well, Alfie too."

He glared for so long that Gloria began to fear she'd badly miscalculated. Then he laughed.

"You's one smart cookie, Miss Gloria. Carlotta wants me ta play nice with our ritzy neighbors, and that could never happen if I sent my own guys over there."

The view spun briefly before Gloria's eyes as she sucked in a breath. Beside her, Alfie exhaled. They'd survive this weekend after all.

Monty went on, "You ain't asked for nothin' but ole Monty likes to show his gratitude."

"No business at the breakfast table," Carlotta repeated. "But I was thinking… we should get some statues for our lawn. Not a pig like that awful man has. Tasteful ones, from Italy. You think so, Gloria?"

The 13th Letter
M
The End

IN A COLD COUNTRY

By Lisa de Nikolits

Toronto, Canada, Present day.

"Yes, Madame. Sorry, Madame. Thank you, Madame."

I woke with a start, covered in sweat.

Something terrible had happened but I couldn't remember what.

I lay in bed, trying to remember what the bad thing was, what day it was, and what I was supposed to be doing.

I pulled my comforter tightly around me. It was dark but that meant nothing. My basement apartment had one window and it was in the single room that served as a living room, kitchen and laundry, with a small washroom in the corner.

I peered at my phone: 3:33 a.m.

I sat up and turned on the bedside light, soaked in a greasy cold sweat. I blinked the sleep from my eyes and got up.

I grabbed my ratty chenille dressing gown and opened up my laptop, gnawing at my fingernails which were already bleeding in places.

I clicked on Facebook, with a sick feeling in my stomach.

As expected, there it was. A new message, from a new account. The privacy settings on Facebook had declined to the point where anyone could message you. There was nowhere to hide.

As always, there was a single line.

This was the twelfth message, posted from the twelfth profile that my stalker had created.

I'll tell you when it's time.

One line a week. Always posted at 11:11 p.m. The time when divine beings have a message for you, or so I'd always been told. Never mind angels, I was being chased by the devil.

When the first message popped up, I thought it was a mistake. Spam.

There was a little girl

But the next message, a week later, stopped me in my tracks.

from a land far away

How did they know? Then, the third week:

not a very nice little girl

My blood ran cold.

I wrote down all the messages as soon as they came in, then I blocked the user.

The lines made a disturbing poem.

There was a little girl
from a land far away
not a very nice little girl
she always got her way
and now that little girl
is so, so alone
in a cold country
like a dog without a bone
old dog, old dog
one day I'll make you pay
you won't see me coming

and now:

I'll tell you when it's time

Time for what? I hurried back to my friend's Facebook page to see if the picture had resurfaced.

But, true to her word, it was no longer there.

I clicked on the profile picture of the latest message and there I was at the museum gala, wearing the necklace. The necklace that I had reported stolen, all those years ago.

I had thought about deleting my Facebook account, but I didn't want to do that, since it was my last lifeline to the world. In any case, my stalker would find another way to get to me.

I was about to block the user when I saw three dots moving. The unknown person at the other end of the Ethernet was typing.

Instead of making me wait for another week, a second message was incoming.

I held my breath and tugged my moth-eaten pink chenille gown tighter around me.

Boston Cream at 10 a.m., on the day of our Lord. You know where.

I waited but there was nothing more. I stared at the laptop, unable to move.

Fight, flight or freeze.

In the past, I'd fought with all my might. Then, I fled. And now, I was frozen.

I was 74 years old, and it was time to account for my sins.

Johannesburg, South Africa, 1977.

"Yes, Madame. Sorry, Madame. I'll fix that, Madame."

I gave her a practiced look of withering scorn. "Thank you." I was gracious. "Next time, make sure to iron the pleat precisely along the seam, not to the side of it. As you know, Lily, my clothes are expensive and we don't want anything ruined, do we?"

"No, Madame. Sorry, Madame."

The truth was, I had no business asking Lily to iron my linen suits. The labels clearly stated *Dry Clean Only*, but Lily was our maid. I expected her to be able to do anything and everything I asked.

Harald, my husband, chose that moment to walk into the room and Lily looked relieved.

"Cup of tea, please, Lily?" he asked.

"Yes, Master." Lily bowed her head and rushed off to the kitchen, leaving me and Harald in the laundry, with my linen trousers on the ironing board.

"Dry cleaners, Cinders," Harald commented, not for the first time.

"She needs to learn." I studied him. "You look very dapper. New tie?"

He grinned and I was reminded why no one could resist Harald's charm. Born into a distinguished lineage, his movie-star good looks rounded out the package and when I landed him, shortly after my debutante's ball, everyone, including me, thought I'd hit the jackpot.

"For good luck. I'm going to head to the track now. You ready or will you join me there?"

It was Saturday. Racing day. Harald was part of a collective that cost a pretty penny. It also meant that on Saturdays, nothing existed except the track.

I enjoyed going. We were in a catered suite with a covered awning, very pleasant.

"I'll come with you," I said. Going to the track involved highway driving and I did as little of that as possible.

"Cancel the tea," Harald sang out to Lily as we gathered our things to leave. "Have a good day and don't do anything I wouldn't!"

I saw a quick smile flash across Lily's face, and I wanted to slap her.

"How will she ever learn her place, when you treat her like a friend?" I asked him, getting into our Mercedes convertible.

I felt Harald looking at me. He'd paused, keys halfway to the ignition.

"Learn her place?" he said. "Cinders, you're a bloody witch. She's a person, for God's sake. An intelligent person who cleans our clothes and gets hauled over the coals for not ironing them exactly how you like it, when she shouldn't be doing it anyway."

"An intelligent person?" I mocked him. "So, you and she discuss existential philosophies while I'm not watching? She's a maid and she's lucky to have a job."

Harald rubbed his face. This wasn't a new argument. Harald hated apartheid. He genuinely believed the Black people should be in power which made me laugh. They'd take our houses and our jobs and the whole country would go to hell in a handbasket.

"I'm not going to argue with you today," he said softly. "I wish you weren't the way you are, but there's nothing I can do about it."

"You're sorry you married me?" I twisted my sapphire and diamond engagement ring on my finger. "You want a divorce?"

I watched him dig his fingers into his eyeballs. He couldn't afford to divorce me. I funded everything. His family might trace their lineage back to the King of England, but he hardly had two pennies to rub together.

He started the car. "No," he said, not meeting my gaze. "I just wish you were nicer to Lily."

"And I wish you were less nice. Let's go."

We drove to the track in silence.

I was 28 and I felt like I was 60. Harald and I had been married for two years and I had no idea why, but my life troubled me. I'd done everything I was supposed to; be head girl at my elite school, graduate from university, marry well and live happily ever after.

Only the happy ever after was a real let-down. Nothing to do but decorate the house and wonder if I should have a baby. So I picked on Lily, which made me feel important.

My parents died when I was fifteen. My father crashed his little Cessna 185 Skywagon and took my mother with him.

My aunt returned from Canada and took care of me until I was 18 and then she left me to it, saying that South Africa was too depressing. She offered to take me with her, but I had my sights on Harald and my perfect life.

We got to the track and I followed Harald into the suite.

"Trouble in paradise?" Berry asked me as we grabbed our race forms and chose our seats outside.

"Same old, same old," I said. Berry was my best friend. We were at school and university together. Harald had studied law, but he spent most of his time protesting apartheid and getting tear gassed. Berry's husband, Teddy, was a political writer at *The Star*, a big job for a young guy. He, like Harald, was anti-apartheid, fighting for change where he could.

Berry was on the fence. Equal rights for all, but keep things the way they were. Mainly, the wives tried not to discuss the situation.

"Let's focus on the positives," Berry would say. "I mean, we're nice to the people we meet throughout the day. It's all we can do."

I happily eyed my breakfast plate from the buffet as Berry and I got settled outside.

"Eggs look great," I said. "They must have a new chef. That last cook, if you can even call him that, was just hopeless."

"Yes, Teddy said they've got a new guy."

Something in Berry's tone made me turn and look at her.

"You okay?" I asked through a mouthful of freshly baked croissant and scrambled eggs with sour cream and caviar.

"Ja, I'm fine." But she wasn't. Berry, for reasons I could never understand, was never interested in the food. It was one of the main reasons I came.

"Bee, what's up?" I was concerned.

"It's just…"

I put down my plate. "Spit it out."

"Teddy heard that Harald's in over his head." She said it quietly and wouldn't meet my eye.

"What do you mean? At work? Harald said the partners love him."

"Ja. Well look." Berry sounded like she was close to tears and just then the boys came bounding out, grinning and clutching their racing cards.

"Did you girls bet?" Teddy asked and we shook our heads.

Neither Teddy nor Harald sensed anything was wrong.

"We knew you wouldn't," Harald crowed. "So I bet for you. Here. Trifecta of Lucky Guy, Spin the Wheel and Your Numbers Up."

"Thank you." I studied his face. In over his head? What did Berry mean? I'd have to get the truth from her, because Harald wouldn't tell me a thing.

Next thing, the horses were out of the gate and the race was done. No winners.

"Ja, well, fine. Better luck next time." Harald was unfazed.

"Ladies room, now." I hauled Berry to her feet.

I closed the stall behind us. "Tell me everything."

"Harald's up to his eyeballs at the bookies. And they fired him from the law firm for taking bribes."

"How long have you known?"

She shrugged. "Teddy told me a few days ago. He was waiting for Harald to tell you himself."

"I can't stay here." I felt dizzy. "Berry, call me a limo. Tell Harald I've got a headache. Actually, I don't care what you tell him."

"Don't tell him I told you," she begged me. "Teddy swore me to secrecy, but I had to tell you."

"Of course you did." My whole face felt numb. I heard myself speaking but I couldn't feel my face.

"Will you be okay?"

"Ja Bee, for sure. Don't worry, you had to tell me. But," I grabbed her by the shoulders, "don't tell anyone else, okay?"

"Sugar, apparently everybody already knows." Berry was miserable. "Only you and me were in the dark."

"Great." Now my social standing was blown to pieces too.

"I'll phone you later," I said, then I ran to the main entrance and found my limo.

I couldn't believe this was happening, and yet, I could.

"Standard Bank, Braamfontein," I told the driver. "As fast you can."

Inside, I demanded to see the bank manager, and of course he ushered me in.

"Coffee, Mrs. Douglas Evans?"

"No." I was brusque. "Sorry, Gene, but this is an emergency. We need to look at my accounts right now."

An hour later, every single aspect of my happy-ever-after was like dust in the wind.

I was screwed. Royally screwed. How had it happened?

I needed to think. I had to come up with a plan.

And along the way, I'd kill Harald for what he'd done.

Kill him and eat his heart.

That boy had no idea what was coming to him.

Toronto, Canada, 1978-2024

I got us out of the mess.

Not easily.

After I finished with the bank manager, I had lunch at my favorite restaurant.

I slowly worked through mussels in white wine, cream and garlic, mopping up the sauce with half a dozen small brioche buns. Then I tucked into a lovely salmon Pernod served on a bed of rocket mash, with white wine, paprika and Pernod-infused cream sauce. By the time I polished off the final crumb of a superb crème brûlée, I'd worked out what to do.

On the way home, I sent a telegram to my aunt in Canada, saying that Harald and I needed a fresh start and that we'd be coming to live in Toronto within a few months. I asked her if she would sponsor us, and reassured her that I'd pay the legal fees.

She lived in a shoebox in Kensington Market, so I told her to get us a furnished apartment and that I'd take it from there.

I also told her to get a storage locker.

I said I was planning to open a shop with African art and knick-knacks, and I'd be shipping boxes of cheap curios to her. I'd undervalue the goods, so she wouldn't have to pay taxes. If she did, I'd repay her.

Her response, a few days later, via a long telegram, was that she was glad I was coming and that she'd do as I asked.

In addition to running our credit cards up to the max, Harald had forged my signature, giving him access to accounts he should never have been near.

I gave the bank manager what-for, for letting it happen. "All these years I've been coming to you *in person*," I hissed, "and out of nowhere, my husband brings in documents by himself? You should be fired. The signature doesn't even match mine."

Gene went an interesting shade of green. "He's your husband," he stammered, as if that explained everything, but I guess that back in the day, in South Africa, it did.

My husband. Who wasn't sober for a day after I learned what he had done.

The only person I could trust was Berry. All our other so-called friends dropped us like we were flies on pig shit.

I took Harald away for a long weekend at Sun City, a gambling resort a few hours north of Johannesburg and before we left, I sat Lily down for a cup of tea.

"I'm sorry I've been hard on you," I said, and her eyes widened in surprise. "I've been struggling. Believe it or not, white people have got problems too."

Her face froze and I think she would have got up and left, but I put out my hand and stopped her. "Maybe we won't ever be friends, but let's have some tea."

What could she say?

"Yes, Madame."

"Ag, I forgot the biscuits. Will you get them, Lily? Bring the big tin."

"Yes, Madame."

As soon as she left, I drugged her tea with some crushed sleeping tablets. Not enough to kill her, but enough to make her sleep for at least ten hours.

"Thank you," I said when she returned. "Come now, drink my tea."

She took a sip and pulled a face. "It is very bitter."

"Add more sugar. Dunk a biscuit. You don't want to hurt my feelings, do you, Lily?"

"No, Madame. Sorry, Madame."

She drank the tea.

Later that evening, I checked on her in the servant's quarters. She was fast asleep. I hadn't realized quite how young she was. Or how beautiful. Her skin was so smooth and she looked like a queen, with her high cheekbones and sensual mouth.

I looked around her room. It was neat and tidy. And bare. With just a basin to wash herself in, and a toilet without a seat cover. Unpainted concrete walls and floor. It was cold and damp and I shivered.

I shook myself. This was no time to turn into a lefty. I had to follow through with my plan if I was going to survive.

I stirred more crushed-up sleeping tablets into the water glass beside her bed. The longer she slept, the better.

Then I phoned Berry and gave her the go-ahead. I took my useless husband to Sun City where he sat next to the swimming pool and got drunk.

When we returned on Sunday night, the house had been burgled. Every single piece of my family's jewelry was stolen, along with several paintings.

"But how did the burglars get into the safe?" The cops were baffled. "Sure, your maid opened the security gates, because no one except you and her and your husband knew the code. But the safe wasn't tampered with."

"It's probably my fault." I looked sheepish. "I worry that I'll forget the numbers, so they're here."

I turned over a coaster next to my bed. "Safe#1950000" was cello taped to the underside.

"I guess Lily saw it when she was cleaning," I shrugged.

"She says she was asleep the whole time," the cop said.

"The whole time?" I was incredulous. "Pull another one."

"We heard you've had a bad run of luck recently," the detective said to Harald who was holding a glass of scotch.

Harald looked confused. "Ja, so what? It's a temporary thing."

"Doesn't sound like it," the detective observed. "Maybe you staged this whole thing for the insurance money."

Harald laughed. "That would take more energy than I've got."

Everyone turned to look at me, accusations written across their faces.

My eyes welled up with tears.

"For heaven's sake. Yes, things are not good, but I've lost all my family heirlooms. If I needed the money, I would have sold them. Instead, they're God knows where and they won't get a pittance of their value. Besides, the insurance value pales to what they're really worth."

Which was a lie. They were all over-valued.

In the end, the cops agreed Lily had to be behind it.

Harald cried like a baby when she was taken away and sentenced to 20 years in jail.

I went shopping with Berry. We had so much fun, buying wooden statues, masks, ostrich eggs, carvings and sculptures. We hid the jewelry in the carvings, boxed it all up and sent it to my aunt.

What Harald didn't know was that I had close to a hundred thousand dollars' worth of Krugerrands in the safe. And they made their merry way to Canada, too.

And we got the insurance money.

The only time I cried was when I hugged Berry goodbye at the airport.

"Come visit, ja?" I asked, but I knew she wouldn't, and I knew I'd never return.

"Of course, yes. You look after yourself, okay?"

I shepherded Harald onto the plane.

We arrived in Canada in the middle of February. I watched the snow falling from the window of our furnished apartment near Bloor Street. It was so pretty and so quiet. I wasn't unhappy to be where I was.

But I still had one problem to get rid of.

And it turned out, I didn't even have to try very hard.

The boy needed his liquor, so he went out in the middle of a winter storm, wearing only his thin-soled leather shoes, his once-lawyerly suit and a raincoat. A raincoat!

It wasn't my fault he died of exposure.

I told the cops I was asleep when he left. I said that he'd been struggling with the drink, and he'd had some bad luck back in South Africa. We came to Canada to start a new life, to work on our marriage and help him get sober.

"But," I said, my eyes welling up with tears, "it was clearly too late."

What the police didn't know was that, before he went out, I took his keys and hid them.

There was no way he could get back inside.

Good thing he had life insurance. The way I saw it, he was repaying the debt he owed me.

Finally, my life was back on track again.

I found a lovely apartment in Rosedale and befriended a lot of other rich South Africans.

Canada worked out just fine, but things were expensive. Over time, I used all the insurance money from the burglary. Then I used Harald's life insurance.

I treated myself to some cruises and those, along with my fine dining, depleted my savings. I thought about getting a job, but I wasn't qualified to do anything.

I was sure one of the rich South African men would offer to marry me, but I finally had to admit defeat.

I gave up my Rosedale apartment and moved to a basement apartment in a rooming house in Lansdowne. You can be sure that none of my rich South African friends came to visit me there.

Bit by bit, I sold the family jewelry. And I sold the Krugerrands.

Nine years later, I had one piece left. The Bulgari necklace.

I was on the verge of selling it when one of my few remaining friends bought me a ticket to a museum gala. I decided what the hell, why not wear it one last time?

My friend unknowingly outed me by posting a pic on Facebook which was quickly followed by the first message.

There was a little girl

And message after message after that, and finally, the thirteenth message asking to meet.

Boston Cream at 10 a.m., on the day of our Lord. You know where.

I'd stared at the screen, soaked in sweat.

I knew what I had to do.

I had to face the music.

Fine, I messaged back. *I'll meet you. Tim Hortons it is. Sunday morning. 10 a.m.*

I gave the address of my local Tim Hortons, but I was sure they knew it anyway.

I wished I could message Berry and tell her what was going on, but she had died.

She and I had reconnected on Facebook a while back, but a year ago, she was taken from me by a vicious cancer that showed no mercy.

I couldn't tell the friend who had taken me to the gala. I had no one.

I was completely alone.

I got dressed. It was mid-winter, so I yanked on my boots. Lack of exercise and an affinity for junk food had wreaked havoc with my body. I was in constant pain and more than a hundred pounds overweight. Fast food was my only friend and it had cost me dearly.

I dragged myself to the Timmie's and sat down heavily. I shed my coat, scarf and gloves and trudged up to the counter for an extra-large double-double, two cheese tea biscuits, two Boston Creams and half a dozen mixed Tim Bits.

I polished those off and was about to stand up and order round two, when I saw her.

Lily and Harald's daughter.

The resemblance was as clear as day. She was stunning.

I plopped back down in my chair, feeling like a pus-filled spider facing an ethereal elf.

She sat in front of me and stared at me in silence for a while. I picked my cuticles, hiding my hands in my lap.

She finally spoke. "For someone so completely evil, you look ridiculously ordinary."

Her scorn reminded me of someone. Right, me, when I was talking to Lily.

I waved my hand at her. "Get it out of your system. I've got nothing left anyway. I did what I had to do. It was what it was."

Her face changed. No longer serene, she looked demonic.

I'd hit a nerve.

"That's it?" she hissed. "You ruined my mother's life. You ruined my father's life. And that's all you've got to say? It was what it was?"

I shrugged. "Your father was a drunk and a gambler."

She looked like she was going to explode.

"You should watch that half of the gene pool," I advised her. "Addictions run in the family."

"He drank because of you!" Her eyes bulged. Not so pretty when she was angry, I thought.

I remembered Harald, so young and beautiful and full of promise. I was to blame for a lot of things, but his demise wasn't one of them. Or was it?

My heart did a feather dance in my chest. "You're giving me palpitations," I said, patting my chest. "You're not good for my health. What's your name anyway?"

"None of your business."

I'd had enough. I just wanted to end this.

My breath was catching in my throat and sweat soaked my armpits. I tugged at my sweater to give myself room to breathe, but my heart pounded faster and my breath came out in ragged, hoarse pants.

Old dog, old dog. Yes, that was me.

"You're quite the poet," I said, trying to buy time before we got down to business.

"I have my Masters in Creative Writing," she said, holding her head high. "I'm going to be a famous poet."

I snorted. "Poets never make money. You'd better take what you came here for."

I reached into my sweater and pulled out the necklace. I undid the clasp with shaking fingers. I put the necklace on the table and pushed it toward the evil elf.

"There. This is what you wanted."

"You're wrong. I never wanted it," she said, and tears filled her eyes. "That wasn't why I came."

She shredded a napkin into a hundred tiny pieces, each the same size.

I sat back and waited. She'd tell me eventually.

"You!" She shook her head. "What a disappointment! I expected a magnificent evil queen, but you're just a doughy, soggy, pathetic mess. What did you do with your life? Nothing."

She was right. What had I done?

and now that little girl
is so, so alone
in a cold country
like a dog without a bone

I tried to think what my life had amounted to, but I couldn't recall much of anything.

The girl picked up the necklace and dangled it from her fingers. "This is paste."

"Rubbish. My mother had the best. That's the most famous piece, which is why I saved it for last."

"My dad sold the real one," the girl smiled. "Luckily for you, it was the only one he got the chance to steal. And he wasn't fired for taking bribes. He was fired because he was working for the ANC, trying to get us our freedom, which is what he used the money for. The gambling was a front."

My mouth dropped open. The African National Congress. Of course! It all made sense.

"But my dad was reckless. Too impatient. He thought he could fund the whole revolution with your money. And then it went sideways."

"Why didn't he tell everyone the truth? Why pretend to be a gambler?" The pain in my chest was getting worse. I grabbed my left arm.

"Ja, like you would have forgiven him for being an ANC supporter. The law firm didn't want to be associated with the ANC, so they put out the lie. He stayed with you because he needed you."

"But how did he get the necklace? I kept it under lock and key."

"He switched it one 'romantic' night after you wore it."

I remembered that night with bile. Harald had told me to wear nothing but the necklace while he made love to me. Which, to be honest, stressed me out big time, but I went along with it, taking it off as quickly as I could, and having a bath.

"Not to be rude, but you people didn't have the wherewithal to make a replica. I can't see you guys sitting around your fires in the townships, making fake rubies and diamonds."

"'Not to be rude.' And yet, you are beyond rude. Others around the world helped our cause. A gem smith in London volunteered time and materials." The girl studied her manicure. "There were pictures in all the society pages, so it was easy to copy. Vintage 18K diamond necklace, pave-set with graduated heart-shaped rubies and cabochon sapphires."

She looked around the Timmie's with disdain. "But you were right about one thing. My father was a weak man. He turned to drink and then he died." She pointed at the necklace. "Still, that picture of you on Facebook came in handy. I couldn't figure out a way to confront you, but then there you were, wearing the very necklace you claimed my mother had stolen. My mother, who died in prison when I was ten."

"If she died when you were ten, how do you know all this?" I managed to say.

The girl gave a snort. "My parents were legends. Everybody knew everything and they told me."

I slid down in my chair. "What's your plan now? I doubt the police would be interested in an old woman like me, for a crime committed in another country such a long time ago."

"They would care. But you know what I want? To hear you say 'Yes, Madame, sorry Madame,' like you made my mother do all that time."

I snorted. "Yes, fat chance of that." I was relieved that the pain in my chest had eased. I could breathe again. I let go of my left arm and picked up the necklace. Could it be paste? My last nest egg. Worthless.

"I read that in Canada, you have to address the judge as 'Madam Justice.' My plan is to turn you in and listen to you say those words."

I stared at the girl in horror. She was serious.

Before I could stop her, she took out her phone and snapped a pic of me holding the necklace.

I squealed in horror and threw the necklace on the table.

"I'll make a deal," The girl said, quietly putting her phone on the table between us. "Say it now, to me."

The red recording light was on. "Have you been taping this conversation?"

"Of course I have. So let's hear you say it, and I won't turn you in. Say 'Yes, Madame, sorry Madame.' Say it like you mean it."

I looked down. Maybe prison life wouldn't be so bad. I was struggling to make ends meet and now my last resort, my necklace, was a fake. Would a prison cell be worse than my basement apartment? Yes, it would. The noise of the other inmates, the thin mattress. I needed my soft bed. I needed my junk food. It was the only happiness I had left.

"I—" I stumbled and couldn't say the words.

The girl folded her arms.

Could I grab her phone and make a run for it? Who was I kidding? She was fast and young, and she'd be on me before I even got out of the chair.

"I'm sorry, Madame. Yes, Madame," I mumbled, clenching my hands and closing my eyes.

"No mumbling. Eye contact." The girl was sharp.

I raised my eyes. "I'm sorry, Madame. Yes, Madame." I said it more loudly and my eyes filled with tears. I felt transported, back in time, back to South Africa, only now I felt like Lily and I felt the humiliation and the powerlessness that she must have felt.

"Again."

"I'm sorry, Madame." Tears flowed down my cheeks. I didn't want to go to prison, but I'd sent Lily there, to her death. "Yes, Madame."

"You're only sorry because you got caught," she commented. "You would have lived the rest of your life with no remorse whatsoever."

"I thought it was the only way for me to survive." Snot ran down my face and I wiped my nose with my sleeve. "I really thought that!"

I sniffed hard. It was time to make peace with the horror of my past.

This was my confession, on the day of the Lord. It was time to repent.

"Yes, Madame. I *am* sorry, Madame." I leaned toward the phone. "I am sorry with all my heart. I confess to you, that I sinned against you and your mother and your father for my own selfish gain and I am sorry."

The girl looked exhausted. "I wanted this for so long, I can't tell you." Her face cleared and she was beautiful again. "You're a worthless loser, but this helped me. Now I can move on with my life."

She stopped the recording and pocketed her phone.

"Goodbye, old dog," she said quietly.

I wanted to ask if she could spare twenty dollars, but I couldn't bring myself to say the words.

She zipped up her coat and I watched her leave.

Outside, the snow was still falling.

> *in a cold country*
> *so, so alone*

I was too tired to move so I decided to rest for a while. Then I'd get myself some doughnuts and a coffee and head home.

But all I could hear were the words ringing in my ears.

Yes, Madame. I'm sorry, Madame.

And then I felt the pain return to my chest. Only this time, I knew it wouldn't go away.

The 13th Letter
M
The End

SCAMMING GRANNY

By Lynne Murphy

Charlotte Manners was taking cookies out of the oven when her phone rang. She thought about letting it go to voicemail, because she was in a hurry to get the cookies to her condo's weekly coffee morning. And the screen said "Caller Unknown." But, as she said later, something compelled her to answer it.

A young man's voice said, "Mrs. Manners? I have your grandson on the line."

Charlotte said, "Justin?" What was he up to?

"Yes, it's me, Justin. I'm in bad trouble." It sounded as though he was crying.

Charlotte's heart skipped a beat. Justin never cried.

"What's wrong, dear? I'm here."

"I've been arrested."

Oh, no. Justin was such a good kid.

He was still talking. And he was definitely crying. "I hit another car. They said I was following too closely. And the other driver was hurt. Bad. They took her to the hospital. The cops let me talk to this lawyer. He says he can help me."

"Have you called your parents?" Charlotte barely managed to gasp this out.

"The cops took my phone, but please don't call them. Please. The car is damaged. Dad will kill me. Please talk to Mr. Pope. Here he is."

"Mrs. Manners?" The young man sounded very businesslike. "I'm Justin's lawyer. I'm sorry to say your grandson is in a great deal of trouble. The other driver was a pregnant woman, and she has been taken to hospital."

"Oh, good heavens," Charlotte said, but the man kept talking. "There's a witness who claims Justin was using his cell phone at the time of the accident. He denies this, but at the moment the police are holding him. We need to post bail. The amount is set at $9400. Justin is determined that his parents not be contacted."

"But—" Charlotte tried to interject.

"The money needs to be in cash and there's a non-disclosure agreement. That means you can't tell anyone what it's for, not your bank or anyone you may get in touch with. Do you understand? We need the money as soon as possible."

He said this very quickly, hardly taking a breath. Charlotte tried to break in and ask him to slow down but he just kept talking. When he finally stopped, she was shaking.

She barely managed to find the words she needed. "Where are you? How will I contact you?"

"Here is the number where you can reach me." He recited it slowly and carefully. "Call me as soon as you have the money and I'll come and pick it up. Please confirm your address for me."

Charlotte had trouble even remembering her own address. Finally, it came to her. Her mind was not working properly.

"Thank you. That is the address Justin gave me. I'll come as soon as you call me. But remember, time is of the essence."

"I'll be as quick as I can," she said.

In the background, she could hear Justin saying, "Thanks so much, Grandma." She hung up.

That was when she came to her senses.

Grandma! Her grandchildren never called her Grandma. She had always been Nana to all four of them.

The truth hit her like the proverbial ton of bricks. This had to be a scam, one of those telephone scams she had read about. Her seniors' club had even hosted a meeting with a policeman who had warned them about these crooks. And yet, she had almost been taken in.

As she calmed down, she remembered that Justin was working nights at his summer job. He should still be in bed. Just to make sure, she called his cell phone. She was very relieved to hear his groggy young voice answer.

"Nana? Wha's up?"

"It's all right, dear," she said. "Sorry—I called you by mistake. Go back to sleep."

She transferred the still-warm cookies to a tin and went down to the condo party room. She couldn't help smiling. How irritated the scamster would be when she never called him back! How long would it take before he phoned her again to ask if she had the money? $9400 indeed! She would have her police whistle handy when he called and blow it loudly in his ear.

She could hardly contain herself until all the ladies were seated with coffee and cookies in front of them. Then she burst out with the story of the morning's drama—how she had almost been fooled into thinking it was Justin calling. It was just by chance that she had been home when the scammer phoned.

"If I hadn't been delayed making these cookies, I would have been down here and missed that call."

"They are really good cookies," Maisie interrupted. "Is that rosemary in there?"

"Fresh rosemary." Charlotte nodded at Maisie. "But to get back to the scammers, I don't know how I could have been such an idiot as to believe them."

"The rosemary makes a big difference to the shortbread," Maisie said.

"Yes it does," Charlotte snapped. She wanted to finish her story. "If it hadn't been for that boy calling me 'Grandma'—"

Bessie cleared her throat, one of those "harrumph" noises she was in the habit of making. Charlotte saw that she was looking smugly at Maisie. Maisie was blushing.

"What's going on?" Charlotte asked.

There was a pause. Finally, Maisie said in a small voice, "I got caught this spring. By a gift card scam. You tell them, Bessie."

Bessie took over. "You gals all know Sharon, I think. She came to our pub nights a few times."

"The one with the purple hair?" Olive asked.

"That's Sharon. From Knox Church where Maisie and I go. Well, her email was hacked. And the hacker was sending out emails asking people to buy gift cards for her."

"Sharon said she was out of town and needed to get a present for her granddaughter," Maisie chimed in.

"It wasn't Sharon, Maisie. It was the hacker," Bessie said. "Anyway, Maisie went over to the drugstore and bought a $250 gift card. Luckily, she couldn't afford any more."

"I couldn't even afford that," Maisie said, mournfully. "But the phony Sharon said in the email she would pay me right back. I had to send her the numbers on the card. And it was awfully hard because of my poor sight. I finally had to scan it and send the scans to Shirley."

"And there went the money," Bessie said. "I hadn't checked my email for a while, so I hadn't read the hacker's message, but as soon as I did, I knew something was wrong. Because Sharon is a real tightwad and wouldn't spend that much on a gift. I phoned Sharon and we started calling people. But it was too late for Maisie. Sharon said she felt awful but that none of it was her fault."

"Sharon said I should have known it was a scam," Maisie said.

"She didn't even offer to pay Maisie part of the money."

The ladies all looked sympathetic. They knew Maisie didn't have a lot of money to spare.

Isobel, who had been very quiet, suddenly exploded. "Lord Jaysus, these scumbags need to get some of their own medicine. Charlotte, what say you meet up with that guy and call him out?"

"How would I do that?" Charlotte asked. "I don't want to have anything more to do with those horrible people." It was enough that she'd almost been taken in.

"We call the police and get them to send a cop to your place. Then when that crook comes to get the money, the cop can nab him. Have you kept his phone number?"

"I threw the paper in my recycling bin, but it's still in the kitchen. I don't know about this, Isobel. It was nearly an hour ago that I talked to him. He may think I'm not cooperating."

Bessie stood up. "That's a great idea, Isobel. Don't be such a wimp, Charlotte. You can think up an excuse for keeping him waiting. It would take you a while to get the money from the bank. If they think they've got you hooked, they'll be willing to wait."

When Bessie thought something was a great idea, it was difficult to stop her. "The police," Charlotte said. "Will they agree to meet the man at my place?"

"I think you should just notify the police and ask them what to do," Olive said. She was the least adventurous of the group. "I don't like to think of that man coming to your place."

Oh dear, Charlotte thought. *Olive ought to know that if you try to stop Bessie from doing something she just gets more determined.*

"Of course we have to involve the police," Bessie said. "But it'll be so much better if the scammer thinks he's got Charlotte fooled. Remember Ryan, that nice cop who came to the club to talk to us about scams? I'm going to phone him. Charlotte, you go contact the scammer."

"You need backup, Charlotte," Isobel said. "I'll come up to your place and hide in the bedroom when he comes and listen in. I've got better hearing than the rest of you. Let's give Bessie time to contact Ryan and then you can call this Mr. Pope."

"I want to be there, too," Maisie said. "After all, I'm the one who actually lost money."

Olive slammed her fist on the table. "You are all crazy as hoot owls. Well, I'm not letting you go into danger alone, Charlotte. I'm coming to your place too."

Charlotte felt as though she'd been caught up in a tornado. Why, oh why, had she told the ladies about the scammer?

"Olive, I want you to wait with me to meet Ryan. I might need you," Bessie said. "I'll call him and tell him the deets." And she hurried off, as fast as a woman of ninety pushing a walker can hurry.

Back in Charlotte's apartment, Isobel went into the bedroom to see where she should sit so she could hear everything.

Maisie insisted on staying in the living room. "What kind of a threat will I look like with my white cane and all? And I can record you on my phone in case Isobel doesn't get things right. You know how she flies off the handle."

"You know how to record on your phone?" Charlotte asked, astonished. Maisie was the least tech-savvy person she knew.

"My grandson showed me. Now you'd better get a bag ready for the fake money. Cut up some paper and stack it together so it looks like there's a wad of cash in there. Then you have to put a big bill on either side of the wad."

"I only have twenties. I never take fifties or hundreds from the machine."

"I have a couple of hundreds I was going to give the nephews for their birthdays," Isobel said. "I'll go up and get them. But I want them back when this is over."

"Of course you'll get them back," Charlotte snapped.

Isobel headed out.

Marveling at Maisie's sudden acquisition of useful ideas, Charlotte called on her to help cut up scrap paper into bill-sized pieces. They had no idea what $9400 in cash would look like, but they knew it would be sizeable. Isobel returned with her hundred-dollar bills when they were part way through the job and pitched in.

"Wrap it in plastic wrap so he can see the big bills and put it in a shopping bag," Isobel said when it looked like they had enough.

Charlotte had just finished doing this when her phone rang. It was Mr. Pope.

"Mrs. Manners? You're back at home so I assume you've been able to get the money. Justin is getting very anxious. They have him in the cells."

"I have it," Charlotte said. "I'm just getting it ready."

"Good. We were afraid you weren't going to be able to get it."

I'll bet you were, Charlotte said to herself.

Out loud she said, "I had to go to three banks. You can't get that much that much cash from any one bank."

"That's fine. I'll be there in about fifteen minutes. You haven't told anyone about this?"

"Not a soul," Charlotte lied cheerfully and disconnected. She discovered that she was almost starting to enjoy being deceitful.

The phone rang again. This time it was Bessie.

"I'm in the lobby. Ryan is on his way," she reported. "He says to wait till he comes before you call the scammer. He doesn't want you letting him into your apartment when you're alone. I told him Maisie was with you and he just snorted."

"Oh, dear. The scammer's on his way, too. I'm sorry, Bessie. He phoned me. I shouldn't have picked up."

"No, you shouldn't. Well, you'll just have to stall him when he gets there. Think of something. I'll call up as soon as Ryan arrives." She hung up.

"That *was* dumb of you, Charlotte," Isobel said. "Put some duct tape around the wad. Make it harder for him to open it if he tries." And she headed for the bedroom.

How had her friends suddenly become so full of larcenous ideas? She had just finished taping the bundle shut when there was a knock at the door.

"Mrs. Manners?" a man's voice said. Mr. Pope hadn't phoned up so someone must have let him in.

Charlotte looked desperately at Maisie, who could only say, "Stall, Charlotte, stall."

She went to open the front door. Mr. Pope was a surprise. He looked so young. He was quite short and had a silly little mustache which, she supposed, was to make him look older. How could he possibly be a criminal lawyer at his age? Then she remembered that of course, he wasn't. He was a crook. And a very young crook.

"Mr. Pope?" she said.

He stood in the front hall, eying Maisie. "I thought you'd be alone, Mrs. Manners," he said.

"This is my friend, Maisie, who I'm taking care of. She can't see you." She pointed to Maisie's white cane. "She's also quite deaf. Please come in."

Mr. Pope closed the door behind him and came into the living room.

"You have the money ready?" he asked, gesturing to the shopping bag Charlotte was holding.

She clutched it to her chest. She had to stall. But how?

"Cookies," Maisie croaked suddenly. "Cookies for Justin."

Charlotte understood what she meant. "If you could just wait a moment, Mr. Pope, I want to send Justin some of my freshly baked cookies. It will only take me a minute to get them ready."

"Mrs. Manners, time is of the essence. Justin's in the cells, as I told you. With hardened criminals."

"They're his favorite cookies." She rushed into the kitchen where she found the cookie tin sitting on the counter. She snatched it up. "Would you like a cookie?" she called out. "Homemade."

"Mrs. Manners, there's no time for this," Pope said. He sounded ready to explode.

She dropped the tin into the shopping bag with the duct-taped bundle. Mr. Pope grabbed the bag from her and opened the door.

That was when Isobel came rushing out of the bedroom. "Stop right there, you shyster," she shouted.

Mr. Pope wheeled around and stared at her. "Mrs. Manners, you lied to me," he said. "This is some sort of scam you've cooked up."

He charged out the door with Isobel, Charlotte and Maisie in pursuit and stopped dead. Between him and the elevator, there was a wall of seniors pushing walkers.

There were actually only three seniors with walkers, but it looked like more. Bessie was in the middle, leading the charge. Their friends, George and Jimmy, were on either side of her.

"Stop thief," Bessie shouted.

Mr. Pope turned around, but Charlotte, Isobel and Maisie were making a wall of their own. Maisie must have appeared to be the most vulnerable, because he gave her a push. She lashed out with her cane, got it tangled between his legs and he fell heavily to the floor.

The bag with the cookie tin went flying. Charlotte picked it up. Isobel rushed forward and plopped down on his legs, but Mr. Pope managed to roll sideways and she slipped off. He got to his feet and advanced on Charlotte.

"Give me that bag, you old witch!" he yelled.

Charlotte had never liked being called names. She drew back her arm, aimed the bag at Mr. Pope's crotch and swung with all her might.

She'd been a softball pitcher as a girl, and she still had a strong right arm. The result was all she could have hoped for. He gave a high-pitched shriek and dropped to his knees, clutching himself.

Isobel, who was still on the floor, grabbed his ankles and hung on. "Call 911," she yelled. "We can't wait for Ryan."

At that moment, the elevator door down the hall opened. Olive rushed out, shouting, "Police." She was followed by two large men, Ryan and his partner, Ed.

Ryan looked at the tableau in front of him and said, "Holy sh—. I thought you were going to wait for me to get here, Bessie."

"We couldn't wait, Ryan. The miscreant was going to escape," Bessie announced.

Ryan moved forward, bent down and took a good look at Mr. Pope.

"If it isn't Dennis!" he said. "What are you and your brother up to now?"

Mr. Pope moaned.

"You can let go of him," Ryan said to Isobel. "What have you ladies done to him?"

"We had to restrain him," Isobel said, getting to her feet. "He was trying to escape."

Mr. Pope shook his head. "I haven't done anything," he gasped out. "They attacked me. I just knocked on the door, looking for a friend of mine who lives in the building. They were waiting for me. That one," he pointed at Maisie, "hit me with her cane. And the other one hit me with her shopping bag. Arrest them!"

"Seriously?" Ryan said. "You want me to arrest these elderly ladies for attacking you? With a white cane and a shopping bag?"

"He pushed me first," Maisie said.

"I believe you," Ryan said. "On your feet, Dennis. You're coming to the station with us." And to his partner, "Put the cuffs on Dennis, Ed, and take him down to the car. I'll be there in a minute." He looked at the excited little group in front of him. "Well, maybe you better take him to the station right away and talk to him there. You need to get hold of his brother, too. I'll be there after I get this sorted out."

As his partner led the protesting man away, Ryan turned to Charlotte. "Can we talk things over in your apartment, Mrs. Manners? Just the ladies, thank you, gentlemen," he added, as George and Jimmy started to follow.

"You know Mr. Pope?" Charlotte asked when the ladies and Ryan were all seated.

Ryan nodded. "I've run into him before. Now, tell me what's been going on. He and his brother didn't get any money from you, right? It's still in that bag?"

"Oh, there's only a couple hundred dollars there," Charlotte said. "And a wad of cut-up paper." She pulled it out of the bag, along with the cookie tin. "And my cookies in here."

Ryan blinked. "Cookies?" he said. "You were giving him cookies?"

"Shortbread with rosemary," Maisie said. "Really good cookies. You should try one."

Charlotte opened up the cookie tin and held it out. "Go ahead, Ryan. And we'll explain to you how we scammed a scammer."

The 13th Letter
M
The End

A HOLLYWOOD TALE

By Ed Piwowarczyk

Nothing fascinates the public more than a celebrity death, especially when it involves murder among the denizens of moviedom. That's when my readers turn to me, Eve Brooks, to deliver the salacious details in my syndicated newspaper column, *Hollywood Whispers.*

So it was when the Los Angeles police found the body of producer Bill Alden in his rambling Spanish Colonial bungalow in Brentwood on a June night in 1935.

Joining him on his trip to the Great Beyond were Alice Simmons, a young actress he'd just married, and Betty Preston, a star with whom he had romantic ties. All three had been fatally shot.

The police's only lead was a statement from a neighbor who'd seen someone lurking near Alden's home the night of the killings. It was a woman, he assumed, although the figure wore a hat with the brim pulled down low, obscuring her face.

All of this gave rise to wild speculation, including rumors of jealous lovers and a ménage à trois.

Such stories—whether true, half-true, or false—are my stock-in-trade, and my fans expect me to deliver the goods.

In this case, I reported most of the story, but not all of it. I knew who did it, but held back the killer's identity from the police. To my mind, they'd find my tale difficult to swallow, and the murderer would walk away.

I vowed I would not let that happen.

***

My association with Bill Alden began about a year after I arrived in Los Angeles.

After a stint with a New York tabloid, I was hired by the *Los Angeles Gazette* in 1930, after the production of talkies had shaken up Hollywood. My *Hollywood Whispers* column was picked up by the Sentinel Newspaper Syndicate, and I was on my way.

Pretty good for my first year in L.A., but the public is fickle; I needed to expand my network of contacts. Landing Alden for an interview helped boost me to the top.

Alden, who was 40 when I met him in 1931, had started out as an actor and director in silent movies. Standing six feet tall, he had dark brown, slicked-back hair, hazel eyes, a cleft chin and a warm smile. A man-about-town, he was frequently seen in restaurants and clubs with a desirable woman on his arm.

With the arrival of talkies, he became a producer at Light and Shadow Pictures. He had a knack for discovering new talent, an eye for good material, and a string of box-office hits to his credit. His golden touch earned him comparisons to MGM's Irving Thalberg, Hollywood's "Boy Wonder."

After leaving unreturned phone messages for weeks, I tracked him down to the studio soundstage, determined to have him sit for an interview. I expected a polite runaround, but he quickly said yes, stipulating that it be over dinner and drinks at the Musso & Frank Grill.

Alden proved to be an engaging subject, not simply plugging his movies but also offering witty observations on the film industry.

As he ordered a round of drinks, he gave me an admiring once-over. "You know, I'm partial to brunettes."

"Blondes and redheads, too?" I teased, and he laughed.

"Good figure, nice legs… 'You Oughta Be in Pictures,' as the song says."

"Flatterer," I said.

That began our secret relationship. Morals clauses in contracts, including mine, were *de rigueur* in and around

Hollywood. Hanky-panky was frowned upon, and everyone had to tread carefully when it came to their liaisons.

Dinner and drinks at hot spots such as Musso's and The Brown Derby were beneficial to both of us. Alden got good publicity for the movies and performers he was promoting, while I heard the latest rumors about who was on the way up—or down.

I was under no illusion, however, that our occasional romps between the sheets would lead to anything permanent.

***

About eight months before Alden was killed, we were having coffee and dessert at Musso's when a buxom, middle-aged woman—five foot seven, green eyes, soft waves of chestnut hair falling to the shoulders of her curve-hugging red dress—strode up to our booth. She smiled broadly as she extended her hand, like a salesman gearing up to make his pitch.

"Mr. Alden, I'm Cora Simmons," she announced.

A bemused Alden rose from his seat. "I don't believe we've met," he said, "but we're just finishing—"

"I shouldn't have interrupted," she said, "but with both you and Miss Brooks here, well, what an opportunity. Allow me to introduce my daughter, Alice." She beckoned to a young woman at the entrance. A five-foot-six blonde, wearing a gold satin dress that accentuated her slim waist and gently rounded hips, approached us.

Alden sighed, sat back down, and motioned for the women to join us. I was about to get up to leave, but he put his hand gently on my arm. "Don't go," he whispered. "I'll need your opinion."

Once they'd settled in their seats, Cora launched into an agent-style promotion of her daughter. "Mr. Alden, I just know my Alice will be perfect for the lead in your new picture. Why, I was reading in Miss Brooks' column…"

Alden, however, was only half listening. He was focused on Alice, entranced by her sapphire eyes, full lips, and pageboy-style hair. She gave him a demure smile.

"You can see, Mr. Alden, that Alice will be Hollywood's next *big* star," Cora concluded. "What do you think, Miss Brooks?"

I gave a noncommittal response. "She'll need to appear in a few hits first."

"That's where you come in, Mr. Alden," Cora continued. "And Miss Brooks, you'll want to sit down with Alice for *Hollywood Whispers*."

"Mother!" Alice interjected. "Don't be so…shameless. It's embarrassing."

Cora scowled, but Alden held up his hands. "Ladies, please!" He paused, then lowered his hands to the table. "Miss Simmons, there's nothing to be embarrassed about. Your mother wants to help you make it. I understand."

He reached into his jacket pocket and handed Cora his business card. "Come see me tomorrow afternoon. I'll arrange for a screen test, and then, who knows? All right?"

Cora and Alice gushed their thanks as they stood up to leave.

"You'll just *love* her," Cora declared. Alice flashed another smile at Alden as they sashayed out.

"Well?" Alden asked. "What do you think of them?"

"Alice is too young for you," I answered. "I don't think she's jailbait, but I'd say she's no more than 18."

"Really?" he said in mock surprise.

"Uh-huh. As for Cora, she's an agent, not a mother. Tonight was no chance meeting. I'll bet she's trailed you for a while, waiting for the right moment to 'introduce' herself and Alice."

"If I get Alice's name on a contract, I'll be signing *her*, not her mother."

"Alice is her meal ticket, and Cora's not going to let her go. It'll be both of them or neither of them." I paused. "What about Betty?"

"What about her? It's not as if I'm going to *marry* this Simmons girl, or anything like that." He patted my hand. "Don't worry. I can handle it."

The way he'd eyed Alice told me otherwise.

***

The "Betty" in question was Betty Preston, a five-foot-five brunette with a bob cut with swooping ends, bee-stung lips, large brown eyes, and shapely legs. Her looks had boosted her to stardom in silent movies, but her prime asset in the new era of talkies was her husky voice, which brought sultriness to her roles in romances and melodramas. Audiences loved her.

She was willing to scrap with directors and producers to secure better roles, earning her a reputation for being "difficult." That hadn't deterred Alden from casting her when his roving eye inevitably fell on her.

A string of box office hits followed, and Betty and Alden carried their relationship from the soundstage into the bedroom. Their arrangement had wedding bells ringing in Betty's ears, but Alden wasn't about to give up his playboy ways.

***

Within a month of meeting Cora and Alice, Alden had signed Alice to a contract for her debut feature, and soon cameras were rolling on *My Tender Heart.* He told me he'd seen an "it-girl quality" in Alice's screen test that prompted him to cast her in the lead role. If it worked out as he hoped, he'd sign her to a new, multi-picture deal.

"The same 'it-girl quality' Betty Preston had when you signed her?" I asked over drinks at the Frolic Room.

He nodded. "But Alice has the potential to be bigger than Betty."

"You really believe that?"

"Yes, but don't quote me. Betty's nose is already out of joint."

"No wonder. She expected *My Tender Heart*, but you gave her *Midnight Rendezvous*. It's the last picture you've got her under contract for, right?"

Alden nodded. "I'll make it up to her."

"You're not worried she'll leave?"

"She knows we've got a good thing going." He tossed back the last of his whiskey as we prepared to go. "Why give it up?"

"Other studios would jump at the chance to have her name on their pictures." I picked up my handbag. "Remember, you don't run the only game in town."

***

"Quite a coup for an unknown, landing the lead in *My Tender Heart*," I told Alice and Cora while interviewing them at the Derby. "Congratulations. That role was supposed to go to Betty Preston, wasn't it?"

"Yes, but once Mr. Alden saw my Alice's screen test, well, there was no question about who should get the part," Cora said.

"He has a lot riding on Alice's success." I turned to Alice. "How do you feel about it? Nervous?"

"A little bit," she answered. "Everything's happening so fast, but Bill—Mr. Alden, I mean—is looking out for me." Suddenly, she paused. "Oops. There's also Mother, of course. How could I forget?" She glanced at a frowning Cora. "Sorry."

Cora replaced her frown with a crocodile smile. "That's all right, dear." She patted Alice's hand, and I could have sworn the young woman winced slightly. "Remember, I always have your best interests at heart."

"Yes, Mother." Alice turned back to me. "Working on *My Tender Heart* has been exciting, but the attention can be overwhelming. That's what I was trying to say earlier. I'm glad I have Mr. Alden and Mother guiding me."

"Once *My Tender Heart* is finished, what's next for Alice Simmons?" I asked.

She turned to Cora. "Mother?"

"Mr. Alden and I are reviewing a few scripts, so it's too early to say," Cora answered.

Addressing Alice again, I asked, "Is there any star you'd like to work with? Can you see yourself and Betty Preston doing a picture together?"

"Miss Preston and I in the same movie?" She put her hand over her heart. "That would be *such* an honor. Maybe Mr. Alden—"

"Let Mr. Alden focus on *your* career, not hers," Cora interrupted.

"Mother, I think it's a wonderful idea," Alice replied. "It could give my career a boost. Don't you think so, Miss Brooks?"

Before I could answer, Cora snapped, "Sharing the spotlight is *not* my idea of boosting your career." She stood, and said coolly, "Alice, we must be going."

As Alice headed for the door, Cora swiveled to face me. "Next time, Eve, keep the focus on Alice. Don't bring up Betty Preston again when you're talking with us."

"It was a harmless question," I said. "Alice is a big girl. She can speak for herself."

"She's immature and needs me to look after her interests. I know what's best for her, not you or Bill Alden. I won't let anyone come between me and Alice."

With that, Cora gave me a curt goodnight, turned on her heel, and followed Alice out the door.

As they left, I wondered how much longer the young woman could stand being under her mother's thumb.

***

My Tender Heart became another hit for Alden. Trade publications were gushing with praise for Alice Simmons. "Audiences will be transfixed by her luminous presence," one declared, while another said, "We haven't seen a screen ingénue like her since Mary Pickford."

Meanwhile, *Midnight Rendezvous* enjoyed only tepid box office returns.

At the same time, Alden was seen squiring Alice and Cora around town to the spots where he and Betty had once turned patrons' heads. For Betty, that stung, and she asked to meet me for drinks at the Château Marmont. "Strictly woman-to-woman," she said.

"Thanks for coming," Betty said as we sipped our martinis. "I just had to talk to someone, get things off my chest. Off the record?"

"You have my word."

"It's Bill." She leaned forward. "He promised me *My Tender Heart*. Giving it to Alice Simmons really hurt. I *deserve* to be treated better, and I don't mean just movie roles."

"You want to marry him?"

She leaned back and nodded. "Ever since I met him, while we were shooting our first picture."

"You two appear to be close," I observed. "Everyone wonders how soon you'll be heading to the altar."

"Bill complains that he doesn't want to be 'tied down' in either his private or professional life," Betty said. "But I'll get him to settle down."

"Good luck." I paused. "What about the affairs he's had?"

"Including with you?"

"What! With *Hollywood Whispers*, I have my image to consider. I wouldn't dare!"

Betty furrowed her brow. "Really, Eve?"

"All right." I gulped down the rest of my drink and signaled our waiter for another round. "I couldn't resist. But it's always been just a fling." I paused. "I thought we'd been *very* discreet. How did you find out?"

"Bill cozies up to you more than to any other member of the press. So I played a hunch just now, and I was right." She glared at me. "Keep your hands off him."

"Strictly business from now on," I assured her.

The waiter returned with the fresh round of drinks, and we clinked glasses in a wordless toast.

"What happens now?" I asked. "Your contract with Bill is up. You could sign with another studio."

"No, Bill is the one for me, and the only contract I want from him is a marriage contract," Betty said. "We can sort the movie stuff out later."

"What if he says no? Decides to marry someone else?"

"He won't."

"How can you be sure?"

"Because I've got this." Betty reached into her handbag, pulled out a snub-nosed revolver with a walnut grip, and placed it on our table. "A Colt Detective Special. I bought it for protection."

I stared at the weapon. "You wouldn't really use that!"

"Oh, no?" She picked up the gun and aimed it at me.

"Whoa!" I held up my hands. "Have you gone *crazy*?"

She pulled the trigger.

Click!

I put down my hands and sighed with relief.

"Next time, it will be loaded," Betty said. "I'm going to be the first and only Mrs. Alden. There'll be no more hanky-panky from Bill." She sounded cool, but she had a strange glint in her eye. "My little friend here—" she tucked the gun back into her handbag "—will help me see to that."

She finished her drink, stood, and smiled. "I'm glad we had this little chat, Eve. I'll be seeing you."

As I watched Betty leave, I feared she'd gone mad.

***

The next time I met Alden, it was in a modest bar across from the Sentinel offices. I figured we were safer there from a pistol-packing Betty than at any of our posh haunts.

When I'd finished describing my encounter with Betty, Alden chuckled.

"I don't see what's funny about having a gun pulled on you," I snapped.

"She tried that gun stunt with me after I suggested she get one," Bill said. "She treats the gun like a prop." He looked hard at me. "She really rattled you, huh?"

I nodded, belted back my drink and waved to the bartender for another. "You didn't see the crazy look she had."

"Trust me, it's all an act."

"Act or not, I told her you and I are strictly business from now on." The bartender placed a shot of whiskey in front of me, and I quickly downed it. "And I meant it."

"No more private visits? I'll miss that."

"So will I. But we'll continue with your *Hollywood Whispers* interviews, all right?"

Alden sighed. "It will have to be." He downed his drink and signaled for another. "I have a more pressing problem. A new contract for Alice Simmons. Light and Shadow is eager to have her on the studio roster."

"Mother Cora stands in the way, I take it. But you've worked out tough deals before."

"Not one that includes marriage—to *Cora* Simmons—for Alice's signature on a contract."

That left me speechless.

"That's her condition for me signing Alice," Alden continued. "Cora says she loves me, and that if anyone's going to marry me, it'll be her." He paused. "What do you think?"

"Why not marry Cora, sign Alice, and get a divorce later?"

"I don't want to hurt Alice. She's devoted to Cora."

Love really is blind. Can't he see that Alice is itching to get away from Cora?

He finished his drink. "There's only one solution." He got up to leave. "First I have to see Alice—alone."

As he said goodbye, it dawned on me what he had in mind. If I was right, Betty and Cora were going to be furious.

***

Two days later, I was at the Sentinel offices when my phone rang.

"Sentinel Syndicate. Eve Brooks speaking."

"Miss Brooks, this is Alice Simmons," the voice on the other end burbled. "I have the most *exciting* news." That was followed by a delighted squeal. "I'm getting *married*!"

Just what I guessed Alden might do. I grabbed my notebook and a pencil. "Who's the lucky guy?"

"It's Mr. Alden. Bill, I should say. We wanted you to be the first to know."

"Thanks, and congratulations. Your mother must be thrilled."

"Well…" Alice hesitated. "Mother doesn't know yet." A hint of worry crept into her voice. "I…I don't like keeping this from Mother, but Bill thinks we should wait until it's a *fait* something—"

"*Accompli*."

"—before we tell her. Bill says that way, she can't raise any objections."

I was about to say Cora could raise all sorts of objections after they were married, but I held my tongue.

"You won't print anything about this yet, will you?" Alice continued.

"Don't worry," I assured her. "I'll discuss it with Mr. Alden."

"Thank you." She blew out a breath in relief. "I wouldn't want Mother to find out about it first in *Hollywood Whispers*. Here's Bill."

He told her to wait in his car, as he had a few things to discuss with me. He'd fill her in later, he promised. I heard her whine of disappointment and complaint, followed by the sound of a door closing.

"Any reason why I should sit on this story?" I asked Alden. "It's an exclusive at the moment. I don't want to be scooped by a rival."

"Nobody knows about this but you," he said. "Let me call you once we've tied the knot. And we're not doing it in Los Angeles, or anywhere in California. The state has a three-day waiting period after you apply for a marriage license. I don't want to give Cora time to stop us."

"So you're heading for Yuma," I said. For the Hollywood set, Yuma, Arizona, with its no-wait marriage option, was a favorite destination for elopements.

"That's right. We're taking a plane this evening, and I've arranged for Earl Freeman to preside."

Freeman was Yuma County's Justice of the Peace. He was called Yuma's "marrying judge" in movie magazines such as *Photoplay* and *The Hollywood Reporter*. His celebrity marriages included screen beauties Loretta Young, Gloria Swanson and Jean Harlow, and cowboy star Tom Mix.

"What's in it for me if I hold off?" I asked Alden.

"I'll call you at home before we fly back tomorrow morning," he said. "You get the news into your column that afternoon. Say we've gone on a brief honeymoon, we wouldn't say where, so that we can enjoy some privacy. That should keep the press and Cora away from the house. In the evening, you drop by for drinks to celebrate and do an exclusive interview with both of us. Well?"

I stopped scribbling. "All right, but I also want to get a photographer out to your place. Readers are going to want to see the happy couple."

"Have him get his pictures in the early evening, let's say eight o'clock, and you arrive around nine to talk with us and have a nightcap."

"Okay. But before you go, tell me one thing. How did you pry Alice away from Cora?"

"You won't print this, right?"

I remained silent.

"I'll take that as a yes." He paused. "Although Alice loves her mother, she finds her…domineering. She needs to be her own woman, she tells me. But she needed my help to get away."

"And that help means marrying you."

"Hey, it was *her* idea. She's smitten with me, and vice versa."

"That's lust, not love." Before he could accuse me of being cynical, I quickly added, "Finish your story about Cora and Alice."

"It was simple, really," Alden said. "You could say we caught Cora off guard. The two of them went out for dinner, Alice excused herself to go to the ladies' room—alone—but headed out the back door into the alley where I was waiting in my car. Then we were off to a hotel where I made the Yuma arrangements."

"Well, congratulations and good luck," I said. "I'll see you tomorrow night."

"Thanks." Before he hung up, Alden added, "Eve, watch out for Cora. She's angry, and that makes her dangerous."

***

"Where are they?" Cora demanded as she stormed into the Sentinel newsroom later that day. "Tell me!"

"Where's who?" I asked innocently as she hovered over my desk.

"Don't play games! Alice and Bill Alden. She disappeared during dinner last night. Either she ran off with him, or he *kidnapped* her!"

"That's ridiculous," I snapped. "If you believe that, you should go to the police."

"I have, but they told me to wait a day or two for Alice to come back," Cora fumed. "You were chummy with that *snake*, Bill Alden." She fixed her emerald gaze on me. "Any idea where they are?"

I shook my head.

She lowered her voice, but her tone was menacing. "To think I wanted to marry him! I suppose he told you that."

"No, he didn't," I lied.

"Well, he's not going to have my Alice, and she's not going to have him," she declared. "I'll make sure with this."

She reached into her purse, gave me a glimpse of a semiautomatic pistol, and stuffed the weapon back into her bag.

Then she spun on her heel and left.

***

Alden's Spanish Colonial home in Brentwood reminded me of Old California. With its white stucco walls, red terracotta-tiled roof and ornamental ironwork adorning windows, stair railings, arches and patio, I pictured it as the set for that silent Douglas Fairbanks swashbuckler, *The Mark of Zorro.*

The Sentinel photographer told me he'd posed Alice and Alden with their arms around each other in the arched front doorway. "Kinda like standing under a wedding arbor," he said.

For their interview with me, they wore the same outfits they'd worn for the photos. Alice was draped in a gold satin dress, while Alden wore a white dinner jacket, white shirt, black bow tie and black tuxedo trousers.

They sat on a couch, holding hands, while I perched on an armchair facing them.

"You two certainly make an elegant couple," I said.

Alice blushed, while Alden thanked me for waiting to release the news of their marriage.

They gave me a lively account of Alice sneaking out of the restaurant and meeting Alden in the alley, the night flight to Yuma, the early-morning exchange of vows before Earl Freeman, and their quiet return to Los Angeles.

"Have you contacted your mother?" I asked Alice. "She'll have read about your wedding in *Hollywood Whispers* by now."

"N-n-not yet." She looked at Alden, gripped his hand, and turned back to me. "We're going to w-wait a little, let her get used to us being together. She will, won't she?"

He smiled and gave her hand a gentle squeeze. "You bet."

"What about Betty Preston?" I asked Alden. "There was talk of romance between you two."

"That was before Alice came along," he replied. "But no, I haven't contacted her yet. Our priority is to smooth things over with Mrs. Simmons, but I believe I can get Betty under contract again with Light and Shadow."

"Congratulations, again." I tucked my notebook into my purse. "That's it for tonight."

Suddenly, there was pounding on the front door. "Bill! Open up, you bastard!"

"Alice, stay here." She sat, frozen in fear. He stood, handed me my hat and purse, and steered me toward his study, where French doors opened onto a back patio. "You'd better go out the back."

Once I was inside the study, he closed the door behind me, expecting me to vamoose. I knew I should have left, but my reporter's instincts took over. I tossed my hat and purse onto a chair and eased the door slightly ajar.

The study door was to the left of the couch and armchair, which stood opposite the front entrance. It opened inward, and from where I stood, I had a view of the living room from the crack between the jamb and the door's edge.

There were more thuds, punctuated by cries of "Bill!" before he opened the front door.

"Betty, give me the gun. Don't do anything you'll regret."

There was a shot, and he staggered back, his left hand clutching his gut, and fell to the floor. Alice screamed and started to rise to go to him.

"Sit down!" Betty ordered, and Alice eased back down onto the couch.

I turned away, pressing my back against the wall, tears trickling down my cheeks. I wiped them away, then peeked out again.

Betty came toward Alden, her gun trained on him. "I warned you there would be only one Mrs. Alden. Me!" She stood a foot away from him, watching the blood ooze between his fingers.

Suddenly, she dropped the gun and threw her hands up to her face. "Oh, my God! What have I done?" She fell to her knees and started crying. "Oh, my God! Bill!"

As Betty sobbed, Alice rushed to Alden's side. He writhed and moaned on the floor.

I was about to rush out to him when there was more gunfire.

Betty fell forward, shot in the back. Her head turned toward me, her eyes widening in surprise.

I ducked back into the study, then cautiously looked out.

There was Cora, outfitted in a black dress and dark wide-brimmed hat.

"Alice, you miserable ingrate!" Cora pointed her small semiautomatic pistol at her daughter. "You knew I wanted Alden. It would have secured both our futures in this town."

"But I *loved* him. He wasn't *using* me—like you."

"Ha! He just wanted to get you away from me. He'd have left you soon enough, for someone like her." Cora pointed her gun at Betty's body, then trained it back on Alice. "However, I'll forgive you. Come with me."

"No!" Alice looked up at her. "You can't make me."

"Get your things. You're coming with me."

"No!" Alice stared defiantly at Cora. "I'm not going."

"I'll count to three. It's your last chance." Cora raised her semiautomatic. "One…" She slowly brought it down. "Two…" Her gun hand was level with her shoulder. "Three!"

"Go to hell, you witch!" Alice spat out.

Cora fired at her point-blank. Alice fell on her side, her eyes and mouth open in death.

Then Cora stepped up and fired two shots into Bill's chest. He stopped moving.

Clapping a hand over my mouth to stifle my scream, I lost my balance and stumbled into a side table in the dark. Landing on my hip, I grabbed the table to prevent it crashing down. I righted it and scrambled to my feet, hoping Cora hadn't heard me.

Looking out again, I saw Cora facing the study. "Someone in there?" She took a step forward, but halted when she heard the wail of sirens in the distance. She hurried out the front door into the night.

I grabbed my hat and purse and was about to leave by the French doors when I stopped. I rushed back into the living room.

Betty's gun was lying near her body. I scooped it up and dropped it into my bag. I figured I might need it if I ran into Cora.

Pulling my hat onto my head, I scurried out the front door, and ran into a pair of uniformed policemen.

"Officers, thank goodness!" I said breathlessly, then pointed to Alden's house. "It's horrible. I think they're all dead."

***

Joe Norris, the detective assigned to the case, and I faced each other in Alden's living room as the bodies were removed for their ride to the morgue. I pegged Norris to be in his mid-50s. He wore an ill-fitting suit, and had a slight paunch and thinning dark hair.

He reviewed his notes. "That's it?"

I nodded. "Believe me, Detective, I wish I could help you more."

"Let's go over your story again."

I repeated it, careful to avoid implicating myself. When I arrived at Alden's home, the front door was open. I called out, but got no response. Entering the living room, I saw the bodies on the floor. Frightened, I hurried away and ran into the two police officers.

"There's nothing more I can tell you," I concluded.

"A neighbor reported seeing someone, possibly a woman, lurking nearby. You didn't see anyone?"

"No one."

Norris went back to his notes. "You were invited to come over, but what about Betty Preston?"

"She's made movies with Mr. Alden," I said. "But why she was here tonight, I don't know."

The detective sighed in exasperation. "Not much to go on." He closed his notebook. "Thank you, Miss Brooks."

Tell Norris about Cora, an inner voice whispered on my way back to my car.

No. It will be my word against hers. No one will believe me. Because what mother could murder her own daughter in cold blood?

***

Fans and the morbidly curious—police estimated the crowd at a few thousand people—gathered for the celebrity interment at Hollywood Cemetery on Santa Monica Boulevard. Alden and Alice were laid to rest in a mausoleum, while Betty was buried in a nearby grave.

Cora presented a spectacle of grief for the press and newsreel cameras. Dressed in black, she collapsed and wailed outside the mausoleum.

I reported her histrionics in my column, but I wasn't fooled by her phony display of emotion.

We hadn't spoken since the murders, and I didn't know what to make of that. Maybe Cora thought she'd been mistaken about hearing a noise in Alden's study. Maybe she'd decided she had heard someone, but not me. Or maybe she knew it was me, and was biding her time before coming after me.

Cora could afford to wait, because the killings had made her a rich woman.

Alden died without a will, and had no relatives entitled to shares of his estate. Had she lived, Alice would have got everything. In court, Cora produced a will, signed by Alice, naming her as her daughter's sole beneficiary.

Had Alice signed it knowing what she was doing? Was the document genuine? Or was her signature forged?

No one came forward to challenge Alice's will, or to claim a share of Alden's estate, so the court awarded everything, including the Brentwood home, to Cora.

How could Cora stand living in that death house?

***

A few days later, I was putting the finishing touches on my column, including the latest no-progress-yet statement on the murders from Detective Norris, when my phone rang.

"Sentinel Syndicate. Eve Brooks here."

"Eve, it's Cora Simmons," the voice at the other end said. "I want to pass along something for *Hollywood Whispers*."

"Is it to do with Alice?" I asked.

"Yes. What happened was so dreadful."

"Alice was a sweet kid." I kept my voice calm, but I was seething inside. *The gall of the woman!* "I'd like to help catch her killer."

"Good." Cora paused. "I'm not happy with the lack of progress in the investigation."

"Detective Norris told me no one's come forward with any possible leads."

"Exactly! So I'm offering a $5,000 reward for information leading to an arrest. Do you think that's enough?"

"If I knew something, I'd go for it," I lied. "Where do I come in?"

"I'd like you to get this out in your column," Cora said. "They can call Detective Norris or myself at one of these two numbers."

Once I'd jotted them down, I said, "You know you'll be inviting all kinds of nuts to come forward for that money."

"Detective Norris and I can sort that out," she said. "What do you say?"

"Sure, I'll do it," I said. "For Alice." *And Bill and Betty.*

Cora was using the reward to deflect attention from herself, playing the grieving mother seeking justice for her daughter. The money was also a means to flush out any possible witness to the murders.

First, phony claimants had to be discredited. Then, if no one stepped up, she'd conclude there had been no one in the study. But if there was another witness, one she thought was genuine, she'd have that person in her sights.

Cora probably thought one of Alden's former flames was a possible witness. Did she count me among them? I had no idea.

Offering the reward was a clever gambit. Maybe I could use it to my advantage.

***

A few weeks passed. Despite the reward offer, an increasingly frustrated Detective Norris was no closer to solving the case than he had been the night of the murders. Meanwhile, Cora continued to voice her impatience with the investigation. I'm sure she believed she'd get away scot-free.

It was time to call Cora. I couldn't risk being overheard at the office, so I made the call at home on my rotary phone.

I dialed her number and put a handkerchief over the mouthpiece to disguise my voice. "Hello, Cora Simmons?"

"Speaking. Who is this?"

"Never mind. I'm calling for that $5,000 reward."

"Oh?" I heard her yawn. "Go on."

"I know you did it. I saw you."

Cora inhaled sharply, but quickly recovered her composure. "How do I know you were there?"

"Here's how," I said, and proceeded to describe the murders. "Satisfied?"

"It would still be your word against mine."

"There's one more thing," I said. "I have Betty Preston's gun. She dropped it, but you didn't pick it up when you ran out. I'm sure the cops would be interested in it. They might start rethinking everything about the case. Do you want that?"

Cora paused. "No."

"If you want that gun, it will be another $5,000."

"All right." Her voice couldn't conceal her anger. "But I'll need some time to get the money together."

"You have a week, then I'll call back."

I hung up. My plan was in motion.

***

Two weeks earlier, I was driving home after interviewing *Dracula* star Bela Lugosi, who lived in the Hollywoodland subdivision of Beachwood Canyon. As I drove, I pondered how best to handle Cora.

In the distance, built on the side of a mountain, was the sign spelling out Hollywoodland in giant white letters. Originally installed to promote homes, it had recently come to symbolize broken dreams. In 1932, Peg Entwistle, an actress who'd failed to find stardom, jumped to her death from the sign's *H*.

Hollywoodland proved to be an enclave of storybook homes. As I cruised through it, I could see houses ranging from vine-covered cottages to Normandy castles. At the edge of the subdivision, I spotted a Hansel and Gretel cottage. I pulled over to take a closer look.

With its steeply pitched gable roof, wooden shingles, small windows, cobblestone walk, and arched front door, it looked like someone was trying to copy the Witch's House in Beverly Hills.

I found the front door unlocked. Inside, the cottage was a shell. There were just a few wooden chairs, a table, unfinished stairs, and a brick fireplace.

The stock market crash of 1929 had likely killed its builder's dream.

Then it struck me: where better to deal with Cora than right here?

***

I waited for Cora, sitting on one of the wooden chairs in a back corner of the cottage. I'd moved myself far into the shadows, hoping she wouldn't see me.

My eyes had adjusted to the dark. It wasn't quite pitch-black inside, but close. The glow from flames of the fire I'd lit in the hearth provided the only light.

Betty's Colt, with its bullets removed, lay on the table in the center of the room. I held a gun of my own, which I'd purchased following the murders. It was loaded and ready to use.

I had called Cora from home in the late afternoon, disguising my voice again.

"Put the money in an envelope," I told her, then gave her directions to the Hansel and Gretel cottage. "When you arrive, knock on the front door."

I'd be ready, but I didn't want to be caught unawares.

"It will be unlocked, so you can go straight in. You'll see Betty Preston's gun on a table. Take the gun, leave the money, and go."

"It's such short notice," Cora complained. "I have to package the money. I have to find the place. I don't know how late it will be when I get there."

"Stop whining," I replied. "And no tricks when you get there. I'll be out of sight, watching you."

There was a knock. I rose silently, pushed my chair to one side, and gripped my gun.

Cora shoved the door open and stood silhouetted in the entrance. Like me, she was wearing a dark jacket and wide-leg trousers.

She peered into the gloom. "Hello! Anyone there?" She reached into her left jacket pocket, pulled out an envelope and waved it above her head. "See? The money. Here it is."

She opened the envelope, removed some bills and fanned them out on the table. "All here." She scanned the room, looking for me, and picked up Betty's gun. "Why don't you come out and count it?"

Suddenly, she whirled and fired into the corner opposite to where I was standing. *Click! Click! Click!*

"Damn!"

She threw down Betty's gun as I stepped out from the shadows. I shot twice and hit her in the right arm. Her gun hand.

She staggered backward, fell on her right side, and rolled onto her back, looking up at me.

"Eve Brooks! I should have known!" She struggled to prop herself up.

She winced as she reached into her jacket pocket with her left hand and brought out her semiautomatic pistol. "Bill Alden was meant for *me*! Not Alice! Certainly not *you*!"

She raised her left arm to fire, but her grip and aim were wobbly. The shot went wide.

I moved forward and stood over her, aiming my gun at her chest.

Bang! "That one's for Bill." *Bang!* "That's for Betty Preston." *Bang!* "And that's for Alice."

After checking Cora's pulse to make sure she was dead, I grabbed the money and Betty's gun, and rushed up the road to where I'd parked my car.

***

On my way home, I stopped at Musso's for a drink and called Detective Norris from their phone booth.

"Who's this?" he growled. "I've had a busy day. This better be good."

"It's about those Brentwood murders and that reward," I said, with my handkerchief over the mouthpiece to disguise my voice.

"I've collected it—the reward, that is," I went on. "I've earned it. You'll find the killer's body in an abandoned cottage in Hollywoodland."

"Wait a minute," Norris interjected. "That Simmons dame never said anything to me about this."

"She's at that cottage right now," I continued. "You can't miss it. It looks like a smaller, shabbier version of the Witch's House in Beverly Hills. You know, the one at Walden Drive and Carmelita Avenue."

"What? Listen here—"

"Better get going, Detective. So long."

I hung up, satisfied I'd done my duty in calling Norris. I returned to my table and ordered another drink to celebrate, while I mulled over what might happen next.

The police would find Cora's gun at the Hollywoodland cottage. Ballistics tests would prove it had fired the bullets that killed Alice, Betty and Alden. The evidence would point to Cora as the killer.

The two shots Betty had fired into Alden would remain unexplained, because I had kept her gun. No weapon to compare the slugs with.

Authorities would be left asking who killed Cora. Witnesses? I doubted there were any, but if there were, their statements would likely be vague. Weapon? None at the scene except Cora's.

The case would be a sensation for a while, but reporters and the public would grow bored with the lack of progress. The story would fade away.

As I sipped my drink, I thought of Alice's dying words to Cora: *Go to hell, you witch!*

I raised my glass in a silent toast.

Rest in peace, Alice. The wicked witch is dead.

The 13th Letter

M

The End

THE BUTTERCUP

By Cat Mills

Edith stands in her kitchen, phone cradled between her shoulder and ear, half listening while her friend, Judy, talks about her kids. She sorts through the mail stacked up on her counter. Bill, bill, junk.

A small white envelope.

Edith flips it front to back—no address, no postage stamp, no markings at all.

The envelope has some girth to it; whatever's inside is larger than a sheet of paper.

Ripping it open, she reaches her slim fingers inside and pulls out a piece of white tissue paper, delicately folded over. She opens it.

A bluebell. Pressed flat.

Edith's heart starts pounding.

"I have to go," she says in a shaky voice. She hangs up and stares at the flower.

***

"It feels like it has been raining for years."

Edith looks up from washing mugs in the sink. It's Ralph, one of the regulars. He's an old cop, a recent widower. Edith suspects he is lonely. Then again, so is she.

She dries her hands on a tea towel.

"Coffee?"

"Yes, please."

He slides onto the stool at the counter. She puts a black coffee in front of him.

"What's new, kid?" Ralph asks.

"Nothing," Edith replies.

It's the truth. Nothing ever happens in her life. She has one friend, she's held the same job since high school, and she has no ambitions. Her parents live in Florida. They gave up on her a long time ago, disappointed with their unexceptional daughter.

Luckily, another customer walks through the door and Edith is rescued from further conversation.

***

Kicking off her boots and squirming out of her raincoat, Edith makes her way into her apartment inside an old Victorian house, today's mail tucked under her arm. Hanging her coat on a hook in the hallway, she collapses onto the couch, nearly sitting on Stuart, her affectionate tuxedo cat. He arches his back in a stretch before crawling onto her lap.

Her clammy hands give the cat a chin scratch, bits of fur clinging to her fingers. She tosses the mail onto the coffee table and spots a small white envelope.

She sits up.

Ripping it open she pours onto her hand another piece of tissue paper. Wrapped carefully within, a pressed snowdrop.

***

"It's a great place to work. The people are nice, the benefits are amazing…"

Edith sits across from Judy at their favorite brunch spot. They have been doing this weekly ritual for several years. It's the only thing that Edith looks forward to, catching up with her best friend.

Judy is filling her in on the latest office scandal, when Edith hands her a white envelope.

"What's this?" Judy asks, peeking inside. She pulls out a violet, a bleeding heart, a crocus—all flattened.

"I've been receiving these in the mail," Edith tells her.

"Why would anyone send you pressed flowers?" Judith asks, incredulously.

"I have no idea."

"How many so far?"

"Seven." Edith watches the rain outside. It's pouring.

"And there is no letter?"

"There is no letter, no writing on the envelope. Nothing."

"Huh." Judy is stumped.

"Yeah." So is Edith.

Judy looks up at Edith, perplexed. She's about to say something, but stops mid-sentence, mouth gaping.

Edith turns around to see what Judy is staring at, a tall, handsome teenage boy with dark hair and eyes. The boy doesn't notice the women gawking at him as he collects his takeout order and leaves.

"Can you believe it?" Judy exclaims.

"Believe what?" asks Edith, confused.

"He doesn't remind you of anyone?" Judy prods.

Edith's blank face tells her he does not.

Judy slaps Edith on the shoulder. "He's Tom's doppelganger. You remember Tom, don't you? Tom Marshall?"

The memory hits Edith like a tidal wave. Tom—handsome, rebellious, mysterious. Her next-door neighbor. Yes, Edith remembers him and the crush that she and every teenage girl had on him. Tom was always getting into trouble at school. Later he moved on to petty crime. Then he disappeared.

Everyone assumed that he'd skipped town for the big city.

"I wonder what happened to him..." Judy muses.

Edith watches through the window as the boy looks both ways before darting across the street.

***

It's sunny. The kind of day that warms your shoulders in a comforting way. The sky is blue with wisps of white clouds. The trees are swaying gently in the wind, shimmering bright green against the light.

And there is a body of a little girl, face down, in the pond.

Edith's eyes drift past the girl and focus on two yellow buttercups floating peacefully on the water.

***

Edith wakes up with a sob in her throat. She cries, long and hard, something she hasn't done for years. Her dreams are getting worse.

With an aching chest, she climbs out of bed and walks into her living room. The morning light is shining through her large front windows. She notices some purple light on the floor. It's transparent, like a shadow.

Glancing up, she sees pressed flowers taped to her windows, all 11 flowers that came to her in blank, unmarked envelopes.

Someone has been inside her house.

No, not inside after all. She takes a closer look. The flowers have been taped to the outside of her window, from her porch.

Who would do such a thing?

***

Coffee is doing little to calm Edith's nerves. The usual customers are sitting at their tables, engaged in lively conversations. When the bell jingles above the door, Edith expects to see Ralph. Instead, in walks a tall thin man with gray hair, cropped close. It takes a minute before she recognizes him as John, her old neighbor, and Tom's father.

He searches for a seat and spots Edith. He looks at her for a minute, then walks over to the counter.

"Edith, I didn't recognize you. How are you? How are your parents?"

John was friends with Edith's father until the year when everything fell apart. After Tom's disappearance, John and his wife divorced. She stayed in the family home in the hopes that her son would return. John moved into an apartment downtown and Edith never saw him again.

Until now.

She starts to answer his questions but is interrupted when the entrance bell jingles.

In the doorway stands the teenage boy she saw the other day, the one who looks like Tom Marshall. He is scanning the menu board.

The color drains out of John's face. He turns a sickly shade of white.

As the boy approaches the counter to order, John turns without a word and slips back onto the street.

***

Edith crouches behind the large tree across the street from her house. She knows her stealth is almost cartoonish, or would be, if she wasn't so terrified. She had already grilled the mailman about the envelopes, but he claimed to know nothing. He pointed out that there were no stamps or addresses, so they couldn't come through the mail.

Edith keeps up an intense watch on her house. Ants crawl on her hands as she grips the tree bark. Her legs begin to ache, and she is on the verge of giving up when she sees a man approach the house. He drops a letter into her mailbox. His coat collar is pulled up and he's wearing a hat, but he's unmistakable.

It's Ralph.

***

Edith's heart skips a beat every time someone walks into the cafe. Ralph has yet to appear. She cleans the counters again, needing to keep busy.

The bell jingles. Edith turns to see Ralph slide onto the stool.

With a cheery voice he asks her for a coffee. Her smile is tight as she places a cup in front of him—and tosses a white envelope onto the counter. Pressed flowers spill out.

Ralph looks at the envelope and its contents. He leans back and crosses his arms.

"I want to know why you are doing this," she says, her voice shaking.

He looks out the window before answering.

"Because I know you killed Sally."

Edith is shocked.

"You think I murdered my little sister?"

He stares at her, saying nothing.

"You have got to be kidding! What is wrong with you?" she spits out in disgust.

Some customers look over at them.

"She had defensive wounds on her hands and a bruise on the back of her neck." Ralph looks her in the eye.

Edith tries to process this new information. The police had declared Sally's death an accident. The evidence pointed to Sally tripping and falling into the pond and drowning. No foul play.

"Why are you bringing this up now?"

Ralph looks at her. "I've been a cop for a long time and most cases are cut and dry. Sally's death wasn't even investigated. Little girl getting killed. It's never sat right with me."

Edith remembers that Ralph lost his daughter when she was very young. Leukemia.

"They told me to drop the case and move on," Ralph continued. "I'm retiring soon and I'm going to find out the truth before I'm done, with or without help from the force."

Ralph pushes himself up and storms out of the cafe, leaving behind a stunned Edith.

***

Heading home, Edith doesn't bother to run, despite the torrential rain. Her coat is soaked through. Her cheeks start to grow hot. She feels a fever coming on.

She hesitates as she approaches her house, hovering in front of her mailbox.

She opens it and breathes a sigh of relief.

It is empty.

***

Edith pushes her head under the hot bathwater. She feels like her lungs will burst but she stays down. Her brain is spinning. A bruise. Marks on Sally's hands.

Ralph thinks she is a murderer.

She sits up and wraps her arms around her legs, trying to think back to that time, 20 years ago. She's blocked out the memories for so long.

What really happened to Sally?

***

Out of the bath, crouched on her knees, Edith fishes under her bed until she finds her old photo album. Dusting off the top, she reluctantly sits on her bed and opens the book. These are memories she has tried to bury.

Herself, a gangly teen with braces and thick bangs. Sally, a pretty girl with strawberry blond hair and muddy shoes. Sally was a tomboy, but she loved girly things like unicorns and kittens. She adored flowers and learned the Latin names of all of her favorites. She said she wanted to be a botanist. She'd collect flowers and press them between the pages of stacked encyclopedias, gluing them into a scrapbook and labeling each.

Turning the pages, Edith takes in photos of her happy family: Sally perched on Dad's shoulder; their golden retriever, Trudy; Sally throwing her hands up in excitement as Edith looks pained to be in the same room as her sibling. Sally looks straight at the camera, her eyes big and innocent, her smile goofy. Her little sister, who was bigger than life itself.

Sally, the golden child. Edith the black sheep.

She closes the album.

***

Edith pulls on her shoes and raincoat and throws open the thick wooden front door. Her eyes try to adjust to the dim morning light.

She takes a step and looks down.

There on the porch is a single buttercup. It's not pressed flat—it is full and golden.

Her feet freeze to the ground.

***

She's unprepared for the deluge of memories that flood into her brain. Edith, curled up on her bed, burying her teary face in her pillow.

Sally bursting through the door with buttercups clenched in her fist.

"I know what happened to Tom!" she screams, a dog with a bone.

Broken-hearted, Edith has no patience for her sister's imagination, for her lies. The boy she planned to marry has run away, and her sister is trying to get attention.

"Go away, Sally!" she screams.

Sally steps back, frightened. Her eyes well up and she runs off. Edith pushes her face back into her pillow and wallows in her misery.

Then Sally's body, floating face down in the pond. Two buttercups floating beside her.

Later the police and ambulance arrive to cart away her body. There's a crowd of people in the yard, offering condolences and taking photos. Edith's father holds her mother as she weeps.

Edith stands in her sister's bedroom, watching a young detective. He examines the flowers taped to the window. He asks Edith questions, which she barely answers.

Her eyes are focused on the other side of the fence, at the neighbor's yard. John is standing there, watching the proceedings.

His yard is covered in buttercups.

***

Edith stares out the window of the cafe. The sun is starting to emerge after what feels like years of rain.

April showers bring May flowers, she thinks.

She spots Ralph through the window. He nods at her and enters the cafe. He sits at the counter in his usual spot.

"You were right," he tells her, shaking the rain off his hat.

She watches him, saying nothing.

"We interviewed John's ex-wife again. She admitted that her son and husband had a huge fight, after which Tom disappeared. She assumed he had run away."

Ralph rubs his forehead. He looks tired.

"He's admitted that he killed the boy. No idea why he is confessing now. I guess he had a long time to think about what he did."

Edith remains frozen, waiting to hear more.

"We found the boy's body in the backyard."

Edith's hand goes to her mouth.

Ralph pauses before he looks up at Edith. "He admitted to killing your sister. Said that she was in the yard collecting flowers and overheard him crying and talking to himself about the boy. He saw her running away."

Edith's eyes have welled up. She says nothing but raises her hand, *stop*. She doesn't need to know more.

"He's been arrested. He's being charged with both murders."

Edith nods.

She pours him a coffee. She and Ralph sit together in silence.

Finally, Edith speaks. She needs to know.

"Did you leave me the buttercup? The thirteenth flower?"

He looks back at her, confused.

He shakes his head.

***

Edith walks up the hill. It is steeper than she remembers, and the rain has made the grass a rich green. She stops to listen to the cardinals in the trees and takes a deep breath. Her parents did choose a beautiful spot.

She kneels, pulling moss from the headstone: *Sally Miner, forever in our hearts.*

The grave has been neglected for too long. Edith puts on her gardening gloves, removes the weeds and digs small holes in the ground. Out of her bag, she pulls a variety of bulbs and seeds: crocuses, tulips, bluebells, snowdrops, and buttercups. She plants them and, pulling a water bottle from her purse, pours water over the soil.

It must be lonely to be in a graveyard, Edith thinks. She imagines the grave covered in her sister's favorite flowers.

She gets up.

"Don't worry, Sally."

She kisses her fingers and places them on top of the headstone.

"I'll be back to visit again soon."

The 13th Letter

M

The End

27

By Blair Keetch

"Looks like alphabet soup."

Halfway up the industrial metal staircase, Moira and I stood side by side as we gazed down to the warehouse below. She was my new partner and while the jury was still out, there were promising signs.

Speaking of signs, this was the display showroom belonging to SOS Signage and underneath us was an array of large letters ranging in size from three feet to twenty feet in a variety of shapes and fonts. Regretfully, the letters did not spell out a clue. Secretly, I'd hoped they would be arranged in 'Ted' or 'Sara', but the life of a homicide detective is never that easy.

***

Dawn was still several hours away, and the area was lit with spotlights positioned by the crime scene technicians. There was a muttered curse below and my focus shifted to the male body crushed by a large twelve-foot sign of the letter 'A'. The victim was completely covered by the large heavy sign except for his right arm which extended outward and pointed toward a grouping of letters. A pool of blood leaked out from under the sign and its acrid smell was still fresh in the air.

"Talk about *The Scarlet Letter*," Moira murmured.

I glanced at her in surprise. Moira was slim and short with dark hair that she wore in a severe bun. Her height had led to sarcastic comments about the falling standards of the police academy and how anyone that slight of frame could tackle a criminal who was more than five feet tall. However, her eyes held a shining intelligence and she moved with deceptive grace and strength.

"I studied American literature before joining the force," she confessed sheepishly. "Hawthorne to Hemingway."

I chose to save it for another time to inform her about my eclectic background, but safe to say that a day didn't go by where I didn't draw upon my 'useless' education.

***

Once down on the warehouse floor, I looked at the massive letter 'A' and stared up at the platform that had been its original display space. "That's at least a ten-foot drop," I said. "You would have thought the sign would have been tethered with a safety wire of some sort."

"An industrial accident?" Moira asked skeptically.

"Doubtful." A low raspy voice spoke from the shadows. Ethel, the chief crime scene officer emerged into the light. With surprising agility for someone her size, she swung herself up the metal handholds at the back of the platform and swiftly climbed. "See this?" She brandished a cut wire. "This was a safety device until someone cut it in half. Nothing fancy, likely a good set of pliers, but I'll know more later."

I grunted and noticed how my breath hung in the air. "Windows open?"

"Plus the roll-up door." Ethel jumped the last few feet to the floor. "Amateur attempt to confuse the time of death."

"Also, the point of entry?"

"Ask the owner. He's the one who found the body." She pointed to the second floor, its interior windows lit up like a beacon. "He's in the office with one of your staff."

"Any clues to his identity?" I motioned toward the corpse.

"This letter weighs at least a hundred pounds if not more," Ethel said. "It will take some time to lift it off the body."

"SOS Signage." Moira read the large sign that dominated one of the walls. "Curious name."

I'd seen the large exterior logo from the motorway and idly wondered if anyone ever interpreted it as a distress call, but a shout from Ethel disturbed my thoughts.

"I told you more light over here. Not tomorrow. Not ten minutes from now. Now!"

Two white-suited technicians hurried past with more portable lights.

Sensing her urgency, I moved closer to the body. "What is it?"

"I think it's what you professionals call a clue." She signaled me over.

Peering past the victim's head and above the outstretched arm, I saw another small puddle of blood. In an untidy scrawl, the victim had written two numbers in his own blood.

"It looks like the number 27." I scrutinized the messy scrawl.

"What does that mean?" Moira wondered.

"You're the detective. Isn't that your job?"

I ignored Ethel's jab and used my phone to take a photo of the numbers written in blood.

"Judging by the amount he bled out," Ethel said, "I'd guess—and this is off the record for now—he probably remained conscious for a minute or so, two minutes tops."

"Long enough to leave a clue in his own blood," Moira stated.

"Twenty-seven," I said aloud. "Maybe he was starting to write a telephone number."

"Including area code?" Moira asked. "Good luck, the possibilities are endless."

"Here's something that may interest you." Ethel gave a triumphant wiggle of her hand which held a slim leather wallet. "Sticking out of his jacket pocket."

I looked back at the mammoth letter 'A' that obscured the body. A corner of a suit jacket peeked out from the other side.

I slipped on a pair of latex gloves before carefully opening the wallet. "Not much. A couple of twenties." I slowly pulled out a driver's license. The photo showed a man in his late forties, hair just a little longer than the current fashion and swept back off his forehead. Even in the formality of a driver's license photo, his expression had a faint smirk. "Dr. Anthony Cook," I read aloud.

"'A' as in Anthony?" Moira offered.

"A bit of a stretch, I would think." I dropped the wallet into the evidence bag that Moira held open. I turned to Ethel. "What does the number 27 mean to you?"

"Psalm 27," Ethel didn't hesitate. "The Lord is my light and salvation—whom should I fear? The Lord is the stronghold of my life—of whom shall I be afraid?"

This unexpected display of Biblical literacy took me aback, but before I could reply, a voice called out from above. One of the uniforms stood at the top of the staircase. "Detective? Mr. Cohen is anxious to speak with someone in charge."

Moira looked at me. "Samuel Cohen. Owner of SOS Signage. He found the body."

"Be right there," I shouted up.

Together, Moira and I wove our way through the maze of letters to the base of the stairs. Once we'd reached the top, I looked down, hoping that the higher perspective would offer some suggestions. No such luck. Just a jumble of letters haphazardly spread across the warehouse floor.

"I'd like to buy a vowel, please," I muttered as we stepped onto the second floor.

***

Sam Cohen was a lean man with a gravelly voice that belonged to a fellow twice his size. He was bald except for a neatly trimmed fringe of red hair and, despite the early hour, he wore a crisp white dress shirt and paisley silk tie. He sat behind a large oak desk clear of everything except a laptop and a cell phone placed carefully to one side.

"About time," he growled. "My studio is supposed to open in four hours."

"Ah, not sure if you noticed, but there's a dead body lying on your warehouse floor." Moira spoke in a firm tone.

"Of course I noticed." He ignored her sarcasm. "I was the one who found Dr. Crook."

"You mean Dr. Anthony Cook?"

"Trust me, Crook is a better moniker," Sam said. "He presented himself as a man of letters. His business card had MBA and even PHD printed behind his name, but for those who knew him well, SOB or WTF would be more fitting."

"If he's so dishonest, why are you doing business with him?" Moira voiced the obvious question.

Cohen looked at me, not her. "Because I figured out his modus operandi a long time ago and made sure he paid fully ahead of time. We weren't best friends, but we respected each other."

"SOS," I said. "Interesting name."

"My brother Silas and I worked at Paramount Signs for several years. We both had a devoted following of clients. When people came in, the receptionist would ask 'Silas or Sam?' When we started our own business, it was easy to choose a name: SOS."

"And your brother?"

"Dead two years now. Throat cancer." He genuinely looked upset. "Horrible, horrible disease."

"Was Dr. Cook your client or your brother's?"

"My customer from the very get-go. My brother had higher moral standards." Cohen noted my raised eyebrows. "I know Cook was a con man, but as I said he was a good customer who paid on time."

"What kind of signs?"

"Anything and everything, but promotional and exterior signs mainly for his various projects." Cohen counted off his fingers. "Cook Industries. Cook Medical Supplies. Cook Critical Care."

"Not exactly modest," I said. Beside me, Moira furiously took notes.

"Not in the least, but he had an engaging charisma that many people fell for."

"Are all these genuine companies?"

Cohen shrugged dismissively. "The signage is genuine. That's all I care about."

"So, what was he doing in your warehouse in the middle of the night?"

"I gave him access."

"You let him in? Why?"

"Because he wanted to look at some of the signage samples. He called me late in the evening and he's a VIP client. And I'd given him the security code before without any issues."

"It couldn't wait until morning?" I pressed.

"Cook may have had dubious ethics, but he was a workaholic. Day and night whenever inspiration struck him. Even though his endeavors were likely frauds, he put a lot of time and effort into all aspects."

"Did Cook have any business partners?"

"Sure did. At least one for each and every failure." He shook his head, maybe in admiration, perhaps in dismay. "Usually a new partner for each business venture. There's no shortage of gullible people."

"What brought you out to your office so early?" Moira asked. I held back a spark of irritation at the interruption.

"Couldn't sleep, so I drove in to tackle some paperwork. Came up by the elevator, so didn't even look into the showroom. Worked for over an hour before I even glanced down into the display area."

I gazed through the interior window. Two stories below, Ethel was still moving around the lifeless body, taking notes and directing the crime scene technicians. I followed the direction of Cook's outstretched hand. It pointed to a cluster of letters, but nothing specific.

"Does the number 27 mean anything?"

Sam answered without a beat. "Trout."

I turned to face him directly. "Trout?"

"Mike Trout," he said. "One of the greatest baseball players ever."

I suppressed a groan. "Regarding his partners, any idea who might have wished him harm?"

"Perhaps you should start with me," a soft voice spoke from the doorway.

***

"I'm Meredith Cook." The mystery woman introduced herself. "Not related to the deceased. At least I hope not."

She was tall and slim and wore a white, sleeveless blouse that showed off taut, muscular arms. Her long, chestnut hair spilled casually over her shoulders. Her poised manner seemed far older than someone who looked to be in her early thirties.

She held out her hand. Her grip was firm and confident, and she held my hand for a split second longer than necessary.

Moira was quicker on the uptake than I was. "Meredith Cook—the swimmer? Olympic medalist?"

Meredith tilted her head in acknowledgment. "The same. As well as Dr. Cook's latest naïve target."

I guided her down the hall to the SOS staff room. "Let's talk here, where it's more private." I pulled out a chair at one of the circular lunch tables. "You're a business partner of Dr. Cook?"

"Regretfully, yes."

Moira snapped her fingers, and I bit back my exasperation. "Against the Tide." She turned to me. "It's this wonderful charity in Africa that builds community pools to develop children's confidence."

"You've heard of us." Meredith's face lit up. "Believe it or not, many children don't know how to swim, and there are a lot of needless tragedies." Her voice was tinged with passion. "Do you know that in South Africa alone, there are well over a thousand drownings a year, a third of whom are children?"

"How did Dr. Cook become involved?"

"He said he had the expertise and resources to build the community centers and that he'd done a lot of charity work all over the world."

"What happened?"

"Our first location, in Nairobi, ran far above budget. No surprise. But the final result was worth it—a world-class facility. I went for the opening, and it was one of the highlights of my life." A cloud crossed her face. "A couple of months later, my overseas contact, Kene, called. He was in Dar Es Salaam, and he'd dropped by the next site."

She paused to collect her emotions. "He called me in a panic. The site was half the size of the proposed blueprints. And all the materials were obviously poor quality."

"So, Dr. Cook was charging full price—maybe even higher—and doing half the work with shoddy material."

"It's not just my reputation." Her eyes misted over. "This charity will eventually fail if it's not done properly. I really want to make a difference in the lives of these kids."

"Wouldn't you eventually find out?"

"Of course," she said. "But maybe not for a few more years. Then it would be too late. Cook would have moved on to another scam."

"Where were you last night?" Moira brought the conversation back to ground.

Meredith's eyes widened in surprise. "At home with a friend. We had dinner and ended up talking past midnight. It was late and we'd had a few glasses of wine, so she decided to crash in my guest room."

"What does the number 27 signify?" I changed the topic, hoping to catch her off guard.

"That's an Angel number," Meredith said. "An Angel number is a spiritual indication that you're on the right path. The number 27 is a sign to continue pushing toward your goal."

"And how does this connect to Cook?"

Meredith shook her head. "Don't be foolish. He was anything but the right path for me or anyone else."

It was late—or maybe early, depending upon your viewpoint—and my brain was beginning to throb with the faint rumbling of a headache.

"Thank you, Ms. Cook. The officer will get your contact info and we'll be back in touch shortly." The window was now tinged with morning sunlight. "And please stay in town."

***

Cook's office was in a drab building in a drab part of town. The skies had turned slate gray, and the litter-strewn, windswept parking lot did nothing to improve my perception.

Fortified by a drive-through breakfast, we gingerly trod through an obstacle course of water-filled potholes to a bland and anonymous lobby. No reception desk, just a directory that was comprised of many indecipherable business listings or names. For the fourth floor, it simply said 'Cook' spelled out in white plastic letters. So much for fancy signage. Like many low-rise buildings, the wait for the elevator was interminable.

"What do you think of when I say the number 27?" I asked Moira as we waited.

She responded immediately. "The 27 Club."

My perplexed expression spoke volumes.

"I used to be a bit of a wild child. Goth with a sprinkling of punk for good measure."

I had noted the array of faded piercings where multiple earrings and miscellaneous fixtures must have once adorned her. I'd even caught a glimpse of a tattoo sleeve on her one arm despite her modest dress style.

"Still have lots of hidden piercings," she offered.

My discomfort was eased by the hiss of the elevator door. "The 27 Club?" I repeated.

"I was also into alternative music. There's a long list of musicians who died at age 27. Jimi Hendrix. Amy Winehouse. Janis Joplin to name just a few."

"Kurt Cobain?" I ventured.

The elevator groaned to a halt and revealed a hallway that was beige and dated. The lighting was dim, and the wallpaper was probably fashionable in the early seventies.

Halfway down the corridor, I could hear strains of Roger Whittaker coming from an open doorway with a modest plaque reading "Cook" beside it.

"Come in," called a raspy voice.

The reception area was sparse and devoid of any signs of life. An Ikea desk, completely bare, no telephone, no computer. The wall was equally barren of decoration—no calendars, photos, or even a clock.

Another door yawned open into the office proper. A woman, likely in her late twenties, stood and held out her hands, which were garbed in white gloves. She wore a pin-striped jacket and form-hugging skirt with black seamed stockings. Her red high heels matched her lipstick.

"I'm Jaye Winslow," she announced. "Cook's Executive Assistant."

"Not Dr. Cook?" I asked.

"I'm not sure if his degrees are real."

"Either way, we're here to talk about your boss."

"Truly a shame." Her voice was flat. "Couldn't happen to a nicer guy."

"You've heard already?"

"A couple of his clients called. Asking if his death meant they were now going to be paid."

We stood awkwardly in the doorway with a view of another plain desk. A shelf held a high-end espresso maker and, incongruously, an old-fashioned turntable playing a vinyl record.

"I thought his office would be a little more…luxurious."

Jaye laughed. "Cook spent as little time here as possible. This office is only for files and business keeping and all the administrative crap I look after. For client meetings, he booked tables at fancy restaurants—preferably at their expense."

"Then why…" Moira started to ask.

"Because he paid well and left me alone."

I thought about the solitude the office space offered and the comfort it provided if you were anti-social. "Any idea which of his clients might hold a grudge?"

She smiled smugly and handed over a folded sheet of paper.

I opened it. A list of names typed—by a real typewriter—in alphabetical order to boot.

I scanned the list. Twenty-six names—the same number as the letters in the alphabet. Looking closer, I groaned aloud.

"What is it?" Moira asked.

"Cici Palmer. Dee Wingfield. G.W. Connor," I recited. "Ai Yakamoto. Half the names are initials or letters."

Jaye smiled brightly. "All the names are authentic, I assure you. And all are former business partners burned by Dr. Cook. Not sure if any of them would kill him, but most probably gave it serious consideration."

I nodded toward the gleaming espresso machine. "May we? I think we need to sit down and chat awhile."

***

Three hours later and after ingesting enough caffeine that I wanted to take hostages, we were no further ahead. All the business partners had good reason to wish him ill, though it wasn't obvious who might have the nerve to follow through.

"You know what surprises me?" Moira asked with a sigh. "Why no one killed the bastard years ago."

"Of all the disgruntled partners surely one or two stand out."

She pushed her notepad across the table. "Dr. J.D. Armstrong. They founded a charity called Cook Medical Miracles."

"Sounds impressive."

"The concept is pretty admirable. As certain types of medical equipment—vents, monitors, pumps—approach their end of life, usually the hospital purchases the newest model with the latest technology. The old equipment is discarded even though they still have some value especially if further preventative maintenance is done on them."

"So Cook asked the hospitals to donate them," I conjectured.

"Exactly." Moira frowned. "But I can't figure how this is fraud."

I stood up. "Let's ask the good Doctor J.D."

***

Southcreek Hospital maintained a reputation as a world-class cancer treatment center, complete with the most cutting-edge technology. However, the corridors were still cinder blocks painted in a depressing shade of green with the smell of antiseptic burned into the walls.

If I'd imagined Dr. J.D. to be a lanky Texan, I contained my surprise when it turned out that J.D. was a petite Vietnamese lady in her mid-thirties.

"Joanie Davina," J.D. explained once we introduced ourselves. "But I always thought J.D. sounded more professional."

"We're here about Dr. Cook."

She nodded without surprise. "So, it's true. Good, I've got a nice bottle of Moet chilling in my fridge for this occasion."

"Sounds like no love is lost for your business partner."

Her voice was unapologetic. "Not any longer. I would've killed him myself if I had the guts or the strength."

I cut straight to the chase. "We can't figure out how Cook Medical Miracles was a sham."

"Neither could I, at first," J.D. said. "But even a free donation is subject to expenses. Custom fees, shipping fees, even bribery for various officials in some third-world locations."

"Nothing overly suspicious."

"Exactly. It wasn't until much later that I realized everything was two, even three times more expensive than it should be, and Cook was skimming off the top."

"How much?"

"It varied, but easily several thousand dollars per piece of equipment, and hundreds of items were donated in the first year alone."

I gave a low whistle. "Who paid for the shipping?"

"Anyone and everyone. Some of the receiving hospitals covered the costs. There were a few fundraising dinners. Even a charity golf tournament."

"How did you discover the fraud?"

"Cook was away on vacation and an invoice was sent to me in error. Most of the donations were large pieces of equipment, but this was something Cook wouldn't be familiar with. There was a donation of cannula tubes which probably could have fit in a dozen shoeboxes, yet the invoice listed and charged for three pallets. That's when my suspicions were raised."

"What did Cook say?"

"He was horrified. Or at least pretended to be." She tugged at her white lab coat in frustration. "He should have been an actor instead of a doctor. I waited a couple of weeks and confronted him again. He cut me off and shut down the charity, but not before cleaning out all the bank accounts."

"And there was nothing you could do?" Moira asked sympathetically.

"I thought about suing him, but my lawyer said it would take years, and there was a good chance it would fail. He could claim to be innocent—a victim as well."

I nodded—the likely winners would be the lawyers who would leave behind a disillusioned and frustrated client. I changed tactics. "What does the number 27 represent?"

J.D. paused in thought, then walked to a nearby whiteboard and scribbled a string of indecipherable numbers. "27 is a unique number, as it is the only number that is three times bigger than the total of its digits: (27 = 3 x (2+7))," she explained.

Both Moira and I stared blankly at her.

"Sorry," she apologized. "I'm a bit of a math geek."

***

The next few days were an endless repeat of the first day.

The 'Kayes' and the 'Elles' and 'Beas' and 'Dees' became a jumble of letters in my mind and, if it weren't for Moira's meticulous note taking, I'd have been lost.

Not only were many of the names similar, but the swindles also shared common traits. Most had a charitable element with an elegant simplicity that usually involved padded expenses or extra charges. While the scams couldn't bear much scrutiny, no one bothered to look too closely, which was the beauty of the whole set-up.

Most of Cook's victims were female, but no romance was apparent other than the opportunity for Cook to flex his good looks and charm. Virtually all the scams involved a medical component, where Cook emphasized his fake credentials to snare his investors.

"Was he really a doctor?" I asked at one point.

Moira looked up from the file she had assembled. "Not a medical doctor. He'd studied General Arts—everything from Medieval Art to European history. It's not even clear if he ever graduated."

I turned back to the folders that contained info on his various victims. We'd conducted eighteen preliminary interviews with the remaining eight former partners either out of town or located in different parts of the country. While all of them had ample reason to want Cook dead, none of them seemed to have a clear opportunity—or the backbone to commit murder.

As for the number 27, it meant something unique to each person, but held no clear connection to Cook or any of the suspects.

"Did you know the alphabet was invented by the Phoenicians?" Moira said. "Strangely enough, there's little evidence of their writing."

"Fascinating." I frowned. Something nagged at the edge of my consciousness. A spoken word or phrase that reverberated within my memory. However, the more I tried to recall it, the more elusive it became.

***

It was a few minutes before midnight, but the light in the upper office at SOS Signage still burned brightly.

The employee entrance door was unlocked, and I quickly climbed the stairs. No alarm system, I noted, but when I entered Cohen's office, he was obviously waiting for me. "Installed security cameras," he explained. Despite the late hour, his dress shirt was still crisp and unwrinkled.

"Good idea, especially if you're burning the midnight oil."

"Look who's talking. Don't suppose you're here to tell me when I get back my showroom."

"I've heard by the end of the week, but that's up to Forensics."

"Who haven't been around for a couple of days," he grumbled.

"I'll make some calls," I promised. "But that's not what brings me here. I'd like to take another look."

"At three minutes to midnight?"

"Whenever inspiration strikes. Isn't that what you said about Cook? Besides, it won't take long."

He wordlessly went over to a wall panel and flipped some switches. "Just let me know when you're leaving."

***

Cohen had turned on only half of the overhead lights, which left the showroom in a gloomy jungle of large alphabet letters throwing surreal shadows.

My footsteps echoed as I walked toward the spot where Cook had been killed. I'd looked at the crime scene—including dozens upon dozens of photos that Ethel and her crew had taken, but had I really seen anything?

The giant 'A' that had crushed Cook to death was now gone—presumably transported to the lab for further analysis, but I wasn't optimistic that any fingerprints or other evidence would be found.

The dusty outline of Cook's body had faded, though the 27 painted in blood remained clearly visible.

I looked toward where Cook had pointed, but nothing stood out from this angle.

Time to change the perspective. Carefully, I knelt on the ground until I was completely prone on the cool concrete floor. I was probably a few inches taller than Cook so I shifted my body back, pointed my hand straight past the 27, and rolled my neck onto my right shoulder mimicking Cook's final resting place.

From this viewpoint, certain letters were more prominent. Directly ahead lay the symbol for 'and.' Nearby were the letters 'Q' and 'Z' although I couldn't recall any connection to the names of any of the suspects.

Moira's words echoed in my mind, on how her university degree in English literature had proven useless in the real world. Cook had a similar background in the arts. My own education had ranged from studying film noir to medieval history, until I decided to sign up with the police. The academic life may not have been for me, but it was certainly not a waste of time.

***

"If I'd known you were going to invite so many people, I'd have prepared some appetizers." Moira glanced from Cohen's office to the crowded showroom below, where over two dozen people stood uneasily amongst the giant letters.

"The key to a successful cocktail party is to invite a diverse group of people and encourage them to mingle."

"By guests you mean suspects," Moira retorted.

In response, I beckoned Moira to follow me down the staircase. The showroom was lit only by the late afternoon sun, but it felt like a spotlight tracked our descent.

I stopped on the lower landing and spoke to the assembled crowd. "Thank you for coming this afternoon. My name is Detective Inspector…"

"Jesus, we all know who you are, as well as your gorgeous assistant." I felt Moira stiffen beside me. "What I'd really like to know is why we're being brought together like some third-rate production of *The Mousetrap*."

The belligerent voice was courtesy of T.J. O'Reilly, a short—and short-tempered—oncologist who was one of Cook's very first victims. If being a jerk contributed to one's status as a suspect, T.J. would be number one with a bullet. However, his overall unpleasantness was driven by the fact he'd fallen for one of Cook's earliest schemes, which he should have realized was a hoax, had he not been caught up in greed. His broken pride only fueled his anger.

"Sorry if this is rather dramatic," I said, trying for diplomacy, "but I wanted to bring everyone together to summarize the case so far."

It was now Moira's turn to speak, in part so I could observe the reaction of the others.

"Now, I don't think it's an overstatement to say that everyone here had good reason to want Dr. Cook dead."

"Isn't that a little exaggerated, dear?" Emma Michaels, known to everyone simply as 'Em', protested. She was elderly, refined, dignified lady who had lost more money than any of Cook's former partners, but she still protected Cook's reputation, likely due to an unrequited crush.

"Then why was the body of Dr. Cook found lying on this very floor?"

Involuntarily, the crowd looked at the faded outline.

I stepped in. "As many of you know, Dr. Cook was able to leave a clue as to the identity of his killer."

"It seems to be a pretty obscure clue," J.D. said.

"Yes, Dr. Cook didn't want to be too obvious. The killer was nearby so he chose something that wouldn't be easily understood. Something from his university years. The number 27 and its true meaning."

Meredith Cook looked at me with her cool eyes and calm demeanor. "So exactly what does the number 27 represent?"

"Well, if you lie in the position where Dr. Cook's body was found, you'll notice several things."

"Such as?" Cici Palmer asked. Of all the suspects, she had the most fatalistic view and blamed herself for falling for the doctor's con.

"Numerous letters are now clearly in the line of sight," I said. "Such as 'Z' and 'Q' and 'X' for example."

Everyone was silent as they tried to figure out whose initials might be implicated.

"But the symbol directly in the line of sight is the ampersand, meaning 'and,'" I said.

"Are you telling us Cook meant everyone?" Meredith's tone was slightly mocking. "Like *Murder on the Orient Express*?"

"No, it was definitely the ampersand that Cook was pointing at. Interesting bit of trivia—did you know at one time there were 27 letters in the alphabet?"

"Interesting if this is Trivial Pursuit," J.D. spoke again.

"And the last letter was the ampersand. Thus the 27th letter. In common use until the mid-1800s."

"I still don't understand what the significance of this ampersand thing is," Sam Cohen said. His voice was curious, but I sensed in his eyes that he knew where I was heading.

"You tell me. You made the signage for him."

Without further prompting, he recited, "Cook Medical Devices, Cook Overseas Medical, Cook Diagnostics, Cook…" Cohen abruptly stopped. "Cook & Cook."

"The only one with an ampersand?" I asked.

Samuel nodded silently.

All eyes swiveled to Meredith. "That's ridiculous. It doesn't prove anything."

"No, it doesn't prove anything, but it's a start," I said. "Why, after all this time, did he acknowledge a partner?"

"Because you two became romantically involved," Moira interjected. "After all this time, he let his guard down and became emotionally entangled."

"What kind of fool do you take me for?" Meredith shot back.

"A fool who enjoys fine dining and weekend escapes." Moira flourished a sheaf of papers. His credit card bills for the past few months. "We've just started, but I'm sure some of the wait staff or hotel workers will remember a pretty girl such as yourself."

"I have an alibi…my friend was over…"

"Who was passed out on your couch from midnight until after breakfast," I said. "We interviewed her yesterday."

Meredith opened her mouth to protest, then thought better of it.

"You arranged to meet him at the warehouse. You knew he'd enter via the door directly under the letter 'A'. Look around you. You're the only one here strong enough to push it off the platform."

Meredith glared at me in defiance, and I decided to change my strategy. "Did it hurt to know you'd been played like all the other victims? That Cook never loved you? You were just another gullible target except, this time, he took pleasure in using not only your money, but your body."

She shook her head. "No, no, it wasn't like that at all."

"Did he confess, hoping you would join in the scheme, or did you find out for yourself that he was lying all along?"

Meredith's face flushed with anger.

"But I have to admit," I said, "you were the only one who stood up to him. The only one with enough backbone to punish him. To give him what he deserved."

Her eyes lit up. "Exactly," she said. "Everyone else—all these losers—they complained, moaned and cried, but no one had the guts to do anything about it. They're all cowards. Only I had the courage to stand up and show what a weak, evil man he truly was."

"Did he know it was you?" Moira asked softly.

"Of course." She grinned in triumph. "After I pushed the sign on top of him, I climbed down and stood over him. I looked him in the eyes, so he knew I was responsible, and his day of reckoning had finally arrived."

"Did he say anything?"

"Why, Meredith, why?" She shook her head in disgust. "Those were his last words and I just walked away. He must have had a last-minute burst of strength to write 27 in his own blood."

I didn't say anything, but let the silence sink in.

Meredith looked at the assembly of shocked faces. She appeared to be relieved at her public confession. A uniformed officer approached, and she offered her wrists for the handcuffs with no objection. She was led outside, and the crowd of former suspects dispersed.

Samuel Cohen paused at the top of the staircase and his eyes met mine. He gave a barely perceptible nod and returned to his office.

Moira and I stood in the showroom and gazed at the 27 written in blood. She looked at me in the fading afternoon light. "Aren't you going to say something witty or cynical?"

I glanced around at the letters surrounding us. "Sorry, I'm at a loss for words."

She shook her head but smiled faintly, and I knew our fledgling partnership would work out fine.

The 13th Letter

M

The End

MY BABY JUST WROTE ME A LETTER

By Catherine Astolfo

The summer of 1982, Saylor Hammett didn't know my secret and I didn't know hers.

Every morning, including that final season, I was her slightly nerdy pal, Zack, an employee of Hammett's Airboat Rides. By the time I reached 30, I had been working there for 10 years.

I had finished my wildlife biology degree. Sometimes, mostly in my birth country of Canada, I accepted contracts to teach courses related to my credentials.

Besides teaching, I was very good at building, painting and refurbishing wooden structures. Since all the docks and fences and even the little gift/cashier shop at Hammett Airboat Rides were constructed of wood, the place constantly needed paint or a new coat of stain. Replacement boards. That was my job.

Saylor and her dad drove the airboats and enlightened tourists about our section of the Everglades, along with Gus, their other guide.

"My real first name is Gwendolin," she said when anyone asked, which sooner or later everyone did. "My mom's maiden name was Saylor, so I got Saylor Hammett as last names. But really, do I look like a Gwendolin?"

She did not. With her curly hair and her tan face where two round, heavily lashed brown eyes gazed out with her trademark frank stare, she looked like a Saylor. Almost as tall as I was, six feet, she was a bit stocky. Not skinny. Not at all overweight. Saylor could lift a huge pile of firewood or effortlessly pull in a line with an enormous fish on the other end.

"My mother died when I was three," she would freely tell tourists. "So, it seemed fitting that I would take her last name as my first. She was black, while my dad is white, as you can see for yourself in that picture."

There was a large poster under plastic on the outer wall of the gift shop, with a tribute to the gorgeous black woman in the photograph. You could clearly see where her daughter got those fathomless brown eyes.

Anthony Hammett stood beside her, a tall skinny white man with ginger hair, who looked surprised to be in the company of such a beautiful woman.

"This property is owned by Margaret Saylor Hammett and Anthony Hammett as a sanctuary, a place where animals and birds can be safe, and humans can find peace in their midst."

Tourists always obediently read the inscription and nodded wisely or smiled.

Saylor was a great salesperson. She tied up the boats, snapped pictures that were sold later at the gift shop, or took payments for trips and tips. Once she reached the age to be licensed, she had a ball doing the tours. She also became a wildlife biologist.

I met Saylor in college. Up until then, we might as well have lived in different states. Her family's property was way down Old Creek Road, toward the south shore of Lake Taho, while my mother and I lived in one of the housing communities at the edge of St. Cloud.

We had moved from Canada to the U.S. when I was ten. My dad stayed behind. Which is why I returned "home" whenever a contract to teach came up.

Back in first year college, I was even nerdier. I still wore thick glasses that, thankfully, I eventually switched for contact lenses. Looking like a stunned giraffe with my nervous lope, I stumbled into the lecture room praying for a seat.

Saylor answered my prayer.

"Want to sit here?" she asked, patting the chair next to her.

"Thanks" was the only word I could choke out.

Despite her odd way of dressing—checkered shirts and polka-dotted pants and a huge red bow in her hair for instance—I soon learned that no one ever made fun of Saylor. Everyone adored her. She had that kind of magnetic personality.

"She's so mannish" was about the only criticism I ever heard. Personally, I didn't get why they said she was like a man. After all, I was a man, and I could not keep up with her nor did I dress like her. Saylor was one of a kind.

"Why don't you come over on Saturday?" she asked at the end of the first day.

That was the beginning of hundreds of trips to the Hammetts'. Saylor and I shared a love of animals and were passionate about the environment. We were best friends from that initial encounter. We encouraged each other and finished college with high marks.

We worked together throughout the year. Eventually, I moved into one of the cabins, so I didn't have to commute.

"Doesn't your mom mind that you're gone most of the time?" Saylor asked me once.

"Not one bit. Since she split from my dad, she's single and dating. She's glad to have the house to herself."

When the buildings surrounding the swamp were all shiny and practically new, I disappeared for months at a time on contract work. Saylor didn't seem to notice my absence. Not once had she suggested writing letters to one another. I was too embarrassed to write one to her. Would I look needy? Nerdier?

Saylor wasn't aware that my feelings had progressed from the best-buddy relationship we'd shared since we met. My affection for her had become far deeper. Romantic rather than friendly. Since I was pretty sure *her* feelings hadn't changed, I was careful to keep my thoughts of kissing her soft lips to myself. At night in my dreams, I could take her in my arms and become her lover instead of her friend. In secret.

"It's so hot," Saylor grumbled in July. "Seriously, Zack, isn't this the hottest year ever?"

It was true. That year's weather hadn't helped my mood. Each day when I stepped out of the cabin it was like popping my head into an oven.

Normally the savior was a breeze that moved over the swamp like a brush across strands of soft hair. That summer was so hot the wind felt heated too. The relentless sun beat on dried-up ground. Succulents and sawgrasses were stunted.

Nothing kept the tourists away. Saylor, Anthony and Gus were far too good at the job. People came from close by and far away. Dozens of repeat customers.

Down the roadway they would drive, kicking up dirt and dust in their path. Over the cattle grate. Toward the outcrop that poked into Lake Taho. Surrounded by swampland, the peninsula housed the Hammett homestead and airboat business.

On the wider side of the cape, a sprawling one-story house, built in the 1940s, had served as home to the Hammetts for decades. Tucked under a grove of Royal Palms, surrounded by ferns and mangrove trees, the place was barely visible. Not to mention that pretty much every tree dripped with Spanish moss.

Anthony stayed in their home. Saylor couldn't stand the lack of sunlight and the swarm of insects at dusk each day. Over the years, we built several huts in an open area near reception. Saylor. Storage. Gus. Me.

I'd been inside Saylor's cabin many times. I often looked longingly at the bed, which filled one end of the hut as though demanding my attention.

Almost every night, we sat on her porch, drank a couple of beers and talked.

"It seems like things are changing. Not slowly, but quickly, as though the land is boiling up," I said.

Saylor took a sip of her beer. She slowly shook her head.

"I know. There's something odd happening."

We couldn't understand the various abnormalities, but other than some quick conversations after dark, we had no time to consider the reasons.

As though driven by the heat to fly across swamps, the tourists lined up in droves. Once the ramps and boards were nearly completed, I was forced to lead tours, too. Not my favorite task.

"You're a snob," Saylor told me more than once. "You expect people to be smart about the environment and they're just not."

It was true. I had no patience for their stupid questions. Their ignorance about the swamp and its inhabitants.

"It can't be the heat," Saylor said one night.

Sweat trickled down her cheeks into the neck of her t-shirt. Her magnificent breasts poked through the wet cloth. I averted my eyes.

I knew what she was talking about. Our shorthand over the years had blossomed so much that our conversations were impossible for anyone else to follow.

"I agree. They should be seeking the water. Half in. Half out. Or mostly in. That's normal. This isn't."

We meant the alligators. They had started to approach land in worrisome numbers. Lumbering onto the cape, far too close to where our docks loaded the visitors.

Despite their fascination with the inhabitants of the swamp, tourists really did not want to be face-to-face with an alligator. We didn't want that either. Very bad for business, to have someone lose a leg or an arm.

Over the last couple of weeks, the reptiles had begun to move. Beginning at dusk, we'd noticed a few of our larger males plodding up from the marsh. Once launched onto land, they moved quickly on those dinosaur legs.

"Where are they going?" I mused.

When Saylor didn't answer, I looked at her face. Her expression was odd. She didn't look at me with her usual probing gaze.

"I have no idea," she answered, but the words didn't sound real.

I had become a bit of an expert on alligators. Not only on up-to-date research about their habits, but I could wrestle and coax them back into the swamp.

The safest routine was to have someone—Gus, Anthony or Saylor—distract the animal while I leaped onto its back from the rear.

With the bigger ones, once they were pinned down, I'd place my hands between the back of its jaw and the front legs. I'd run my hand along its neck and grip the jaw to keep it firmly closed. I'd use tape to keep that mouth shut. In this position, I could lift the neck toward my chest and hug its powerless head.

Someone would secure its arms and legs. After which we made our way, clumsily, back into the water.

The babies were easy to wrangle because we could pick them up and hold their mouths shut. When they grew to bigger than twelve inches, I used all precautions. If I was alone, I'd throw my t-shirt over their eyes for some temporary blindness. By myself, I'd only try to wrangle one that was small enough for a cage.

I loved alligators, which is why I'd studied them so thoroughly. Despite their rough exterior and gaping mouths, I thought their telescope eyes sparked with intelligence. I'd watched them gather twigs and carry them on their snouts to lure birds. They were good at hiding under trees or in mud to capture prey. I was fairly certain that one of the older males—whom I called Caiman—recognized my favorite shirt. When I wore something else, he ran away.

That summer I had to wrangle some big ones by myself. We were busy and short-handed. Few young people wanted to come out to Lake Taho to work. There were jobs in town, where the drive was short, and alligators weren't involved.

When I was alone, I spent a long time stroking the alligator's neck as I clasped the jaw with the other hand. Then I'd roll the animal over, clutching the mouth shut, then quickly tape it. As the weeks went by, I discovered that the gators were calm and drowsy. Which was strange in the extreme.

We were so busy that I didn't spend too much time worrying about the issue. There were docks to mend, fences to paint. Tours to conduct.

Saylor buzzed back and forth between the boats, the ticket counter and the gift shop, handling all these jobs with cheerful energy. Every once in a while, she'd fly past me or stop to make a comment.

"Do you think scientists could be wrong about alligators? Maybe they do care about each other," she said one morning.

Her father and I were preparing the airboats for the day. We stood on the dock in the stillness of another freakishly hot day. Anthony shrugged.

I didn't like to give Saylor a lecture on any wildlife subject, but she hadn't studied alligators the way I had. I knew she respected that.

"They have a low level of intelligence in the human way. They don't seem to care if one of their group disappears or dies. But you know, we *Homo sapiens* don't have a deep understanding of reptiles. Most animals, really."

"Okay, so coming to see how one of their group is doing would be unusual."

Anthony and I looked at each other.

"Yes, that would be quite unusual," I said, "at least in our experience. Why? Have you noticed something?"

She shrugged her shoulders. "Not really. Just curious."

In August, I received a very lucrative contract offer to teach at the University of Toronto for two months. Part of me was thrilled, while the rest of me was worried. The drought and heat had not abated, nor had the number of tourists.

However, Saylor was excited for me.

"Zack, this is fantastic. You'll kill this! And who knows what this contract might lead to? You could be a famous speaker on behalf of wildlife. Your circuit could be all over the world."

I didn't really want to be a famous speaker who traveled. I wanted to be here with Saylor. I pictured building a small house on this property. Teaching our kids to shepherd the environment…

But she was so obviously encouraging me to go away again that I said nothing.

Before I left, I was crushingly busy. I completed the refurbishing. Guided loads of tourists.

Saylor became more and more distant. I got the feeling she wanted me out of the way. She disappeared in the evenings, eschewing our usual conversational time. When I tried to look at her directly, she averted her eyes.

The night before I left for Toronto, I thought about following her to see where she was going. Unfortunately, Gus and Anthony decided to give me a small farewell party, complete with beer and nachos. We gathered dockside in chairs reserved for tour groups awaiting their turns.

The sun had gone down, but the heat was relentless. No breeze stirred the marsh or the lake. The birds were nearly silent. Every bit of vegetation drooped. The water had receded enough that we'd been forced to add an extra length of docking.

"Where's Saylor?" I asked.

"She had an errand to run. I forget what. Checking some nests? You know how obsessed she is with that kind of thing," Anthony answered.

His reply struck me as strange. More words than he usually said in a day. Spoken in a stammer, as though he struggled to make it up as he went.

I sipped on the beer, feeling the cold alcohol zing through my tired, overheated body. Not for the first time, I felt afraid to leave.

"Your mother didn't want you to visit with her tonight?" Gus asked.

"She's picking me up tomorrow and taking me to the airport," I said. "She's got a shift tonight."

Gus shook his head. "Poor nurses. Those shifts must be brutal. I guess you'll see your dad in Toronto."

"I'm staying with him."

It was the first time Gus had ever mentioned my parents. I gazed around at the strange scenery and stared at the two men. Their heads were lowered toward the beer bottles that were nearly out of liquid inside. Their eyes were fixed on the ground.

I had a terrible sensation in my stomach, but I couldn't give voice to what was happening inside my guts.

Just then Saylor raced up to the dock. She grabbed a beer from the cooler and traded our three empties for full ones. No one said anything other than "thanks."

Saylor's curls were long and wild. She looked as though she'd gone for a dip in the lake. Sweat stained her underarms and lathered her forehead.

"Where'd you get to?" I asked her, trying to sound nonchalant.

"Oh, one of the scientists who visited this summer asked me to take a few pictures of areas she didn't capture."

It was a different story from Anthony's, but he hadn't really known what she was doing.

Her brown eyes skidded past mine as she took a gulp of the beer.

"Last night for a while, huh?" she said, as though this might be news for a discussion.

"Yup. Two whole months."

"Did I tell you we got a guy from the college to take your place?"

Take your place. Not *fill in for you while you're gone*. I choked a bit on the sip I'd just tried to swallow.

"Great. Good. I won't feel so guilty."

Saylor didn't reassure me. For the rest of the "celebration," we made insignificant small talk.

Little did I know the college hire was a fabrication.

After everyone went to bed, I lay staring at my ceiling. My nerves tingled. Finally, I got up and crept outside. The stillness of the swamp seeped into my flesh like influenza. I felt feverish and achy.

The moonlight was shaded by clouds, but it was bright enough to see where I was going. I walked along the shore of the promontory, listening for sounds of life. Nothing. No movement. No muttering. No reaction to my presence. It was as though the marsh had died.

Suddenly along the bank, highlighted in the glimmer from above, a rustle began in the short grasses. Something was headed toward the water. I stopped, making my breath shallow and quiet.

Slowly I realized it was Caiman. He held his head up, nostrils, eyes and ears probing the dark. His mouth hung open to show his long upper teeth. He didn't lumber as usual. He crashed through the vegetation, such as it was, to race into the swamp. His bent legs propelled his enormous body as quickly as they could. At around eleven feet long and likely weighing half a ton, his progress was a heart-stirring sight.

I waited in silence as Caiman reached the shore and plunged under the water. All I could see was the ripple of his movements underneath.

I was about to move when I heard the sound of another gator moving along the same path as Caiman. Smaller, likely female, the animal followed the exact same route and ended in the marsh.

I watched in awe and fright as they came, one after another, from the same direction into the water. I lost count, but at least ten or twelve alligators passed me.

Saylor's comment echoed through my mind. *So, coming to see how one of their group is doing would be unusual.* Is that what this collection of alligators had been doing? Checking on one of their own?

I shook my head. All the research would reject that theory.

When it had been quiet for several minutes, with no other alligators coming down that path, I tried to follow it. Lit only by the cloudy moon, the route was difficult to see. Despite the fact that literally tons of alligator flesh had passed that way, and the vegetation was stunted and sparse, I couldn't seem to find my way. The trail was no flatter than the surrounding vegetation. It wound into a clump of trees. Spanish moss hung everywhere, feeding itself on the dying cells of the older trees and plants. It was plenty dark as I stumbled forward.

When my shoe met mossy water, I knew I had wound my way back to the swamp. Sure enough, I stepped into the moonlight not too far from where I had started out. My sneakers were sopping.

As soon as I got back from my nighttime journey, I peeled off my wet clothing, drenched now with sweat. The heat was unbearable. I put my face close to my fan and sank into a deep sleep.

Naturally, I slept in. When I finally roused myself, I had to take a quick shower, finish packing and gather my documents. By the time I emerged, tourists were lined up at reception. On the dock, Saylor, Gus and Anthony checked the airboats. My mother's car roared down the road in a fit of dust.

I dropped my bag and ran out to the dock. A shake from Gus, a shoulder punch from Anthony and a quick kiss on the cheek from Saylor and I found myself sitting in the front seat beside my mom.

When I landed in Toronto, the temperature difference was stunning. I breathed in the clear, cooler air and felt energized. Maybe this gig was going to be all right.

And it was. Incredibly busy. I called the Hammetts a few times, but Anthony was vague and Saylor unavailable. After a while, I buried myself in work and tried to keep her halo of hair and deep brown eyes out of my dreams.

***

The letter arrived seven weeks after I'd left. It had been sent by express airmail two days earlier than the postmark. Florida. No return address.

Only three words and her signature on the small sheet of paper inside the envelope.

I need you. Saylor

When I told the University that I had to leave a week early due to a family emergency, they were very understanding.

My dad was ridiculously wealthy, so a last-minute flight back to Florida meant nothing to him. When I landed, I rented a car and raced from Orlando to Old Creek Road in record time.

Dirt and dust flew around the car like a cloud. I bumped over the cattle grate, jolting my head toward the roof. At the sign to Hammett Airboats, usually a colorful welcome to tourists, I slammed on the brakes. Pasted across the billboard was a huge "closed until further notice" banner.

Ahead, the trees seemed to have bent even closer to the ground. A burial shroud of Spanish moss had thrown itself over everything. The water had receded past the extended docks.

Across the horizon, the sun had painted a deep orange band that was slowly sinking into the lake.

I pushed the gas pedal and careened into the nearly empty parking lot. Gus's truck was covered in grime. Anthony's car, I assumed, was in his garage. Only Saylor's pick-up appeared to have been used recently.

When I stepped into the oppressive heat, I heard nothing. Not a sound from the birds. Dormant insects. Lack of breeze. Exactly as I had left it.

No. Worse than when I had left. More collapsed vegetation. Greater stillness.

Of course, the absence of tourists made the place feel deserted, but the air was dead, too. My stomach twisted. I could barely breathe.

"Saylor!" I began to yell as I walked around the small houses.

She popped out from her cabin after my third screech. Her hair was wiry, stuck to her head with sweat. No sparkle touched her eyes. Her face was drawn and waxy.

"You came," she said.

"Of course I came," I answered. "You wrote me a letter."

I stepped forward and she fell into my arms. For the first time, I embraced her strong, luscious body. Held her close. Felt my love flow from me to her.

She trembled and clung to me as though otherwise she would topple over.

"Tell me everything," I whispered.

Saylor looked at me, our eyes level.

"I have to show you," she said.

When we parted, one of her arms stayed around my waist. We walked as one toward her father's house. Darkness began to fill the air around us.

As we entered the thicket of Royal Palms and mangrove trees, a cloud of black made progress not only difficult but terrifying. I could hear the frightening buzz of flies and mosquitoes; mouths open to suck the life from us.

We kept our own lips sealed. Our eyes became slits for enough vision to keep going, but not wide enough for invasive bodies to enter.

Under the Spanish moss, the house looked crushed by the weight of heat and invaders. My heart pounded from lack of oxygen and fluid. The scene that awaited us ramped my blood pressure into the danger zone.

We stepped into the living room that had once been a comfortable gathering place.

Anthony's rocker lay on its back, with him in it. The only way I could tell it was him was by his boots and jeans. A towel had been placed over his face and head.

Gus was sprawled across the sofa, a neat bullet hole through his forehead.

The walls and floor were plastered with gore that had dried like a macabre painting. From the stench, I assumed they'd been dead for at least two days or more.

I stumbled on the doorstep and gagged. Saylor held *me* up this time, her face placid.

"This is why I had to show you," she said. "It's impossible to describe. Dad and Gus had a huge fight, as you can see by the wreckage. When Gus took the axe and flung it into Dad's head, I got my gun and shot him."

I let go of her and bent over, fighting the urge to vomit. Hands on my knees, I tried to speak.

"You…didn't call the cops…?"

Saylor heaved a big sigh, as though responding to the stupidest question ever posed.

"Of course not. You know Sheriff Watson. He's a bully. Plus, he's asked me out at least a dozen times and hates me for turning him down."

"But…"

After one more useless word, I felt able to straighten up. I refused to allow my eyes to stray over the bodies. Hopefully, I'd never have to look again.

I finally found my voice. "They were best friends. What the hell could they have been fighting over that would cause Gus to…to…"

I waved in the direction of poor Anthony. Glanced over at Saylor, noticing the details. There was a feral look about her. Her eyes had a wild glow. Her lips were pulled back from her teeth.

"Gus wanted to sell the Queen. Dad was adamant that we would keep her. Allow her to grow up in private. To live a normal life. She's another reason not to involve law enforcement."

"The Queen…?"

Saylor turned away from my stare. She began to pace back and forth. Insects flew up from the floor and buzzed around us.

"She's a leucistic alligator."

I was stunned into silence once more. A white alligator. Not albino?

Leucistic alligators are extremely rare. If this was one, it would be among only about a handful worldwide.

"Blue eyes?" I asked.

"Yes. And one patch of regular skin color on her belly. Pinky white mostly. She's unquestionably leucistic, not albino. I do know the difference, Zack."

"Sorry. I'm just…"

My head hurt. I couldn't process all the information swirling around. Buzzing flies. Human remains. A white alligator.

"We could sell her for an enormous amount of money. Gus wanted to do just that. Or turn the airboat business into a kind of zoo for the Queen. Dad and I couldn't do either of those things to her."

"Why didn't you tell me about her?"

She'd told her father and his friend obviously.

"I didn't tell *anyone*. Dad followed me one night. How Gus found out, I don't really know."

"Can I see her?"

"Of course. We'll go to her palace now."

This time both my head and my heart pounded with shock. Saylor said "palace" as though it were a normal word to use on this promontory surrounded by marsh.

We followed the trail that I remembered from my last night here. At some point, we veered off under a palm tree laden with Spanish moss. The weeds and leaves formed a large, round hut.

In the middle of the shelter, a seat had been formed from mud and leaves. Resembling a throne, it had a basin of water as well as grass and weeds all around it.

The white alligator lay half in the pond and half out. She was small, about cage size. She opened her huge blue eyes fixed at the top of her head, but she didn't move. She appeared quite comfortable in the presence of two humans close to her nest.

She was beautiful. A sight I had never expected to see in my lifetime. I wanted to reach out and stroke her chin.

Saylor caught my astonished, appreciative breath.

"Isn't she amazing?"

"Yes. Breathtaking. I can see why you and Anthony wanted to protect her."

"And you agree, right?"

I nodded my head, though part of me wanted to argue that her magnificence should be shared with the entire world. When I looked into Saylor's obsessed eyes, though, I knew I would never challenge her viewpoint.

"She's the real reason I didn't call the sheriff, Zack. Can you imagine what they would do to her?"

"People can be cruel."

"Yes, whereas animals can be surprising. They come to pay her homage every day."

I had a difficult time moving my eyes away from the Queen.

"Who does?" I finally asked.

"The other alligators. They come to visit at dusk."

Suddenly the memory of Caiman and the numerous gators lumbering through the trees flashed behind my eyes.

"They come to visit her?" I asked, though my question was redundant.

"Yes. They sit with her for a while and then go back to the lake."

I looked around at the pile of fish, frogs and snails in pails and cartons. I immediately thought I understood why the gators came to visit.

Saylor, however, clasped her hands in prayer formation and bowed her head.

I felt sick to my stomach. Saylor had become entranced to the point of neurosis. I wondered if she would ever be able to shake this unhealthy obsession. What could I do to release her? To change her back to the woman I loved?

"If you keep her here, what will happen when she's fully grown?"

"Oh, I wouldn't do that to her. I'll build out onto Lake Taho. She'll be able to see everything and splash in the water, but no one will see in. It'll be hard without Dad, but now I have you, and you're so skilled at construction. I've researched a type of canvas that…"

"But you won't be able to reopen the airboat business," I interrupted. "How will you survive?"

"My mother was a very wealthy woman. I have an enormous amount of money in a trust I inherited when I reached thirty. I didn't spend any of it. Now I realize that I was waiting for the Queen."

She smiled over at the gator, who had closed her eyes once more. Saylor went down on her knees in front of the throne. She began a rumbling sound in her throat, pushing out air resembling the bellow of an alligator.

The oppressive heat, airless hut and the odd sounds coming from Saylor pressed down on my head. I could barely see through the pain that zinged from temple to temple. Without explaining, I stepped out of the palace and drew in a few breaths. The air wasn't much better out here, but my headache subsided marginally.

A few minutes later, Saylor emerged. She leaned against me. Despite her odd behavior, my body stirred at her touch.

I finally found my voice.

"What…what do you plan to do with…about…Anthony and Gus?"

"The gators are hungry. There hasn't been enough food. Most of what I've scavenged, I've given to the Queen. What you saw in there…I think that's the last of what the lake has left to give. This drought shows no sign of stopping."

This time I did vomit. Dry heaves to be more accurate. The thought of what Saylor was implying made me sick.

"You have to help me, Zack," Saylor said. "No one will come out here to check up on us. Dad and Gus rarely went anywhere. If anyone does show up, I'll say they're in South America on an environmental mission."

I gazed at her. From her wild halo of hair to her huge brown eyes framed by long lashes. Down to her thick lips formed in a pout.

I leaned over and kissed her. To my surprise, she returned my passion with an equal pressure. When we lay down in the soft, wet grass, I was transported beyond the dreams I had had for years. Her response to my lovemaking was greater than anything I could have imagined.

Afterward, we lay for a few minutes enjoying the sensations, but were soon chased upward by insects. They too were hungry for anything.

"Will you help me, Zack?"

Saylor looked at me with a plea in her eyes. I had a terrible feeling that she would even make love to me for the sake of the Queen. I tried to shake off the thought.

"I love you, Saylor. I've loved you for years."

"I love you, too, Zack," she said, but it was automatic, as though she were agreeing that it was a hot day.

At that moment, I knew it was too late to return this new woman to the one I had always adored. But I also realized that I would do anything for her. I would never abandon her. Nothing she asked of me would be too much.

Even using my saw to slice up human flesh for alligator food wasn't beyond me. Though I was unable to eat for a couple of days before and after.

As the oppressive heat continued to flatten every living thing in the area, we worked by day. By night, we made love. At least, I persuaded myself it was love and not bribery.

Occasionally, a load of tourists would try and persuade us to reopen, but it didn't take long for word to spread. We changed the banner at the entrance to read, "Closed Permanently."

With Anthony and Gus gone and me in compliance, Saylor turned to delivery for supplies. Special fabrics that kept the sun out for the palace yurt. Poles that would form the new structure. Groceries and cartons of beer. Tons of fresh meat. Only these trucks were allowed to pull up past the cattle grate. Saylor and I never left the property.

The Queen's cage began to take shape. Of course, I never dared refer to it as anything but the palace. Poles were driven into the bottom of the swamp. Covered with fabric on all sides, it was a prison, in my opinion. There were flaps everywhere, but only humans could untie them and get in. No better than the zoo in which Saylor feared the Queen might be placed. I said none of this, of course.

The Queen never stirred even when the panels stood wide open. She stayed at Saylor's side.

As the weeks went by, the gators became more restless. They still visited every evening, but too often the flaps were closed. I was more convinced than ever that we were feeding a dozen or more alligators whose homage to the Queen had more to do with hunger than any fantastical belief Saylor held.

Rats are not usually good news, but in our case, they were. They showed up in droves once the house had been deserted for a couple of months. They took care of any leftovers and most of the garbage. When Saylor worried that the local butchers might become suspicious, I took care of the rodents.

By June, I was exhausted and depressed. I had begun to imagine our lives spinning along in constant care of a leucistic alligator and all her friends. Cutting up meat. Trapping rats. Each day, tons of feed to prepare and deliver.

I wondered if Saylor's inheritance would last until we were old. What would happen if we became ill?

Once the Queen was ensconced in her palace, Saylor spent most of her time out on the dock we'd built alongside it.

Though small by normal standards, the alligator had grown. Perhaps because she'd never had to fend for herself, she was a quiet, sleepy sort. She'd blink her bright blue eyes at Saylor or me. Her jaws would often erupt in a huge yawn.

I couldn't deny that she was beautiful. Mesmerizing really. Saylor's obsession with her only grew. She spent hours praying or bellowing. The Queen responded quietly. Royally.

Very soon the alligators began to swarm over the promontory in search of the food that had been available before the new palace was built. Saylor and I spent a lot of time wrestling them back into the lake.

"I think we have to feed them," I said after a particularly exhausting fight to get a gator nearly as big as Caiman into the water. "At least until this drought is over."

Saylor looked worryingly at the darkening sky. "It's been going on for over a year now," she said. "Do you think the climate has simply changed and we'll never be normal again?"

Normal. I wanted to bite back at her, *we'll never be normal as long as you worship that white alligator*. But the nights in her arms kept me from contradicting anything she did or said.

"The climate is definitely changing," I agreed. "But I don't think this drought will last forever. In the meantime, we're going to have to feed the alligators. You get that, right? They're dependent on us. For now, at least."

I pictured the nightly line of giant heads and bent legs, telescopic eyes alight with want. Saylor must have visualized them, too, for she nodded in agreement.

"When the drought ends, we'll have to train them to go back to their usual habits," she said.

I wondered how one trained an alligator to return to hunting instead of being fed without effort, but that was the future. One I didn't want to think about.

Saylor turned and looked out over the shrunken marsh. The sun had left a red stain across the horizon. Herald of another hot day to follow.

We had cut ourselves off from the world for months. We had no warning of what was to befall us that night.

The tornado bounced over the Atlantic and hit Florida in the middle of the night. We'd never had a tornado touch down in our area before. When it punched our little cape, the results were catastrophic.

I awoke at the first sound of the locomotive that was the wind. Saylor's cabin rattled and moved. I rolled over to the other side of the bed, but she wasn't there. On my hands and knees, I crawled through the shaking hut and flung myself outside. To avoid being blown away, I huddled underneath. Watched the whirling wind brush the edge of our home. The storm flattened the reception area and restrooms before turning Anthony's house and all the trees around it into piles of debris. It danced in no discernible pattern, ruining this area, saving that one.

My cabin was shaken loose of its roof but stood erect. Some of the others around Saylor's place were spared as the storm passed by.

When the wind subsided enough to allow me to stand upright, I crawled out and looked around. The tornado had plowed the lake sideways, picking up water as it moved. Leaving a muddy marsh behind and flooded grassland to the north of us. Already some water was trickling back toward our area. Seeking the low point.

Finally, I realized that something was missing from the horizon. The palace. Either it had been flattened into the mud or carried away on the wind.

"Saylor! Saylor!"

I was frantic. I began throwing debris out of my way as I marched toward the lake. Suddenly I heard her. Bellowing.

I turned and saw her behind one of the untouched cabins. At first, I thought she was grieving the death of the Queen, which I had to admit gave me a surge of hope. But when I got to her side, I saw the white alligator lying next to Saylor. The animal turned her eyes toward me and blinked.

I knelt and put my arms around Saylor.

"I'm so sorry, sweetheart," I said.

She stopped bellowing and nestled into my arms.

"It's ruined," Saylor wailed. "Everything is gone. The other gators have disappeared. What if they're all dead?"

"You rescued the Queen," I whispered in her ear. "And your house is still standing. So are some of the others.

We'll find a place for the Queen to stay. She doesn't seem to want to leave your side."

It was true. The alligator chumpfed, as though her gator's cough were an agreement. She didn't move more than a few inches away.

Saylor reached out and stroked the pinky-white skin, her face drawn and sad.

As I gazed over the mostly ruined point, and remembered the busy, thriving business that used to hum here, I was filled with distress too. Mostly because of the question that kept reverberating through my head. What would we do now?

Then the rain began.

We soon discovered that even money wouldn't help us. Many of the local businesses were closed. Damaged from winds and floods. Even the rats seemed to have deserted us.

"Your truck is still filled with gas," I said to Saylor on the third morning of foraging in pouring rain. "We should leave for a while. My mom escaped to her sister's place up north and it's all good there."

We were close to using up all the cans of food we'd discovered in the surviving cabins or buried under debris.

"How do you propose to travel anywhere with an alligator in the back seat?"

"I thought we could design a cart for the Queen and put her in the cargo bed. Some water along with a dry area. Use the cloth tarp so air gets through."

Saylor sat on her porch steps, which were slightly crooked but otherwise stable. She looked out over the ruined peninsula that used to be her family legacy.

"Where will we go? If you think we can go over the border with the Queen, you're delusional."

She laughed. The alligator gave a short chumpf.

I tried to convince myself that this communication between them was only in my imagination. When I looked at Saylor, her hair wild and eyes distant, I wondered if the nights in her arms were worth what amounted to condoning her obsession with this animal.

"We'll travel north until we get past the tornado's destruction and the rain. It shouldn't be far. We can be back in a few days. Fill up with supplies. The stores around here will reopen soon."

"I'll have to think about this. Discuss it with…"

Even Saylor wouldn't say out loud that she would consult an alligator.

That evening the rain suddenly stopped. I used up the remainder of the food in a stir fry. I opened a big can of cooked chicken for Saylor to serve to the Queen.

They had both moved off to a section of the point where water was returning in a slow, narrow stream. They were quiet when I brought the chicken, but I had my suspicions.

Saylor and the Queen bellowed and chumpfed together constantly. They always stayed some distance away from me, but I knew. The sounds sent shivers all through my body.

Saylor stood and smiled when I arrived at their meeting point. She wrapped her arms around me. Almost as tall as I was, her hair tickled my cheek. In spite of everything, I felt a surge of love.

"Alright," she whispered. "We'll come with you. I'll help build the crate so we can leave tomorrow."

She stood back a bit, hanging onto my hand.

"I think this is our only choice, Saylor. We'll be okay and we'll take good care of the Queen. We'll find a private place where no one will question what we're doing."

"I have the money to rent a house for a few days. Something away from prying eyes. Maybe close to the ocean."

"Are you okay financially? I can always ask my dad for…"

"No, it's fine. We're good."

"Let's get started on the crate. There's enough wood strewn around to use. Luckily the tools are in the untouched shed. That tornado sure was fickle."

I grinned at her.

"We have four beers left. We can drink while we work."

Saylor gave me a real smile. The kind she used to give. One that lit up her beautiful face. She put her hand on my arm.

"Thank you, Zack. The Queen is terrified to leave, of course, but this is the right thing to do. We must get to where there are food and resources."

She leaned into me. "I love you, Zack."

This time it sounded real. Soon our kisses led us to a sweet sojourn in her cabin.

When we reemerged, I looked over at the white alligator. She sat half in and half out of the water that had started to refill this side of the marsh. Her snout moved in our direction. She blinked her blue eyes.

I glanced at my lover and noticed her nodding her head. A message to and from Saylor? I shook off the dread that filled me.

Suddenly I noticed there was a breeze that swept away some of the humidity. In the dusk, I could see the outlines of birds poking in the muddy marsh for insects that had survived the storm.

"We won't have to stay away long," I said. "Look at how life is already returning to the outcrop."

Saylor gave me that spectacular smile once again.

We began to gather wood, rebars and other items we thought we could use. It wasn't long before the crate started to form inside the truck bed.

"I think there's a nice flat piece of wood under here for the bottom," Saylor said as she lay on the ground near one of the damaged huts.

I laid down beside her. "Let's drag it out and have a look. Might be perfect."

I pulled and wiggled the board, trying to loosen it from under the debris.

Saylor got to her feet. Suddenly she jumped on my back, as though I were an alligator. Her knees pinned my shoulders. I had no time to react before she pulled my head backward. She was strong enough to hold me in place. The knife in her hand would do the rest.

"The Queen liked the meat from Dad and Gus, didn't she? I'm sorry, Zack, I no longer need your help. It doesn't matter how I feel about you."

I tried to speak, but no air got past my pinned upper body. Only a squeak and a huff came through.

"Don't fight it. You know this is the right thing to do. As difficult as it is. By the time we're finished with you, my love, the resources will be available right here at home. We won't ever have to leave. And in a way, you'll be here too. At least, parts of you will."

She placed the knife at my throat and stared upside down into my eyes.

My brain went dark.

The 13th Letter

M

The End

HATCHECK BINGO

By Therese Greenwood

It was Friday the thirteenth, so the girls at the speakeasy switched up the squares on their Hatcheck Bingo cards.

Case Doyle and Lele Broussard had been on the job for two months. The first week they realized checking hats at a speakeasy was a bore, even at a high-class joint in a fake castle on a heart-shaped island in the St. Lawrence River.

Every night at nine o'clock the first boat from the American side of the river pulled up to the dock, ferrying fancy-dressed punters ready for what they considered a wicked night out. They swanned up the carefully raked stone path to the double oak doors at the grand entryway, where they were met by the one-armed greeter.

"Gunboat Merkley," a punter would say. "I saw you score the winning goal for The Cup with a slapshot from the blue line!"

At half past nine, the first boat from the Canadian side of the river came in and the punters said the same thing in a flatter accent but with even more enthusiasm.

By their third day of work, Case and Lele were keeping score whenever someone mentioned The Cup. By the end of two weeks, they made Hatcheck Bingo cards at the start of each night. Each square was filled with a stupid thing the punters said. First to check off every square on their card won bragging rights.

Eight weeks in, most of the staff were playing. It cost a penny a night to buy in and the pot rolled over until someone got a full card. Now it held fifteen bucks, more than a month's rent for the old carriage house Case and Lele had been lucky to lease behind the shipyard on the mainland.

When they asked Gunboat to play, he almost smiled. He insisted the card have a square with "Where's your arm?" That comment usually came at the end of the night when Gunboat was directing punters squiffy with tiger milk toward the last boat home.

One of the rules of Hatcheck Bingo was that players never correctly answer a stupid question, so Gunboat always said, "It's in my other jacket."

The hatcheck girls loved Gunboat, partly for his joke answer, and partly for the real answer, that the little bit of his arm left for the army surgeon to saw off was fertilizing a field near Passchendaele. Gunboat didn't talk about that, or about hockey. He did his job, greeting punters and bodychecking anyone up to shenanigans. Luckily, he did not see Hatcheck Bingo as shenanigans.

"Monkeyshines," he called it after picking up a handmade bingo card that fluttered off the counter during a furious barrage of hats and coats. "Make sure the punters, and the boss, don't see it."

It was good advice. The hatcheck girls were on thin ice. Case had been caught doing her Charlie Chaplin impression with a hat and walking stick belonging to the Under Secretary for Transportation. She should have known a Transportation Under Secretary had no sense of humor. Luckily, his wife found it hilarious.

Case and Lele knew they were bad hatcheck girls. Two years before, in the Argonne Forest with General Jack Pershing's signal corps, they were good soldiers. They were dab hands at connecting generals to the front lines over telephone wires hastily strung across battlefields. They coded and decoded telegraph messages about troop movements. Case, who spoke six languages, did lightning-fast translations. Lele, who had a chemistry degree from the women's college at Tulane, could calculate artillery distances in her head.

But they stunk at checking hats.

So, they took Gunboat's advice. For a few nights they filled the Hatcheck Bingo cards in French. But they were on the St. Lawrence River, halfway between Canada and the United States, and there were French Canadians *de tous côtés.* One night a lanky Quebec City brunette in a mink coat glimpsed the bingo card on the counter, winked a kohl-smudged eye, and shushed her butter and egg man when he pointed at Gunboat's empty sleeve.

Now they used a dead easy Level One Alternating Cypher from their first week of Signals Corps training. They taught it to Gunboat, the cigarette girls, the barmen, the band, the cleaners, the gardeners, the janitors, the washroom attendants, the cooks, the waiters, and the dishwashers, everyone but the boss. The staff easily deciphered it as they cleaned ashtrays, dispensed linen towels, and ladled Thousand Islands salad dressing.

Tonight, as staff members dropped by to pick up their bingo cards, there was a lively discussion about the center square.

"This must be your lucky day," said the barman Billy Large, handing over his penny. "Why is that the center square?"

"Someone is sure to say it on Friday the thirteenth," Lele said.

"It will be catnip to them," said Case, who came up with the idea.

"I have my doubts," said Billy Large. "They hate the Number Thirteen hatcheck tag."

The punters were a superstitious lot, especially the gamblers who came for the roulette wheel imported from Monte-Carlo. No one wanted the Number Thirteen hatcheck claim ticket, so Case and Lele made up extras for particularly obnoxious punters. A man who saw the number thirteen in his hand expected bad luck and went on to lose all night. Psychological warfare, Case called it. She wanted to smuggle in a black cat to shoo across the path as punters strolled up from the boat, but Billy Large would not hear of it.

Billy Large, whose real name was William Patrick O'Reilly, had a tender heart devoted almost exclusively to animals. He was slender, well below average height, and not at all large. His fellow soldiers in Flanders nicknamed him for his regular pub order of "Glass of beer, large."

Case and Lele had a soft spot for Billy and his adorable Boston accent. When he was nine years old, he started work in the stables of a Beantown Brahmin. When he was eighteen, the army trained him to kill and sent him across the ocean. Every night he was away, his mother prayed the rosary that he be spared from the trenches. Her prayers were answered when he was assigned to tend the horses that pulled telegraph wires across the battlefields.

Billy Large fed them moldy hay, hauled pails of brackish water, and scraped the Flanders mud from their spent bodies. Then he drove them through machine guns, artillery shells, and sharpshooters. In the two years since the Armistice, he had not buckled a harness or hitched a wagon. He tended the First Bar at the speakeasy entrance, directly across from the hatcheck, and talked about a farm for retired horses.

"I want you to win," said Lele as Billy handed over a penny for a card that included "be quick about it," which at least a dozen punters said to him every night.

"I want to win," said Case. "But if it's not me, I hope it's you, Billy, for your old age home for war horses."

"Warhorses don't live to old age," said Billy. "It's a refuge for all abused horses, a sanctuary after a life of hard service."

"I want a refuge," said Lele.

"Don't we all?" said Case.

Their palaver was interrupted by the roar of a high-powered boat engine, and they glanced down at the wristwatches they'd brought back from Europe.

"It's only half past eight," said Lele. "We still have half an hour before the first boat of punters."

"Gunboat is scowling," said Case. "That's his I-expect-shenanigans face."

Their version of catnip was Gunboat's scowl, which signaled excitement was afoot. They scampered to his post by the door, Billy trailing behind.

Gunboat had a clear view of the waterfront, allowing him to keep an eye out for splifficated punters determined to fall in the water, as well as American patrol boats trying to enforce the liquor ban. He had drawn back the brocade curtains on the floor-to-ceiling windows on either side of the door. The setting sun sent orange and pink diamonds of light flickering over the dark river that stretched west to the Great Lakes.

"It's like an orange macaroon dunked into a cup of coffee," said Lele. "I miss macaroons from that little bakery on the *Rue de Sucre*."

"I miss French coffee," said Case. "What I wouldn't give for some java from *La Closerie des Lilas*."

"My landlady makes a fine butter tart," said Billy. "I could bring you some."

"That would be lovely, Billy," said Lele.

The sleek speedboat roared out of the setting sun, its varnished wood gleaming in the golden light. The engine throttled back as it approached the wooden dock, a whiff of fuel drifting through the screened-in windows. It putt-putted to the slip reserved for Big Cheeses, and they saw their boss stand up to flip rubber bumper guards over the side.

"Did you know the boss was on board, Gunboat?" Billy asked.

"Yup," said Gunboat. He was one of the few staff members the boss spoke to.

"What's he up to?" asked Lele.

"Business," said Gunboat.

They watched the boss step easily onto the dock, rope in hand. A few quick tosses of his wrist and the boat was secured.

"Poetry in motion," said Case.

When they weren't badly checking hats and making bingo cards, Case and Lele killed time surveilling Marten "Dutch" Vos. The Amsterdam-born Dutch had a matter-of-fact dedication to unvarnished truth that the hatcheck girls found hilarious. The night before they had eavesdropped as a punter who owned a box factory in Oswego walked into the boss's office after a dizzying loss at roulette.

"Do you think my luck will change?" the punter asked.

"No," said Dutch. "You are not good at gambling. You should stop."

He was unapologetic about his accent, too, though it sounded German to men who had recently fought the Hun. He even used Dutch spelling in the speakeasy's name, and the ashtrays bore the words The Oranje Tulip. There was a bingo square that said "Orange is spelled with a *g*."

Dutch had bought the island and its castle for a song when an American railroad baron put it on the market after losing three sons to the *Saint-Mihiel salient.* It was the perfect location for a swanky juice joint, exactly halfway between the United States and Canada. The international border ran smack through the middle of the castle, the dance floor in the United States and the hatcheck in Canada. The giggle police on both sides of the border bickered over jurisdiction, neither keen to enforce liquor laws against the rich and powerful.

It was a perfect setup and Dutch made sure it stayed that way. He strictly maintained his rock-solid reputation for high-end liquor, discreet staff, and zero shenanigans, especially those of the legal variety. He was a smart cookie, and Case would have liked the chance to dunk him in a glass of milk and soften him up. He was six feet tall, with a castle on a heart-shaped island, Dutch frankness, and British tailoring.

"That's an exquisitely cut pair of pants," said Lele, as Dutch bent over to retrieve his suit jacket from the boat. "Likely from that expensive Saville Row tailor who makes suits for the Prince of Wales."

"Money well spent," said Case. They watched their boss toss a close-fitting, broad-shouldered jacket over his bright white shirt like he was flipping a cozy blanket over a freshly made bed.

"How much does a suit like that cost?" said Billy.

Lele named a figure that would clean out several hatcheck bingo kitties and then some.

"For one suit?" said Billy.

"Clothes make the man," said Lele.

"And how!" Case said.

The man piloting the boat switched off the engine, and Dutch leaned over to offer him a hand stepping onto the dock. The hand was waved away, and the skipper hopped out, revealing himself to be a foot shorter than Dutch.

"Isn't that Maurice Hinault?" said Case.

Gunboat grunted, and Billy said, "Who is that?"

"The bootlegger from Montreal," said Case. "He has his fingers in lots of pies."

"I miss mushroom pie," said Lele. "*Le quiche aux champignons.*"

"You wouldn't miss these pies," said Case and ticked them off on her rather small fingers. "Rum running, prostitution, racetrack cheats, and probably hatchecks."

"Racetrack cheats?" said Billy. "Like that horse dosed with cocaine in New York yesterday?"

"The horses in New York get cocaine," said Case, "and I can't afford a bottle of Miss Pinkham's magic elixir."

"It's no joke, Case," said Lele, seeing Billy's face.

"That horse died a horrible death," said Billy. "Its heart exploded."

"I'm so sorry, Billy," said Case. "That is absolutely tragic. I was wrong to joke about it."

"What's with the hatchecks?" said Gunboat.

"The big-time rackets in the States are taking over hatchecks, pocketing the girls' tips," said Case. "If the girls want to earn more, the options are nasty and nastier."

"Trust my fellow Americans to take something as boring as a hatcheck and turn it into something ghastly yet lucrative," said Lele.

"Yankee enterprise," said Case. "I tip my hat to it."

Billy muttered about racehorses as he headed back to the First Bar to lay out the ingredients for a whiskey sour, Dutch Vos's tipple. He placed an egg, a lemon, and a sugar bowl next to an empty silver shaker and full ice bucket. Then he took down a bottle of J.P. Wiser's Deluxe rye whiskey from the top shelf. There was no cheap moonshine at the Oranje Tulip. Americans were the experts at free enterprise, but Canadians knew how to write a liquor law so profitable distilleries, especially those owned by Members of Parliament, kept operating "for export only." It was perfectly legal to send Canadian whiskey out of the country. If the Americans had a problem with it, they could use their Yankee ingenuity to figure out a solution.

"Billy Large has the right idea," said Gunboat, as the boss and the bootlegger began walking up the path from the dock.

"Time to get a wiggle on," agreed Lele. She and Case were behind the counter of the hatcheck looking as if butter wouldn't melt by the time the two men were standing in front of Gunboat.

"Monsieur Hinault, perhaps you know Mr. Richard Merkley?" said Dutch, the only person who used Gunboat's real name.

"I saw Gunboat win The Cup," said Hinault. Case and Billy crossed squares off on their bingo cards. Lele marked her own and the one she kept for Gunboat. "It was a spectacular goal."

"Richard's victory is often remarked upon," said Vos. "I understand it was a splendid achievement."

"Not for me," said Hinault. "I took a lot of action expecting Montreal to win. I lost a pile."

"To the victor belongs the spoils," said Dutch, guiding his guest toward the hatcheck. Dutch was not sporting a lid, but Hinault was wearing enough hat for both of them.

"That's a top-line beaver felt Borsalino," Lele murmured through the gritted teeth of her punter smile. "He worked in that brim himself. Nice job. Sharp edges."

The girls had checked the hats of Wall Street tycoons and Hollywood actors, but none of those expensive lids were a match for Hinault's topper. This was even more impressive considering he was decked out in tan spats, a colorful tie, and a soft-shouldered pinstripe suit.

"Italian tailor," murmured Lele. "Neapolitan by way of Montreal. Look at the stitching on the sleeves."

"Good evening, Miss Doyle, Miss Broussard," said Dutch.

"Good evening, sir," they said in unison.

"Welcome to the Oranje Tulip," said Lele in French. She always spoke first, unless one of Case's languages was needed. So far, there had been little call for Russian or German, but Spanish and Italian sometimes brought in a few more tips.

"*Enchanté, Mademoiselles,*" said Hinault, removing his magnificent hat and giving a slight bow as he held it out. He had manicured fingernails, a luxury the girls could not afford, which didn't matter to Case, who hated anyone touching her hands. Lele, who missed manicures, took the hat, and Case handed him a Number Thirteen claim tag.

"*Numero treize,*" said Hinault. "*Quelle bonne chance.*"

"You think it will bring good luck?" said Case.

Gunboat, who had the ears of a bat, shifted one foot. It was against the rules to repeat the phrase on the bingo card, although you were allowed to ask leading questions.

"I make my own luck," said Hinault.

"Except when Richard is making his," said Dutch, as Hinault set his walking stick on the counter and began to remove his blue woolen overcoat with its luxurious collar of Arctic fox fur.

"Beautifully tailored to hit above his knee, excellent choice for men of shorter stature," Lele murmured. The bootlegger was the same height as Case, five foot four, but threw himself into every inch. Case picked up the walking stick, also made to match his size, and balanced it in her hand.

"Be careful with that, *ma cherie*," Hinault said. "It cost a pretty penny."

"Worth it. The carving is flawless," she said, examining the elaborate ivory wolf-head knob. She pressed down on it, twisted her small wrist, and pulled out the sword embedded inside.

"Incoming!" said Billy Large, keeping a close eye from the First Bar.

"How remarkable," said Hinault. "You certainly have a head on your shoulders, Mademoiselle."

"This is sharp enough to slice my head clean off," said Case, her small fingers wrapped firmly around the sword handle, cutting edge facing out.

"That would be a waste of a lovely head," said Hinault.

Gunboat appeared beside Case the same way he had once materialized next to the star forward of the Montreal Canadians. He held out his only hand, and Case slid the sword back into the cane and handed it over.

"Thank you for securing our guest's property, Richard," said Dutch. "We can leave it here to be retrieved later."

Gunboat looked grim as he dumped the weapon into the receptacle in front of the hatcheck. The ivory knob peeked over the top of the elephant foot's umbrella stand that Billy Large particularly hated.

"Monsieur Hinault, may I escort you to my office?" said Dutch in flawless Parisian French.

"*Bien sur*," said the bootlegger, his Canadian joual accent slightly more pronounced in response to Dutch's patrician one.

Hinault followed Dutch into the office on the other side of the hatcheck, the door closing as the first boat of American punters pulled up to the dock. The engine cut out, the sound replaced by the tittering induced by the free cocktail presented to punters when they boarded.

The laughter grew louder as they surged up the path. Case and Lele met the onslaught head-on, tossing hats with abandon, pausing only to properly admire a matching pair of ermine fur coats made on the Big Apple's 27th Street. The furs were warm for a mid-September evening, but Case and Lele would have donned them in a New York minute, weather be damned.

The punters were a chatty bunch. By the time they streamed into the ballroom, Case and Lele had crossed off "a pair of hotsy-totsy tomatoes" and "it's the third time this week I paid for my own hat." Despite handing out three Number Thirteen hatcheck tags, they had not succeeded in getting a lucky day. But the next boat was due in twenty minutes, and in the meantime, they decided to treat themselves to some Dutch surveillance.

"The bingo pot might roll over again," said Lele, closing the shutters over the hatcheck counter.

"Soon there will be enough for Billy to buy that old age home for horses," said Case, taking a framed photograph from the wall.

"Refuge," said Lele, reaching under the counter for an earphone headset.

Case looked down at the framed photo of the Prince of Wales wearing a cowboy hat, a memento from his post-Armistice tour of Canada. Case had once danced with the Prince, and Lele had once danced with Tom Mix, the King of the Cowboys, so they both felt connected to the picture.

"The prince needs a refuge," said Case. "He looks sad."

"We all look sad," Lele said, plugging the headset into the listening device hidden in the ladies' lost and found box.

"We do," said Case, turning on the microphone in the hole usually hidden under the photograph. On the other side, in Dutch's office, the microphone was concealed behind an enormous mahogany filing cabinet.

Having the boss on the other side of the hatcheck wall had been too tempting, especially after they found the railroad baron's old Dictaphone gathering dust. They jury-rigged the machine the same way they had in Versailles when General Jack ordered them to get the inside dope on French plans for the Treaty. They did it partly to keep their skills sharp, partly to find out if Dutch had a paramour, and mostly out of boredom.

So far, their eavesdropping yielded mixed results. Gunboat's shenanigans report usually entertained with its litany of champagne coupes smashed in fireplaces, Oranje Tulip ashtrays stolen as souvenirs, and tight punters tumbling off the dock. They learned nothing about Dutch's love life, the shadowy suppliers of his excellent liquor, or the truth about the ruthless lengths he was said to take protecting his business. Hinault's visit promised excitement, and the hatcheck girls shared the headset, their heads together as each used an earpiece.

"We pay the girls a small wage and keep the tips," Hinault was saying.

"How enterprising," said Dutch. "But the Oranje Tulip already has hatcheck girls."

"I will consider keeping them," said Hinault. "They could be rather pretty with a bit of makeup."

Case and Lele raised their eyebrows and mouthed "rather pretty" at each other.

"They are bad at checking hats," said Dutch. "And our women employees do not wear makeup."

"I supply makeup," said Hinault. "I supply it all. Whiskey. Beer. Cigarettes. Flowers. And the skirts, of course. Cigarette girls, hatcheck girls, flower girls, good-time girls."

"You are a true entrepreneur," said Dutch.

"You understand me perfectly," said Hinault. "We are cut from the same cloth. Together, I supply the goods, you supply the well-paying customers, and everyone wins."

"Except the hatcheck girls," said Dutch.

"Not so, *mon ami*," said Hinault. "We are creating a great deal of work for young ladies."

"That is one way to look at it," said Dutch.

"Opportunity is knocking at your door," said Hinault. "This, *mon ami*, is your luck—."

He was interrupted by a knock on the office door.

"They only knock when it is urgent," said Dutch.

"Of course," said Hinault. "The Tulip is renowned for its well-trained staff, with the apparent exception of your lovely hat-checkers."

A chair pushed back. Muffled footsteps crossed the dark red Persian rug that Lele called "exquisite." A doorknob turned. A door opened.

"The banker from Albany is harassing Mary Pickford again," said Gunboat.

"I will see to it," said Dutch. "Monsieur Hinault, would you care to join me while I attend to this matter?"

"As much as I would enjoy meeting the delightful Miss Pickford, I am needed elsewhere," said Hinault. "Sadly, we entrepreneurs must sacrifice our personal pleasures for the sake of our organizations."

"Well, that's that," said Case, switching off the microphone. "The charming Monsieur Hinault won't put up with our shenanigans."

"Or our monkeyshines," said Lele, putting away the headset.

"Every time we find a way to make the smallest crust of bread, some goon comes along to eat it," said Case. She replaced the photo of the cowboy prince as Lele tucked the listening device under silk scarves at the bottom of the ladies' lost and found box. They opened the shutters and plastered on punter-friendly smiles as the boss, Gunboat, and the bootlegger stopped in front of the First Bar.

"William, my business with Monsieur Hinault has concluded," said Dutch. "Richard and I have a matter to attend to. Would you please escort our guest to his boat?"

"Yes sir," said Billy Large, who still stood at attention when a superior gave him an order.

"I will consider your offer and be in touch," Dutch said to the bootlegger as Billy came out from behind the bar.

"Things move fast in our business," said Hinault. "I advise you to be quick about it."

Case and Lele crossed out the second-last square on their card, leaving only the lucky day to come.

"You have given me much to think about," Dutch said to Hinault, shaking his hand. "*Au revoir.*"

Dutch and Gunboat entered the ballroom, closing the double doors behind them, and Hinault turned to the hatcheck.

"Whoopsie-daisy," said Case, accidentally-on-purpose dropping the magnificent Borsalino on the floor. A telegram slipped from its hiding place in the hat's brim and landed in front of Billy Large, who picked it up, glanced at it, and went pale.

"I will take that," said Hinault, fussily brushing off his hat even though the foyer's marble floor was spotlessly clean that early in the night. "You will not be able to read it."

"Hayburner a goner." Billy read out loud, slowly making out each word. "All good third race Aqueduct."

"*Tabernac!*" said Hinault, looking up. "Why does Monsieur Vos have such a bright young man tending bar when you would be more useful in other areas of his organization?"

"I think he killed a racehorse," said Billy, handing Lele the telegram.

"It's the Level One Alternating Cypher," Lele told Case.

"That code is not secure enough for a criminal enterprise," Case said to Hinault. "A simple letter swap based on the day of the month is too vulnerable."

"It is an army code," said Hinault. "Women do not understand these things."

"The ladies' washroom attendant can read that code," said Case. "So can the cook, the cigarette girls, and the canary with the band. They know today is the thirteenth, so each letter swaps with the thirteenth after it. A is M, B is N, and so on."

"What sort of crazy outfit is Dutch running?" said Hinault. "He has a reputation for exceptional staff, *mais c'est incroyable.*"

"Did I read it right, Lele?" Billy asked. "He killed a horse to fix a race?"

"It looks that way," said Lele, scanning the telegram.

"You are correct," said Hinault. "But if you think you can blackmail me for disposing of my own property, you are beating a dead horse."

Hinault laughed cheerfully and alone. Case turned for his coat and Billy reached into the despised stuffed elephant foot to pull out the walking stick.

"Fix bayonets," Billy said. He pushed the ivory knob, twisted, pulled out the sword, and stabbed Hinault in the side of his neck next to his Adam's apple, severing the carotid artery.

For the first time in a long while, Case and Lele froze. The bootlegger dropped to the floor, his hands to his throat. Billy kicked him twice and stepped back.

Case came to herself and vaulted the counter, already too late, Billy's aim doing his boot camp instructors proud. As she crouched over Hinault, his heart stilled and blood stopped pumping.

"Billy," said Lele. "Are you all right?"

"I'm good," he said, wiping clean the sword blade and reinserting it into the cane. Then his teeth began to chatter.

"It's a Calais Overcoat situation," Case said to Lele.

"With a Marseilles Goodbye," said Lele, handing over an enormous coat belonging to a fat bastard from Ithaca, an overnight guest who had offered them money to come to his room together.

"Come on Billy," Lele said, "let's get you looked after." She took him by the arm and led him into the hatcheck.

Case began to drag the body, surprisingly heavy for such a small man, into the hatcheck. She had barely moved when Gunboat walked through the ballroom doors.

"I've seen some shenanigans in my time," he said, "but this takes the cake."

"Don't just stand there," said Case. "Grab his leg. There's only eleven minutes before the next boat of punters."

Gunboat locked the ballroom doors, then wrapped his hand around Hinault's left leg and pulled the body into the hatcheck. Case followed behind, mopping up the blood trail with the coat. When Gunboat came out of the hatcheck, Case was moving two large aspidistras to hide the blood on the wall.

"I'm never going to clean up this blood pool and execute a Marseilles Goodbye in the ten minutes left," she said. "Do you have a key to the boss's office?"

"Yup," said Gunboat.

"Get the red rug and throw it over the blood stains," said Case. "Pour beer where the blood soaks through, enough for people to smell it."

"Shame to ruin such a nice rug," said Lele. "It's eighteenth-century."

"And please, please, Gunboat, let us get a running start before you tell Dutch," said Case as she headed into the hatcheck. "Just eight minutes, that's all we need. Then you, the boss, and Hinault's mob will never see us again."

As Case closed the hatcheck shutters, Gunboat went to fetch the rug. He covered the blood stains with it, then pulled a pitcher of draft from the First Bar. He poured it over the rug and a hoppy, malty smell filled the air. While he worked, he heard a kerfuffle inside the hatcheck, a jumble of muffled instructions, clicking wooden hangers, and cursing. Then he left to get the boss.

The foyer was empty when the trio emerged from the hatcheck. Billy Large was wearing Hinault's coat and hat, the brim of the magnificent Borsalino pulled low over his face. He held tight to the walking stick, which perfectly matched his height. Case and Lele were bundled in full-length ermine coats and sporting the latest cloche hats, the bell shape perfect for hiding their hair color. They had masked their faces with layers of makeup from the ladies lost and found.

Billy Large protested as Lele pulled up the fox-fur collar to cover the bottom of his face. "Fur makes my skin crawl," he said. "It's barbaric."

"I know," said Lele. "But you only have to put up with it for seven more minutes."

"Billy, do you speak any French?" said Case.

"Glass of beer, large," said Billy, in the worst accent they had ever heard.

"Never mind," said Lele, lighting a cigarette. "We'll do the talking. Keep this cigarette in your mouth as we walk down to the boat. When you get aboard, make a show of flicking it into the water."

"Cigarette butts are bad for fish," said Billy.

"Fish don't feed in an onshore wind," said Case. "They will be fine."

"There are turtles, too," said Billy.

"Grind the butt under your heel," said Lele.

"There's the boat," said Case, as they heard the familiar whine of the engine approaching. "Curtain up!"

They went out Gunboat's door and stepped into a breeze that had cooled since sunset, making the ermine coats bearable. The pathway to the dock glowed under lanterns that had been lit by the grounds staff as the sun set. Through the open windows came the sound of the band tuning instruments, preparing for the first set of the night.

Case and Lele flanked Billy's sides, snuggling in close and half-carrying him while they pretended to flirt. Even at this early hour, it was not unusual to see a fellow unsteady on his pins with a girl on each arm. When the engine of the incoming launch had throttled back and their voices would carry, Case and Lele giggled like schoolgirls. They put on a big production for the approaching punters as they made it to Hinault's boat.

"Maurice, oh you kid!" said Case in English, playfully slapping Billy on the arm.

"Monsieur Hinault, you are a scamp," said Lele in French.

They kissed Billy on his cheeks, making a show of wiping off lipstick stains as they reminded him to stub out the cigarette. Billy stomped on the butt and started to pull at the fur collar, but Lele grabbed his hand before he could pull it down. Billy was stepping into the boat when they heard a voice shouting from the steps in front of Gunboat's door.

"Stop!" called Dutch Vos, starting down the path. "Stop! Do not leave!"

"No sign of a weapon," said Case, as Dutch came down the path, moving at lightning speed without looking like he was hurrying.

"Wave at him in a friendly way," Lele said to Billy. He raised the walking stick in salute and brought it down by his side. Then he twisted the knob and slid the blade an inch out of the cane.

"Hold steady, Billy," said Lele.

"He's not close enough," said Case.

"I am glad to catch you, Monsieur Hinault," Dutch called loud enough for the boat of punters to hear. He strode confidently up the dock, and leaned over into the boat, looking Billy in the eyes.

"William, I made a terrible error in judgement," Dutch said quietly. "I should not have left you alone with Mr. Hinault."

"I wasn't alone," said Billy, his hand surprisingly steady on the sword stick.

"Indeed, you were not," said Dutch. "The ladies have done us both a favor with their quick thinking. We can still all come out of this in one piece."

"I'm sorry, boss," said Billy, clicking the blade back into the cane. "I don't know what came over me."

"I think I do, Billy," said Dutch.

"You've been good to me," said Billy. "You took me on with my bad nerves and no experience, and then I put you and the girls in an awful spot."

"What's done is done," said Dutch. "But for it to end here, I need you and your clever companions to clean up your mess."

"Yes sir," said Billy, standing up straight again. "What do you need?"

The door to the Oranje Tulip flung open and Gunboat burst forth pushing a cart containing a large wooden crate labeled "French Champagne."

"Champagne," cried Case loud enough for the punters to hear. "Just what the doctor ordered."

"Ooh, how lovely," said Lele. "A drinky-poo to share when we are on our way."

Case was careful not to transfer any of the blood smears on her hand as she leaned in to touch the sleeve of Dutch's jacket and asked whether the crate contained an item requiring disposal.

"It does," said Dutch. "Is this something you and Miss Broussard can see to?"

Case turned to Lele and said, "It's a Seine Sightseeing Cruise."

"All aboard," said Lele.

Gunboat pushed the cart alongside the boat, and he and Billy loaded the crate. It landed with a deep thud. Dutch showed Case an open envelope with several American hundred-dollar bills inside and slipped it into the pocket of her ermine coat.

"That's the biggest tip we ever made," said Case. "It has been a pleasure working with you, Dutch Vos."

"I cannot say the same," Dutch said. "You were terrible hatcheck girls."

"We know," said Case.

"Don't come back," said Dutch.

"Wouldn't dream of it," said Lele.

Lele started the boat while hanging on Billy's arm, Gunboat leaned over to cast off the ropes, and Case pulled the rubber bumpers onto the deck. As they pulled out, Case and Lele blew kisses and waved merrily at the two men on the dock. Gunboat surprised them by blowing back a kiss.

As they motored off into the dark night, Lele kept the boat steady and Billy tossed the fur-collared coat overboard. They headed for the deepest part of the river, where a crate would sink to the bottom and never come up.

"What next?" said Lele.

"We find our refuge," said Case, showing her the envelope of C-notes.

"Maybe," said Billy, "this was our lucky day."

The 13th Letter

M

The End

ON MOON MOUNTAIN

By Lorna Poplak

Wendel Williams could not believe his luck. Here he was, at night, on the mountain, with Enemy Number Three lying unconscious at his feet!

It was the summer solstice. Everyone was on Moon Mountain for the annual Lunar Party. There were bonfires all over the place and a barbecue at Orion's Point.

Wendel was standing in a little clearing, looking down at the twinkling lights of Kingsville in the distance. The moon, his ally, was darting playfully behind dark clouds and peeking out again. He heard footsteps behind him. He turned silently and saw her—Katy Marshall, all alone. At that moment, the moon disappeared. Katy stumbled blindly towards him. He stuck out his foot and bingo! She tripped over it, fell, banged her head, and there she was, lying at his feet, totally in his power.

There were three people Wendel hated more than anyone else in the whole world. They were always sticking their noses into his business. Take Katy, for example. For the longest time, Wendel had thought she was kind of okay, but lately she'd become very hostile over that pathetic little creep, Oswald Ottley. So Wendel mentally cranked up her punishment quotient.

Wendel had a system of judging his enemies, based on the amount of punishment he felt they deserved. The punishment quotient, or PQ for short, was a number out of ten. Katy now had a PQ of eight.

Tania Dodd was Enemy Number One, with a PQ of ten. He'd hated her from the very first moment he'd set eyes on her. She had also started bugging him about the Oswald creep, and his patience finally snapped. The time had come to teach her a lesson. Three weeks ago, they were both riding their bikes through the Kingsville University campus. Bracing himself, Wendel crashed into her from behind. Her bike went in one direction, and she went in the other. She came down hard and broke her leg. Pity it wasn't her neck.

He was so concerned about her! He even went to visit her in the hospital. But inside he was cracking up with laughter. She probably suspected that he'd bashed into her deliberately, but she couldn't prove a thing.

Then there was Collin Ferguson. Enemy Number Two. PQ of nine. Getting that idiot into trouble was a snap. Collin had organized that ridiculous night-time stunt just before the end of term. Climbing up the outside of the university's Chapel Tower to hang a Kingsville U sweater from the flagpole was strictly against the rules. And guess what? The campus police had caught him red-handed. Wendel didn't have to do much—just a few words in the ears of the officers hanging about in their cruiser outside the dorm building.

And the best part was how well the punishment of these two enemies suited their crimes. Tania was all puffed up with pride—she thought she was such a great cyclist. Well, she fell off her bike. No hike up Moon Mountain tonight for her. She was still hobbling around on crutches.

Collin was a lawbreaker. A danger to himself and others. And that's what the police were for—to deal with that kind of person.

Unfortunately, Katy's punishment would not be entirely appropriate. But sometimes you just had to go with the flow. Wendel's eyes gleamed with satisfaction. It was his grand plan to punish his enemies one by one, and it was coming together beautifully.

There was a cliff at the edge of the clearing where he was now standing. Not enough to kill anyone if they rolled over it, he was sure, but enough to give them a few scrapes and bruises. Perfect. He grabbed Katy's shoulders and dragged her over to the brink of the precipice. He stood up. A well-aimed kick would do the rest.

At that moment there was a sound, like a little peep, behind him. Senses tingling, he whipped around. At the opposite end of the clearing, eyes huge with shock and terror, stood Oswald Ottley.

Wendel glared at him. "What are you doing here, you little freak?" he hissed. "Just stay where you are. I'll take care of you later."

Nothing was going to spoil his grand plan.

***

Oswald Ottley swallowed painfully, his mouth dry. His thoughts flashed back to his first day at Kingsville University, two weeks after the term had started. He was standing outside a classroom, his back pressed up against the wall. Just then Tania, Collin, and Katy came up, sharing a joke. The three of them stopped and looked at him.

"Hi there," said Tania. "Haven't seen you before. Your first day?"

Oswald nodded.

The three friends introduced themselves.

"And what's your name?" asked Collin.

Oswald's eyes fluttered rapidly three or four times. "Oswald Ottley," he said in a soft voice. "But some people call me Owl."

"Owl? Why Owl?" asked Katy.

He knew she was just being polite. He knew that with his small round body, his brown hair parted in the middle, and his big round eyes, he looked exactly like a pathetic little owl.

"Well, owls are useful creatures. I've always wanted to meet one." Katy broke the silence with a smile. "But tell me, what do your friends call you?"

"Ozzie," he said.

"Okay," said Katy, "then that's what we'll call you."

"Hang on a sec," said Collin. "I just want to check something out with you. Last night I watched a program about owls on TV. Bottom line is that owls are vicious predators. They swoop down on their prey silently in the middle of the night, rip them apart with their talons and devour them. Do you do that kind of thing?"

"Not usually," replied Ozzie. "Only when I'm very, very angry."

"Do you get angry often?" asked Katy.

"No, not really."

"Well, that's a blessing," said Katy.

"We've got an English lit class now," said Tania. "Then we're all going to the cafeteria. Would you like to join us? I can't promise you any delicious treats like rats or mice or beetles. It's just plain cafeteria food."

"Thank you," said Ozzie, his eyes lighting up. "I'd like to come with you. I prefer cafeteria food to rats and mice any day."

Since then, he'd led a seesaw existence at Kingsville U. On the upside was his friendship with Katy, Tania, and Collin. They laughed and joked with him and did their best to protect him. But on the downside, there was the ever-menacing presence of Wendel Williams and his gang of bullies. They zoned in on him from day one. A push on the stairs, a sticky drink spilled over his laptop, jeers, threats, a missile flung at his head—all of these had become commonplace in Ozzie's life.

Katy would get mad. "Take a look at poor Ozzie's bruises," she complained to Tania. "Wendel and Erik tried to push him down the stairs!"

"Wendel has become much more violent since he started hanging out with Erik," said Tania slowly. "I hate to blame the victim, but I'm sorry to say that part of the problem is you, Oz. You're such an easy target. If you would only stand up to him—just once! —he'd back right off, for sure. But I know that'll never happen."

"One of these days that disgusting bully will get his comeuppance," said Katy fiercely. "And when he does, I hope I'm around to see it."

Ozzie was very grateful to all three of them. They accepted him despite his differences.

But he adored Katy.

"What do your friends call you?" she'd asked him that very first day, when he was feeling so alone and frightened.

She gave him sympathy and understanding. Her warm brown eyes and ready smile had helped, ever so slightly, to chip away the cold hard block he carried around at the center of his being.

And now, on Moon Mountain, Wendel Williams—that beast, that monster who tormented him so mercilessly—was getting ready to kick Katy over the edge of a precipice. The tiny spark of anger flickering inside him suddenly caught flame. Hot blood pounded in his temples, and he felt his heart would burst.

***

"Katy, Katy! Oz!" The voice was quite close. "Ozzie! Katy! Where are you?"

Katy stirred and moaned slightly.

Wendel glanced down at Katy's limp figure. Not a moment to lose. He put his foot against her back.

Just then, he heard a crackling, hissing sound behind him. Shards of fire lacerated the back of his body, and he spun around.

Oswald Ottley, the object of his contempt, had not moved from his spot at the other end of the clearing. But somehow, in the moon's bright light, he seemed a lot bigger. As Wendel watched, he threw his arms up, and, as he brought them down again, he began to change. Feathers sprouted all over his body. His chest puffed out, his arms lengthened, and his eyes became tawny. Another flap of his arms—now they were wings—and he was airborne.

And then, on the mountain, in the moonlight, there came a high-pitched screech and the sound of powerful wings beating the air. Wendel shrieked. A hideous creature was swooping down on him, talons curved and extended. Its eyes were huge, round orbs, transfixing him malevolently.

Wendel staggered back, his arms folded across his face to blot out the terrible sight. He stumbled over Katy's body and lurched towards the cliff's edge. He clawed the air, desperately trying to regain his balance, and, with one last cry, he fell. A crunching, tearing noise marked his passage down the mountainside.

When Collin burst onto the scene moments later, Katy was sitting up. She clutched her head groggily. Ozzie was kneeling beside her, his eyes rounder and more surprised than ever.

The moon slipped behind the clouds again, and a couple of brown feathers drifted lazily to the ground.

The 13th Letter
M
The End

THE BELL TOLLS ONCE AGAIN

By Madona Skaff

Leonard the Great, now simply known as Lennie, inhaled the sea air. He needed this holiday to rethink his decision to give up his successful life of crime and become a struggling PI.

But mostly he had to take a break from dealing with ghosts.

He wandered around the deck of the whale-watching boat. They were 45 minutes out of Halifax, and, with nothing but water all around, his pent-up stress was draining away. He scanned the ocean for the telltale signs of whale spouts. Nothing on the port side. He meandered over to the starboard side and joined the few people leaning on the edge of the boat.

They waited in hushed anticipation of their first whale encounter—live and in person. Honestly, so did he.

Without warning, less than a hundred meters away, a humpback whale breached the surface and splashed into the water, accompanied by a chorus of "oohs" and "ahs" by everyone, including himself. Even some of the crew joined in, proving that a sight like that could never get old. With the breeze, the salty splash reached the boat. Many wiped their faces.

Smiling for the first time since he'd arrived last week, Lennie strolled aft, stopping near a couple in their late 20s. Once he realized they were arguing, he moved away before he got caught up in their drama.

Then the man cried out, "She's there! You have to look!"

Lennie spun around and looked where he was pointing. Two hundred meters away, he saw a ship with billowing black smoke.

Lennie waved a nearby crew member over, calling out, "There's a ship in trouble!"

The sailor raced over. After scanning the waters for several seconds, he asked, "Where?"

"Just past where we saw the whale!"

How didn't the guy see it? Sighing, Lennie muttered, "Unbelievable." Then said, "I'm so sorry. Guess it was a trick of the sun."

The crewman gave him a polite nod. "That's all right, sir. Happens a lot when people aren't used to being surrounded by endless water." He nodded and left.

Lennie turned back to watch the burning vessel that only he and the other man could see.

The wife snapped, "There's nothing there!"

She turned to Lennie. "And you! This isn't some joke!"

"Believe me, I wish it was." To the man, he said, "She's a two-masted schooner with square sails, right? The sails are on fire. Oh! The bow just plunged and the entire ship sank."

"Yes," the man whispered. "You saw it, too. A ghost ship. Then, I'm not crazy?"

"No, you're not."

"That description…" The wife paused to pull a sketch pad from her backpack. "It matches your drawings. I'm so sorry I didn't believe you."

She turned to Lennie. "We came here to celebrate our first anniversary. We took a whale-watching cruise on our first day and that's when he claimed…when he *saw* it. That was *five* weeks ago. We've taken one tour after another every day."

"You didn't have to come with me," the man said.

"Oh sure, I'm supposed to let you go off on your own. What if you decided to swim out and meet your ship?" she huffed.

"These drawings are amazingly detailed," Lennie said. "Drawn from different angles. I don't see a name, though."

"I could only make out the first letter, 'M'. The rest of the name was burnt off or hidden by thick, black smoke," the man said. "I've charted the sightings. This is the only place the ship appears. And at this time."

Lennie pulled out his cell phone to get a GPS reading. Then he photographed the drawings.

The man laughed. "You don't know what a relief it is to have someone else see her."

"Does this mean we can go home?" the wife asked.

"Home sounds great." He hugged her. To Lennie he said, "Thank you."

"Sure." Lennie watched the happy couple walk away.

What happened to getting away from ghosts that needed his help?

***

But Lennie was curious and a little research wouldn't hurt. Besides, he had planned to visit the Maritime Museum of the Atlantic at some point. Located downtown, it was the oldest and largest maritime museum in Canada, home to over 30,000 artifacts, 70 small craft as well as larger ships, such as a schooner and steamship.

More important, the huge reference library was open to the public. Using his memory of what he'd seen, plus the many sketches, it shouldn't take long to identify the two-masted schooner whose name began with the letter 'M'.

But no luck. At dinner time, he left the museum in search of some fresh catch of the day. That, he found with no problem.

The ghost ship, however, remained a mystery.

***

The next day, Lennie woke early and rented a motorboat. The rental guy told him it was perfect for deep-sea fishing.

Lennie resisted the urge to say, "You have no idea how deep."

He arrived at the GPS coordinates two hours early, just in case. Idling the engine, he maintained his general position and kept watch. So far, nothing but a brisk wind under clear blue skies and a few choppy waves.

Then at 9:45, like yesterday, a thin mist appeared off the starboard bow. Despite the wind, the mist remained stationary.

Soon the schooner sailed out of the mist, moving as though through calm waters. He moved his boat to 50 meters abeam of the sailing ship and cut his engine.

Lifting his binoculars, he stood. He leaned against the seat to keep his balance, hoping to get a better view. But as he adjusted the focus, the view went black. He lowered the binoculars.

Someone was standing in front of him! Startled, he stepped back, tripped and landed on his butt. It was a pirate—a female pirate. She wore tight brown pants, knee-high boots and a billowy white shirt with a vest. Around her waist was a red sash, into which she'd tucked a short-blade sword.

She whispered, "Can you see me? My shipmates abandoned me."

"How? What happened?" He climbed to his feet.

"I was fighting the flames... the crew... was helping the tourists to disembark. I almost had the fire out, but it lit up again. I saw an empty gas can rolling around on the deck. Then I saw my business partner. We locked eyes before he jumped off. That jerk-face killed me!"

"What date did you…uh…your ship sink?"

"Date?" Her gaze became distant.

Looking past her, Lennie saw the ship start to sink, bow first. Suddenly the pirate was yanked back to it, as though a rope had been tied to her waist. She and the ship slipped below the surface.

Other than the Hollywood version of pirates saying, 'argh' and 'shiver me timbers,' he had no idea how pirates spoke.

Somehow, though, he doubted that 'jerk-face' was accurate pirate lingo.

***

He pushed the speed boat to the red line and headed for shore.

Back at the library, using their faster Wi-Fi instead of his hotel's, which seemed to be racing a turtle for last place, Lennie started searching news records. He found a three-year-old article about the sinking of the schooner, *Marilla*. There was one casualty, a woman, Carter Samson, the co-owner of a small company that organized parties on the schooner. She was survived by her three co-workers. Danny Simons had given up the glamorous life of advertising campaigns and now worked for a construction company. Wes Doherty, who had been in charge of contracts and other legal paperwork, was now part of a small firm running sight-seeing cruises. The third partner, Julie Hamilton, who had handled the company's finances, had gone to work for a loan company.

A couple had booked the *Marilla* for a four-day pirate-themed cruise to celebrate their daughter's 18th birthday with nine of her friends. On the third day, an explosion in the galley tore a hole in the hull. With the exception of Carter, everyone made it into the life rafts mere moments before the ship sank.

The *Marilla* was owned by the Nautilus Corporation, so Lennie decided to start there. Nautilus owned several yachts of varying sizes as well as two tall ships, operating along the eastern seaboard. Moving to a private corner of the library, he called its head office in Toronto.

He debated mentioning that he was a private investigator. Sometimes people clammed up when he told them, but if he said he was a journalist…

Billie, the woman who answered his call, proved to be professional and approachable when he identified himself as a reporter doing a story on the *Marilla.*

"Carter was also a good friend." Billie took a breath before continuing. "I remember when she and her partners pitched us their idea for party-themed cruises. Danny and Wes' presentations were, well, let's just say reading cereal ingredients would have been more interesting. I was about to send them on their way when Carter jumped to her feet and took over the presentation herself."

"Obviously you changed your mind."

"She added the missing human touch. She knew that I was born in Nova Scotia, so she adjusted the pitch to emphasize how it would bring money into the area. My instincts were right, because they showed a profit within four months."

"That's amazing."

"Between the more complicated three-to-four-day cruises, she'd do single-day tours for smaller events like children's parties."

"So everything went smoothly?" Lennie asked.

"For four years, yes. But one week before the accident, during one of our quarterly check-ins, I noticed she seemed a bit off. More subdued."

"Do you know why?"

"She wouldn't say. I suspected it was some disagreement with her partners. But everyone loved Carter, the crew and especially the clients."

Billie had little more to add, so Lennie thanked her and ended the call.

He returned to his chair to consider his next move. An outsider's impression of the partners would be useful. He called the clients who had booked the *Marilla*'s last trip and made an appointment to see them in the afternoon.

In the meantime, he decided to talk to Carter's surviving partners.

Wes was out on a local sightseeing tour and wouldn't be back on shore until suppertime. Danny couldn't be reached at the construction site, but Julie agreed to meet him for lunch when he mentioned he was a reporter. She told him that she was glad someone was doing a news story on the *Marilla*, so Carter wouldn't be forgotten.

When Lennie arrived at the restaurant, he was surprised to see Julie sitting with a man. It was Danny.

"I asked him to come with me for moral support," Julie said.

"I was planning to talk to him as well, so this is perfect," Lennie said.

Even though it had been three years since the tragedy, they were probably still feeling the effects of their life-threatening experience. And from their pained expressions, he didn't doubt they were grieving the loss of their friend.

The ghost hadn't given him a name to work with, only that it was a man, but that didn't mean Lennie could discount Julie. Any one of the partners might have been involved in the explosion that led to Carter's demise.

"Can you tell me what you remember?" he asked, wondering who would take up the tale.

"It happened so fast," Julie said. She cleared her throat and continued. "One moment we're all on deck doing swashbuckling stuff. The next moment there's an explosion. The ship was rocking so much, we didn't think we could get to the life rafts before... in time."

Lennie noticed how Danny put a comforting hand on Julie's. More than friends?

"Chaos all around us!" Julie went on. "The teens were screaming. Both parents were crying. Carter kept everyone together while the crew got the life rafts ready. She asked me and Danny to keep an eye on them."

"Why didn't she join you in the life raft?" Lennie asked.

Julie closed her eyes tight for a moment. Then after a tiny sniffle, she said, "As we were evacuating, a fire started on the deck. Carter insisted that Danny and I get into the boats to care for the guests. The last I saw, she grabbed a fire extinguisher and went to put it out. Why would she do that?" Julie's voice broke. "The ship was sinking."

"I'm sure she was trying to give everyone more time to get to safety," Lennie said.

"Yeah." Danny nodded and patted Julie's hand again.

Julie dabbed her eyes with a napkin. "That's what she was like. Always looking after everyone."

So far, Danny had been quiet. The dark look in his eyes told Lennie that the man was hiding something.

"I know it's a painful memory," Lennie said. "Do you have any idea what might have caused the explosion?"

"The inquest concluded that the propane tank valve in the kitchen—I mean the galley—was defective," she said.

Lennie looked to Danny, who remained silent.

"It's nice that you're supporting each other," he said.

"Danny and I stayed friends... after..." she said. "It makes the pain easier."

"Does Wes feel the same way?"

She shrugged. "He handles grief differently."

Lennie noticed Danny's shoulders tense as he slightly pulled away from Julie. He looked angry.

This guy deserved a deeper background check. Also a second chat, without Julie. Lennie could read people as clearly as a book. And this guy was definitely more than a footnote.

***

On the way back to the library he called the captain of the *Marilla*, but had to leave a message.

A deeper dive into Danny's background revealed nothing. In fact, there was nothing out of the ordinary for any of the partners.

Lennie leaned back in his chair, thinking. Might something in Carter's background suggest a motive?

He found the usual stuff at first, but then he noticed something strange. Her details and history seemed too perfect. Using the search skills he'd learned at the private investigators' course, he peeled back Carter's fake profile. And there, on the screen, was her real persona.

She was a grifter. A woman after his own heart.

He laughed, feeling a sort of kinship with her. She'd been running scams and con jobs her entire adult life. She'd been arrested a couple of times, but the alleged victims refused to press charges. From what people had told him, Carter's charming personality was probably the reason she'd been able to skate.

However, if she'd been running cons her entire adult life, a past victim might have found her. Or someone figured out that the party cruise was her latest scam.

He wanted to know more about her. It meant using the skills he'd honed as a con man and some search methods on the twilight side of legal.

He opened Carter's juvenile record. Just like Lennie, she'd started her illegal activities when she was barely eleven years old. He'd have to wait till morning to talk to her at the usual time. The ghosting hour.

In the meantime, he headed over to see the couple who had been on the *Marilla*'s last voyage.

Rachel and Nelson warmly invited Lennie into their home. Nelson brought cups of coffee for everyone.

"We're glad you're doing a story about our nightmare trip," Rachel said.

"The pirate theme was pretty interesting," Lennie said, accepting his cup.

"Our daughter has loved pirates since she was a child. We thought what better way to celebrate her eighteenth birthday than with a pirate-themed cruise," she added.

"It was a few of her closest friends, and four days at sea," Nelson said. He joined his wife on the sofa.

"Carter loved the theme and worked so hard to make it perfect." She broke off. After a moment, she continued, her voice shaky. "We worried that our daughter would have nightmares forever. She was in therapy for a while..."

"We all were," Nelson said.

"We're okay now." Rachel jutted out her chin in defiance of the dark memory. "Carter made sure we were safe. No one realized she was left behind until..." she broke off.

"I'm so sorry you went through that." Lennie regretted coming. He added quickly, "I'm sure you have some wonderful memories."

He hoped they would concentrate on the fun and leave the pain at a distance. It worked. They actually smiled as they recounted the cruise.

"Everything was amazing!" Rachel said. She pulled out a tablet, opened it to photos from the cruise and passed it to Lennie. "It was a good thing I had my cell in my pocket when, when..."

"Carter organized several swashbuckling activities," Nelson said. "She'd hired a sword master to teach everyone how to fence."

Rachel, calm now, added, "Yes, and that's when Nelson discovered he's not good at quick reflexes!"

"Attacking my wife with a weapon wasn't a good look." He laughed. "I did much better at following clues to a buried treasure on an island."

"Yes, so much better at the digging part," Rachel said.

As Lennie scanned the photos, he said, "I see that the organizers were on deck a lot of the time."

"Sure," Rachel said. "All four of them helped with the activities."

"So, the organizers were great?" Lennie asked.

"Carter was," Rachel said. "We could tell Julie wasn't really into the pirate thing, but she made a good effort, and the kids liked her. But the other two, Wes and Danny..." She rolled her eyes.

"They were in a sour mood even before we set sail," Nelson said. "I caught them arguing very loudly a couple of times on deck. I had to tell them to go below."

"At least none of the kids noticed," she added.

"That's the main thing," Lennie said.

They chatted a bit more, and after taking a photo of the itinerary, he left.

As he drove back to his hotel, he wondered why the ship sank so fast. It had been dressed up to look like an ancient pirate ship, but the *Marilla* was still a modern vessel built to current specs.

He'd read all the news reports. What he needed now was information not available to the public. But to get more answers meant walking through the doors of the last place he'd ever willingly go.

A police station.

***

He hesitated outside the Halifax Police Headquarters, reminding himself that he had an honest job as a private investigator now. There was no reason he'd be arrested the second he stepped inside.

At the reception desk he gave the young officer, Constable Michaels, his reporter cover story, hoping the cop wouldn't try to confirm it. However, as soon as Lennie mentioned he was researching the *Marilla*'s accident, the officer gave him an excited smile.

"There are almost as many ghost stories as there are shipwrecks in these waters. In fact, a man came in here, a little over a month ago, reporting that he'd been on a whale-watching cruise where he saw a ship with flaming sails that vanished. Right where the *Marilla* sank."

"You didn't tell him?"

"I realized it after he left," Michaels said. "His wife dragged him out before I got his name. She looked pretty embarrassed."

"Were you part of the original investigation? Anything you could tell me?"

"No, I was a rookie then. But I heard a lot of the senior officers talking. And I got to see the accident report and the evidence."

"I know there was an explosion in the galley that ripped a hole in the hull. Witnesses said it sank too fast."

"Unfortunately, the water-tight doors below deck were left open. It happens sometimes with party boats. People get tired of opening and closing them. Nothing could've stopped her sinking, but she'd have had a few extra moments."

"Was Carter Samson's body ever recovered? And was there anything, well, odd in the autopsy?" He really wanted to ask about evidence of murder.

Michaels turned to the computer. "Let me bring up the report."

Lennie tried to peek nonchalantly at the screen, only to have Michaels adjust it so he could read along.

"I don't suppose I could get a copy of the file?" Lennie asked.

"Should be okay, but I'll check."

"Thanks."

Michaels was happy to discuss all the details of the case, including the autopsy results. Cause of death, drowning. Injuries consistent with a shipwreck.

Lennie left the station with a digital copy of the report which included several measurements, descriptions and underwater photos of the damaged hull.

He checked his watch. Wes' tour boat would be returning to shore soon and Lennie planned to greet him when he docked.

***

Once again Lennie introduced himself as a reporter covering the accident. Wes' reaction was one of indifference. More accurately, he showed no reaction at all. But he accepted Lennie's invitation to grab a beer at a nearby pub.

"I've talked to several people already," Lennie said when they were halfway through their beers. "Everybody really liked Carter. It's sad that she didn't get off the ship."

"Yeah, she was a good business partner."

"That's nice to know."

Lennie still had no idea what kind of person he was dealing with. Was Wes an active participant in Carter's death? Or was he simply a hapless bystander who jumped ship to save himself?

"I guess it's hard to lose someone after you've spent so much time together on these trips. It must have made you closer than regular co-workers."

"Not really. I was only on board in case any legal questions came up."

"What kind of legal issues could there possibly be on a boat?" Lennie asked, his eyebrows raised in surprise.

"I would double-check before each shore excursion that the right permission forms were signed, and our insurance was up to date."

"For each port of call? Wouldn't you only need to do it once, before you cast off?"

"Sure, for official ports. But the clients usually wanted isolated beach excursions. Those contracts needed to be detailed. Last thing you want is a Karen slipping on the beach and suing us."

"I see."

Lennie didn't see. Those kinds of contracts would be standard and signed before anyone left shore. And as for beach excursions, they'd be the same from one trip to the next with minor changes. Logic, not his intuition, told him the guy was lying.

"Can you tell me what you remember about that day?" he asked.

"I was in my cabin reading."

"You weren't on deck?" Lennie asked, incredulous.

"I hate interacting with clients. I stayed in my cabin unless a legal issue came up."

"Okay."

The party photos proved otherwise. Lennie was amazed at the guy's talent for lying. Not one tell-tale micro-expression showed on his face or in his body language.

"I heard a loud bang," Wes said. "I thought they were firing fake cannons on deck. You never knew, because Carter rented all kinds of weird stuff. But when the ship's alarm sounded, I grabbed my life jacket and went up on deck just as everyone was getting into the rafts. The old man wanted me to get off so that he could live that old cliché, you know, of the captain being the last off the ship. I was worried about him, so I pushed him overboard. The ship started to lean forward, so I jumped. I had no idea that Carter was still on board."

Lennie noted an expression on the other man's face. One of disdain. Did this guy like anyone? How could someone be so indifferent to the death of a person that he'd worked closely with for four years?

Then Wes added, "She was good at her job. Really organized."

Finally, a nice thing to say, Lennie thought. Maybe he'd judged the guy too harshly.

"I made a hell of a lot more in tips back then than I do now with these tightwad tourists."

Nope, not harsh enough.

They finished their beers. Lennie paid the tab, and they went their separate ways. As he strolled back to his car, Captain Jaeger returned his call. They agreed to meet at another bar near the pier.

Walking distance, so Lennie took his time, stopping to buy a burger from a street vendor. He couldn't drink as much on an empty stomach like he used to, and he wanted a clear head when he spoke to Jaeger.

The bar also had a nautical theme, but this one felt more authentic. Of course, a sailor would know the bars that didn't cater to tourists.

Lennie found Captain Jaeger at a table in a corner. After they exchanged greetings, the captain mentioned that he'd returned from a cross-Atlantic cruise the previous week.

"Commanding a large sea-faring vessel is something I've always wanted to do."

"I bet it's a lot harder after a smaller ship," Lennie said.

"Keeps me busier, definitely. Though I have more officers to share the tasks." Jaeger paused to drink his Glenfiddich.

Lennie sipped his beer, believing that he understood what Jaeger meant. That there would be more people around to help in an emergency.

"Do you mind telling me what you remember?" he asked, keeping his tone as 'reporter neutral' as possible.

"After the explosion, I gave the order to abandon ship," Jaeger said. "I made sure everyone was out of the cabins below. Up top, Wes was waiting for me. I ordered him into the lifeboats so I could clear the deck. When the ship listed, he panicked. Tossed me overboard before I had a chance...." his voice trailed off.

"It wasn't your fault that Carter was left behind," Lennie added gently.

Jaeger said, "May I ask you the reason for doing a story on the *Marilla*?" Before Lennie could answer, he continued, "You've heard the reports of people seeing the *Marilla* on fire? And sightings of a ghostly woman pirate?"

"Yes, I have," Lennie said.

"More than heard, I think." Jaeger leaned forward. "You've seen them both, haven't you? I can tell from your eyes. I've never seen the ghost ship. Or her."

He drained the rest of his whiskey, and paused a beat. His jaw tight and his voice rough, he added, "I saw her on deck. As I went over the side, I never went back for her. Don't you see? I'm the reason why she haunts these waters. Why Carter can never rest."

***

The next morning Lennie woke early to rendezvous with the ghost ship. He needed to talk to Carter.

At the appointed time she appeared.

"Quickly, before the ship disappears, I want to ask if you remember anything else. Small or insignificant." She didn't answer. "You said you made eye contact with someone before they jumped off the ship. Who was it?"

No response.

"No one sinks a multi-million-dollar vessel to kill *one* person. They'd knock you on the head then throw you overboard. Easy with no mess."

She continued to stare past him.

Frustrated he snapped, "Look, we only have a few minutes before the ship disappears! Focus!"

She looked at him, her chin quivering.

He softened his voice. "I'm sorry I yelled. I can't imagine how hard it is believing someone wanted you dead, but..."

"It's not that. I had no idea Captain Jaeger blamed himself for leaving me behind."

"Wait. One. Minute!" His voice was quiet, deep and furious. "You're scamming me! You pretended to be tied to the ship, but you've been following me."

"I didn't think you'd help without an aura of mystery around me," she said lightly.

"Oh, cut the crap! Once a scammer, always a scammer. That's right! I know all about the *real* you."

"Okay, it's true. I've never been tied to the ship. I go where I want. I've even talked with a few sensitives, like sailors or regular people. The last three years haven't been that bad, well, except for the being dead part."

"Why lie to me?"

"When you showed up, I knew you were different. I've asked others to help before, but they couldn't, or wouldn't. I didn't want to risk you leaving me. So I thought if I played a poor wretched ghost then you'd be more willing to help. Besides," she paused, looked at him pointedly and added, "*You*, of all people, know that when you're getting someone to do what you want, you never tell the full truth."

"How do you know about my own less-than-pure background?"

"I can feel things," she said.

"Reading minds?"

"Nah, not that exciting."

"Too bad. Then you could find out if someone actually murdered you, and why."

"I know Wes killed me."

"I need more..." he broke off, gasping when the schooner's bow dropped below the surface. Instinctively he reached out to keep Carter with him, but his hand passed right through her.

She glanced over her shoulder, sighing as her ship disappeared underwater.

"I've been running cons for as long as I can remember," she said, turning back to Lennie. "Then I met these people with an idea for a party ship. Easy pickings since only super-rich people would rent it. I never expected to start enjoying myself. The rich were nice, most of them anyway. And generous with tips. With my quarter share of the profits, I was making a hell of a lot more than I could pilfer. Besides it was nice to finally drop the act."

"I know what you mean. About finally relaxing," Lennie said, thinking back to his own decision to go straight.

Returning to the present, he said, "There's no proof your death wasn't an accident. Why didn't you just get into the life raft? Julie said you were trying to give everyone more time to get off, but was it necessary?"

"I was about to get in, but then I saw the flames. I don't—it's not clear."

"When we met, you mentioned seeing an empty gas can rolling on deck."

"That's right." She stopped, looking off in the distance as though searching for a lost memory. "I think, I think I saw Wes near the flames. I wanted to warn him to get away. I grabbed the fire extinguisher and... then I see Wes looking at me just before he leaves."

"Sure, he was a jerk for leaving you, but cowardice isn't murder. Maybe your past caught up with you."

She laughed bitterly. "Nothing that exciting. We were anchored overnight off an island to be ready for a sunrise breakfast. I had trouble sleeping, so I went on deck to get some air. I saw boxes being loaded from another ship. Wes was there directing everything. He told me Chef had forgotten that this was a four-day trip and he'd run short. He made me promise not to tell the captain, or Chef would be fired. And not to embarrass Chef by mentioning it."

"Sounds reasonable."

"The thing is, Chef always ordered two extra days of supplies in case we got stuck due to weather. Later I found the new boxes tucked away behind the inflatable water slide."

"Could you have tipped Wes off somehow?"

"Do I look like a civilian to you?" Carter said. "I'd never make a mistake like that."

"No, but it doesn't make sense to destroy an entire ship just to kill you."

"If I went missing, they'd do a ship-wide search," she said. "This way, he could get rid of me, scuttle the ship and come back with divers for the cargo."

"Too bad we don't know what he was smuggling."

"It was drugs," she said matter-of-factly.

"Nothing like burying the lede," he said.

She gave a slight shrug. "Didn't I mention that?"

"We should be working together, so stop hiding things from me," he said, struggling to keep his anger out of his voice.

"Sorry." She became serious. "As the others were being rescued, I kept calling out. I couldn't understand why they ignored me. I thought I was saved when a speed boat arrived. They didn't even see me. There were three men, two of them divers hired to retrieve Wes' boxes. On their boat, when they opened the boxes, I saw they were filled with bricks of cocaine, wrapped in waterproof plastic. I managed to stay with them as they headed to shore. I lost them when they sped up. It was as though a strong wind threw me back into the water."

"Anything about the boat to help identify it?" he asked.

"It had a very unusual tie-dye paint pattern on its deck," she said.

"Too bad you can't testify in court. We need hard evidence."

"You mean like a record of all his illegal activities."

"You happen to know where Wes keeps it?" When she nodded, he added, "We need to figure out a way to make him get it. Ideally in front of a credible witness."

"I guess that leaves you out," she said, chuckling. "Too bad that cute cop can't help. What's that smirk for? Just because I'm dead doesn't mean I can't appreciate a great-looking guy."

"No, no, of course you can. You just gave me an idea." Lennie smiled and said, "We've been so busy living an honest life, that we forgot something important."

"Like what?" she asked.

"We are *not* honest."

***

When he turned the boat back to shore with Carter beside him, Lennie wondered if Danny might be Wes' accomplice. That would explain why Danny had looked angry when Lennie had mentioned Wes' name at the restaurant. He planned to ask him about his arguments with Wes that the clients had witnessed.

Thanks to Carter, he knew which construction site Danny would be working at that day.

Danny put his chain saw down, much to Lennie's relief, and removing a work glove, he shook Lennie's hand.

"Nice to see you again," Lennie said, nonchalantly moving the two of them out of reach of the potential weapon. "I need to fill in some details for the article. Then I'll let you get back to work."

Lennie paused, in case Danny wanted to offer something. He didn't.

"I spoke with Captain Jaeger yesterday," Lennie said. "He told me he saw Carter on deck just before..."

"What?" Danny snapped.

Lennie was sure his look of surprise was genuine.

"Wes told me she died when equipment fell on her after the explosion," Danny said. "The captain kept ordering us to go back, almost getting hysterical, right up to the time the ship went under. I always suspected that Wes had lied about Carter being dead. But I couldn't be sure."

"You think Wes had something to do with her death?"

"We'd been arguing all day about what to do about her," Danny said. "She saw the smuggled boxes on the last trip. Wes was worried she knew what was inside. He thought she'd go to the cops. I warned him not to hurt her. That we'd figure something out. Pay her off." He shook his head. "I thought the explosion was just an accident."

Lennie looked at Carter's pained expression. He couldn't imagine what it felt like to realize that she'd turned her life around only to have it cut short by crooked partners.

"Danny, I know you didn't want to kill her," Lennie said. "I strongly suggest that you turn yourself in. Tell the police everything. Otherwise, I'll make sure they'll arrest you in the morning."

Back in his car, Lennie turned to Carter and said, "We have Wes on smuggling. But we still need to prove he killed you."

"Any ideas?"

He nodded. "We need to make one more stop before we talk to Wes."

***

At the police station with Carter by his side, Lennie approached Constable Michaels at the desk.

"Do you have a minute? We'd like to talk to you."

"We?"

"If we go somewhere private, all will be clear," Lennie said, as Carter chuckled.

Several minutes later, Constable Michaels stood blinking at Lennie, his mouth open as though ready to speak.

Eventually, he cleared his throat and with a forced smile said, "A great imagination does help when you're a journalist. Makes the words engaging."

"What?" Lennie said. He looked at Carter. "What's wrong?"

"I don't know. This was your idea!" she snapped.

"Nothing's wrong, sir," Michaels said. "It's just that you don't really believe that the ghost of Carter Samson is here, do you? And that she told you, just now, that she was murdered?"

"Try harder," Lennie urged her.

"I *am*!" She closed her eyes even tighter.

"Sir, asking me to try harder to believe you, well, that's not how the law works. I need proof. Or at least probable cause for the police to investigate." Michaels took Lennie's elbow and guided him to the office door.

Lennie was getting tired of being thrown out of places.

They stepped into the corridor, in time to see Danny walk through the main door. Lennie breathed a heavy sigh and smiled at Carter.

Then he turned to Michaels. "Your probable cause just walked through the door."

***

Wes opened the door, showing no reaction at the sight of Lennie standing on his doorstep.

"Sorry for showing up unannounced," Lennie said.

Wes ushered him into the simply furnished living room. He certainly wasn't spending his ill-gotten gain on his living space.

"More details to fill in?" he asked. His perfect poker face never wavered. Something every grifter aspired to.

Lennie turned down the offer of a drink. He sat on the sofa as Wes took the armchair across from him.

"I have a message for you. From Carter."

"Didn't realize you knew her," Wes said.

"We met recently."

"Trying to be funny?"

"She jumped off the ship in time." Lennie settled comfortably into the sofa and continued. "Floated for hours clinging to flotsam. Luckily a speed boat came by and plucked her out of the water. What are the chances, eh? But it wasn't really a coincidence, since it was the boat with the divers you hired to salvage the crates."

"That's an amusing story," Wes said.

Giving him a tiny smile, Lennie added, "She told me that she loved the hand-painted tie-dye pattern on the deck."

Wes' eyes tightened slightly. Not quite a squint. Not a frown.

"Yeah, I bet you're thinking that you should have made sure the boat you hired was less flashy." Lennie put an arm on the sofa back before continuing. "She knows about the record book."

"Everyone keeps a business record."

"I mean the record of your drug smuggling. In a hidden safe."

"Oh yeah, the secret safe behind my Rembrandt," he said, deadpan.

"No." Lennie gave a quick ha-ha, then equally deadpan replied, "The safe under the bathroom floor tiles."

That got a reaction from Wes. A deep frown. His eyes darted from side to side. Lennie could only imagine the thoughts racing around in the other man's mind.

"I bet you're wishing you'd told the men you hired not to pick up any survivors. Just dive down, grab the three crates and leave."

Wes' eyes snapped back to Lennie as his frown deepened. His expression became threatening.

Lennie forced himself to remain outwardly calm. Inside, he wanted to run.

"If there is a book," Wes said, "and I'm not saying there is, why doesn't she go to the cops with it?"

"And explain where she's been for three years? Nah, but for 60% she'll be your *silent* partner."

"Nice story," Wes said. His poker face was long gone. "But I can smell a con man a mile away."

"Think about it. How would I know any of this if she didn't tell me?"

"Time to go." Wes grabbed Lennie's arm, pulled him to his feet and shoved him out the door, slamming it shut.

"I think that might have been a waste of time," Lenny said.

"No," Carter said as she materialized beside him. "He nearly broke the sound barrier rushing to check the safe. I gotta watch."

And she vanished.

"Wait..." Lennie hurried around to the back of the house, which was surrounded by a waist-high wood fence.

Seconds later Wes rushed out of the house, clutching a blue notebook to his chest. He fired up the gas barbecue.

"No!" Lennie yelled. He jumped over the fence and landed on a bush. He scrambled to his feet and rushed forward.

Wes froze with his hand poised over the barbecue flames. His eyes were wide as multiple flashlight beams lit him. Several cops, led by Constable Michaels, dashed forward.

"I'll take that book," Michaels said.

Panting, Lennie reached them saying, "That was close."

Wes pointed, eyes round and unblinking as he said, "You can't be here."

"Sir, we have a warrant," Michaels said. "Let me read you your rights first." Once he finished the cautions, he asked, "You want to talk?"

Wes never looked at the cop, as he said, "It's impossible. I knocked her out. Hid her behind some rigging. Carter has to be dead."

Two officers handcuffed Wes and led him away. A third officer held an open evidence bag for the record book.

"Well," Lennie said, "that was easy."

"Just like the movies, eh?" Michaels said. "Now we can tie in every new influx of drugs to the dates in these records.

As for killing Carter, with Danny's testimony, let's just say Wes will need a good lawyer."

"Thank you for listening and for believing us," Lennie said.

"You've got an interesting gift." Looking around the backyard Michaels said, "Tell her I'm glad I helped bring her killer to justice."

Lennie looked at Carter who was smiling. He said, "She heard you."

The cop laughed as he shut off the gas on the barbecue. "Don't want another explosion. I'll see you around, Lennie."

As the forensics team arrived to process the evidence inside the house, Lennie returned to his car. He looked at Carter in the passenger seat.

"I'm also glad you finally got justice," he said.

"I guess Danny's going to jail for smuggling?" she asked.

"He's agreed to testify against Wes, so he'll get a reduced sentence," Lennie assured her.

"I'm glad to hear that." She paused, then smiled as she looked off into the distance. "I see a light..."

"Really?" Lennie leaned excitedly on the steering wheel squinting into the distance. "That means you can rest..."

Carter started laughing. "You are *so* gullible." She sobered and said, "Thank you for hearing me."

She faded away before he could answer.

Laughing, Lennie wondered if he should extend his vacation and actually rest. Or maybe he should go home and just help out his local ghosts.

The 13th Letter
M
The End

WHERE ARE YOU, MARILYN?

By Sylvia Maultash Warsh

It was 1962. We didn't know it then, but we were living on borrowed time. Post world war optimism had morphed into the Cold War. People were scared and built bomb shelters, not knowing things were going to get a lot worse. JFK hadn't been assassinated yet, nor his brother Bobby, nor Martin Luther King Jr.

I was fourteen and my parents had just moved us from an old downtown semi to a small suburban bungalow with the personality of a wet noodle. With six weeks to go, I was terrified to start a new school where I knew no one.

Moping on a lounge chair in our new backyard, I closed my eyes and lifted my face to the August sun. At least I could get a tan.

"Hi there!" someone called out.

My eyes popped open. A perky girl with a blonde pageboy smiled at me behind the fence ten feet away. She reminded me of Marilyn Monroe.

I sat up at attention. "Hi."

"I'm Marsha." She held a cigarette between two fingers of one hand. "I'm jazzed another girl moved in next door." She blew smoke out the side of her mouth.

I'm usually nervous with new people, but Marsha put me at ease with her open face, her eager hand planted on top of the chain link fence.

"I'm Sophie."

"What school you going to?" she asked.

It felt rude sitting in the lounger, so I stood up and approached the fence. "Lawrence Public."

"Me too!" She had curves in all the right places in her white-fringed bikini, making me feel like a stick figure in my blue one-piece.

Was she really my age? Lawrence Public only went to Grade 9. I dreaded going into the last grade of a school where all the kids knew each other after years of hanging out.

"What grade you going into?" she asked, as if reading my mind.

"Nine."

"Me too. Hey, you wanna come over and smell the roses?"

I thought it was a metaphor until I stepped into her yard and inhaled the heady perfume. She'd disappeared, but soon exited her back door carrying a turquoise kitchen chair, setting it beside the one already on the grass. Red roses dotted the bushes that grew along the back fence.

She lifted her chin at the roses. "My dad planted them years ago. They were supposed to be pink. He really wanted pink roses, he was so ticked off. You never get what you want. That's what he said."

Up close, I saw she had on full makeup: foundation, eye shadow and mascara. My mother didn't like me wearing makeup, said I was beautiful without it, though it wasn't true.

We sat down, breathed in the fragrance.

"We can walk to school together," she said.

I grinned. "How long have you lived here?" I was keeping up the conversation.

"Oh, years! We moved here when I was seven. I live with my dad."

I didn't ask where her mother was. It felt rude to pry.

"He works at Al's Diner near the school. I eat dinner there every night."

That impressed me. I'd only eaten in restaurants a few times and only for lunch, when my mother and I visited the print shop where my father worked. We didn't have extra cash because my mother stayed at home like most women in those days.

"I'm serving tables there for the summer," she said.

Very grown up. I was just a counselor-in-training at a kid's day camp.

We both had our faces lifted up to the sun, when a large brown dog bounded into the yard.

"Well, if it isn't the neighborhood mutt." She sat up and held out her arms.

He stood on his hind legs, licking her face. She laughed and rubbed his head around the floppy ears.

"You're going to eat all my makeup off!" She pulled him away and made funny faces at him. "Just started coming around a few weeks ago. Must be lost."

I giggled, patting his soft fur.

"Go away, Bowser!" She pushed him away. "Dad'll kill me if you take a dump on the grass."

***

We both had Sundays off, so we started going to the movies or walking to the park together. When Marsha came to the door to pick me up, my mother hung back, cleaning the kitchen counter with quick movements. But she wasn't invisible. Marsha would call out, "Hi, Mrs. Gilman! What's up?"

To my surprise, my small bird-like mother enjoyed the attention, her face lighting up. I knew her high round forehead and elegant nose by heart, but like all teenagers I was embarrassed by her. She was self-sufficient to a fault, cutting her own hair and coloring the gray. She even made all our clothes. I took her for granted until I met Marsha.

We had been friends for a few weeks, and I still hadn't met her father. One day heading for the park, we'd only taken a few steps down the road (no sidewalks) when Marsha remembered she'd left her wallet at home. We turned around. I hovered in the tiny hall while she sprinted to her bedroom. From where I stood, I could see the layout was exactly the same as our house, but it wasn't cozy like ours. A dark old sofa stood against the main wall of the living room.

Above it hung a poster of Joe DiMaggio at bat in his Yankees uniform. Above that, sports trophies stood on a shelf, tiny gold figures holding baseball bats.

When Marsha returned, she followed my eyes. "My dad was a baseball hero when he was young. He hurt his arm and never made it to the big leagues."

A Yankees' jacket draped a dining chair, a baseball bat across the seat.

Outside, it had started to rain. She turned to appraise my face like she was taking inventory. "Why don't we hang around here and I'll do your hair and makeup?"

The place made me uncomfortable, but I wanted to please her. She told me her father coached Little League on Sundays, so we had the house to ourselves.

Her unmade bed was scattered with clothes. A musical instrument lay on her dresser. "That looks like a guitar but it's too small."

"It's a ukulele."

"You play?"

"I'm trying but I'm bad at it. Marilyn Monroe taught herself to play it for *Some Like it Hot.* And she sings this song, 'I Wanna be Loved by You.' I go crazy when I hear it."

So there *was* a connection. "You look a little like her."

"Really? I *love* her! When I'm older, I'm going to Hollywood to do makeup for movie stars. It's my dream to do hers."

She sat me down in front of her dresser mirror. Her head tilted as she examined me, lifting a strand of my curly mousy-brown hair, letting it drop.

"I can fix this."

I was a late bloomer and oblivious to my looks then. I usually brushed my hair in the morning and forgot about it.

She sprayed my hair lightly with water, then rolled strands of it around large rollers. Next thing I knew, my head was inside a fabric hood attached to a contraption with a hose.

"This is going to be loud."

She was right about that. We couldn't talk once she turned it on, but I watched in the mirror as she applied foundation and blush to my face. Every now and then she stepped back to inspect her handiwork. Next was eye shadow, mascara and lipstick.

She turned off the hair dryer, removed the rollers, and combed out my hair. It was lovely, falling softly around my face, but the makeup made me look like a clown. I stared at myself, stunned.

"You're gorgeous!" She beamed.

"Groovy," I said, trying to sound hip. I hated the makeup.

"It's too bad I'll have to wash it off before I go home. My mother doesn't want me wearing makeup. Says I'm too young."

I expected a rolling of eyes, but she gave me a bittersweet smile. "You're lucky you have a mother who cares."

Now was my chance to ask. "What happened to yours?"

She crossed her arms and stared over my shoulder. "She took off for Hollywood so she could be discovered."

"Discovered?"

"She wants to be an actress. Like Lana Turner. Some big shot discovered her in a soda shop in Hollywood. My mother's a looker and figured it would happen if she went there."

"It didn't?"

Marsha grimaced. "She left when I was eight. My parents sent me up north to my Aunt Kay's for the summer and when I got back, she was gone. Got postcards for a while but then they stopped. My dad says she won't come home because she flamed out. Too proud, he says. She got a job as a waitress."

Marsha pulled a small black-and-white photo from a dresser drawer. A striking blonde woman stood with her arm around a young Marsha with dark hair. She looked like a normal girl.

"You look like her," I said. "Except your hair's not blonde."

She touched a curl as if someone were taking her picture. "I started dyeing it last year." She stared at the photo as if she didn't know it by heart. "She's the spitting image of Marilyn. I was sure she'd be in a movie by now."

"Didn't your dad want to bring her home?"

She shrugged. "He won't talk about her. He said her dream was more important than us. It hurt him a lot when she left."

"Maybe you could find out where she lives. Write her a letter."

She blinked at me. "Wouldn't know where to start."

I wanted to do something for her. I was so grateful to her for being my friend. "I could help you. We could be like detectives."

"I don't know. Dad would kill me."

"What's her name?"

"Alice."

"Did she have a job here?"

She paused, thinking. "She worked for Towers. You know, the department store. Head office. Tried on the samples before they bought them."

"We could start there. Talk to people she knew."

She stared at me as if I had two heads. "I don't know. It was six years ago." She hesitated. "She had a friend there. Nora." She gave me a sheepish smile.

We both heard the front door open. "Gee, I didn't know it was so late," she said.

"Marsh? You home?" A man's voice.

She led me out into the kitchen. "Hi, Dad."

I don't know what I was expecting, but he wasn't it. Tall, well-built with quizzical eyebrows and brown hair parted neatly on one side. He wore a striped Yankee's shirt like the one in the Joe DiMaggio poster.

"Who's this?" He looked at me, but I got the impression my presence didn't make a dent and he only asked because it would've been weird not to.

"My friend, Sophie. She lives next door."

"Did you hear the news? Marilyn Monroe is dead. She killed herself."

My heart did a flip-flop. Marsha's hand flew to her mouth. Tears welled in her eyes as she switched on the radio in the kitchen. All the news was about Marilyn. Marsha sank into a chair and sobbed.

"Don't take it so hard," he said, grabbing a bag of potato chips from the cupboard. He threw some in his mouth, his long nose moving as he chewed. "I'm sorry, Marsh. But she's just an actress."

***

After that, Marsha changed her mind about looking for her mother. She looked up Towers in the phone book and found their head office was still on Orfus Road. She remembered her mother took her there on days when school was out and there was no babysitter.

We were both free that afternoon, so we rode the Dufferin Street bus south. School hadn't started, my camp job was over, and Marsha had sneaked out ahead of the dinner rush at Al's Diner.

I followed her off the bus toward an ugly brick building. *Towers* was printed over the front door. The slatted blind on the window to our right was pulled up halfway; people, mostly women, were working quietly at their desks.

Marsha stopped dead in her tracks.

"I can't," she murmured.

What had happened to the confident Marsha? "What was the name of your mother's friend here?" I asked.

"Nora Blake. But I don't know if I'd recognize her. And maybe she's not here anymore." She was talking too fast.

"Don't be scared." I took her hand and opened the front door.

We stood on the threshold of the office, listening to its low hum. I took Marsha's arm and pulled her inside, wondering at my own nerve. It was like our roles had reversed.

The middle-aged woman at a desk near the entrance looked up. "May I help you?"

I swallowed. "We're looking for Nora Blake."

She stared at us over her glasses. "She doesn't work here anymore."

Marsha flinched. I went on. "Do you know where we can find her? We'd like to speak to her about… a missing person."

The woman glanced from me to Marsha and back again. "Maybe you should talk to the police."

I stood my ground. "She knew Alice Palmer, my friend's mother"—I touched Marsha's arm— "when she worked here six years ago. Maybe someone here knows where Nora is."

The woman must've recognized the name because she called out, "Deb!"

A youngish woman approached us. When we explained what we wanted, she motioned us to her desk. We all stood around it.

"Nora got married and had a kid a few years ago. I think we have a forwarding address." She gave Marsha an embarrassed look. "I only worked here a few weeks before your mother left. She was gorgeous! Could've been a model. I heard she went to California. Whatever happened to her?"

Marsha took a breath. "We lost touch."

***

We took the Dufferin bus further down to Lawrence Avenue, then walked three blocks to a low-rise apartment building that had seen better days. The halls reeked of dinners being cooked behind closed doors. We stood outside a first-floor apartment, listening to a child's cries inside. Marsha didn't move.

On the bus, she'd told me her mother and Nora had become friends because people called them both "glamor puss" with their model looks and blonde hair. I was thinking of that when I knocked, so when a drab woman in green cotton shorts appeared in the doorway, I thought we had the wrong place.

"*Nora?*" Marsha stood with her mouth open.

The woman's shoulder-length hair had been blonde once, but dark roots had grown out and it looked like it needed a wash. Her glum face took on some life when Marsha addressed her.

"Do I know you?"

She hesitated. "I'm Marsha Palmer. Alice's daughter."

The woman stared for a long moment. Then her eyebrows shot up. "Marsha? Little Marsha?" She smiled, though it appeared forced. "Do you want to come in?"

She opened the door a little and we squeezed by into the dim interior, drapes closed against the August sun. A little girl with curly blonde hair stood in the living room, her finger in her mouth.

"Andrea!" her mother said. "No finger." The little girl put her hand at her side guiltily. "This is my daughter. Say hello to the nice ladies."

The girl stared at us.

"How old is she?" I asked.

"Five."

Nora motioned us inside, throwing the toys off the worn living room sofa into a corner. "Excuse the mess."

We sat across from Nora, awkwardly quiet. She crossed her legs and smoothed down her hair self-consciously.

"How did you find me?" Another forced smile.

"Mummy…" Andrea started climbing into her mother's lap.

"Go take a nap, baby."

"Aw, mummy…"

"*Now!*"

The little girl rubbed her eyes and wandered down the hall.

"Towers had a forwarding address," I said. She watched me until I added, "I'm a friend of Marsha's."

She uncrossed her legs and bent forward, elbows on her thighs. She had dark circles under her eyes. "So, what can I do for you?"

"I'm looking for my mother," Marsha said.

Nora did a double take. "Oh." She let out a breath I didn't realize she was holding.

"You were friends. I thought you might know where she went."

Nora shook her head. "She's in Hollywood, isn't she? Trying to make it as an actress."

"She didn't get in touch with you?"

Nora shook her head again. Then as if just remembering, "Got a postcard from her a few months after she left."

"Where from?"

"Hollywood Boulevard."

"You still have it?"

"No, it got lost when I moved."

We all looked at each other some more.

"What time does your husband come home?" I asked.

Nora blushed, flustered. "Oh, we're separated."

"Mummy!" A little voice from the bedroom.

"I gotta go," Nora said, standing up.

"Could I have a glass of water?" Marsha said.

She motioned us into the kitchen, suddenly the gracious hostess. "Where are my manners?"

We followed her into the galley kitchen, the sink full of dishes. Marsha inspected the fridge door: a small calendar, a photo of Andrea, and a kid's crayon drawing of a family—a man, woman and a child, all holding hands.

Sitting on the Dufferin Street bus heading back north, I asked Marsha, "Did she seem off to you?"

Marsha stared out the window, adrift. "Some people shouldn't have kids."

***

A few days later, Marsha invited me to the diner for coconut cream pie in the afternoon, their slow time. The mouth-watering smell of burgers and fries hung in the air. We were sitting in a booth, filling our faces with the best pie I'd ever tasted, sipping *Coca-Cola*, when Marsha's father came out of the kitchen. He had a presence, even in an apron.

He poured himself a cup of coffee from a carafe and slid into the booth beside Marsha. Pulling a pack of Marlboro cigarettes out of his shirt pocket, he offered it to us. I shook my head, but Marsha took one. He lit it with his lighter.

She exhaled a cloud of blue smoke, then turned to him. "Do you know where Mom is?"

The air deflated out of him. His gray eyes narrowed. "Where's this coming from?"

"I want to write to her."

He took a gulp of his coffee. "Give it up."

"I know you get upset talking about her, but she's my mother. Maybe she wants to see me even if she is a washout. Why are you so against—"

"Because she doesn't want to see you. Or me."

Marsha took in a sudden breath. "You—you've talked to her?"

He put the palm of his hand flat on the table and leaned in. "She has a new family now. Kids. She wants to leave everything else behind. Including us."

"She—she told you that?"

"Leave it alone."

"You've known where she is all this time!"

"Look, Marsh, I didn't want you to get hurt."

She stabbed out her cigarette in the ashtray with a vengeance. "I don't believe it. You lied to me all these years."

"It was for your own good."

She jumped from the booth and leaped out the door.

"Marsh, wait!"

I ran to catch up to her. Tears streamed down her face, black rivulets of mascara ruining her makeup. Nothing I could say would make things better. Her mother didn't love her. There was hardly anything worse than that.

She slowed down a few blocks from home. By now she was gulping air and catching her breath.

The neighborhood mutt bounced toward us and tried to get her attention, emitting a tentative woof. She stopped, wiping the tears viciously from her face, letting the dog jump on her. His paws rested on her arms, his tail wagging. When the dog started to lick her face, she stopped crying.

"Okay, okay," she mumbled.

I took her to my house where my mother fussed over her, asking what was wrong. To her credit, she immediately stopped with the questions when I shook my head. She brought out a cloth and gently washed Marsha's face until all the messy mascara and makeup were gone. I'd never seen her without makeup. She looked like an ordinary girl, not the Marsha that had dazzled me. Not Marilyn Monroe.

We went into the backyard to get some sun only to find the dog digging up my mother's tomato plants.

"No!" I yelled. "Stop!"

Marsha smiled for the first time. "Bowser! No!" She pushed the dog away and he relented, sitting down and panting, his long tongue hanging out.

***

I had trouble sleeping that night, the conversation in the diner playing itself over in my head. In the morning, I was woken by barking and screaming coming from Marsha's backyard.

I rushed out in my pajamas. Bowser cowered in the corner while Marsha sat whimpering on the grass beside a large hole. The dog had been busy, digging beneath the rose bushes. It was a mess, but I didn't understand until I approached and saw the bones. Some small ones lay in the soil, but she frantically began to sweep earth off a skull.

My heart leaped in my chest. Her mother had never left.

I felt like gagging but took her hand and led her into the house away from the horror, thinking to call the police. She wouldn't let me; instead, she phoned her father. Then she pushed me away and stumbled back into the yard, falling to her knees on the grass, tears pouring down her cheeks.

In less than ten minutes her father rushed into the yard toward her. He stopped when he took in the scene, the hole, the skull.

He gulped a breath. "I'm sorry, Marsh. I'm sorry!"

"You killed her!"

"She wanted to leave and take you with her. To Hollywood. She had a job lined up—I didn't want to lose you. I did it because I love you."

Marsha stood up, her eyes on fire. "You killed her because you *love* me?" Tears streamed down her face. "You sent me up north to Aunt Kay's so you could do it, didn't you?"

He brought his hand to his forehead. "We were going through a rough patch. I needed time to figure things out."

She made a face. "A rough patch?"

He shrugged.

"Was it another woman?"

He chewed on his lip.

"Did you get someone pregnant?"

He closed his eyes.

"Was it Nora?"

I sucked in a breath.

He shook his head but didn't deny it. "I was stupid. I'm sorry, baby—"

"Is that where you go on Sundays? To see your brat? She's five now. Looks like you."

I turned to stare at her, shocked. That's what she'd meant after we saw Nora. It wasn't Nora she was talking about when she said some people shouldn't have kids.

"Marsh, please, I love you—"

"How did you do it? How did you kill her?"

His eyes grew large. His mouth opened, but nothing came out.

"It was the bat, wasn't it?"

My stomach lurched. I ran home to throw up.

***

After Ricky Palmer was sent to jail for murder, Marsha disappeared up north to live with her Aunt Kay. In the beginning, we wrote letters every week. The following spring, it was every other month. Then one day I realized I hadn't gotten a letter from her in four months. I wrote to her, saying I missed her and maybe she could take the bus into town at Christmas. A few weeks later I was thrilled to get a letter back.

Only it wasn't from Marsha. It was from her aunt.

In a large round hand, Aunt Kay wrote that she was sorry to tell me that Marsha was dead. She'd been killed by a new boyfriend. I stopped reading there, unable to take it in. I reread it hoping I had misunderstood, but the words kept coming out the same. *I told her he was bad,* Aunt Kay said, *but she wouldn't listen. I don't think she cared anymore, she'd lost her sparkle.* She prayed the boyfriend would rot in jail. Marsha was an unlucky girl who never had a chance in this sorry world. It was better now that she was in heaven.

I wish I believed in heaven. Then I could picture Marsha touching up Marilyn's blonde hair while she played the ukulele and sang "I Wanna be Loved by You."

The 13th Letter

M

The End

CHOPS AND THE DOUGH RE MI

By Caro Soles

The Pit was jumping. All the tables were packed with citizens having a great time and smoke hung thick in the joint like a London fog. It was just past midnight and Julie's boys had stopped pouring hooch into the teacups scattered forgotten on the tables and were handing out glasses instead.

I was wailing on my sax, halfway through my second solo when The Babe sashayed into the joint. She had a figure that could stop traffic and gams that went on forever and the dress… How could she walk in that thing?

Beside me on the tiny stage, Toots missed his cue. Bibsy took over. I wailed on. Toots looked like he'd just seen the Second Coming and I knew he had it bad for The Babe. I saw the drummer reach down and scoop up his brown paper bag and take a quick nip. He had seen The Babe, too.

Meanwhile, space had miraculously opened up at several tables and the tomato was having a hard time deciding which group to join. Her hat swept up on one side and down on the other, so when she turned one way, I could barely see any of her long gold-white hair. That was fine by me. I know trouble when I see it. By this time, Toots had pulled himself together and The Saints were marching golden out of his trumpet, like usual. The whole joint erupted in cheers as we finished the set. The babe was on her feet jumping up and down. I was afraid for a moment she might jiggle right out of her expensive tiny black dress and Toots wouldn't be close enough to scoop her back in.

The crowd thinned out around two, and by three in the morning, we were packing up to go home. The broad was still there, but now she was sitting right up in front of the stage watching Toots. He was rattled. He wasn't used to an audience after the gig.

"Chops, she wants to talk to you," he whispered as I closed the sax case. "She wants to hire you."

"Tell her to come to my office tomorrow," I said.

"Ah, come on. I can't ask a dame like her to go to a dump like your office, Chops. Come on."

"She came to this joint, didn't she?"

"That was for the music."

I looked over at the dame. She was looking right at me, her eyes large and blue and deep. I knew a bookie with eyes like that once. He was bad news, too, and I was having none of it. I picked up my sax and walked out the door.

The next day I ambled into the office I share with Cuddles Lajoya, a broad who does insurance investigations for a living and a lot of other things just for fun that might get a regular citizen in trouble. Cuddles has nerves of steel and a great line in blowing smoke rings with her cigars, but she can't make a cup of java worth a plugged nickel. What she turns out could be used as engine oil for your old Tin Lizzie.

"So Chops, how's it hangin'?" Cuddles lifted her army boots off the desk and kicked a chair in my direction. "Take a load off. I have a client for you."

Cuddles is known for her big hips, not her big heart, so I assumed this client had wanted me in the first place, me being the private dick.

"So where is this swell chick?"

"Planted in the inner office." She pointed to the door behind her as if I might have forgotten the layout of the joint. "You owe me a finder's fee, don't forget." She grinned, and the light caught her one gold tooth.

"Sure, toots, as soon as you pay me for all the bootleg hooch I lug in here in my sax case on a regular basis."

"You don't do nothin' on a regular basis except piss me off," Cuddles said and pinched my bum.

She's a bawdy dame and that's the truth. I scurried past her into the inner office where who should I find perched daintily on the edge of a chair but the swell chick in the tight dress, only this time the dress was the vivid green of a fresh slice of lime in a long cool glass of gin and tonic.

"Well, aren't you the bees' knees," I said, sitting behind the small desk. "My name's D.D. Domingo, but everyone calls me Chops."

"Don't I know it, sweet thing," she said, and her voice purred like a lazy kitten on a hot day. "I just hope you have the chops to help me."

She sat back, pulled a gold case out of her beaded bag and fitted a cigarette into a long holder that was blood red at one end.

I fumbled with my lighter, managing to drop it once. Finally getting it working, I leaned over the desk and lit her smoke. Then I pulled out a Philip Morris and joined her.

"So, what's your moniker?"

"You can call me Lady M," she said. "I have a problem and I hope you can help me."

You ain't no lady, I thought, but kept that idea to myself. What would a genuine lady be doing in my office anyway, right? A regular tootsie could still have a cheating husband, boyfriend, sugar daddy. I didn't really care, so long as she kept sitting there, leaning towards me at just the right angle.

"I got a problem, Chops," she said.

I pushed the ashtray closer to her glowing gasper. "Your sweetie cheatin' on you?"

She tossed her head as if this suggestion wasn't worth considering. "I've lost something. A very important something."

"This isn't the lost and found, doll."

"I wouldn't be here if it was." She sat back and crossed her legs. I could hear the silk stockings sigh as her skirt rose higher. Then she reached into her cleavage and pulled out a roll of dead presidents that looked fresh out of the mint. "How much will it take to hire you to find it?"

"It's a lot cheaper to go to the fuzz."

"Why talk to them when I can talk to you?" She waved the dosh back and forth in front of my face.

"One of your gentleman friends give it to you?"

"What do you care? Just find my lost property and this is all yours. Meanwhile..." She began to slowly peel off a few bills at a time, like a stripper taking it off in a club. Then she batted her eyelashes at me.

"It might be easier if I had a description."

"A single two-carat pink diamond with a pear-shaped cut surrounded by small marquisettes set in platinum on a yellow-gold ring." She rhymed it off like it was all one hyphenated word.

"Insured?"

"I hadn't got around to that." She began to push the bundle of greenbacks in my direction with one long red-lacquered fingernail.

The smell I was getting from this whole story was a lot stronger than the perfume coming from her warm cleavage, but it wasn't my nose that was doing the thinking. And anyway, that wad of greenbacks looked big enough to float my boat for some time.

"Why the deadline?"

"My sweetie will be back from his business trip then, okay?"

"Who's your sweetie? Bugs Moran?"

"Don't be silly."

But she looked uncomfortable for the first time, and that made me uncomfortable, too. I was pretty sure Bugs Moran was in Chicago where he belongs, but there were plenty more mobbed-up citizens right here in our fair city who carried heaters and they all had itchy trigger fingers. That made me uneasy.

"There's just one teensy weensy little thing," she said, before sliding off the chair. "You might want to check with Boodger's Pawnshop first."

She winked and was gone before I could gather my wits enough to say anything more.

Boodger's Pawnshop is one of two on the main floor of the old building where I live. The second floor is a pool hall. I'm on the third floor, a big warehouse space that suits me just fine. And the fourth floor...well, it used to be inhabited by a citizen named Andy the Handyman Griffith, but he met his Maker in an untimely fashion a while ago and the place is still empty. Makes it real quiet up there at night.

Next afternoon when I finally got up and faced the world, I sauntered down to the pawnshop to have a chin wag with Boodger.

"Chops, my man," he cried. "How's tricks?"

"Fair to middlin'."

"Need to pawn the horn again?"

"Nope. Not for a while."

"You got another gig?" He perked up and wiped perspiration from his mottled face as he pushed up closer to the cage that surrounded him and the merchandise. "You want I should let you in for a hit of java?"

"I'll pass this time, thanks," I said, not willing to face the industrial-strength sludge he brewed up back there in his rat's nest of an office.

"So, what can I do you for?" he asked, settling his bulk onto his high stool.

I told him about the tomato and that pink diamond I was beginning to think she never did own.

The Boodge shook his shiny bald head. "Some dames, you know, they think the rules don't apply to them."

"Ain't that the truth?"

"It looked like a handcuff?"

"I doubt the upstanding citizen who gave it to her was thinking of marriage, Boodger. So come clean. Who ended up with the ring?"

"Not the kind of solid dude who'll let it go for a fair price, know what I mean?"

"How about an unfair price?" I asked. "Apparently, money is no object."

"It sure was when she pawned the thing," he shot back. "Temporary cash flow."

Just to satisfy my curiosity, I asked, "How much did you give her for it?"

"One thousand smackers. I'm a sucker for a pretty face."

I spent another fifteen minutes with the Boodge chatting about this and that and he gave me a hot tip on the fourth at Belmont. Fancy Pants. How could that filly lose? Finally, I wormed the name and address of the buyer out of him. Neither meant anything to me, but that was no surprise.

By this time, I was feeling the need of a little sustenance. What with one thing and another, I hadn't had time for breakfast and by now it was after four o'clock. I dropped into Mindy's and read my Racing Form while I shoveled a Reuben sandwich into my stomach. The tall drink of water who refilled my cup of java informed me solemnly that Fancy Pants had just limped in fifth.

I was so dejected I gave dessert a pass. I hoped Boodger lost a bundle, too. I had just enough of the jingle left to show my tootsie a good time at Shardow's tonight before dropping into the back room at Minnie the Mooch's joint on 42nd Street.

And that's where I saw the pink diamond ring for the first time—on the finger of a red-headed doll who looked far too young for serious jewelry. It was dim in that room, so how was I to know that she belonged to Mat "The Maestro" Milanese? Or that she wore a stiletto in her garter?

"Whoa, there!" I backed away from her, holding my hands out in front of me to show I wasn't packing. "I was just admiring your ring, baby!"

The Maestro loomed out of his seat, glowering. "Admire it from over there," he snarled, pointing three tables away.

I had just begun to slink away when suddenly the lights went out.

"It's a raid!" someone shouted.

A panel in the wall slipped open near me, letting the ones who knew about it make a clean getaway.

I was still looking at the little doll wearing the pink ring. In a moment of madness, I reached out and grabbed her arm, pulling her after me into the darkness of the tunnel that led into an alley two doors down.

She made a little yelp of surprise, then shut up and followed on my heels until we emerged into the quiet back alley. In the distance, we could hear the outraged shouts of citizens who were being rounded up by the heat out in the street.

Did the little doll thank me? She just tossed back her head and the tiny feather on her tiny hat quivered. Then she marched off like Sousa himself was leading the band and she was leading the parade. Dames. What can you do?

When I told Cuddles about it the next day, she howled with laughter.

"You're a Class A chump," she said, lighting another cigar. "If you ever bothered to read anything but the Racing Form, you'd know about the hold-up at Tifiano's last week. Seems, among other things, a valuable pink diamond ring was taken in the heist. From now on, stick to following the cheating sweethearts."

She leaned back and blew a perfect smoke ring.

So, there you have it.

I felt like the chump Cuddles already thought I was for falling for a doll like Lady M, who had fallen for a major low life like Mat "The Maestro" Milanese. Who knew the mobster had already traded her in for a younger model?

As for me, I was left with my memories, the smarts to not go near Minnie the Mooch's joint for a whole month and a bit of the dough re mi.

The 13th Letter

M

The End

ONE HELLUVA LADY

By Rosemary McCracken

When two Toronto police officers took chairs across from my desk, I wondered what trouble I was in.

"Ms. Tierney," Detective Inspector Neil Hardy began, "we understand that Luella Cruickshank was your client."

"Luella was my client for a long time," I replied. "But it's been a year since we worked together."

Hardy's blue eyes bored into me. "Mrs. Cruickshank was found dead in her home yesterday."

"No!" Luella was 78 years old, but I thought she would go on forever. She seemed to be an unstoppable force.

I took a deep breath, let it out slowly. "What happened?"

"Her death is under investigation," Hardy said.

The police don't investigate deaths by natural causes. "You're saying she was *murdered*?"

"Her death is under investigation," he repeated. "That's all we can say right now."

I leaned back in my chair, my heart hammering in my chest.

"We found a note in her study," Hardy's partner, Detective Mario Mancini, said. "'Call Pat Tierney first thing on Monday,' it says. That's today: Monday, May 20th. Any idea what Mrs. Cruickshank wanted?"

"No idea at all," I said. "I haven't seen Luella since I left Norris Cassidy to run my own practice."

"You were in contact after you left?"

I smiled, remembering Luella's frequent phone calls. "She called me from time to time, but not in the past few weeks."

"Why didn't she follow you here?" Mancini asked, looking around my office.

"Norris Cassidy claims clients belong to the firm, not to the financial advisor," I said.

"*Belong* to the firm?" Mancini looked affronted.

I threw up my hands. "I know, I know. Clients can take their business wherever they like. But I may need to network with Norris Cassidy someday, so I didn't want to rock the boat. I purchased a financial planning practice from an advisor who wanted to retire. And I took on his clients."

I had a question of my own. "Did Luella surprise a burglar?"

The officers exchanged a glance. "We're looking into that," Hardy said.

I wasn't going to let him shut me down. "Is anything missing from her home?"

They looked at each other again. "Mrs. Cruickshank's daughter should be able to tell us about that tomorrow," Hardy said.

"Signs of forced entry?" I pressed on. "Broken window, jimmied lock?"

Neither officer replied.

"You read Luella's note," I said. "How did you know where to find me?"

"Mrs. Cruickshank's housekeeper told us you were her former financial advisor. We found your website." Hardy took a notepad from his jacket pocket and flipped through it. "Her son, Arnold, flew in from Vancouver yesterday, arrived at the airport around noon. We need to speak with him."

"He's not staying at Luella's home?" I asked.

"No. We're checking hotels, but he may be with friends." Hardy returned his notepad to his pocket.

"Sounds like you've been in touch with Luella's daughter in Calgary. Caroline doesn't know where Arnie is?"

"She hasn't heard from her brother in a while," Mancini said.

"But she may have an idea where he's staying. She probably knows his friends."

The detectives stood and handed me their cards. "Give us a call if you figure out why Mrs. Cruickshank wanted to speak with you," Mancini said.

I nodded and looked at their cards. Beside their names and rank were the words Homicide Division.

"You're homicide detectives!" I cried. "So, Luella *was* murdered."

"Her death is under investigation," Hardy said.

***

Luella was on my mind all morning. Difficult and demanding as she could be, the elderly widow had had a big heart. Her enthusiasm for everything that caught her interest almost made up for her lack of common sense. If I hadn't been her financial advisor, trying to protect her money and make it grow, I might have found her delightfully eccentric.

It was so damn sad, I thought, wiping away tears. Luella had been robbed of precious time she could have spent with family and friends.

She had no enemies that I could think of, so money had to be the motive for her murder. Was it a burglary gone wrong? There were also the legacies she'd bequeathed in her will. Her Toronto home, her vacation home in Muskoka cottage country and her investments added up to $10 million, give or take a hundred grand. She had divided her estate equally between her two children, so Caroline and Arnie would be coming into serious money.

I'd met both of them many times over the years. Caroline Loomis was about 50, a senior editor at a Calgary newspaper and married to an oil industry executive. Ten years her junior, her brother, Arnie Cruickshank, had held a number of jobs, none successfully. He had moved to Canada's West Coast the previous year. The last I'd heard from Luella, he was managing a surf shop on Vancouver Island.

Now he was back in Toronto, and his mother's death was being investigated by homicide detectives.

Caroline was understandably weepy when I reached her in Calgary that afternoon. "Mom refused to have a home security system installed." I heard her shaky intake of breath. "She must've confronted a burglar."

Luella had always insisted on doing things her way. She'd even arranged her own funeral.

"Your mother made her funeral arrangements at Montgomery Charles," I said, naming a funeral home favored by Old Toronto.

"Montgomery Charles is ready to proceed, and Mom's pastor suggests Thursday morning for the funeral Mass. All we need is the green light from the police. Troy and I will arrive in Toronto tomorrow, just the two of us. Our son, Zach, is taking a gap year before university, traveling across Canada. He's planting trees in British Columbia this month."

"Have you spoken to Arnie?"

"No, but he's in Toronto. Mom met him at the airport yesterday, but Mary Dilworth, Mom's new housekeeper, said she returned home alone. Arnie wanted to stay with friends for a few days."

Caroline let out a ragged sigh. "My brother has never been reliable, but this takes the cake. He doesn't even know Mom is…gone."

She paused for a few moments. "Pat, would you try to find Arnie?"

I was taken aback. Toronto is Canada's largest city, home to three million people.

"I wouldn't know where to start," I said. "You must know some of his friends here."

"Not really. I've lived in Calgary since Arnie was in high school. The only thing I can think of is his fitness club.

Mom bought him a membership at Bay Street Fitness. She told me he was a regular there before he left Toronto."

"It's a long shot," I said with an inward groan, "but I'll try the club." It wouldn't give out the names of its members; that would breach client confidentiality. But Caroline was under a great deal of stress and having me onside might ease her mind.

"I knew I could count on you, Pat."

It was almost 3:30. In another hour, the after-work crowd would be heading for the gym. Now was my opportunity to speak to its manager.

***

I'd read about Bay Street Fitness in *Toronto Life* magazine. It boasted eight tennis courts, a saltwater pool, and the latest and greatest fitness technology. Post-workout, members could unwind at a full-service spa, or at its private bar and restaurant. All for just $25,000 a year.

At the granite reception desk, I asked for the manager. The receptionist spoke on the phone, then pointed to an office across the lobby. Heather Blakey, a shapely brunette in spandex, greeted me from her desk. But her smile vanished when I told her I was looking for Arnie Cruickshank.

"Arnie moved to western Canada last year, but he's visiting Toronto right now. There's a family emergency, and we need to locate him. His sister thinks he may be staying with friends who are members here," I said.

"He's no longer a member," she replied.

"So you remember Arnie?"

Heather frowned. "Oh, I remember him."

I handed her several of my business cards. "Would you ask his friends to contact me?"

"I can't do that."

"I'm not asking for their names. I'm asking *them* to contact *me*."

Heather shook her head. "Sorry."

I glared at her until she said, "Arnie left here under a cloud. We're a 24-hour facility, and locks were being cut off lockers during the night."

"You have security cameras?"

"Sure, in public areas such as the weight and cardio rooms. But not in the changing areas where the lockers are located."

And where members expect privacy. "What was taken?" I asked.

"Wallets containing cash and credit cards. Personal ID."

"And Arnie was in the building when the thefts occurred?"

"That's right, and the break-ins stopped after he left Toronto."

"But other people must have been here on those nights."

"That's right."

"Including staff?"

She nodded.

"So, the thief could have been any one of a number of people," I said. "Did the police speak to everyone who was here when the thefts occurred?"

"They did. Took fingerprints too, but nothing came of it. The thief must've worn gloves." She smiled. "Maybe Arnie didn't break into those lockers. But no Arnie, no thefts. You connect the dots."

I left, my mind clicking away. The police had found no hard evidence linking Arnie to the thefts, but I wouldn't put breaking into the lockers past him.

Outside, I squared my shoulders. I'd visited Bay Street Fitness. It was time to move on. Maybe Arnie had turned up at the Cruickshank home by now.

***

I parked my Volvo in front of the handsome red-brick Rosedale home that had been the Cruickshank residence for four generations. I rapped the brass lion's head on the front door. On my second rap, a platinum blonde in an oversized black T-shirt, black tights and black lace-up boots opened the door. She wore a nose ring and metal spikes studded her ears.

"Yeah?" she said.

"Is Mary Dilworth in?"

"I'm Mary Dilworth."

I'd expected Luella's new housekeeper to be a prim woman in tweeds, not a punk rocker, but Luella had always been full of surprises.

"I'm Pat Tierney, Luella's financial advisor," I said. "Could I speak to you?"

"You're Luella's *former* financial advisor. But she liked you better than that dude the company saddled her with." She held the door open.

I followed her across the hall and into the living room where a white marble fireplace held pride of place. Mary pointed to the marble tiles in front of the grate. "Here's where I found Luella last night."

I looked down at the tiles and shuddered.

Mary's kohl-rimmed brown eyes brimmed with tears. "Sunday's my day off. I met up with friends after Luella returned from the airport. If I'd been here, she might still be alive."

"You were entitled to your day off." My heart went out to this young woman, who'd found her employer dead on the living room floor. Now she was rattling around this big Victorian house filled with knickknacks and doilies.

I drew her down onto a sofa. "Luella thought the world of you, Mary. The last time we talked, she told me how good you were to her."

She ran a hand through her short platinum hair, her face twisting in pain. "I've only worked here four months, but it's the best job I've ever had."

I waited until she'd pulled herself together. "Is anything missing from the house?" I asked.

Mary pointed to an empty space on a wall covered with paintings. "The D.J. Papineau painting hung there. Luella said it's valuable."

"It is. Papineau is a famous Indigenous artist," I said. "Anything else missing?"

"It looks like someone went through her dresser drawers. Caroline may know if anything is missing."

So it had been a burglary gone wrong.

"The police dusted for fingerprints," Mary said with a grimace. "It was some job cleaning that up."

"Has Luella's son come by?"

She rolled her eyes. "Darling Arnie! Luella was so disappointed that he didn't come back from the airport with her. No, he hasn't called or dropped by."

"He probably doesn't even know his mother is dead. Did Luella tell you where he's staying?"

"I don't think he told her."

I got up from the sofa. As I was leaving the room, I passed a glass cabinet stuffed with antique dolls. Luella had been a pack rat. Teddy bears, miniature Toby mugs and ceramic roosters covered every flat surface in the living room. A yellow surfboard leaned against a wall.

"If you hear from Arnie, have him call his sister right away," I said to Mary. "She should be the one to tell him about Luella."

We were back in the front hall when a door banged shut upstairs.

"What was that?" I wanted to know.

"I left a bedroom window open," Mary said. "The wind must've closed the door."

At the front door, I asked, "Have you met Arnie?"

Mary's jaw dropped. "How could I have met him? He hasn't visited his mother since I've been here."

I stepped out into a beautiful May day. The sun was shining in a clear blue sky. And there wasn't so much as a breeze ruffling the leaves on the trees in front of the house.

***

The police released Luella's remains the following day, and plans unfolded for a Thursday funeral. Caroline called me after she and Troy arrived in Toronto on Tuesday evening. She still hadn't heard from Arnie.

The organist was playing "Ave Maria" when I arrived at Our Lady of Lourdes on Thursday morning. I took a seat in the grand old church and surveyed the mourners. Many of them were prosperous and powerful-looking people. Caroline was seated in a front pew. Mary walked down the center aisle and took the pew behind her. She'd cleaned up nicely. The nose ring and the ear studs were gone. She was wearing a black leather skirt, a matching jacket and black high heels.

A priest in a purple chasuble appeared at the front of the church. A procession led by four girls holding candles, followed by six men pushing a casket on a metal bier, moved down the center aisle toward him. To my surprise, one of the pallbearers was Arnie Cruickshank. He was decked out in a gray Armani suit, his fair hair streaked by the sun.

The priest sprinkled holy water on the casket. The pallbearers headed for the pews, Arnie and two others joining Caroline. I assumed the big guy with the salt-and-pepper hair was Troy Loomis, Caroline's husband. The young man with the dark ponytail had to be their son, Zach. His shoulders were shaking. Caroline put an arm around him.

The priest introduced himself as Father Fred Jaworski. He told us he had worked with Luella on a number of parish projects. "She was an admirable woman, with a real concern for her fellow human beings," he said.

The Mass began and my attention drifted. After the final blessing, Caroline delivered the eulogy Luella had written, then invited everyone to a reception at the Cruickshank home. Father Fred sprinkled more water on the casket. And the organist launched into "Amazing Grace."

As I turned to watch the casket leave the church, I spotted Hardy and Mancini in a back pew.

***

I had an appointment to witness a client's signature back at my office, so I arrived late for the reception, at about 12:30 p.m. From the front door, I saw men and women in the hall and living room, plates and glasses in their hands. Caroline was chatting with Father Fred in front of the fireplace.

Mary came to the door to greet me. "Good to see you, Pat!"

She took me into the living room where a bar had been set up at the back of the room. "Can I get you a drink?" she asked. "There's food in the dining room."

"A Coke would be good," I replied, and followed her to the bar.

"So Arnie surfaced," I said. "Where was he?"

Mary snorted. "Staying with friends. He walked in here yesterday morning. Thought it was time he visited his mother."

"Did he speak to the police?"

"Caroline called them. They came right over."

Arnie joined us and draped an arm across my shoulders. "Pat Tierney, my mother's favorite financial advisor."

I removed his arm. "I'm sorry for your loss, Arnie. Your poor mother." I shook my head. "She will be missed."

He bowed his head. "Mom was one helluva lady. They don't make them like her anymore."

The kid with the man-tail came over. "Where's my surfboard, Mary?" he asked.

Mary and Arnie looked daggers at him.

"You must be Zach Loomis," I said brightly. "Zach the traveler. How do you like Toronto?"

"Toronto's cool."

"How long have you been in town?"

Arnie and Mary were eyeing me nervously.

"Since Sunday," Zach said.

"And you and Arnie have been staying here?" I asked.

Zach looked at Arnie, then at Mary who was shaking her head. "Yes…ah, no. I mean…"

Caroline hurried over to us. Once again, I was struck by her resemblance to her mother—the same chiseled features, fair skin and lively green eyes. "Pat, I would've come over sooner, but Father Fred was talking my ear off. It's so good of you to come."

"Can we have a word in private?" I gestured to include Arnie, Mary and Zach.

Zach took a step back. "I have a train to catch."

I placed a light hand on his wrist. "This won't take long."

"Zach, your train doesn't leave for three hours, and your dad is driving you to the station." Caroline pointed to a door beside the bar. "We'll go into the kitchen."

She paused at the kitchen door. "Troy," she called out, "we're having a short meet-up in the kitchen. Look after our guests please."

I excused myself and headed to the washroom. While I was in there, I made a call on my cell.

In the kitchen, I took a stool beside Zach at the butcher-block island, and got right down to business. "Arnie and Zach, you've both been in Toronto since Sunday. Luella met you at the airport, and you both returned here with her. You've been staying here for the past few days."

Caroline stared at her son, then at her brother. "Arnie, you knew about Mom all along!"

Zach's eyes were darting around the room.

Arnie lifted his chin. "I flew in on Sunday and stayed with friends for a few days. Zach got in on Tuesday."

"A yellow surfboard was leaning against the living room wall when I dropped by on Monday," I said. "Luella wouldn't have had any use for a surfboard. But, Arnie, you run a surf shop."

"That's my board," Zach blurted out. "I bought it at Uncle Arnie's shop."

Caroline's green eyes were blazing as she turned to her son. "So, you lied about planting trees, Zach. You were visiting your uncle on Vancouver Island. You took the same flight on Sunday, but you walked into this house soon after your dad and I arrived on Tuesday. You told me you'd just got into town."

Zach hung his head.

Caroline went on. "Zach, your Nana called me last week and asked how you were. I told her you were fine, but I knew she had something on her mind. She said you'd called asking her for money. You told her you'd been in an accident and needed work done on your car. So she wired you $5,000."

I saw the back door open, just a little, but nobody came into the house.

"Luella must have been a victim of one of those granny scams," I said. "Seniors get a call from someone pretending to be their grandchild who needs help. They send money, sometimes a lot."

"It was a scam all right." Caroline's eyes were troubled. "But a stranger wasn't behind it. You made that call, Zach, didn't you? Your grandmother recognized your voice. And she realized what you were up to when I told her you don't own a car. You're taking trains and planes on your travels this year."

Zach was blinking back tears. "We were just—"

"Taking advantage of a woman who loved you." Caroline shook her head. "To think I raised a son who would fleece his own grandmother."

She glared at her brother. "Runs in the family."

Troy stepped into the kitchen. "People are starting to leave," he said. "Everything all right in here?"

Caroline waved him away. "We won't be long, dear."

I turned to Mary. "Meanwhile you were here, keeping an eye on Luella. How did you land this job, Mary?"

Arnie threw Mary a warning look, but she didn't seem to notice. "Luella ran a newspaper ad looking for a housekeeper and Arnie had me apply. Luella and I hit it off from the get-go."

Arnie shook his head. "That's a load of bull!"

"Tell us what really happened on Sunday," I said.

"Mary," Arnie growled.

She closed her eyes for a few moments. "Luella came back from the airport with Arnie and Zach," she began. "I saw she was upset. She told me to have dinner ready for seven, and spent the rest of the afternoon in her study."

"So, you didn't go out with friends after all," I said.

"Mary's got it all wrong!" Arnie shouted.

Zach hung his head.

"Luella was quiet at dinner," Mary continued. "Afterwards, I served coffee in the living room. Luella poured brandy. Then she blasted Arnie and Zach for the story they'd cooked up about the car accident."

Arnie raised an eyebrow. "*We* cooked up? Pitching that story was your idea, Mary."

"Go on, Mary." Caroline was barely containing her fury.

"Then Luella turned on me," Mary said. "She'd figured out that Arnie and I knew each other. She accused me of spying on her. Maybe that was the idea in the beginning, but Luella and I became friends. I really liked her."

Mary glared at Arnie. "She called us a pack of leeches. Said she was calling her lawyer in the morning. She was going to write Arnie out of her will. Then she picked up the long poker by the fireplace and started waving it around."

"Nana was right," Zach whimpered. "We *are* leeches. Uncle Arnie told Nana to put down the poker. He said someone could get hurt. He tried to take it away from her, but she held on. He jerked it away from her and she went flying backward."

"Her head hit the mantelpiece," Arnie said. "It was an accident. A horrible accident."

Tears glistened on Mary's face. "Arnie made me tell the police that his mother was alone here on Sunday. Said it would look like she'd interrupted a robber."

"A robber who took the Papineau painting," I said.

"And Mom's diamond necklace and earrings," Caroline put in. "They're not in her jewelry box upstairs."

Mary shot Arnie a look of pure loathing.

The back door opened, and Hardy and Mancini came into the kitchen.

"We caught a few minutes of that," Hardy said, taking a stool at the island. Mancini stood by the door.

"Then you know Mom's death was an accident," Arnie said.

"You may have had no intention of killing her," Hardy said, "but you're looking at manslaughter."

"Manslaughter!" Arnie cried.

Zach looked at his watch. "I have a train to catch."

"The only place you're going, young man, is to police headquarters," Hardy said. "We'll talk to everyone there. We'll even provide transportation. Cars are on their way."

"Zach is only 18," Caroline protested.

Hardy ignored that.

"Ms. Dilworth's alibi for Sunday was our first clue to what really happened here," he said. "She told us she went out with friends that afternoon, but she couldn't produce anyone to back up her story. Later, Arnie couldn't name the friends he was staying with. And we found his fingerprints when we dusted here on Sunday. They were a match for some of the prints we took when lockers were broken into at Bay Street Fitness."

Mary looked at Arnie out of the corner of an eye. "Arnie hadn't visited his mom for a year, so his old fingerprints were long gone from here." She tossed her head. "And I didn't bother wiping down the new ones."

"We also learned that Zach Loomis flew into Toronto on Sunday, not Tuesday," Hardy said.

He looked at me and smiled. "And Ms. Tierney told us about the surfboard she saw in the living room."

"You knew all this," I said, "yet you haven't laid charges."

"Until now," he replied. "Out of respect for the Cruickshank family, we waited for the funeral to be over. Luella's late husband served as a city councilor for many years."

Mancini opened the back door, and two uniformed officers entered the kitchen.

"Ms. Dilworth and Mr. Cruickshank, you'll take the first car," Hardy said. "Mr. Loomis, you're in the second one." To the officers, he added, "Cuff them."

At the door, Arnie turned to face the room. "I never intended to hurt Mom. I loved her."

Ignoring his sister's look of outrage, he added, "She was one helluva lady."

The 13th Letter

M

The End

SWEET CORAL BELLS

By Jane Burfield

Scrolled iron gates, closed with a rusted padlock, blocked the entrance to the long drive up to the old family home. Abby ran her finger over the flaking black paint, then shook the gate. How could she get the attention of her great aunts when their phone wasn't working?

She locked her car and started to walk around the perimeter, following the fence through overgrown bushes and burrs. After 10 minutes of walking and slipping in spring mud, she stood on a tree stump, scrambled over a broken section of wrought iron, and headed toward the house.

Red brick abutted the four-square windows beneath the petticoat of gingerbread wood trim. Lace curtains hid the inside rooms. Flowers, surrounding the front porch, added color to the faded house's façade. Above the wrap-around verandah, a turret on one side of the shingled roofline added a Victorian touch.

Centered on the second story, at the front of the house, was the suicide door. As a child, Abby wondered why they had built a door that opened into nothing.

With some hesitation, she climbed the worn steps to the porch. Several broken boards were covered by empty flowerpots. How could her great aunts live here safely? She decided to have a discreet look around this weekend to see what else needed repair.

She opened the screen door and knocked, peering through the front door's glass into a dark hall. Aunt Pearl, her apron dusted in flour, opened the door and pulled her into a sweet hug. The house smelled of baking, coffee, and bees' wax. Pearl still had the same grizzled hair with mid-part, the same small frame, wrinkled face and sweet smile that Abby remembered.

"Abby! My Lord, girl, it's good to see you. I forgot you were coming this afternoon."

Hugging her again, Abby said, "Oh, Aunty Pearl, I've missed you! How are you? Where's Aunt Ruby?"

"Ruby's resting upstairs. She gets tired in the afternoon. Come in, come in! How was your drive? I've got flour all over you."

In the kitchen, whisks and flour-dusted bowls covered the table. Cooling on a rack near the window, two apple pies and a quiche made Abby's stomach rumble. She loved the old wooden cupboards and linoleum countertops. The dark green walls had felt claustrophobic when she was a girl, but she was over that now.

"I remember spending so much time with you in this kitchen. And it smells as good as it did then."

"Sit down, girl, and I'll pour us a cup of tea. I've made shortbread."

Abby scooted the calico cat from the chair and sat beside Pearl at the kitchen table. Calli, disgruntled, settled on a mat under the window next to her food bowl.

After a leisurely chat, Abby got to the reason for her visit. "So, what's going on with the property? Edie's phone message last Thursday had me worried."

"Bell is coming next week to fix our phone line, thank heavens." Pearl warmed the teapot with hot water and waited for the kettle to boil. "Your brother, Ian, has wanted us to move out for some time. He wants to develop the farmland for housing."

"I know Grandpa left it to Ian and me, but it's yours and Ruby's to use for as long as you want."

Aunt Pearl smiled. "Ian wants it now. I think his company needs this project."

"He can't do anything without my agreement, Aunt Pearl. And I won't let him force you out."

"Ian has always tried to sidestep the rules, Abby. He does what's best for himself. Always has done."

A slight scraping sounded above them. "That's Ruby, getting up. I'll help her down the stairs," Pearl said as she moved toward the kitchen door.

"Let me help."

"I'd appreciate that. I'm a bit tired from the baking."

They climbed the front hall stairs to find Pearl's twin, Ruby, hovering at the top step, looking unsteady. Her disheveled white hair seemed to mirror the vagueness in her clouded blue eyes.

Abby gave Ruby a big hug and, together with Pearl, helped her downstairs. As they moved into the kitchen, Pearl whispered, "Don't say anything about Ian. Ruby doesn't know."

Abby wasn't sure if Ruby knew much about anything current these days. Her mind seemed to be retreating to earlier times. But every now and then, she surprised the family with a cogent remark about a current topic.

***

Later, Abby walked down the driveway, unlocked the gate and brought her car up from the road, thinking that a horse and buggy would look more appropriate next to the house. Dinner was cooking in the crock pot, a delicious aroma of wine and chicken filling the kitchen. She prepared the vegetables, then set the dining room table for the three of them.

She found Ruby watching television in the lounge with Calli curled on her lap. The windowpane afghan made many years ago by their elder sister, Eleanor, lay on the sofa beside her, unnecessary on this warm spring day.

"I'm so glad you're here, Abby." Ruby patted the sofa. "Sit with me."

Pearl joined them.

Abby fingered the soft wool of the afghan.

Eleanor, the twins' older sister, had seemed distant when Abby was a child. Her sophistication probably stemmed from her marriage, a runaway one, to a preacher. After her husband died, she'd moved back in with her sisters. Her no-nonsense manner added balance to the twins' lives. She gave advice freely, even when it wasn't wanted. But that was over 40 years ago. Now she lay buried with her parents and grandparents in the little graveyard on the farm.

Suddenly, Ruby asked, "Where is Ian, Abby? Is he coming to visit?"

"Not for a few days, Ruby." Abby shared her surprise with Pearl who'd just joined them. "Do you remember seeing him last Christmas when he came for dinner?"

"Yes, I do. He's a strange one. Always has been. He walked around the whole house and yard. He even went to the family cemetery. I was surprised that he wanted to go out there when it was so cold."

"You remember that?" Pearl asked, looking surprised.

"Ian can be pushy," Ruby replied. "Not like our Abby."

***

In the front lounge after dinner, Abby and Pearl settled in to watch a British mystery series, but Ruby's mind slid into another world until bedtime. After her aunts retired, Abby looked out at the night sky. The many recent changes in her life made her yearn for the familiar simplicity of farm life. She locked the front door and went to bed. Calli joined her, settling down beside her on the quilt.

Abby slept more deeply than she had in weeks. The next morning, she awoke early to the sound of birds singing in the large oak tree outside. Wrapped up in her blue robe, she went downstairs.

She was making tea in the kitchen when her cell phone rang. She picked it up quickly before the sound woke her aunts.

"Ian! You're up early."

"Hi, Abbs. I'm driving to the farm today. Should be there by early afternoon."

"We didn't expect you for a few days," she said, "but I'm sure it will be okay. I'll tell the aunties."

"How are they today?" Ian asked. "I'm worried about them."

"They're not up yet. Pearl was busy baking yesterday, so she was tired. We had a good talk, though. Ruby was her usual self."

"They should move to a retirement home. They're too old to live alone."

"I'm not sure it's time yet, Ian. Let's talk about it when you're here. I'll look for you after lunch. And please stay for dinner."

"Good of you to invite me, Abbs. Since when are you the one to issue invitations?"

"Well, since I'm here." Abby was not looking forward to another fraught conversation with her brother. She knew Ian would be upset if she didn't support his idea of developing the land. He could be abrasive when you didn't agree with him.

After the call ended, Abby brewed tea and took a cup upstairs to Pearl in her bedroom.

"Good morning, Aunt Pearl. It's a lovely, bright day."

Pearl struggled to sit, sore from too much activity the day before. She smiled as Abby handed her the cup. "Tea always makes me feel better, my love."

"I remember you bringing my morning tea. It always helped me get moving." Abby pushed the curtains back from the window. "Ian phoned this morning. He'll be here this afternoon." She looked at her aunt's dismayed face. "I'll try to keep him from upsetting Ruby."

"Heavens," Pearl said. "He can be so pushy. Ruby and I talk about that."

"Ruby may be napping when he arrives. Hopefully, he can talk to us about his plans while she is asleep."

Pearl shook her head. "I doubt it, but we can try. Now, I must get up and feed the chickens."

"Don't worry, Aunty. I'll do that. How wicked would it be to have pie for breakfast?"

Pearl laughed.

Downstairs, Abby got the chicken feed ready, put on her sweater and went out to the coop. The chickens looked happy, strutting around their enclosure. She scattered their feed and filled their trough with fresh water from the hose. While they were eating, she collected eggs. As she shut the enclosure gate, she wondered how much longer Pearl could keep up with even these small chores she so enjoyed.

After breakfast, Abby mixed bread dough, making the kitchen smell of yeast and sunshine. She left it covered in an oiled bowl and put on her hiking boots and jacket. The farm was now just 50 acres, since her late grandfather, Charles, had sold off most of their land to nearby farms. Down the road, she could hear bulldozers shaping another new housing development. Soon, Pearl and Ruby would be the only holdouts in their area as the city rolled north.

Abby walked up the east side of the property, smiling when she saw the old hut that held farm tools. She'd used it to hide from Ian when they were children. Her brother had delighted in playing tricks on her then. She remembered how much she had wanted to pay him back, but he was always taller and stronger than she was.

She looked inside and picked up an old scythe, probably from the 18th century, and was surprised to see the blade was still sharp. Other tools were hung up or stacked against the back wall. Near the door, a shelf held dusty bottles and tins of old chemicals. The place certainly needed a cleanout and a lock on its door.

Further north, near the concession road, lay the family graveyard, no doubt covered by long grass and leaf debris. She hoped the forget-me-nots and lily of the valley had survived the winter. The cemetery had been another favorite escape of hers.

She continued walking, the fields bringing her peace. Nearby, she saw the stream, much smaller in its ditch than 30 years ago. Nothing had been more fun than poking the bottom mud with a stick until Ian started to poke her. The stream fed a pond and beside the pond lay the icehouse. Cut into the hillside for insulation, it had been used to keep milk and meat cold in the summer. On hot July days, stealing ice chips was a glorious way to cool off.

Soon Abby came to an area she could not access; dense shrubbery blocked the way to the back fields. She must arrange to have it cleared. She cut back toward the farmhouse, and after removing her muddy boots, went to the kitchen to check her bread dough. Pouring herself a glass of water, she was startled it didn't smell of sulfur. The new hook-up to the township water lines, replacing the well, made for better water. So much about the farm had changed with the encroaching reach of the city, but it still reflected the simple lifestyle she loved.

She began to write down a long list of tasks in her notebook. She must talk to Pearl about hiring a handyman to do the repairs. Hopefully, it wouldn't cost too much.

She finished kneading the bread and made a baker's dozen of rolls. Calli, the cat, led her into the lounge for morning coffee with the aunties.

Abby told them about her hefty maintenance list. "Perhaps I can ask Ian for help. We could start this weekend."

Pearl looked skeptical. "I doubt he'll do much. He's never been interested in fixing up this home. But we'll manage, Abby, like we always have."

As Abby made soup for lunch, she wondered how she could improve the aunties' nutrition. She knew there were days when they lived on sandwiches. She must investigate food delivery services.

She'd changed jobs recently and was now working remotely, so she would have more time to visit them, but she doubted it would ever be enough. She could move in with the aunties if they'd have her, but she didn't want them to lose their independence—and she worried about losing her own. What would be the best path for all of them?

Pearl pulled out some cheddar sold at a nearby farm stall, and Abby sliced tomatoes for their sandwiches. After lunch, Ruby went upstairs to nap, while Pearl and Abby sat in the kitchen, waiting for Ian to arrive.

"I know why he's coming. He's been talking about development for the last year," Pearl said. "What should I say to him?"

"What do *you* want to do, Pearl?" Abby asked. "Living here on your own has become difficult for both of you."

"I know, Abby. I've thought about moving, but we've lived here most of our lives. I doubt Ruby would be happy in a retirement home. I know I won't. I just don't know."

Abby looked out the front window and saw Ian getting out of his car. He looked annoyed.

"Well, look who's here. Don't agree to anything you don't want to do. It's perfectly fair for you to think over any of his ideas," she said.

Ian pulled open the screen door and walked into the house. He handed Pearl a wrapped bunch of flowers. "These are for you and Aunt Ruby." He air-kissed Abby before seating himself at the table.

Well, at least he's trying, Abby thought.

"That driveway is terrible," Ian said. "I thought I'd lose an axle. But it smells good in here. Any leftovers from lunch?"

"We can always find lunch for you, Ian. Abby baked rolls and made vegetable soup," Pearl said.

"Energetic of you, Abbs. Maybe we can talk while I enjoy your cooking." Ian placed some files from his briefcase on the table. "I think you are finding this old farmhouse a lot of work, Pearl. I've given it some thought."

Indicating the files, he said, "Here's some research on retirement homes. There's one near here that looks nice."

"Finish your meal, Ian." Pearl smoothed her apron and sat beside him with a warm cup of tea.

Ian bit into a fresh roll and started to talk again, but a look from Pearl left him silent.

Abby admired her aunt's ability to exude authority, even wearing an apron. All those years of teaching young dancers, no doubt, had honed her sense of power.

Sunlight through the kitchen window lit Ian's fair hair like a halo. His light blue eyes stood out in his tanned, weathered face. If he were an angel, he'd be a hard-used one. He looked much older than his 41 years.

Ian sipped the last few spoonsful of soup before pushing his bowl aside. He turned to face Pearl. "I want to talk to you about moving somewhere more comfortable. Abby and I are worried…"

"No, Ian. This is on you," Abby said.

"Can you be quiet and listen for a minute, Abbs?" Ian growled.

"Let's hear him out, Abby, dear," said Pearl.

"When I visited last time, Pearl, I saw so many things that needed fixing. Time catches up with us. I'm worried that you can't manage this property anymore. You need to move into a place where you can relax and be taken care of. Aunt Ruby, especially."

"I appreciate your concern, Ian. But I'm managing. Before you came, Abby and I were talking about hiring a handyman to do some repairs."

"It needs more than fixing up, Aunt Pearl. I almost went through a board on the porch. The handrail on the steps is loose. I had trouble getting over the ruts in the driveway when I drove up to the house." He looked around the kitchen. "I can see wood rot in that wall," he said, pointing near the sink. "Termites, I think."

"No, just carpenter ants. They always reemerge in spring." She looked a little uncertainly at Abby. "We'll spray again. It can be fixed. Can't it, Abby?"

Ian huffed when Abby said, "I'm sure it can, Aunty."

"Think of the cost of fixing this house up! A fortune. And after Ruby and you leave, it'll be pulled down."

"I'm sure our neighbors will help out. That will keep the costs low," Pearl said.

"Most of the neighboring farmers have left." Ian stood and swore when he accidentally kicked Calli's food bowl. "And where are you going to get the money for repairs?" He stood behind Pearl.

Pushing back her chair and forcing him to step away, Pearl said, "I hear Ruby upstairs. Hush now, Ian. She finds the thought of moving very upsetting."

She went upstairs to help Ruby come down.

Abby leaned toward Ian. In a low voice, she said, "Sit down for heaven's sake! Why the big push to get them to move now?"

"My partners and I," Ian said pretentiously, "have an opportunity to sell the land at a top price to a developer. But it must be now. When we split the money from the sale, Abbs, you and I will be left with a fortune. And I need my share. Now."

"It's our aunts' right to stay here as long as they like. It's in Grandpa's will. And if the land is valuable now, it will be even more valuable in five or ten years. We should let them stay here."

Ian pushed his chair back violently just as Pearl and Ruby came through the door. Ruby looked alarmed, but Pearl gave her a reassuring nod and led her to the kitchen table.

"Hi, Aunt Ruby," Ian said, picking up his chair. He kissed her cheek. "We were just talking about plans for the future."

Ruby sat in her customary spot facing the window. "Hello, Ian. I didn't know you were coming to visit today." She absently brushed her cheek. "What plans are you talking about?"

"No need to worry about them, Ruby," Abby said, glaring at Ian.

"It's time to think about moving you into a nice retirement home," Ian said, glaring back at her. "There's one in this area. I bet some of your friends are there."

"But why, Ian? We're happy here, aren't we, Pearl?"

Pearl nodded reassuringly at Ruby. "This is our home, our lifelong home. We belong here."

Abby put an arm around Ruby. "You can stay here, Ruby. Don't worry."

"My friend, Tony, is coming here this afternoon. We have a proposition for you both. At least hear us out," Ian said.

Pearl took Ruby's hand and squeezed it gently. "I guess we could listen to your idea, Ian. What do you think, Abby?"

"I think, you should do whatever you want to do," Abby said. She looked down the driveway as a red sports car rolled slowly up to the front door. "Your partner is here, Ian. I suggest you let him in."

As Ian left the kitchen, Ruby whispered, "We have secrets here, Pearl. We *need* to stay."

"Don't worry, dear," Pearl said.

"Remember what Eleanor told us. About Inge's letter. We must stay here to look after that. We can't leave."

Abby looked at the two sisters. She surprised herself by saying, "I've been thinking. I could move in with you if you want. I've just started a new job, a remote one." To Ruby's puzzled look, she added, "I can work over the computer from here. I don't have to go into the office."

They heard the front door open.

Ian led Tony into the kitchen, introducing him.

Abby looked at the too-smartly-dressed man smiling too broadly at everyone. His slick hairstyle reminded her of reality show actors. Calli came into the room and sniffed Tony's gabardine trouser cuffs before moving into a corner, her eyes narrowed. With the manners of her upbringing, Pearl invited Tony to sit.

"How long have you lived here, ladies?" Tony continued to smile brightly. "It's a lovely old home. Although your driveway is like a roller-coaster."

Pearl busied herself at the sink, pouring hot water to warm the teapot. Ruby looked surprised, as few people addressed questions to her now.

"Our family settled here in the late 1880s," Abby said. "My great-grandfather emigrated here from England in 1882. Our property was far outside the city then."

"Original settlers," Tony said.

Ruby eyed him, but didn't say anything.

"It's a big piece of land. Lots of development going on around you," he continued. "Have you thought about doing something with it?"

"We enjoy being here," Pearl said as she poured out the water in the warmed pot and put five teabags in before refilling it with boiling water. "We grow our own vegetables and raise chickens. Lots of eggs. We are quite self-sufficient."

Tony looked around the table. "I believe you lease some of your land to farmers?"

"They rent just over 40 acres for crops, and for pasture," Pearl said. "That brings in some income. It's quiet here, even with the housing construction up the road." She energetically swirled the tea in the pot.

"I don't want to sell. Or move," Ruby said sharply.

Scowling at Ian, Pearl said, "Ruby, we're not moving anywhere now." She handed mugs to the men and put a Wedgwood cup and saucer in front of her sister.

"I don't like strong tea, Pearl," Tony said. "It bothers my stomach."

Abby hoped Tony's veneers would be covered in tannin scum.

"I need to check on the chickens, gentlemen," Pearl said. "We can discuss this later."

"I'm staying overnight, Auntie," Ian said. He eyed Tony. "Can you stay for dinner?"

"I'm not sure. There's a storm forecast. It will be rough, driving back on dark roads in the rain."

"I've heard there's a wind warning," Ian said. "We can put you up tonight as well, can't we, Abbs?"

"If you leave now, Tony, you could get home before it begins," Abby said.

"Don't be silly, Abby. Of course he'll stay," Ian said.

"You'd better show him to the guest bedroom then, Ian. Get him some towels and find a spare toothbrush in the linen closet." She noticed Pearl and Ruby seemed less than pleased.

Abby set the dining table with the better china and glasses that evening, hoping a more formal meal would help them manage Tony. She set a fire to combat the evening chill and found a bottle of red wine in the cellar. Stuffed loin of pork, roast potatoes and minted peas reflected childhood meals here. Pearl's applesauce, put down last fall, was fragrant in an old-fashioned beaded glass compote.

After apple pie and tea, Ruby and Pearl went into the lounge while Abby cleaned up the kitchen. Neither Ian nor Tony had offered to help, but she was just as glad not to have to make conversation with them. She heard them go upstairs to Ian's room to discuss their development plans.

She draped the damp tea towel over the stove handle and went to her room for a few quiet minutes to think about strategies for tomorrow. Tony seemed to be the dominant partner. What exactly was his relationship with Ian?

She pulled out her crochet work. Eleanor had taught her how to crochet when she was a child and keeping her hands busy allowed her to think freely. She settled back into the rocking chair to gaze at the painting on her bedroom wall. It was of two women walking on a softly lit beach. Both had silky blond hair and a Danish complexion like her own. Extraordinary light glowed from the canvas. How had the artist made the paint appear so translucent? She felt her anxiety lessen under the magic of its art.

A hum of conversation came from the next room; Ian and Tony were talking. Pushing aside her qualms about eavesdropping, she quietly moved her chair nearer to the door so she could listen.

"How can we make the old ladies move?" Tony asked. "There's a fortune here for the taking. Two developers are interested in participating."

"The land will sell itself," Ian said. "If I could get Abby to agree, she could talk the aunties into moving. They listen to her, Tony."

Tony walked up and down the room, stepping on the squeaky floorboards on each pass. "You need to make this work, Ian. I'm tired of waiting for you to pay what you owe me. And the interest is growing."

"Abby has to agree as well. We both inherit the land when the aunties move."

Too many thoughts and the residual smell of cigarette smoke from her brother's room made Abby's sleep elusive. What should she do for the aunties? What could Ian do to get out of his financial mess? And what was the "treasure" Ruby had referred to cryptically for years? She would ask Ruby in the morning when she was more lucid.

Wind blew hard that night, rattling the loose gingerbread on the roof above her room. Slashes of rain could be seen in the lightning flashes outside her window. A crack of thunder scared Calli, who hid under her bed.

Abby went downstairs to check that the doors and windows were secure, then sat in the kitchen, looking out at the rain strafing the glass. At least she wouldn't have to worry about watering the plants for a few days. When she returned to her bedroom, she noticed the bathroom nightlight was off. Another flash of lightning made her hope they wouldn't lose power.

In the morning, the storm clouds were gone, and the sun shone brightly. She put on slippers and a tartan robe and crossed to the window. Looking east, she saw several boards had blown off the chicken coop. She hoped there wasn't any damage to the main house.

She quietly opened her bedroom door and listened, but no one else appeared to be up. Downstairs, she had a quick look out on the porch. Flowerpots and several chairs had blown over, but there didn't appear to be any serious structural damage. In the yard, branches from the old oak trees littered the drive and yard.

Calli came running down the stairs to give her head butts in the kitchen. She ate some kibble and groomed herself, a good sign she was over last night's trauma. Abby turned on the Keurig coffee machine for a much-needed first cup. She'd given it to the aunties for Christmas.

At the kitchen table, she got out her laptop and was pleased to see the internet was working, albeit slowly. She read about the storm and researched repair companies.

She took her second cup of coffee onto the porch. The sun had started to radiate warmth through the cool air. What should she do?

Back in the kitchen, Abby found Tony looking at the coffee machine with focused lust. As she made him a cup, she asked about his plans.

"After getting permits from the township, we will develop the land in parcels, eight or ten houses at a time," Tony said. "We might be able to finance it without a developer. That would be ideal."

"If and when we agree to sell, isn't there a risk in not using a developer?"

"We can make more profit by doing it ourselves. I understand from Ian that you have an equal interest in the land. What do you think, Abby?"

She sat at the kitchen table, turning her mug in her hands. She was surprised to be asked, and she knew she would have to answer carefully. "I'm sure Ian has told you that the aunts have a lifetime interest. It is their family home. I'm not opposed to some development down the road, but I want them to stay here as long as they like."

"This area will be fully developed within ten years or so. Your land is worth a fortune."

"I want to hold off. Our land will only get more valuable," Abby said firmly.

Tony looked annoyed. He walked over to the porch steps, giving Calli a firm push with his foot to move her out of his way. He pulled a packet of cigarettes out of his pocket and lit one with a silver lighter. "You don't have a choice. Ian owes money."

Such a hypocrite, she thought. She couldn't let him know she knew he was the money lender. "Gambling?" she asked.

"That and other matters."

Abby didn't want to know what other matters. She suspected drugs. She needed time to think.

"Pulling the storm debris off the drive will be a big job," she said. "Local roads will take time to clear. I'm afraid you'll have to stay another night."

Tony inhaled deeply. "I'm fed up. Ian needs money immediately. He does not have a choice. And so, neither do you."

"That's Ian's problem, Tony." She turned away to leave. "And don't smoke in the house."

He looked at his burning cigarette. "Fire is dangerous in old buildings, Abby." He flicked his lighter twice. "Tell Ian."

He threw his cigarette into the wet garden, went indoors and upstairs to his bedroom.

***

Pearl and Ian came down around nine. Abby asked Ian and Tony to help move the bigger branches off the drive and to inspect the outbuildings for damage. A limb had blown onto the front roof. She decided to check the roof and tend to the chickens while the aunties listened to weather reports. Another heavy storm was predicted to land that night.

Abby ran upstairs and got dressed. Carefully she opened the suicide door so she could see the roof. The fallen branch had indeed shifted some shingles. She gathered her tools and tethered herself with a rope attached to the staircase banister. Taking a deep breath, she stepped out onto the roof.

She managed to tack down a tarp over the damage. Breathing easier now, she climbed back into the house and locked the door.

Tony was standing in the hall outside his bedroom.

"Why is there a door there, and nothing on the other side?" he asked. "Has anyone ever fallen out there?"

"Pearl says great grandfather was going to build a gallery out there, but avoided paying taxes by never finishing the house. Only one person ever fell. He got nasty when he was courting Ruby and Grandpa literally threw him out. He broke his leg but survived."

"Wow," Tony said. "I hope you keep it locked."

"Of course we do," Abby said. "We're careful."

After lunch, Ruby looked at the plants in the porch beds. "The lily of the valley is growing well, Pearl," she said. "Let's put our herb garden in a little early this year. I want to make some tinctures again."

Pearl smiled at Ruby's enthusiasm.

When the men came out onto the porch, Calli hissed at Tony. She swatted at him with outstretched claws.

"Damned cat." Blood speckled Tony's bare leg above his ankle. He went indoors to wash the scratches.

"That man is repellent," Abby said. "And he's presumptuous. What's going on, Ian?"

He shrugged. "I'm in trouble. I need money. And soon." He glanced at her, knowing he would see her disappointment yet again.

"I overheard your conversation with Tony last night. How are you going to fix this?"

"Selling some of this land would get me out of a tight spot right now. The aunties don't need it. I can't think of anything else. Tony wants his money. And he can be really nasty about debt."

Abby didn't want to think about what that meant. "I wish I could help, but I don't have much money. I've just started a new job. Could you mortgage your home?"

"Already mortgaged. I lease my car. I thought about Mother's jewelry, but it's not worth enough. I have nothing."

Abby moved to the porch railing. Mixed emotions roiled inside her—resentment for the many times when Ian had gotten into trouble, and his unfailing ability to lose money or overspend. Would it ever stop? She was tired of having her life upended by his problems. At times, she wished he would move to the other side of the world and leave her in peace.

"What are you thinking, Abby?"

She shook her head. "I'm mulling over what you can do. And I'm tired of your drama."

"I just need to find my way out of this one. I won't do it again."

She shrugged. He'd made the same promise many times. "Let's talk to our lawyer. He might come up with an idea."

"I already have," Ian said. "This farm is the only way."

Abby turned to face him and was startled to see Ruby through the front screen door. How long had she been there?

Abby motioned to Ian to be quiet until Ruby moved away toward the kitchen. How much had she heard? What would she remember?

Ian retreated into the house to get some papers, but Tony came back out onto the porch and sat in the yellow Muskoka chair.

"I made some calls," he said. "We have a meeting with the planning committee tomorrow morning. One of the developers, Ben Dixon, will be there."

"Planning committee?" Abby said. "Aren't you getting a little ahead of yourself? Unless the aunties agree, they will not be moving."

"We know there's a problem thanks to that blasted will. We'll find a way around that. We're getting information, nothing else," Tony said. "Look, I don't need Ian to make this deal. You have an equal share. And the aunties trust you."

"What do you mean?"

"I think you know. You and I can leave Ian out of the negotiations. He'll get his money when we sell."

"I can't do that, Tony! I won't do that to my brother, or to our aunts." She sat on the bench, her shoulders rigid.

"It's just a thought, Abbs."

"My name is Abigail to you. You presume too much!"

Rising quickly from the bench, she went inside and sat in the kitchen, trying to control her temper. How could this mess be solved?

Sensing her distress, Calli ran to her. The little cat jumped onto her lap with soft purrs. A few minutes later, she heard Ian and Tony leave.

She needed to talk to the aunts.

She found Ruby in the parlor reading old letters. Envelopes and notes had been pulled from a large basket and lay in piles on the floor. Some seemed to be old cards, yellowing bills, and recipes. One pile, in her lap, was still wrapped with pink ribbon. The room smelled of roses, Eleanor's favorite scent.

"What are you reading, Aunt Ruby?"

"Some of Eleanor's letters. She kept in touch with all our relatives."

"Correspondence like that was part of a more gracious world. I wish my generation still wrote real letters, and not just emails," Abby said as she sat down beside Ruby.

"You are such a dear, Abigail. You always were."

Abby leaned over and gave her aunt a gentle hug. "I treasured my time with all of you. Summers here when I was a child kept my world working. Whenever I was upset, you would sing 'White Coral Bells' to me."

"Upon a slender stalk," Ruby crooned. "Lily of the valley outside my garden wall."

"That song always calmed me. Their scent reminds me of you."

"You were bullied at school, weren't you?" Ruby asked.

"Yes. I was miserable. Mom and Dad didn't realize it. They weren't around much. After they died, Ian and I managed on our own."

"We always looked forward to your visits. Eleanor was particularly glad to see you for the summer. She said you resembled your mother."

"And here I am again, visiting," Abby said with a laugh. "Do you need any help with these papers?"

"I'm enjoying sorting them."

Pearl came in and sat on the sofa arm next to her sister. "Are those Eleanor's letters?"

Abby nodded.

Pearl picked up the bundle Ruby was holding. "These are from Inge, your mother's cousin, Abby. She wrote as often as she could during the war."

"She had beautiful handwriting. And she wrote in English, thank heavens," Ruby said. "Eleanor kept them all in order."

"Was that when Denmark was occupied by the Germans?"

"Yes, they just marched in and took over." Pearl passed the ribbon-wrapped package to Abby.

"Inge's father was killed by the Germans," said Ruby. "He was in the underground, fighting against the Huns, as he called them."

Abby was surprised at how lucid Ruby was. Talking about the past was easier for her than the present.

"In 1943, the Germans became more aggressive in Denmark. The Nazis confiscated art and sent it to Berlin. Inge secretly smuggled out a number of family paintings. They were rolled up in a package to us along with information on the German troops. We were lucky it got through."

"What happened to the paintings?" Abby asked.

"One of my favorites is in your room," Pearl said. "The two women walking on a beach. We have another one in my bedroom. The rest are in Eleanor's old blanket box in Ruby's bedroom. It has a secret compartment." She sorted through the letters. "In this one, Inge asks us to hide the paintings until after the war. In her next letter, the thirteenth one, she asks us to keep them hidden. There was some controversy about how Inge's family got the paintings out of Denmark," she added.

The letters explained so much, Abby realized. The art must be the treasure Ruby talked about. And it might be the answer to Ian's immediate need for money.

Ruby went for her usual nap after lunch. Abby continued listing the jobs that needed to be worked on immediately. She'd look at the barn, the cemetery and the icehouse, too, out of sheer curiosity.

Bright sunlight lit her way there. Cut into a hill, the icehouse looked intact though wet, but it would dry out quickly. Memories of stealing chips of ice from the blocks cut and saved during the winter to preserve food in summer heat took her back 30 years.

The exterior of the barn looked good. Calli ran inside as Abby opened the barn door. She smelled dried sweet grain, evoking more childhood memories. After securely latching the door, she walked to the cemetery. Calli seemed delighted to be exploring with her.

The cemetery, a rough rectangle around a large walnut tree, looked peaceful if ill-kempt. There were more graves than she remembered. Her favorite stone was a carved cherub marking the resting place of babies. Too many babies. She remembered helping Ruby remove lichen and washing the gravestones when she was a kid. Next week, she'd come back out here with the scythe and plant pansies and daisies to go with the forsythia and lilac bushes.

Calli played in last fall's leaves. She began to eat a small lily of the valley leaf, but Abby stopped her.

"That will make you sick," she told the cat.

With very wet shoes and a long list of to-dos, she headed back to the house.

Pearl was rocking in the porch swing with Ruby. "You're wet from your knees down." She looked at Calli, washing herself on the mat in the sun. "And Calli, you look like you've had an excellent adventure."

"We both have, Pearl. I love this place."

"We had good times here. Not always. Farming is hard work. But we have so many good memories with you kids."

Abby heard the front door open. Ian and Tony came out onto the porch.

"Were you able to get to your meeting with the developer?" she asked.

"Yes, at a coffee shop up the road. Their company can't take on another project for the next year," Ian said.

"But I can negotiate with the senior partner. I know him well," Tony said. "We'll get your property sold soon."

"That's not your decision to make," Abby said.

Tony moved a step closer to her. "You need to agree, Abby! It's best for the aunts. And it's imperative for Ian and me. We all benefit."

"How dare you, Tony! You have no say in this decision," Abby insisted.

Pearl looked at Ruby's white face and turned to Ian. "Let's talk later. Maybe we can work this out. Dinner's at six."

Tony quickly disappeared upstairs. Reluctantly, Ian followed him.

"Do you think he'll leave tonight?" Pearl asked Abby.

Ruby looked frightened. "We must do something. We've always managed in the past."

"The women in our family are like your lily of the valley, Ruby. We appear fragile, but we can be surprisingly resilient," Abby said.

"I'll arrange some flowers for the table tonight. We'll make dinner special," Ruby said.

That evening, the dining room evoked the genteel steel of farm families. Stalks of white bells and soft greenery sat in a small vase at the center of the mahogany table. The roast chicken was simple but delicious.

Ian helped Abby clear the table and bring in the coffee in demitasses.

"I can't drink that coffee. I'll be up all night," Tony said.

Ruby looked at Pearl, and said, "We'll make you our special coffee. You'll like it."

"As long as there's no caffeine."

"You won't have to worry about that, Tony. We make a special brew for our guests like you." Ruby giggled.

Tony didn't look at them as he held out his small cup. "That's one way you can be useful, I suppose."

As the aunts left, Abby turned to Tony. "How dare you treat Ruby and Pearl like that! They've earned any peace they want. And you can't bully your way into upending their world!"

"Abby, be quiet!" Ian put his coffee cup down, his hands shaking. "We can't do anything for more than a year. The developer said he couldn't start till next year."

"You be quiet, Ian. You've caused enough trouble." Abby poked at the fire hard enough to cause sparks to fly up the chimney.

She went into the kitchen to find her aunts.

"We're taking care of the coffee, Abby," Pearl said, reaching for a coffee pod for the Keurig.

"That man is a boor, Pearl," Ruby said. "Charles would not have liked him."

When Tony's special brew was ready, Pearl added caramel creamer and Abby carried it into the dining room.

As light faded from the sky, the group continued to argue about Tony's proposition. Finally, Abby stood up, turned to face Tony and said, "That's enough! We will contact you when and if we want to sell. I suggest we go to bed now. We're all tired and upset."

With a sly look toward Abby, Tony pulled out his lighter, flicked it twice, and left the room.

Ian appeared dejected as he went upstairs.

Abby and Pearl helped Ruby up to bed, but by the sounds of her footsteps in her room and the hall, she was having trouble settling down.

They cleared the table but decided to leave the dishes for the morning.

Before going to bed, they readied the house for the threatened storm that night. Calli stayed downstairs, settling into her favorite chair on Eleanor's afghan in the lounge.

The storm was intense. At midnight, lightning struck a local hydro pole, and their power went out.

Upstairs, Abby was again repelled by smoke from Tony's room. About an hour later, she heard him rush into the bathroom to vomit.

She waited for him to stop and knocked on the bathroom door. "Do you need anything, Tony?"

"You bitches have already made me sick. You'll hear from my lawyer soon."

He opened the bathroom door and walked unsteadily through the darkness toward his bedroom.

Lightning lit up the hall briefly. Abby saw Calli, crouching to attack their guest. The hall turned black again just before she saw Tony lunge in the direction of his bedroom door.

He screamed.

Abby groped her way through the dark hallway.

The suicide door was standing open.

Through the bursts of lightning, she saw Tony lying in the flower garden among the new lily of the valley plants.

***

The police had many questions about Tony's death. Why was the upstairs door not locked?

In a small, sorrowful voice, Ruby said she had unlocked it to get some fresh air. Tony's cigarette smoke had made her feel nauseous.

Later, after the police left and power was restored, the family gathered in the kitchen. Ian sighed deeply. He no longer owed Tony money, but he didn't know if anyone else would come after him.

Pearl sat next to her twin, patting her hand and sipping tea. "I wouldn't use the Keurig just yet," she told Abby. "It needs to be cleaned."

That's when Abby noticed the empty vase beside it, the vase that had held the lily of the valley flowers the previous night.

Ruby had a renewed gleam in her eyes as she stroked Calli. Abby wasn't sure when Pearl or Ruby had replaced the key in the lock of the suicide door, but it was now securely latched. She decided to get a quote on having that upper gallery constructed.

Safety first, after all.

Raising her orange juice glass in a toast, Ruby said, "Well, that'll teach them not to mess with the women of this family."

Pearl hugged her.

Abby smiled. She knew the aunties could take care of themselves, and she looked forward to living here with them for as long as they wanted.

The 13th Letter

M

The End

THE CURSE SCROLL

By Cheryl Freedman

The day started out like most days at Goslin & Marlowe, Finders & Private Investigators (Specializing in Missing Royalty and Strayed Magic Items) in Arkady, one of the Seven Kingdoms: me trying to write up notes from a previous case, and Marlowe, my partner, muttering and cursing as he tried to finesse a new sleight of hand card trick. It wasn't so much his muttering and cursing that bothered me; it was his periodic "Hey, babe, cast your peepers over this" interruptions.

On one hand, I had to admire his persistence. Cheating at cards is difficult without opposing thumbs, which Marlowe, being a ferret (albeit a two-foot-tall bipedal, talking ferret) lacks. But enough was enough.

"Marlowe, this is the third bloody time you've interrupted me. I'd like to finish what I'm doing...if you don't mind, of course."

Marlowe, ever cheerful, ever oblivious to sarcasm in any form, continued, "No, really, babe, I've almost hit the jackpot this time. Lemme show you." Tossing the deck of cards on my desk, he leaped onto his chair, which he had shoved over without my invitation.

I sighed and resigned myself to the interruption. I did a lot of that with Marlowe around. Nothing I could say or do would deter him from bothering me once he had his mind set on something.

"Go ahead."

Shoving my neatly arranged notes to one side, ignoring the pages that had fallen to the floor, he dealt five cards to each of us. "Poker, toots!"

Mab's tits! I must have seen his poker cheat trick a million times already. Sighing again, I reached for a card, looked at it, and settled in for what I hoped would not be a long session. In fact, writing up that case, boring as it was, was actually calling seductively to me.

I got my wish. After three or four minutes, Marlowe smirked and crowed, "Four kings. Beat that, toots."

"Not a chance, Marlowe. Let me see." I reached to turn over the cards arrayed in front of him, studiously ignoring his smirk. He had obviously cheated—his goal in life was to become a card sharp—because I was pretty sure there was a king in the discard pile. I just couldn't figure out how he'd done it without opposable thumbs and with me watching him like a hawk.

Suddenly, he pricked up his ears. "Crap, we're in dutch now," he muttered as he dropped his cards and vaulted over the desk to cower behind my chair. "I'm not cowering; I've taken strategic cover," came his sotto voce comment.

I had just enough time to look at his discarded hand before the door flew open and in swept Dilnavaz, my fairy godmother.

She slowly and majestically made her way to the client's chair, pushing Marlowe's vacated ferret-sized chair out of the way with a disdainful sniff. Most of the time, my godmother is an elegant fairy of substance: a scant four foot ten inches tall with a plump but well-proportioned body; an ageless face with a peaches-and-cream complexion and deep blue twinkly eyes; and pure white hair arranged in some kind of complicated up-do that could only be accomplished by magic. Where Dilnavaz breaks the fairy godmother mold is in her fondness for, number one, ale and wine, and number two, gambling. Not necessarily in that order, but usually both together.

When she is in her cups, her peaches-and-cream complexion curdles, her hair looks like the aftermath of a goose fight, and her baby blues turn into rabid reds. And while she still walks in her slow, stately fashion, it's obvious that this is the only way she can keep her balance.

Unfortunately for me, this is usually when she ends up on my doorstep with some rather odd and often unpleasant task for me.

Don't get me wrong. I adore my fairy godmother. Most of the time, that is. Today, however, I sensed was going to be an exception. I stood to greet her anyway.

"Goslin, child, I have a job for you," she said, thrusting a much-folded wad of paper at me.

"I'm fine, Dilnavaz dear, and so is Marlowe. Thank you for asking. And how are you?"

"That's enough from you, child," she snapped. Then she glanced at the cards scattered on my desk and sniffed. "I smell a rat," she pronounced, enunciating very carefully.

I could hear the gnashing of tiny teeth behind my chair.

"Don't start," I warned her, but it was too late. Marlowe—all two feet of him—exploded out from behind my chair, hissing furiously. I reached down, caught him by the scruff, and held him firmly under my arm. Stepping away from my desk, I grabbed my godmother with my other hand, dragged her around the desk, and pushed her into my own chair. Then tossing Marlowe into his small chair, I plopped myself into the client's chair.

"Drunken floozy," Marlowe spat.

"Stinking excuse for a prince," she returned.

Prince? Marlowe a prince? That little weasel never let slip anything about his background.

"Well, I don't get caught cheating at cards, ya grifter," he snarled.

"You can't even play cards properly."

"Yeah? Well, yes I can, and where are the opposing thumbs you promised me, ya double-dealing boozehound."

"Nonsense. And I do not cheat."

"Enough!" I shouted.

It was time for me to jump into the fray, or it would have continued for another three days. For some reason I couldn't fathom, Dilnavaz and Marlowe hated each other. I think it must have all started before my time when Marlowe was possibly something other than what he is now—a two-foot-tall walking, talking ferret with a penchant for fedoras and strange slang, who just happened to decide one day that he was meant to be a P.I. He might once have been a prince, or a frog, or, for all I knew, always a ferret, but for better or worse, he was now my partner.

"Now that we have the pleasantries out of the way, Dilnavaz darling, why are you here?"

"What? I can't come visit my favorite goddaughter?"

Marlowe snorted.

"Of course, you can. But why are you really here?"

"Well, I need your help."

"Well, strike me speechless," came the hissed comment from next to me.

"Do continue. Please tell me you aren't in trouble with one of your questionable cronies."

Dilnavaz is a terrible poker player; her face always gives away what she is thinking. And I had guessed correctly.

After briefly hemming and hawing, she gave up and got to the point. "I need you to find something for me, dear."

She hesitated a moment, which gave Marlowe a chance to mutter, "Get on with it, ya dumb dame," loud enough for her to hear.

"What do you need *us* to find, and more importantly, who's putting you up to this? Because otherwise, you would have just shown up as you usually do, told me to do something, balked at the cost as always, and then everything would proceed."

My godmother wriggled her tush into a more comfortable position, sighed, and started. "You remember King Raoul of Carcassonne?"

"Yeah, Randy Raoul. Quite the object of gossip for a few years, what with his penchant for extra-marital rumpy-pumpy, but I haven't heard anything about him for a couple of years, at least. Rumor had it then that he had decided to stick to conjugal bliss with Maeve, his queen. But I think I also heard that she died a while ago."

Dilnavaz shifted again in her chair. "Yes, she did, but not before…well…getting back at Raoul. She…" She hesitated again, then turned and looked pointedly at the collection of bottles on the shelf behind my desk. "I'm so dry, child. Perhaps a wee drop of something to help the story along?"

A muttered "lush" came from Marlowe next to me, but fortunately, only I could hear him. I didn't need him and my godmother renewing their hostilities, at least not until I had coaxed the whole story out of her. I had to admit that I was curious about how and why Randy Raoul had suddenly come up in conversation. The story I'd heard a couple of years ago was that his queen, knowing she was dying and tired of his extra-marital antics, had cursed him. No one knew for sure what the curse entailed, although whispers within the royal circles of the Seven Kingdoms favored impotence. And now, with any luck and a great deal of patience on my part, we were about to hear the actual story.

I allowed Dilnavaz to take a sip of her wine. "Now, darling, to the case at hand. You're here to ask Marlowe and me to do or find something. What and why?" My stomach rumbled; it had been a long morning. "And please make it quick and brief. I haven't had lunch yet."

After some more beating around the bush, Dilnavaz finally spilled the whole story. First, the rumor about Randy Raoul not being able to get it up was true, but it was unclear who had put the curse on him. Rumor also had it that this was no verbal curse, but a full-fledged serious curse written on a lead scroll and hidden away. Where, no one knew, or at least no one was saying. The catch now, and why Dilnavaz needed our help, was that the king, finally past the prescribed year of mourning for his dead queen, wanted to remarry, and there was a princess interested in him. Whether she and her family knew about Randy Raoul's problem, my godmother didn't know, but obviously the king couldn't remarry if he was unable to perform and beget little princes and princesses.

"But why are you coming to me, darling?" I asked after Dilnavaz finished. "Are you telling me that no one else knows about the curse-scroll? And considering Raoul has been under the curse for over a year, are you telling me no one has looked into how to lift it? Maybe even searched for the scroll, assuming there is one? And what's your concern with him anyway? Is he one of your godchildren?"

I certainly hoped not, because, to Dilnavaz's mind, all her godchildren are related to each other by virtue of having her as a godmother. And if we're all related, then we have to help each other and her.

Alas, Raoul was indeed a fellow godchild of Dilnavaz, but this wasn't why my godmother was coming to me for help. It was because his intended's fairy godmother was Malvoisine, one of the nastiest fairies around, but also one of Dilnavaz's cronies to whom my godmother, because of her addiction to but lack of skill with gambling and drink, owed many, many favors.

When Dilnavaz fessed up about Malvoisine, this was too much for Marlowe who leaped out of his chair and onto the desk, railing at her. "Ya dizzy dame, what the hell do you think you're doing? Why are you even pestering us? Just take a powder. Why do we have to rescue your sorry keister?"

"You nasty little rat," shouted my godmother, heaving herself to her feet. "I'm talking to my goddaughter here, not to a stinky unnatural thing like you."

Before they could come to blows, I stood and bellowed, "Sit down and shut up, both of you!"

They did.

"Dilnavaz, darling, let's get this straight. You want us to find the curse-scroll and lift the curse on Randy Raoul so he can marry his little princess, right?"

She nodded.

"What do you get out of this? How deep into hock are you with Malvoisine?"

"Uh…if you can do this, it will help me considerably."

"Fine, and what do we get out of it? Never mind, I'll tell you what I want. The seven-league boots free and clear plus another credit toward Marlowe's opposing thumbs."

"Yes to the boots. An absolute no to the opposing thumbs. That rat doesn't deserve them."

Marlowe's tail went into full bottlebrush mode, with all the hairs bristling. He was royally pissed now. He bared his teeth and was about to light into my godmother again, but I grabbed him.

"Credit for the opposing thumbs is non-negotiable, darling," I said mildly.

Dilnavaz's face again gave her thoughts away. She was stuck. She needed us. "All right," she conceded. "How long will it take you to find the scroll? Raoul wants to announce his betrothal in a week."

"Depends on how much information you can give us about its whereabouts. Have you any idea where it might be?"

She looked down at her hands resting in her lap, and I knew the answer before she said anything. "No."

"In that case, darling, let me get started. We have a deal, right? I'll be in touch after I get the curse lifted." I walked around my desk, bussed Dilnavaz on both cheeks, and escorted her to the door. I could hear Marlowe muttering some obscenities relating to my godmother's ample frame and tiny brain.

My stomach rumbled again, this time louder than ever. "Let's get lunch and then figure out what we're doing with this case," I suggested to Marlowe.

He grabbed his fedora from the ferret-sized coat rack and slapped it down on his head.

"Let's dust, babe."

After lunch, we settled down to figure out our plan for tackling Randy Raoul's problem. Carcassonne was six hours away by horse from Arkady, so we could set out tomorrow. I could probably get in to see Raoul right away if I played on my own royal status through my mother as well as using the we-have-the-same-godmother angle. I was curious whether he knew about the curse and the curse scroll. If he did, had he looked for the scroll? Or did he think his…uh…performance problems might be caused by something else?

"What about that Maeve dame?" Marlowe pointed out. "Did she write the curse scroll all by her lonesome or did she put the arm on someone to do it for her?"

"You know, what if Malvoisine wrote the curse for her?" I suggested.

"Sounds hinky to me. Especially since that Malvoisine broad had nothing to do with her, so what would she get out of it?"

"Could Malvoisine be playing the long game? After all, she's Raoul's intended's godmother. If the old queen died—and do we even know that she did? —then Raoul would eventually be in the market for a new queen. And then Malvoisine gets to run things through her goddaughter, the new queen."

Marlowe dislodged his fedora and scratched his head. The fedora fell to the floor, and he muttered a curse, then picked it up and flung it onto my desk. "But then what was the point of making sure Randy Raoul couldn't get it up?" he said.

"To make sure he didn't marry someone else, someone whom Malvoisine couldn't control."

We tossed around a few more ideas, then I went back to my paperwork and Marlowe to practicing his card sharp tricks.

***

The next day was pleasant, so I decided to ride to Carcassonne. The ride was uneventful, and Marlowe and I continued to speculate about this case. I planned to visit Randy Raoul while Marlowe was going to sound out all the animals around the palace to get an idea of what kind of person his late queen was.

Raoul's seneschal announced me to the king as Princess Goslin of Arkady, which I had once been, at least before my mother had given up her claim to the Arkadian throne. But Raoul didn't need to know the details. A man perhaps in his mid-thirties, he bent over my hand and kissed it before escorting me to a throne-like chair almost as large as his.

"Welcome, Princess Goslin. How may I help you?"

"Your majesty, first I bring greetings from our mutual godmother, Dilnavaz, who inquires after your happiness. We have heard about a possible betrothal between you and a certain princess, and our godmother is a little concerned about your…health."

I was impressed. Raoul's face twitched at the words "concerned" and "health," but he didn't react nearly as badly as I thought he might at my deliberate bluntness.

"Concerned?"

"About your possible new wife. May I be blunt with you?"

He nodded.

It took a little time plus a lot of throat-clearing and downcast eyes, but in the end, Randy Raoul did confirm all the gossip and rumors: the incessant rumpy-pumpy while married, the curse, the subsequent impotence. To be truthful, he did try to downplay the impotence part, but he was obviously very embarrassed.

I did my best to soothe his feelings with much hand patting and sympathetic grunts. Then I got to the point. "I'm here, Raoul, to fix things. We need to reverse the curse and return you to normal. But you have to promise Dilnavaz and me—and your wife-to-be—one thing."

"Anything, princess."

"Just keep it in your breeches, okay? Because if you don't…" I left the threat hanging.

Oh yes, he understood and nodded frantically in agreement. I didn't know if I could reinstate the curse once it was lifted, but if he thought I could, that's all that was important.

Raoul rang a bell and called for refreshments. When they came, I was pleased to see that they included a bottle of wine. We both needed it. Finally, however, it was time to get down to the problem at hand.

"Lovely wine, Raoul, thank you. Now, about the curse and your, uh, problem. Who do you think was responsible?"

Mab's tits. If I thought he was uncomfortable opening up about the curse and his "problem," that was nothing compared to his behavior now. He looked around the room, wriggled in his chair, reached for the bottle and swigged back the rest of the wine.

"Do you think it was your late queen?" I asked to break the silence.

He looked shocked at the suggestion. "But Maeve loved me. She said so. Over and over."

"But Raoul, you did betray your marriage vows."

"Still, she said she loved me. And I loved her. Truly. And I tried to remain faithful to her in her last year. I might have been with other women, but I never loved them as I loved my queen."

"Sorry, I don't think 'tried' is good enough in this case. But for the sake of argument, do you think she could have cursed you? Did she know anyone who could actually create the curse? A witch, perhaps? Her fairy godmother? Anyone?"

"No, no, she couldn't have."

He had stopped fidgeting and looked directly at me as he said that. For what it was worth, he truly believed that the curse hadn't come from the queen.

"What about one of your girlfriends? Could one of them have been angry because you left her for someone else?"

He shook his head vehemently at such a preposterous thought. We were getting nowhere at this point, so it was time to start looking around for the scroll ourselves. I hoped Marlowe was more successful in finding out something useful. I arranged to search the late queen's apartments in the palace, which sentimental Raoul (maybe he really did love her) had ordered left as-is after her death. But I did have one more question for him.

"Who was your queen's godmother?"

His answer didn't thrill me one bit. The queen's godmother had been Malvoisine.

***

Marlowe and I searched for hours for that damned curse-scroll: outside the palace, aided by Marlowe's animal and bird friends; inside the late queen's apartments, which, as Raoul had intimated, hadn't been touched at all since her death. We knocked on walls, ceilings, and floors; pulled apart anything that could be pulled apart and put back together again; even had some flies and mice helping us. Nothing!

As we searched, Marlowe brought me up to date on what his contacts had revealed. They did confirm that Randy Raoul had indeed come by his nickname legitimately, frequently being sighted wandering off to some other woman's bed. At the same time, many of them confirmed that he almost always went to the queen's rooms as soon as he returned to the palace to apologize and profess his love for her and that she appeared to forgive him. That forbearance on her part, however, according to most sources, including her little dogs who were helping us, lessened as time passed. The dogs thought that she may have indeed cursed her wayward husband as she drew closer to death.

The most interesting thing Marlowe learned from the dogs was that several strangers had frequently visited the queen in the few months before her death.

"The deal is, babe, the dogs fingered all the strangers as one and the same person."

"And I bet we both know who these 'strangers' really were."

"Malvoisine," we said together triumphantly.

Our feeling of triumph was short-lived. If Malvoisine was behind this entire farce of the curse, then why couldn't she find the scroll and lift the curse herself? Why did she have to call in some markers and get Dilnavaz to ask me to find a way to undo the curse? And the biggest question of all: Where was the scroll?

Only two places left to check: Raoul's apartments and the mausoleum where Queen Maeve was buried. Because I really didn't feel like dealing with Randy Raoul right now, I decided I would check the mausoleum and leave Raoul's rooms to Marlowe, the queen's dogs, and any of Marlowe's friends who could locate and squeeze into assorted nooks and crannies in the rooms and furnishings.

I borrowed one of the dogs to check the mausoleum with me. Raoul must really be missing his queen because the crypt was full of flowers that I assumed, rightly or wrongly, were from him. The sarcophagus itself had a beautiful bas-relief of the late queen that was almost hidden by even more blooms. I just hoped I wouldn't have to shift them by moving aside the lid. Besides, it would have been far too disrespectful, and something only someone like a nasty fairy would do, to interfere with Maeve's final resting place.

Mab's tits! Deciding not to disturb the queen was the right thing to do because further down in the mausoleum, where I assumed Raoul would be laid to rest, was a small but heavy tightly rolled-up scroll tucked into an almost invisible cavity in the stone wall. The dog and I took off running back to the palace to tell Marlowe the good news.

Except before I even reached the king's rooms, I saw Marlowe running toward me, one paw clamped down to hold his fedora in place and the other paw holding…a small tightly rolled-up scroll that looked uncannily like the one I was carrying.

"Found it!" we both yelled as we neared each other. Except that "it" was "them" and from no scrolls, we ended up with too many. Things got worse when we found an empty room where we opened the scrolls to see what we had. We were so excited that it didn't strike us that this might have been a stupid move for both of us, seeing as we had no idea of how a curse-scroll worked and whether the curse could be transmitted to anyone who read it. On the other hand, neither Marlowe, being a ferret, nor I, being a female, had to worry about not being able to get it up.

It was a moot point anyway. Because when we looked at the tiny letters inscribed into the lead that made up the first scroll, we couldn't read them. Whatever alphabet they were in wasn't one that either Marlowe or I recognized. We compared the two scrolls. The letters looked as if they were from the same alphabet, but they were arranged differently. This was very bad. In other words, we were probably dealing with two curses, and we weren't even sure if either one of them was the one aimed at Randy Raoul.

We had two options: Return to Dilnavaz with the scrolls, let her figure them out, and collect our payment, or…

Marlowe and I were on the same page. We both shook our heads at the second option: visiting Malvoisine, who was almost certainly up to her nasty sneer in this little predicament, but who would almost certainly be able to read the scrolls. Mab's tits, she probably wrote them.

We ended up having to speak with Malvoisine anyway because Dilnavaz, my beloved fairy godmother, was being very sticky about the terms of our deal. First, we get the curse on Randy Raoul lifted, then she pays us. She wouldn't budge from her position, not even after I plied her with my best wine and Marlowe was uncharacteristically polite to her. She tossed back three cups of wine, looked suspiciously at Marlowe being mannerly, then told us that we still had to complete the deal.

The next day found me carrying Marlowe and the two curse-scrolls, striding cross-country in my godmother's seven-league boots to visit Malvoisine. The visit wasn't as horrible as we had anticipated. In fact, Malvoisine was surprisingly pleasant and hospitable, although we did refuse her offer of refreshment; our trust went only so far. Sure enough, the scroll Marlowe found in Raoul's rooms was the curse scroll; the alphabet belonged to some demon language, which Malvoisine could both read and write. Her eyebrows went up as she glanced at the other scroll, then she smirked and tucked it away in her apron.

Whatever this second scroll said, it put her in a good mood, so she was happy to tell us everything…after we signed a nondisclosure agreement, of course. She detailed how she had persuaded her goddaughter, the queen, to put a curse on her wayward husband. Then when the queen died, Malvoisine would arrange for the curse to be lifted just in time to put forward another of her goddaughters as Raoul's new queen. But because Malvoisine didn't want to be seen as manipulating Raoul, she conned Dilnavaz into asking me to find the curse-scroll and thus lift the curse from the king who could then remarry.

To sweeten the pot, she paid Marlowe and me off handsomely: me with a *tarnkappe*, invisibility being useful in my line of work, and Marlowe with a promise that she would tell Dilnavaz to add yet another credit to his opposing thumbs fund.

Another case successfully concluded. We got back to the office where I was writing up my notes about the case and a bill for Dilnavaz, when Marlowe who was messing around at his desk suddenly shouted, “Hey, babe, cast your peepers over this!” All was back to normal at Goslin & Marlowe, Finders & Private Investigators.

The 13th Letter

M

The End

LEARNING TO LIE

By Rosalind Place

I always think it was the lawyers who were the first ones to ask. But it wasn't. It wasn't my husband either, standing outside the courthouse in the rain the first day of the trial, turning to me and blurting out the question he'd been holding onto for so long.

When was the first time you knew she was lying?

It was my brother, Eddie. On the telephone. Calling long distance from out west; a call he couldn't afford to make. When did you know? When was the first time you knew for sure?

And I was back in my third-grade classroom, a parent-teacher interview. My brother was there as well. I remember him sitting at one of the little desks in the first row, his long legs stretched out. He was drawing circles with his finger on the surface of the desk, over and over again. I don't remember what my teacher asked, or what my mother answered, but whatever she said, I knew it wasn't true. I looked over at Eddie and he just shook his head. I didn't say anything of course, and neither did he. We were co-conspirators, both of us, and only later, much later, were we unwilling ones.

My brother was the one who raised me. Our mother left us for good when I was twelve years old and he was fifteen. Walt had already gone. She waited longer than one might have expected to finally cut us loose. Various relatives stepped in from time to time over the years, but mostly it was my brother who was there every day, making my lunch for school, showing up at parents' night to explain why no parent was there.

I have often wondered why she ever had children. She was so supremely uninterested in us, and we were such a complication in her life. In the end, I decided it was just carelessness. They were very careless people, Walt and my mother: careless with money, careless with the truth, and so very careless with other people's lives.

It was my brother who made sure the rent was paid and I never went hungry.

We lived in a tiny, dark basement apartment. Eddie worked in construction. Long hours and low pay, it supplemented the money our mother occasionally sent. Hard as it was, he needed to work outside. Whenever there were layoffs, he would still leave the apartment early in the morning, not returning till after dark. He was looking for more work of course, but he also hated being cooped up inside, always had.

When I think of that apartment now, of the years we spent there, my clearest memory is of Eddie's pictures. Ever since I could remember, he had collected pictures of mountains, all cut from magazines: blue skies above green foothills, snow-capped peaks, summits barely visible behind walls of snow, hiking trails winding around rock faces, mountain lakes surrounded by firs. At the apartment, he'd pasted them above the living room couch that was his fold-out bed. They were his hope for the future.

He kept the money my mother sent us in a box under his bed, taught, as was I, from an early age never to trust banks. I can't even imagine what it must have been like for him, a teenager entirely responsible for his little sister, keeping all those secrets.

"You know, Jo," he'd say. "She'll be back sooner than you think. Walt, too. That business of theirs, well, it's gonna take off one day soon for sure."

That business of theirs. And what a business it was.

From the time I was 12 until I was 23, my mother wrote to me once a year, always at Christmas. I think it was easier than trying to remember my birthday. The letters were always sent to the same post office, addressed to general delivery, with no return address. They were colorful letters, full of promises. She would be home soon. The big payday was coming, and we would be reunited. The things she would buy me! The trips we would take! She'd describe whichever city they happened to be in at the time. Their "business" took them all over the country, to places I could barely imagine.

I read them, tucked them away in a shoe box. I'd never have to answer any more awkward questions when my mother came home and I wouldn't have to tell any more lies. What an exciting life she had, I thought then, and what a glamorous person she must be. I never questioned why it was that she had to work away from us. It was just a fact. I didn't resent her and, even as I got older and memories of her began to fade, I still held her in some kind of awe. She was like this little bright light. She would knock on our door one day and sweep me away from schoolwork and from our dark little apartment and my increasingly impatient and demanding brother.

Eddie waited a long time to set me straight. In the end, he had no choice. It was just before Christmas, my last year of high school, when I got my annual letter from my mother, the letter that almost tore my brother and me apart.

I was sixteen, a rebellious teenager, and he'd been my parent for so long that he always got the brunt of it. I wanted out, away from him, from school, from my boring job at the hardware store down the street. In her letter that year, my mother told me that she wanted me to come live with her. Eddie knew where she was, she said. She'd put a one-hundred-dollar bill in the envelope.

I showed Eddie the letter right away.

I'd never seen him so angry. He said he didn't know where she was, and he wouldn't tell me if he did. He demanded I give him the money she'd sent. It was a long, bitter argument that continued on and off for days. I was going to finish high school, no matter what. I was going to keep my job and keep saving for university next year. He was never going to let me live with her. *Never.* I didn't stop though; I brought it up again and again until he had finally had enough.

I can see him still, standing at the hot plate, his baggy work clothes shedding dust each time he moved, pouring milk into the mac and cheese saying, "You still have all your letters, Jo?"

I thought it was the first sign that he was giving in, so I got them for him. I watched him read through them, laying each one down on the table as he finished, folding it carefully and handing it back to me without looking up.

He set me straight that night. I remember that I wasn't actually shocked but I wanted, desperately, for him to stop talking. He was very clear, never raised his voice when I tried to interrupt. He was relentless though, and with each word he spoke, I saw the bright light that my mother had been grow dimmer and dimmer until it disappeared entirely. It felt cruel at the time. It was only later that I understood he was trying to protect me. It's who he was then and who he still is now. It's what got him into so much trouble.

Their "business" was no business at all. It was blackmail of a particularly nasty kind. Easy to pull off, if you knew what you were doing, and they did. My mother, with her gift of drawing people to her, men particularly, was the bait. Walt was the aggrieved husband, the one who would burst in at the right moment and threaten to expose everything. She was good as the vengeful ex-wife as well, apparently, just as convincing as any angry husband might be.

Walt had his own set of skills. They were always careful to cover their tracks.

I never wanted to take the money, Jo, he said that night, looking down. I watched his dirt-encrusted fingers as he drew circles on the little kitchen table. I thought of those bills, tucked into that box under his bed, the money she'd sent us over the years, money paid by heartbroken, desperate people. *I never wanted to have to tell you.*

"Look at the postmarks," he said as he rifled through the letters. "They're moving all the time. Never in the same place twice. It's what they were doing when we were little kids. It's what they've always done. I didn't want to take their money, Jo, but I had to. It's dirty money and it makes us dirty too. These letters are all lies."

It makes us dirty too.

That night, sitting at the little round table in the tiny kitchen, the mac and cheese cold on our plates, he made me face the truth and I hated him for it. I didn't speak to him for weeks. He just accepted all the anger I threw at him. I don't know how he did it; how, left to care for his little sister with no apparent life of his own, he had the patience and the kindness to let me turn all my pain and anger against him.

My mother never mentioned my coming to live with her again. I suspect she simply forgot she had ever asked. I don't know what would have happened to me if Eddie hadn't stopped me. I don't know if I would ever have found my way back.

I still went to the little post office to pick up her letters every Christmas. After Eddie told me the truth, I came to dread their arrival, but couldn't resist. Eventually, I stopped opening them, just put them in the box with all the others. Twelve years of letters in the end that I carried with me through college, my first apartment, my first job, my marriage, our first house. A box of dirt that wouldn't let me go.

I have another memory of my brother from that time. Between my part-time, sometimes full-time work, Eddie's salary, various grants and loans, we scraped together the money for me to go to university. It was Christmas break, my first year, and I'd left residence to come back and stay with him. They had been a stressful few months and I remember collapsing into the armchair in the little living room with a feeling of relief. But when I looked across the room that day, expecting to see his mountain pictures, there was only a bare wall. The pictures were all gone. They'd always been there, and I was afraid to think of why he might have taken them down. It was the first thing I asked him when he got home. He laughed, looked over to the wall then back to me, a big smile on his face.

"I don't need pictures anymore, Jo. I'm going to find the real thing."

I remember jumping out of the chair and running to him. I remember the cold, clean smell of his jacket, the strength of his arms as he hugged me. I knew I'd be on my own from then on, but I felt such joy for him in that moment, and such regret that he'd had to wait so long.

So we went our separate ways, my brother and I, on to live better, cleaner lives. We spoke regularly, eagerly sharing our news. We never talked about the past; we never mentioned our mother at all. Whatever she was doing had nothing to do with us.

And then, there it was, the phone call in the middle of the night. The moment I heard his voice, I knew something had to be terribly wrong.

"She *conned* me, Jo. She conned *me*. I'm in a lot of trouble…."

He didn't say anything more for so long that I thought he might have rung off, but then this: "We were going to lose our home, Jo. We were going to be on the street. I couldn't let that happen to Ellie, to my kids."

His voice was hoarse, almost breaking. He sounded absolutely exhausted. "They were going to take the lodge and everything in it. And there she was…. It was so much money, Jo. I never thought, I never thought she'd do it to *me*."

I'm still surprised at how calm I was. I must have been waiting for the reckoning, I suppose, without realizing it. I went down to the kitchen, pulled a notepad and pen from the shelf and sat down at the table.

"Start at the beginning and tell me everything," I said.

My mother's fingerprints were all over it.

I had never thought of her as a long-term planner, but this sounded like a years-long setup to me. Her escape plan, I suppose, in case she had to run.

When Eddie moved out west, my first year of college, he was determined to live among those mountains. And he did. He found work almost right away. Within a year he'd put a down payment on the old lodge and started the renovations. By the time I graduated, he was married, with his first child on the way. He was the hardest working person I'd ever known so it just didn't occur to me to ask him how he got the place, how he got it all going so quickly.

That night, I didn't ask him why the mortgage suddenly came due either. But by then, I didn't need to.

"Walt disappeared, Jo. He left her high and dry. She swore this was the last time. All that was left was to pick up the cash and she really needed that cash. But she was scared. The guy was angry, she wasn't sure she could handle him. I told her I'd do it, but if she ever called me again, I'd go to the cops. I'd tell them everything."

This was the last time.

There were so many things wrong with his story, but that was the worst of it—not just that he'd done it, but that she'd convinced him to do it, or something like it, before. How she'd found a way back into my honest, hardworking brother's life, I didn't want to think about. I'd always believed that, like me, he'd cut her out of his life.

"I believed her, Jo," he said. "She got the mortgage for me in the first place. She got the lodge for me. No one would give me a loan. She said she was paying me back. She said it was all legit."

They were going to foreclose. He was going to lose the lodge, their home, his livelihood and more.

"How did she get the guy to finance you in the first place?"

He didn't answer right away. Maybe he realized how it would sound when he said it out loud.

"He was a friend from the old days. She loaned him money years ago, helped him out. She thought he'd want to return the favor."

The more questions I asked, the clearer it became. The money pick-up wasn't that important on its own. It was simply a way for her to blackmail him into helping her get away. It was the mortgage. She, and this "friend" of hers, had been laundering her dirty money through the lodge for years. They were trying to cash in because they were about to get caught.

I think he understood it at the same moment I did. He was going to lose everything and that wasn't all. They were setting him up to take the blame for something he knew nothing about. By the time he rang off, I knew enough to see how she had manipulated him, on and off, for years, a pick up here, a phone call there. She knew where he was vulnerable and how to take advantage of it. She had made my brother lie to me. *To me.*

When I was still in middle school, I told Eddie I wanted to go to university and become an accountant. He couldn't stop laughing. When I got my certification and told him I was going to work for a bank, he laughed until he cried. I couldn't blame him. I was laughing then, too. But there was a certainty about numbers that had always entranced me. A good friend of mine, a classmate back then, was fascinated by the forensic side of things and specialized in it. I could never have done that. I couldn't bear the thought that numbers could be made to lie. But as that good friend told me, lies can always be undone, you just have to know how.

The night my brother called me, it was impossible to sleep. I sat at the kitchen table for the rest of the night, trying to figure out how to help him, my oh-so-innocent husband asleep upstairs. By the time he came down, bleary-eyed, looking for coffee, I knew what I was going to do.

I went up to the attic and dug out the old shoebox. I sat down at our dining room table and spread my mother's letters out before me. I have never understood why she wrote them. Perhaps she was playing at being a mother the way she played at being a jealous wife, carelessly, heartlessly. Or maybe she needed an audience, someone to witness her fabricated life. On darker days, I've thought they were merely a series of alibis she thought she might need one day.

Twelve letters, one a year from the time I was 12. The early ones were pretty much how I remembered them. She described lavish parties, occasionally dropped names of semi-famous people. They read in part like travelogues, in part like rather nasty gossip columns. She flattered and complained. They often veered into an odd kind of self-pity and self-justification that I didn't grasp at the time. *I love you so much, my beautiful girl. Walt says the business needs me. But why must I be away from my precious children?* We went here, we went there. Business is good, business is bad. *I am so sad to be away from you all the time.* But we have to go. We have to move on. *It isn't an easy life, Jocelyn, and Walt isn't an easy man. I love you so much, my beautiful girl.*

At times, she was more serious, giving me advice, trying to seem like a mother after all. *You must never use a bank, Jocelyn. If you have too much cash on hand, you must find someone you trust to invest it. There are investments out there, Jocelyn, that no one knows about. Even the banks don't know about them. When we meet, I'll let you in on a few secrets!*

I barely looked at the one where she invited me to live with her, only glanced at the one she sent the year after where she didn't mention it at all. They were both too painful to read.

There were six letters, the later ones that I had never read, never even opened. They were quite different from the rest. There were no more travelogues, no more flattery, just self-delusion and bitterness. *Walt was a very smart man, Jocelyn. We were a very good team for many years. No one could fault us. He needed me as much as I needed him. He meant the world to me.* If I hadn't just talked to my brother, I would have assumed Walt had left years ago. Then this. *If people are stupid, how are we to blame? They are no better than us and what do they know? Nothing! There are so many liars out there. You have to get in there before they do. Walt let me down. He let me down badly. Something had to be done. I'm on my own now, Jocelyn. Your mother is on her own. The things I've done, Jocelyn, I had to do.*

She never admitted anything, of course. It felt like she was trying to bring me on side somehow, trying to make me part of some more elaborate lie I couldn't guess at. It was only when you knew what she'd been doing that any of it made sense. She'd scrawled her addresses on the bottom of these letters, as if expecting me to write back.

I read them over and over again. There wasn't enough there, on their own, to save my brother.

You could say that I'd learned to lie years ago, sitting at that parent-teacher interview in grade school; that my knowledge was refined over the years by necessity. When I printed out my mother's last letter, the thirteenth letter, you could say I was following in her footsteps. But I know the difference between right and wrong, taught by the brother who raised me. My mother went after the wrong person and I had to stop her, that's all. I should have done it a very long time ago.

In her last few letters to me, my mother skirted with revelation. She walked up to the line and then backed away. It was a kind of manipulation, an invitation to conspire. *I will tell you one day soon, Jocelyn. One day you will know what I did and why I did it. I cannot tell you now. I'm sure you would understand. You must protect the ones you love.*

Is she talking about herself? Her lover? Surely not my brother. If you didn't know her, you would think she was preparing to make some kind of confession.

Thirteen letters. I put them all in a large brown envelope and took them to my brother's lawyer. *I just found these. The last one just arrived. I thought you should see them first.*

The police interviewed me, of course, as did all the lawyers. And then they looked away from my brother, as I'd hoped they would, and began to pull at the threads that would untangle it all. Liars, especially the careless ones, eventually lose track of their lies. Inevitably, they make a mistake.

My mother no longer writes to me. I get a weekly call instead. I can safely say that I've talked to her more in the last two months than in my entire life. I never say very much myself, something she doesn't seem to notice, but I always take notes.

She has never asked me directly about the last letter, the one she didn't write, the one that got her arrested, that put her in prison. She hints at it sometimes, as if she's trying to figure out who wrote it and why. She knows, of course. Who else could it have been?

But it's a hard thing, facing the truth. I take notes because I don't know, after all, who else might be out there, waiting to trap us. I'll keep taking notes until I know we are safe, and then I'll never speak to her again. She doesn't deserve anyone's sympathy, ours least of all.

Eddie's the one who writes to me now. He says it helps him to think things through. He's still in the mountains with Ellie and the kids. They had to start over, but they're doing okay. We're going to visit them this spring. I'll get to see his pictures come to life at last.

When was the first time you knew she was lying?

The memory is so clear and immediate now that it's hard to believe there was ever a time I couldn't remember it. I was standing on the sidewalk outside our house, watching two men argue. They looked like they were about to fight each other. Walt was one of them. My brother was there too, standing back, looking scared. There was a car parked next to me. The window was down, and I could see a woman sitting in the front seat. She looked like she was crying. As I went closer, I could hear her sobbing, saying the same thing over and over again. *Just pay. Just pay. Just pay.*

It didn't make any sense. Then my brother was beside me, grabbing my arm and pulling me away and Walt was shouting, "Get the fuck back in the house!"

My mother was standing in the doorway.

"Everything's fine," she said, closing the front door behind us.

"But that lady's crying. That lady in the car…"

"You tell her, Eddie. You tell her." She turned to my brother, but he just shook his head and looked away.

She turned back to me. I felt her fingers digging into my shoulders.

"Everything's fine," she told me. "It has nothing to do with us."

The 13th Letter

M

The End

THE MALEVOLENT MASTERPIECES

By Kevin P. Thornton

The body lay in the studio, face down, stretched across the paint-mottled floor as if laid out on a surrealist mosaic. Sergeant Benderby looked at the crime scene with jaded detachment. He had seen too many dead bodies in his career, and he had hoped that this final assignment to Fort Clearwater meant no more murder investigations. Unless.... He looked at the room again. There was no actual sign of murderous activity. The body was dead, sure, but there was no bottle of poison, no large *assegai* sticking out of the corpse's back.

"Why exactly was I called out?" he asked.

"It's a suspicious death," said the Corporal in charge of the scene. "Procedure requires the senior investigator to be informed so he may assign a subordinate to the case."

"And yet that choice, the whole assigning a subordinate part, was not mentioned?"

"Well, I thought I would save you some time. In this town, on this detachment, you are the sum total of the investigative team."

"So there is no subordinate to assign."

"Correct. I believe that particular sub-section refers to larger detachments. I thought it was all explained to you in your orientation this morning, I mean yesterday." She yawned. "Sorry, I've been on call all night."

"I have been to too many orientations, at too many detachments, over far too many years to pay attention anymore," said Benderby. "Tell me what you know, starting with your name."

"Corporal Sheelagh Delorme. The deceased is Silas Tomkins. He is a painter of some fame in the art world, portraits being his specialty. His stepdaughter, Meredith

Tomkins, woke at about 2 a.m. and noticed Tomkins hadn't come down to bed so she went and checked on him. The studio door was locked from the inside. This was unusual. Silas always locked his studio when he was finished, but as there was only one key to the room, she was worried. She knocked and yelled, to no avail, then she fetched the housekeeper, Jamina Tomkins, who went to the garage and brought a pry bar. While Jamina tried to force the door, Meredith called 911. As luck would have it, one of the emergency responders, James Sutcliffe, lives around the corner so he was here within minutes. According to the stepdaughter, Sutcliffe and the housekeeper eventually broke open the door and found Silas on the floor, dead."

"Hmm," said Benderby. The studio was on the top floor of what was a rather decadent tract mansion. It had been built to impress with its excess, and was in a small exclusive part of town. Once it had been a pig farm before the *nouveau riche* needed somewhere to flaunt their wealth.

"Is this the artist's home? It doesn't seem Bohemian enough."

"He has been renting it for just over a year," said Delorme. "It is part of his method. He moves to a community, lives in it, paints his portraits, then leaves. When he departs, all his work is exhibited, mostly to critical acclaim. His paintings usually command very high prices, but he doesn't make many friends along the way. His portraits are not always flattering."

She looked at the screen on her phone. "The *Globe and Mail* art critic called his last exhibition a riotous *tour-de-force* that peeled back the ugly of small-town Canada. Like a raging Lucien Freud with a permanent hangover."

"That's a lot of information, Corporal. Well done," said Benderby.

Corporal Delorme colored a little.

"I took art history," she said. "When I heard Tomkins was coming here to do his latest series, I became interested.

He is a fascinating artist and he's unusual. He paints very quickly and he doesn't like people posing for him. Instead, he takes pictures and projects them on a screen."

She pointed to the computer setup and blank wall beyond the easel. "He finds people who let him take their photos, then he paints, working always on his own. The subject is never in the room and doesn't see the work until all paintings are displayed at the end of his test opus."

"I can understand why he didn't make many friends. If Tomkins was considered more dyspeptic than Lucien Freud, his work may have made many of the subjects angry. I wonder why they would agree to let him paint them. The Warholian fifteen minutes mayhap?"

He walked over to the artist's position.

"So he would stand here," said Benderby, approaching the empty easel, "and look up at the portrait he was projecting on the wall. Then he would paint." He looked around, saw the palette on a stand next to tubes of oil. "He was painting under artificial light, with a projected picture that, no matter how good his equipment was, would not be the sharpest of images. It seems like an awful lot of effort for mediocre work. Tell me, Delorme, was he any good?"

"You described his art as if you had seen it," said Delorme. "His images were fuzzy, deliberately so. Blurred lines, colors melding together. All except one part of the painting, generally the face, which was as sharp as if it came from a different lens. It was an unusual style, but very successful for him. His exhibitions regularly sold out and quite often they went for thousands of dollars."

"That's fairly lucrative," said Benderby. "How many did he do a year? Six? Ten? A dozen maybe?"

"His last exhibition was called *Leery Labrador City*, and he displayed over two hundred paintings."

"Two hundred? Why that's, that's…" He screwed up his forehead in concentration, unsuccessfully. Math always made his head hurt.

"That exhibition realized more than $4 million," said Delorme.

"And how many of these guerilla art projects has he done?"

"Fort Clearwater would have been his thirteenth. He named them sequentially and alphabetically. It's twee, perhaps the only part of him that is, but he is—was—a marketing genius. Apparently, he made a tidy sum in official prints. Give the people a sequence, and they'll want to collect them all."

"By alphabetically, what exactly do you mean? Like *A is for Alibi*?"

"Not quite," said Delorme, "but I'm impressed with your Grafton line. His first collection was called "Arduous Ardor," followed by "Boorish Bedlam," "Captivating Calumny" and "Deviant Devilment." Shall I carry on?"

"No need. Interesting, but hardly helpful. In summary, then," he said, looking at the Corporal. "Erm, could you take some notes please?"

"I am," said Delorme. "I have a lapel microphone wirelessly connected to my phone's voice-to-text application. It records everything and I transcribe the salient parts later for my report."

She saw the Sergeant's eyes glaze over at everything she said from "lapel" onwards and felt sorry for him, until he gently reprimanded her.

"That's all well and good, but if you take notes now and then give me the piece of paper once we are done discussing the case, I will have something to work with." He reached into his pocket and brought out a leather-bound notepad and a stubby pencil and handed them to her. "Now, let us review the case, if indeed it even is a case. Questions to be answered include: If you find a dead body in a locked room, surely one should apply Occam's razor first. Did he die of a heart attack, a stroke, or some other medical matter known to strike down men who live excessively? Why are we even looking at foul play?"

"Ah," said Delorme, making a note to find out what an "Occam" was. "Perhaps I should have mentioned that."

She leaned over the body and pointed at Silas's eye. "Here," she said, turning on her Maglite to illuminate the face.

There was a paintbrush sticking out of the victim's eye socket. The bristles pointed outward to the world while the sharp end, judging by the approximate length, was lodged deep inside his brain.

"Indeed," said Benderby. "Probably not a heart attack then."

***

The coroner came and did what coroners do. The crime scene people finished dusting and tweezing, leaving the grisly tableau for the two investigators, Benderby and Delorme, who went back into the studio.

"Why do you think it wasn't just an accident?" said Benderby. "A heart attack followed by a stagger forward clutching his chest, only he has a Windsor & Newton Number 5 in his hand. As he falls, it jams into his eye. Gravity and his not-inconsiderable weight do the rest. Natural causes, case closed, let's go home."

"Did you see the brush end of the paintbrush?" said Delorme.

"I did," said Benderby. "I was wondering if you had."

"If he had accidentally fallen on it, the bristles would have been crushed with his weight."

"And there is nothing wrong with the bristles," said Benderby. "Well done, Delorme. Unfortunately, that makes our job harder. If someone came into the room and jammed a brush into his eye, how did they lock the room behind them? Are we sure there is only one key?"

"The lock is a special one, made in Quebec. They only ever have one key. It is their trademark. Every key is unique."

"You know a lot about locks," observed Benderby.

"I remember reading about the lock company in a Rosemary McCracken short story. Or maybe one by Lisa de Nikolits." She saw the puzzlement in Benderby's eyes. "I'm surprised. If you know Sue Grafton, surely you've heard of the Mesdames of Mayhem? No? Your loss. Anyway, I read a lot of mysteries. A company that makes a lock with only one key is a useful plot point in locked room mysteries. It's turned up more than once in books I've read."

"You're a cozy fan, are you?"

"We prefer the term 'traditional mysteries.'"

"I see. Well, it has been my experience that there is no such thing as a locked room mystery."

Corporal Delorme looked as heartbroken as if Benderby had stolen her dreams. "But…" she said and pointed to the room then to the door.

"What I mean," said Benderby, "is that they are always solved. The mystery of the locked room is inevitably the mystery of why people actually believed the room was inaccessible in the face of all evidence to the contrary."

Delorme still looked unhappy. "Silas Tomkins installed it when he first moved in. He was very private and kept his work a secret. The key is still in the lock. On the inside."

"Unless the door was never locked at all," said Benderby. "But that would require collusion between the stepdaughter and the housekeeper. Possible, but then they would also have to be in cahoots with the emergency responder, who they did not know would get here so quickly."

"Cahoots?" said Delorme.

"It's an ancient policing term. Back in the day, mounted police roamed the land looking for miscreants and their fellow travelers. They were often found to be in cahoots."

Changing to a more relevant subject, he said, "What are the chances they pretended to force a locked door that was not, in fact, locked?"

"Unlikely," said Delorme. "I've known Jimmy Sutcliffe all my life. He is the most unassuming person in the whole world. I mean he's twenty-six and still lives at home with his mother, yet no one thinks that's strange. That's just Jimmy. It's probably never occurred to him to get his own place."

"You think him unlikely to be involved in a conspiracy," said Benderby.

"I think it's impossible. The only time I ever saw him angry was once when he was twelve. Someone at school called his mom a mean word. He was fuming mad, clenching and unclenching his fists, telling the boy to take it back. But he never did anything. It was as if he didn't know what to do next. Losing his temper was a new experience for him."

"What of the stepdaughter and the housekeeper?"

"They're downstairs," said Delorme.

"Well then, let's not keep them waiting. And while you are taking notes, here's one to add to the list. Silas Tomkins had been up all night painting. Why else would he have had the palette and brushes out? So where's the painting? The easel is empty."

"I didn't think of that," said Delorme.

"And if his last exhibition earned $4 million, and we can assume the five before that did as well, then there is a large pile of money waiting to be inherited. I wonder if the two ladies Tomkins know anything about that."

***

Meredith Tomkins was 21 and had a body granted by youth and good genes that, if left untended, would decay into middle age earlier than most. She didn't have a job, but drove an expensive German car, took regular trips down to the city to go shopping, and in fact, was missing a trip today because of this inconvenience. All this was in her first tirade at the detectives. Delorme wondered what the going rate was for allowances paid by indulgent stepfathers.

"I'm the daughter of his second wife," said Meredith Tomkins.

"You took his name," said Benderby.

"I didn't mind," she said. "He may have been my father, if the rumors are true. I met my mother's ex-husband once and even though he was supposed to be my biological father, there wasn't a hint of it in our looks. He was a mousy little man, while I," she stretched and shrugged her shoulders, "look like the daughter of a real man. Like Silas Tomkins."

She did have the same hair color, thought Benderby, although that wasn't always conclusive. She may have shared other features. All the Sergeant had seen so far of Silas was his corpse on the ground.

"Did that bother you," said Delorme, "being taken for his child?"

"No, it was what everyone thought anyway. Better to be thought of as his daughter rather than the daughter of Julius Cohen, CPA."

"Yet Silas and your mother divorced, and you stayed with him."

"My mother decided that if Silas was the goose who laid the golden eggs, he was doing so in secret. She took as much as her prenup allowed, then left *him* for an Albanian Count, and then left the Kont (their word, not mine) for a Sicilian car dealer. I believe she has moved on again." She shrugged. "We're not close."

"So I gather. How much do you stand to inherit?"

"I'm sure I have no idea. Some, most, maybe all. I was his favorite after all."

"You realize you'll get nothing if you're found guilty of his murder?" said Delorme.

"Murder, wait…what? Silas was murdered? How? He was locked in his studio."

"That is what we mean to establish," said Benderby. "Until then, don't leave town."

He waited until Meredith Tomkins had been escorted out before turning to the Corporal. "I take it you don't like Miss Tomkins, or maybe you like her as a co-conspirator?"

"I'm sorry. That was unprofessional. I just wanted to wipe that smirk off her face."

"Well, you did that. She didn't think she was a suspect until you rattled her. But does that mean she's innocent, or does she think she's too smart to be suspected?"

"She strikes me as someone who's never had reason to believe she was too smart," muttered Delorme. "I know, I'm showing my inner prejudices here, but people like Meredith Tomkins, the entitled for no apparent reason, have always irritated me."

"So do we think she did it?"

"She could have," said Delorme. "After all, she may be more than just a stepdaughter. How else did she notice that he hadn't come to bed?"

"My thoughts as well. What's the word that describes such a situation?"

"Icky?" said Delorme.

"I was thinking incestuous, but icky works. Let's talk to the housekeeper."

***

Jamina Tomkins was no fan of the late artist. She was also his first ex-wife. "He was a terrible man. He misused me, then threw me over when he met that little brat's mother." She pointed at the ceiling.

She was a stocky woman who seemed both capable and unafraid of a hard day's work. However, there was a whining tone to her voice, as if the fates had dumped on her and left her with no means to clean herself up.

"By little brat, do you mean Meredith Tomkins?" said Delorme.

"I mean the slutty daughter of the slutty woman who took my husband."

"I'll take that as a yes," said Delorme.

"And yet you stayed on as his housekeeper," said Benderby.

"I had nowhere else to go," she said. "When I met Silas, he was too poor to go to art school, so he sat in the back of classes and watched, trying to learn. I supported him. I left school to get a job, then another job. I kept him when we were first married, working those jobs so he could paint and hang about with all the hoity-toity ones on Whyte Avenue. And when he started to make some money, well, I wasn't good enough for him anymore, was I? Not artsy enough."

She paused as if she had finally listened to herself and for a moment it appeared she was trying to rein in her bitterness. She failed. "I didn't wish this kind of death on him."

"Why, what kind did you wish?" asked Delorme.

Jamina Tomkins stared at Delorme through dead black eyes and said, "A long, lingering, painful one."

"Is that why you killed him?" said Delorme, trying the same trick again.

Jamina Tomkins was made of sterner stuff though and wasn't rattled by Delorme.

"Like I said, if I had killed him, you'd have heard him screaming. It wasn't me, but when you catch who did it, tell them I said thanks." She snickered a little.

Delorme said, "You find this funny?"

"It will be. There's gonna be plenty of people who would have wanted to murder him if they knew about his latest collection. When we broke down the door, he had a painting standing on the floor next to his storeroom. You go and take a look at it, and you'll find all the motives for murder you need."

"Don't leave town," Delorme said to Jamina.

"I can't," she said. "I have nowhere to go."

***

"Do you remember a painting?" said Benderby as they walked back up the stairs to the studio.

"No," said Delorme, "and for good reason."

She pointed to where Jamina said she'd seen the painting. Nothing.

"Look at the floor," said Benderby. "That's where he would put his canvases to dry. Standing in the corner, next to what Jamina called the storeroom."

He tried the storeroom door. "Locked. At least it's not a fancy lock like the outer one. I assume no one found the key."

Delorme checked her phone. "The crime scene guy said it's a simple Yale-type lock, no key as yet." She looked at the door. "If someone put the latest painting inside the storeroom then pulled the door closed, it would lock automatically. That's how these locks work."

"Then we need to get in there," said Benderby.

"I can call for a locksmith," said Delorme.

"No need. There's an old-school way of opening locked doors. Would you like me to show you?"

"Please do."

Benderby, in response, leaned back and crashed his size 11 foot into the door slightly above the lock. It splintered with a loud crack and swung open.

"Great," said Delorme. "How are we going to explain that in the report?"

"Put it down to exigent circumstances," said Benderby.

"What does that even mean?"

"I don't know. I've been using it for years and no one has ever questioned it. I think it's a polite way of saying 'too impatient to do things properly.'"

***

The storeroom may once have been an oversized parlor in the original plans for the house, but it was now a room filled with canvases, all standing on the floor, gently leaning into each other, facing away from the door. They were neatly racked, as if someone had taken a ruler to the lines they formed and measured their spacing precisely.

"Can you estimate how many there are?" said Benderby.

Delorme scanned the room. "About two hundred, I'd say, or as near as."

"He was just about done then." He picked up the nearest one and turned it around. "My, my. Didn't you say he was a portrait painter?"

"Yes. What did you find?"

"A new string to his bow, apparently." He turned it and showed it to Delorme. It was a nude, middle-aged woman. As per Tomkin's style, most of the painting was slightly fuzzy, as if seen through intoxicated eyes. With two exceptions.

"You said his previous collections always had one section sharply in focus, normally the face?"

"That's been the pattern of his work," said Delorme. She looked at the picture more closely.

"Well, there are two clear parts to this portrait. The face, and the, ah, the parts that make a nude painting nude. Do you think the artist was making a point?"

"I've seen some of his previous work and his anger has always shown through, as if he hated his subjects. He's never been the kind of artist you'd like to hang in your boudoir. But this, wow! This is so angry that it's ugly." Delorme picked up another. "It is as if he's doing tabloid portraiture. Naming and shaming."

"That's a good description," said Benderby. "I wonder if one or more of the subjects found out about these works and decided to come and take a look. Can you get the housekeeper back up here, please?"

Delorme sent for the constable on the door, and a few minutes later Jamina Tomkins came into the room.

She looked at the few visible paintings. "Whoa," she said, "he's done the whole collection nude? That's going to cause some trouble. You let me know when this becomes public, will you? I want to get out of town before the village people storm the castle with flaming torches."

She took a few steps closer. "Still, it's his best work artistically. Powerful strokes, bold brushwork."

"Why would he change his methods? Do you think he was trying to torment the community?"

Jamina Tomkins laughed. "Their feelings wouldn't occur to him. He wouldn't care, he never did. To Silas, his art was always a progression. Every series he's done has been greater than the one before. That's the nature of his work."

"So why the nudes?" said Delorme.

"It's the next step, isn't it? All the greats study the naked human form and eventually they paint it. Also, he had the opportunity here." She pointed out the window. "I never knew why he rented this particular place until now. It wasn't his style, but the back of the house leads out onto a *cul-de-sac.* His previous collections were fueled by meeting people on the street and taking their photos. With this set, he would have needed a place where the women could take off their clothes, discreetly. It explains all the traffic over the last year."

"Weren't you curious?" said Benderby.

"No," she said. "I thought it was about his rampant sex drive." She stared at the paintings. "These aren't about lust though, are they? They're angry. This is the true Silas Tomkins. The man who hated women."

After she went back downstairs, Benderby said, "I was hoping she might narrow down the suspect pool, but she's just increased it by about two hundred. Maybe we should look at the how rather than the why. There's still a slight chance it was a heart attack, and he fell on his brush. Or was it either a planned murder or just a fortuitous opportunity?"

"And don't forget the locked room part," said Delorme.

"I think if we look at the murder, the mechanics of the locked door will be revealed. What we need now is an actual cause and time of death."

"The coroner will send me the preliminary findings as soon as they can. I'm just waiting for the ping on my phone," she said, holding it up.

They continued looking at the pictures. Benderby, not knowing the community, tried to categorize them according to age, to no avail. He tried other refinements, hair color, size, ethnicity, and found nothing that formed a pattern.

"This is an eclectic collection. Apart from the anger and naked nature of the works, there seems to be nothing in common."

"There's something," said Delorme. "Oh, dear."

She picked up another painting and looked at it. "This one is the Reeve, Diana Formby. What on earth was she thinking to pose like that? And this is the credit union manager, while this," she said, holding up a picture of a gray-haired woman, "is my former Sunday school teacher."

She put it down and spread her arms as if encompassing the collection. "There is a theme. They are all prominent women of the town."

"Meaning?" said Benderby.

"Meaning that you would find these women at the art gallery cheese and wine receptions, or the library poetry evenings. They vote for the best non-profit of the year, and they are involved with the school board, the town council and every single fundraiser going. They're the ones who raise money for the Sudan or Senegal, Somalia or Syria."

She seemed to be gathering steam, so Benderby interrupted. "Your point, Corporal?"

"Sorry, yes. My point is there is no way that these women didn't boast about their naked *tete-a-tetes* to each other. In addition to being the prominent women of the community, they are also the biggest gossips."

"So, they all knew what was coming," said Benderby. "And our list of potential suspects continues to grow."

They carried on sifting through the paintings. All of them were nude. All of them, while artistically brilliant, displayed the same harshness and ugliness of the first ones they had seen, as if Tomkins had opened their souls and found only blackness.

"This is what Jamina Tomkins meant," said Delorme. "Two hundred portraits, two hundred subjects painted in the most unflattering light."

"Two hundred motives for murder."

Delorme showed him a picture of a younger lady. "This one is of Agnes Wood. We were at school together. She was the prom queen and went on to a modelling career. She is the most beautiful person in the world, and kind as well. Yet if you were to look at this, she appears as if she were evil personified. Why did he do that? At first, I thought he was painting them as they really are, as if he was looking into their souls. But he wasn't here in Fort Clearwater long enough to get to know them. And this one of Agnes is just so wrong. That is not her at all. She is kind and warm. Why did he do that to her? Why did they all pose nude for him? That's what I don't understand."

"It's intoxicating, the idea of being immortalized on canvas," said Benderby. "We'll probably never know how he managed to do it, but whatever he did, whatever he told them, it worked. The evidence speaks for itself. Unless, maybe he just took photos of their faces and added the rest later, painting them nude without their knowledge or permission. But then why did he need to have them visit?"

"Eww, that's creepy," said Delorme. "Besides, I don't think that's what happened. He had the opportunity to take nude photos of them, so I think that's what he did."

She paused, thinking aloud. "Tomkins had just created the most startling body of work he had ever done. Regardless of these women's feelings, the art world was going to sit up and take notice of these works. He painted them naked, I'm sure of that."

She nodded at one of the paintings. "Agnes and I were at school together for six years. We played on the same teams, showered afterwards." She pointed toward the high upper thigh. "That birthmark is part of Agnes. I know that, and a couple of former high school basketball players know that. But for Tomkins to have painted it, well..." she let her sentence trail off.

"It means he knew about it as well," said Benderby. "No doubt with a close examination of the paintings, a task best left to others, we could establish that fact conclusively. But it doesn't help us discover who the murderer is, does it? Remember, no one has seen these paintings. It is quite likely that none of these women anticipated what a high-scale exhibition this would be. Then, and only then, would these two hundred reasons for murder become valid. Are there any anomalies?"

"Nothing that sticks out," said Delorme.

There was an uncomfortable pause as though Benderby's mind was working so hard, his body had frozen. It made Delorme feel that she had missed something, or messed something up.

"Wait," he said. "Say that again?"

"Nothing sticks out," said Delorme.

"That's it," said Benderby. "That's what I was missing. Something does stick out. Get your phone and show me the photographs you took of the paintings in the storeroom before we moved anything."

Delorme did as asked.

"There," said Benderby. "Jamina Tomkins said there was a painting standing on the floor next to the storeroom. It must have been the one he was working on all night. He took it off the easel, stood it there to dry. Later on, he would have put it away, in a perfectly organized and tidy row, with all the others. Except for this one. Look at it."

Delorme tried to see what Benderby was seeing. "It sticks out a bit, but it's barely noticeable."

"To you and me, maybe. But Silas Tomkins lined up his works in the storeroom with a precision bordering on fanaticism. He would have noticed that one painting, and he would have fixed it, unless…" He paused, waiting for Delorme to catch up.

"Unless he was already lying on the floor of his studio, which means the killer tried to hide it."

"Correct," said Benderby. "What's so special about it?"

Delorme fetched it and brought it into the studio. She held it in such a way so as not to see it, as if she already knew. Benderby knew who it was as well, even though he had never met her. It could only be one person.

"I think we need to go and have a chat downstairs. Delorme, why don't you gather them together downstairs? Let's see if we can get a confession."

***

Meredith Tomkins sat at one end of the dining room table, Jamina Tomkins at the extreme opposite end. The emergency responder James Sutcliffe, Jimmy as Delorme had called him, sat in the middle, an inadequate barrier should warfare erupt. Whatever presumed civility had gone on while the artist was alive, had dissipated in the few hours of his passing. The two women looked as if they could kill each other for sport.

"I need to create a timeline," said Benderby, "and to do this I need your help."

He was interrupted by a ping from Delorme's phone. She read the message, then passed the phone to Benderby, who read it and nodded. It confirmed what he had suspected.

Now he just needed to close the case.

He turned to the stepdaughter first. "You say you noticed Silas hadn't come down from the studio at what time?"

"It was a little after two in the morning," she said.

"How did you notice?" said Delorme, as pleasantly as she could.

Meredith Tomkins looked uneasy. "Erm…"

"Because the other side of the bed was cold," said Jamina. "The slut has been sleeping with Daddy for years, probably far enough back to qualify him as a pedophile."

"He wasn't my father," said Meredith. "He was, once, my stepfather. That is all. And at least he wanted to sleep with me," she said to Jamina. "He gave you up years ago."

Delorme moved in between them as if to protect Jimmy Sutcliffe, but the expected explosion didn't come. Jamina looked like Meredith's words had slapped her in the face, but she waved her hand and said, "Whatever." She leaned back, distancing herself from her life.

Delorme looked at her notes. "You called on Jamina to force the door. Why didn't you try yourself?"

Meredith Tomkins held up her hands. "Hell-o-o. Brand new nails. I wasn't going to damage them. I left her to find a way in while I called 911."

"And you responded?" Benderby said to Sutcliffe.

"Yes, that's right. A call like that would be texted to all of us in Emergency Response. I said I was on my way as I lived nearby. When I arrived, Jamina was trying to force the door, so I helped her."

"After you broke through the door," said Benderby, "what happened next?"

"I went to the body on the floor to see what I could do," said Sutcliffe.

"And you?" said Delorme to Jamina Tomkins.

"I, er, I just stood there. I saw the painting leaning in the spot where he put all his work to dry. I remember thinking, Holy Geez, he's done it this time."

"It was the first you knew that Silas was painting the women of Fort Clearwater as nudes?" asked Benderby.

"So help me God, it was the first I knew," said Jamina.

"And you never went near the body?"

"Never touched him."

"And you," he said to Meredith.

"I never even went in the room," she said.

"Which leaves one person," said Benderby. "How did you feel, Jimmy, when you entered the artist's studio and the first thing you saw was a naked portrait of your mother?"

It was an appropriate moment for a cliché—the silence was deafening, you could have heard a pin drop. Benderby always liked the phrase 'a deathly silence', and this one held on and was interrupted only by Sutcliffe saying, "I wanted to kill him."

"And so you did."

"And so I did."

He had seen the picture as he knelt. At first, he didn't recognize his mother. He didn't want to believe it.

"There was a star-shaped scar on her hip, from a biking accident when she was a girl. You could only ever see it if Mom wore a swimsuit, and she hadn't done so for years."

"But you recognized it, and then you found that Silas Tomkins was still alive. He was in poor shape, and if you had left him alone, he likely would have died anyway from the heart attack he had suffered. According to the coroner's preliminary report, it was a miracle he was still alive."

"But he was," said Delorme.

"But he was," said Benderby.

"I was so angry," said Sutcliffe. "How dare he do that to my mother? She didn't deserve that."

Left unsaid was that she had been a willing volunteer in the artistic process. Perhaps that was too hard for Jimmy to wrap his head around.

"So, you stabbed him with the first thing you could get hold of," said Delorme. "Oh, Jimmy, why?"

"I didn't mean to. I was just so mad. I didn't mean to." When the uniforms took him away, he was still muttering, "I didn't mean to."

But it was too late.

***

"Poor Jimmy Sutcliffe," said Delorme. "He only lost his temper twice in his life. He should have done what he did last time. Clenching your fists is much smarter than stabbing someone with a sharp object."

"And in the end, it wasn't a locked room mystery after all," said Benderby.

"Of course it was," said Delorme.

"Not really. If you recall, at the point when the murder occurred, when Sutcliffe applied paintbrush to eyeball, the door was already open."

"Ick," said Delorme.

"Indeed," said Benderby. "Did you discover what this collection was going to be called?"

"There was a note found by the crime scene guys. They didn't know what it meant, but we do. *Malevolent Masterpieces*."

"Pity he didn't wait for N," said Benderby. "He could have gone with *Naughty Nudes*. Oh well, like Grafton's Z is for... we'll never know."

The 13th Letter

M

The End

CARDIOPULMONARY ARREST

By Melissa Yi

Rainier Hetherington crossed his arms while his wife kissed the air around her ancient father-in-law's cheeks. Frieda always pursed her lipsticked mouth into a perfect pout before she sighed, "Mr. Hetherington, *you* look *wonderful*."

Of course, Rainier's "wonderful" father, William Hetherington III, appeared paler and more wrinkled than his bedsheets. He smelled like morning breath and Listerine. The old man's oxygen hissed because his mask didn't fit properly over his mustache and beard.

William Hetherington III stretched his wrinkled hand upward to stroke Frieda's cheek. She flinched before she could check herself and covered it up with a small laugh. "You still have life in you yet. I mean..."

"I know what you mean," William breathed into his mask, and Frieda jerked back from the bed with a nervous grin.

"Children! Say hello to your grandfather!" Frieda told Harry and Pippa.

Harry held out his hand to shake, but he was trembling. William touched his grandson's palm with his gnarled fingers.

Pippa bobbed a curtsey.

"Give him a kiss," said Frieda.

Pippa shook her head, wide-eyed. She glanced at Rainier.

"How about a hug?" said Rainier, hating himself, but the old man banked over a billion dollars. That was worth some last-minute TLC.

Pippa threw her tiny arms around the old man's neck and squeezed. He closed his eyes and grinned, showing off his nicotine-stained teeth. Then he said, "Time for some father-son time."

"Of course," said Frieda, hurrying the children away, but not before she air-kissed the old man on the cheek again and said, "Love you, Pops."

After the door closed behind them, William said, "Quite an actress you got there, son."

Rainier pretended not to know what he meant. "Yes. She wanted to go to Hollywood at one point."

"Better for her to stick with the Hetheringtons, though. We're the sure bet." William started up one of his coughs.

Rainier stared at his laced fists, waiting for the fit to end. At long last, William yanked his oxygen mask aside and horked some sputum into a blue plastic cup. "Want to see?"

Rainier shook his head.

"That's the problem with you. You never wanted to face things head-on. You were always your momma's boy. I was sure I'd have another kid, someone with a little more—"

Rainier stood up. "Your corporation cleared a seven percent profit under my reign. In your final two years, you hemorrhaged $2.7 million."

William waved his hand. "Accounting, boy. That's not what I was talking about anyway."

Rainier sat back down. Not talking about business? When did that happen?

"I have something much more important for you. An early bequest. Very hush-hush. Something that's helped make the Hetherington name into the empire it is today, a legacy that you will pass on to your two children." William pointed at a black computer tower in the corner of the room, a non-descript antique about the size of a filing cabinet, with two closed doors on top, an open slot near the bottom, and a green light on its front indicating that it was on.

"What is it?" Rainier expected some sort of stock fund predictor. His father also funded inventors and entrepreneurs and took their patents in exchange.

"My father named it Azreal."

Rainier didn't know whether to laugh or curse after he managed to decode the name. "The Angel of Death? Is this a joke?"

"No, it's a nickname for an instrument that analyzes reams of data in order to answer a question. Your grandfather struck upon the idea to ask only the most specific and pertinent question of all. With a blood sample and the correct inputs, Azreal will deliver unto you your most likely cause of death."

Rainier didn't move.

William cracked a grin, even though he was breathing hard after that speech. "Azreal's been working on you since you were born. It interfaces with the nanobots in your bloodstream to analyze your hormones and rate your nutrition. It watches you through your webcams, security cams, and public records. It scrapes data every time you click your watch or take a dump—yes, I understand that your gut flora tells quite a tale. Still, there's no substitute for good, old-fashioned hemoglobin."

Rainier said nothing. He remembered private doctors taking blood from him more than once.

"I can tell you what your card says."

Even when he screamed and kicked.

"That's what it does, it prints out a word or two on a little card."

Once, Rainier wrenched his arm away, dislodging the needle, but they simply brought two more goons in to hold him down while William stood over him and said, *Do that one more time and you'll pay for it, boy.*

"Oh, boo-hoo," William snapped, before he broke off into a long cough. "My father did it to me, too. That's how we built the Hetherington name and fortune. We collected money, we found influence, but it's more than that. Our family controls the *future*. There are no secrets from us. Better than a private detective, although I hired those too, of course, for those women of yours."

Rainier met his father's cold blue eyes.

The old man bared his teeth. "We had to break those off. Only the best for a Hetherington. You remember that one you had in college?"

Sarah, the socialist who wrapped her legs around Rainier's waist and whispered, "Fuck your father. We belong together."

"Her card said 'SUICIDE.' We couldn't afford mental illness in our gene pool."

Rainier licked his suddenly dry lips. "She died in a car accident." He'd sent white lilies, her favorite flower, with no card.

William waved his hand. "Single car accident. 'Died suddenly.' Azreal told me the truth."

Rainier said a silent prayer for Sarah, even as he moved on to the only other woman he'd loved. "Did you test Susan Jensen?"

William's lips smirked under the oxygen mask. "Of course. Name her, we tested her."

"How did you get Susan's blood?" Rainier wanted to rip the mask off his father's face and smother him with a pillow. Instead, he assumed a look of amusement.

William laughed. "We sent someone to pose as an insurance agent needing an extra sample. She never missed it."

Rainier remembered Susan applying for disability insurance. She had insurance as a teacher, but she was very cautious. Not to mention kind and remarkably willing in bed, but she never recovered after he broke up with her. Not suicide, or at least not overtly—

William laughed. "Aren't you going to ask what her card said? I'll tell you. 'MYOCARDIAL INFARCTION /

OBESITY.' Can't have that. Not in the Hetherington family. No way, no how."

Rainier forced his voice to stay cool. "I trust that Frieda's card was acceptable?"

"Of course. 'CARDIOPULMONARY ARREST.' Say that one three times fast." William coughed a few more times before he removed the mask and spat into a sample container. "Huh. Beige. Wonder what that means."

Rainier could smell the purulent phlegm from where he stood. He waited.

"We consulted some doctors about the diagnosis. It simply means that your heart and lungs stop working. That's how everyone dies. It seemed too generic. I wondered if Azreal was malfunctioning after all this time, but we retested your wife three times, and it always came out the same."

Rainier closed his eyes. His witch of a wife would live to a ripe old age, as he'd always feared. He opened them again. "Why are you giving this... instrument to me now?"

"Couldn't just leave it to you in my will, now, could I? Azreal is one of a kind. No official records exist of her creation. She runs military-grade algorithms, cutting edge even now. My father's company was born trying to hide her presence from prying eyes, even as he used her to build his empire. Simple questions with extremely complex data. Stocks, bonds, pending natural disasters… combine Azrael with human actuarial tables and analysis, and that's how we got the reputation for reading the future. She's that good. More than once, the FEC investigated us, but they couldn't make anything stick. If they knew about Azreal, though... the privacy violations alone… Good God, the Feds would've strung me up!"

Rainier raised his head in recognition. Illegal. Contraband. Multiple violations. At long last, there was something there, something he could use.

Then William continued, "Or they would have, if I hadn't already bought them off. Now, son, you need to practice with Azreal, make sure she works for you. Simple questions, useful ones. For all her power, she requires a gentle touch. Almost like a woman." William's eyes glittered, high on more than morphine. The old man thrived on other people's discomfort and fear. "All you need is a drop of blood and you can see her power for yourself."

"I don't want to know how I'm going to die." Rainier swallowed back the acid at the back of the throat.

"You don't have to." The old man held out his quavering yet still imperious index finger. "You can practice on me."

Rainier shook his head. "I'll take away my legacy, thanks." He strode toward Azrael and touched the black plastic case. It—he refused to call it *she*—felt cool but hummed under his hand, almost like a live thing, even though it wasn't plugged in to any wall and didn't have any obvious solar panels. It must run on battery power, then.

He crouched to lift it, and found it heavier than expected. Older devices tended to be surprisingly dense.

"No. Stay here and test her on me, boy."

Rainier didn't answer. He wouldn't linger in the same room as his father for one second longer. He only took the thing with him to shut the old man up. And to show that the old man was too weak to stop him.

Rainier strained his back loading the thing onto a nearby cart and wheeling it out of the room. Perhaps he was destined to die trying to move it.

"Don't you want to see this?" said William. He yanked a yellow cardboard card, its edges brown and weathered with age, from his front pocket and held it up like a prize.

Rainier didn't falter.

"Look at my card. It hasn't changed since the day you were born. I check it every year. Come back here, boy, and look at my card. Azrael's never wrong!"

Rainier closed the door behind himself and Azreal, shutting out both the old man's commands and his next coughing spasm.

The next day, Rainier tested Azrael's algorithm. When he popped open a small plastic door level with its surface, it revealed a tiny keyboard and a monitor window that said, READY FOR YOUR QUESTION.

Rainier hesitated.

ASK YOUR QUESTION.

He typed into the little keyboard with the fingers of his right hand, since his left held a tube of blood: *cause of death?*

The screen turned black for a moment before the instrument replied, ADD DATA? Y/N

Rainier didn't know how to input any further information. He'd left before his father could demonstrate. He pressed N.

A second, even smaller, door opened to extend a needle-like tube, like a proboscis.

INSERT BLOOD

Rainier held up the tube of cow's blood.

The proboscis drank the burgundy fluid.

PROCESSING

Internal motors whirred before he heard a click, and the instrument issued a fresh yellow, rectangular card through the open slot:

MURDERED

"Doesn't pull any punches, does it," murmured Rainier.

He turned over the three-by-five card, but it seemed like a regular index card. He noted a paper tray beneath the open slot, where he could load 100 of them. On the left side, he opened another door for printer ink.

What an odd little machine it was, opened up. He wondered what lay deeper inside it. After his father died, and he was done with the thing, he resolved he'd gut it and find out.

First, he wanted to test its limits. It also decreed another vial of blood from the slaughterhouse, this one from a pig, as MURDER.

However, his daughter's dog, Scruffles, was going to die of LYMPHATIC CANCER.

After Rainer's animal trials, for the twelfth test, he bribed a lab tech to pull an extra vial of blood from his wife, Frieda, at her annual physical exam.

CARDIOPULMONARY ARREST

Rainier's breath hissed out between his teeth, but he'd already begun to feel intrigued, despite himself, when the butler announced a special delivery from William Hetherington III.

Rainier opened the box and exposed the ice packs. He already knew what he would find even before he pushed the packs aside: a vial of burgundy blood labeled with his father's name.

"No," said Rainier, as his watch chimed with an incoming call. He listened to the doctor describe his father's course. COPD exacerbation... pneumonia... possibly ARDS... intensive care... all possible measures.

Why should he run the sample in the face of three different deadly diagnoses? His father had finally landed at death's door.

On the other hand, revenge would taste very sweet. Even in the form of a yellow card.

"Would you like me to come now?" Rainier asked the doctor.

"Yes, as soon as possible. You see, he asked for all possible interventions, but I'd have to send him to a tertiary care center ICU—"

Rainier let the words wash over him as he opened the little door on Azrael and let its needle suck up his father's blood.

"—once the bill is settled. Your father had no health insurance."

"What?" said Rainier, nearly spilling the sample.

The little needle had already drunk enough. Azreal's motor began to spin and hum, processing the blood.

"Yes. Of course, that's not a medical matter, but our finance department will be in touch with you. He paid us individually for each treatment."

Rainier's mind whirled. Many people bankrupted themselves after cancer diagnoses. Exactly what kind of health care debt had his father run up—and was still planning to incur?

"Your father listed you as his health care power of attorney."

"Yes." Rainier's first impulse was to stop the financial hemorrhage in the swiftest fashion possible, even if it meant unplugging his father himself. But was that what Azrael had predicted?

And was that the reason the old man had hated him his entire life?

The doctor continued, "Before your father took a turn for the worse, he made it clear that when he became unable to speak for himself, you would make the final decisions about his care."

If the old man had drained his fortune, then Rainier had spent his entire life kowtowing to him, shoveling his life into the company, courting shareholders, marrying and having children with the iciest stick of a woman for nothing.

Nothing.

Nothing.

Except revenge.

Rainier smiled. He'd become a better player than his father had ever credited. He'd prove the old man and Azreal wrong in one blow.

First, Rainier pinged his personal accountant, then pitched his voice as soft as uncertain for the doctor. "That's right. I'm his health care POA. I already hired a new nurse. You should have met her today."

"Yes." The doctor sounded dubious. "She seems very attentive. She refuses to leave his side."

"Excellent," said Rainier. "That's what we wanted. Someone who would tend to his every last need."

"Yes. Well, when will you be coming in, Mr. Rainier?"

"I need one thing first. When I last visited, there was a little yellow card floating in his front pocket with a word or two written in capital letters. I need you to find it and read it out to me, please. It's a… password for an old computer file for the company accounts. I forgot to take it from him while I was there. I need it as part of my duty as POA."

"You want me to look for what, now?" The doctor sounded astonished,

"Never mind. I'll talk to my nurse." He messaged his private nurse, who immediately reported that she'd found two of those yellow cards and had stowed them away for safekeeping.

Of course, the old man had two. The codger checked his means of death every year, like an annual exam. However, since William claimed that the cause never varied and that Azrael was always right, the other card must be Rainer's.

Rainier suppressed a shudder, imagining his own fate already printed on a yellow index card. That knowledge would warp him the way it had his father and perhaps his father before him.

Before Rainier could become morbid, his accountant pinged back. William Hetherington III could and probably would siphon his wealth down to every last penny, but none of those debts would be transferred to the next generation.

"If you could come in now," said the doctor, "we need to talk about your father's level of care. You see, although we provide sedation and analgesia, resuscitation can be extremely … uncomfortable."

"Choking on the breathing tube? Broken ribs? Punctured lung? Brain damage?" Rainier had turned off the video, so he examined his manicure as he raised his voice to convey anxiety.

"We try to avoid it, but yes, all of the above. So you see, we have to discuss Mr. Hetherington's code status. To be honest, I wouldn't want these kinds of measures on my own father, if he were in this kind of condition with little chance of meaningful survival. Sometimes prolonging a life only means suffering, Rainier, and—wait. That nurse of yours. Patricia. Stop that, Ms. Jensen! That's *not* how you use the suction!"

Click. The doctor disconnected the call.

Click.

This time, the sound came from the black box in front of him. Rainier leveled his gaze at the machine, waiting for the thirteenth message.

Azreal spat out his father's final diagnosis on a single yellow card.

ARDS PNEUMONIA

Rainier accepted the card and patted the box. "Thanks, Azrael."

He would ask the doctor to step up the antibiotics and work on whatever ARDS was. He messaged the nurse to check if either of her cards said ARDS PNEUMONIA, while explicitly instructing her not to reveal the precise content of her own cards back to Rainer.

She replied that neither of the cards matched that diagnosis.

Azrael had changed her—no, *its*—mind.

Proof that the algorithm could alter with new input.

And buying more time with dear old dad.

If the old man pulled through, he'd eke out the remaining moments of his life broken and penniless and struggling to inhale and exhale every breath of every hour of every day and night.

Rainier would enjoy every one of those moments. So would nurse Jensen, who'd proved extremely interested in tending to William Hetherington III once she'd learned how he'd treated her sister, Susan.

"To us," said Rainier. He poured a glass of single malt Scotch. "To Sarah. To Susan and Patricia Jensen. To me."

He performed a mocking bow toward the open slot of the black box. "And naturally, to you."

He tipped his glass to the black tower and drank deeply, already calculating how he could next employ Azrael to change the fate of the lovely, empty Frieda and remake his own life.

The 13th Letter

M

The End

THE BOY IN THE PICTURE

By M.H. Callway

It began with the photograph.

I was searching for my missing swim goggles when I spotted Mother's keepsake box. There it was, a fixture in the bottom drawer of our dresser in the spare room. Normally I was oblivious to it, but today, hot on my quest, I lifted it out.

I'd always loved that box. It was soft, padded, covered in ivory pleated silk and edged with pink fabric roses: the treasure chest of a lady. Now, though, the silk was disintegrating, and the roses had faded to a pale beige.

I opened the box. The tattered lining on the inside of the lid gave way. Out fell an envelope I had never seen before. I traced my finger down a line of tiny perfect stitches at the edge of the lid, recognizing Mother's fine needlework. But why hide the envelope under the lining?

I shook out its contents. That's how I found the boy.

The photo was black and white. It showed a small boy about two years of age standing in a wading pool in a garden. He wore a cotton sunsuit that clung to his body from the wet. In his hands, he held an absurd inflatable toy that resembled the Loch Ness monster.

"Why on earth did you think that your swim goggles were hiding in your mother's old treasure chest?" asked Gordon, my partner, that night over dinner.

"Desperation." I laughed and shrugged.

"What else did your mother hide inside the lid? A secret bank account with a million dollars?"

"Hardly. Here, take a look." I passed him the envelope and watched his slender fingers search through it.

"Cute kid," he said, holding up the photo of the boy. Next, he pulled out a piece of folded drawing paper, which he carefully smoothed out.

"You must have written this to your mom," he said, passing it to me.

The words, *Mom, I love you, Helen,* were printed in elongated childish letters. I'd surrounded them with red hearts and blue flowers like daisies.

"I'm surprised she kept it," I said. "When I gave it to her, she scolded me because I called her 'Mom' instead of 'Mother.'"

"Seriously?"

"Ronald was adamant about upholding British traditions. It was always 'Mother' and 'Father.'"

"Daddy Ronald." Gordon found it amusing that I referred to my father by his Christian name. "So, what's this?" He pulled out a thin blue paper. "Looks like a letter."

"It's an aerogram, a letter and envelope combined. People used them to save on air postage."

"Well, it's 1990. The way email's taking over, these aerograms will become antique collectibles before you know it."

Gordon spread out the blue letter, trying to decipher it.

"It's not written in English," he said at last. "Your mom's family was from Europe, right?"

"Yes, from Poland. After my grandparents immigrated to England, they became more British than the British themselves."

"Maybe that's what this is, Polish." Gordon squinted at the letter. "Any chance you can read it?"

"Absolutely none."

"Too bad your mum's gone. See, the letter's addressed to her, Mrs. Ronald Pierce." He pointed to the name printed on the back.

"Enough nostalgia." I took the letter from him and shoved it, my childish greeting note and boy's picture, back into the creased envelope. "Let's have our tea."

***

But that night, I dreamed about the boy. I could feel the grass in the garden prickling my bare feet and the sun hot on my face—the heady perfume of lilacs was everywhere.

The boy splashed in his wading pool, smiling at me. His damp sunsuit was yellow with the white thread of a check running through it. I bent down and took him in my arms. I could feel his sandy hair against my cheek, smell his sweet scent…

"Helen, wake up! Helen!"

I was sitting up in bed. My face was wet with tears. "I know that boy, Gordon. *I know that boy*!"

"It's a dream, a vivid dream, that's all."

"I know that garden. It had a boxwood hedge. Black bugs would stick to the leaves like bits of licorice. And there was a garage by the back alley, all falling down."

"OK, OK, so you knew the little boy. But you were an only child, right?"

I nodded. "My parents didn't even want *me*."

"Could he have been a relative?"

"We didn't know anyone when we moved to Canada. Vancouver Island was as far from our London relatives as we could get without moving to Australia."

"Well, then, he was probably a neighbor's child. Some Brits your parents got friendly with."

"Yes, that makes sense." I lay back down, wiped my eyes with the back of my hand. "But why would my mother keep the photo? She was never sentimental."

Gordon snuggled up against me. "Maybe she was, but you were too young to see it. I mean, she died when you were just a teenager, right?"

"Seventeen, I was seventeen."

That April day was forever seared in my memory. I was at boarding school in Victoria though my parents lived only a short distance away in Nanaimo. Mrs. Blake, the headmistress, summoned me to her office in the middle of my science lab. Ronald was there, without Mother.

"I'm afraid we have some very bad news," she began before Ronald took over.

Ramrod straight, brown moustache perfectly trimmed, he informed me Mother had died of an aneurysm. The funeral was tomorrow.

All the breath left my body at once. Death happened to other people. I should cry and scream, but I couldn't. All I said was one word: "Mother…"

Mrs. Blake helped me pack my overnight things into a small white cardboard suitcase with a red handle. At the school's front entrance, she squeezed my shoulder, a rare gesture of warmth, before I climbed into Ronald's blue Austin for the journey home to Nanaimo. All the way back, Ronald refused to answer my questions as he stared straight through the windshield at the two-lane highway.

I barely recognized our house, I'd spent so little time there. A heavy-set, white-haired woman was waiting for us at the front door to tell us dinner was ready. She introduced herself as Miss Whitton, the housekeeper.

"She's made up the spare room," Ronald told me. "You can sleep there."

The service was held the next day in a downtown church with gray brick walls. Church of England, of course. It was sunny, I remember, not at all in keeping with a funeral. Inside the walls were white, the stained-glass windows shimmering with red and gold. I looked everywhere for Mother.

Miss Whitton touched my arm. Close by the entrance stood a table covered with a white damask cloth. On it stood a vase of red roses and a photo of my mother as a young woman. She had long dark wavy hair and large expressive eyes, more beautiful than I could ever hope to be.

"But where is she?" I asked.

Miss Whitton threw a sideways glance at Ronald, lowered her voice and said, "In the box, dear. Behind the roses."

I saw it then, the gray cardboard box, so small, too small to hold a human being. I should have known; lately Ronald had become a strong advocate of cremation.

I remember very little of Mother's service and the reception in the church hall afterward. The large crowd felt suffocating: all middle-aged, no children or young people that I could see. Most were parishioners, because Ronald was popular with the church community. At Morning Prayer he'd read the gospel with verve and drama, or he'd lead the choir in rousing versions of "Onward Christian Soldiers." And he was an enthusiastic participant in Bible Study during the week.

As the reception wound down, Miss Whitton came over to me. "You look so much like your mother, you know."

"No, I don't. My hair is blond and straight."

"You have the same eyes." She squeezed my shoulder, the same way Mrs. Blake, the headmistress, did on the steps of my school. "Good luck, my dear," she whispered. "Use this if you need it." She slipped me an envelope.

"Aren't you coming with us?"

"My services are no longer required, now that your mother's left us."

Ronald was flushed, angry on the drive home. Even in the fading evening light, I could make out the web of capillaries in the skin stretched tight over his cheekbones. He poured himself a stiff gin and tonic as soon as we got in through the front door.

"Right, you won't be going back to that ridiculous school," he said.

"But term doesn't finish until June," I protested. "I graduate in June."

"Doesn't matter. I can't bloody well afford it, can I? It was your mother's money paid for it."

I wanted to say that Mother's money would be his now, but thought better of it.

"And another thing, now that you're of age, you'll start paying me room and board."

"I don't understand. What do you mean room and board?"

"Don't get cheeky with me, Miss Clever-sticks. My father," he took a deep breath, "my father charged me room and board the minute I signed up with the Navy and started earning my keep. You'll do the same."

"But I haven't any money."

"Be quiet! Don't contradict me! Now get out of my sight."

I fled back to the spare room. It had an old-fashioned lock with a turnkey, which I now quietly withdrew. Through the walls I could hear the blare of the radio turned to the CBC news. Even though it was 1967, Ronald was a holdout against television, calling it a demonic American invention.

I locked the door from the inside and packed my suitcase. In the top dresser drawer, I found Mother's white silk keepsake box. There was nothing inside it, but I took it anyway, the only memento I had of her.

I opened the window of the spare room, lowered my suitcase to the soft grass outside then climbed out myself. The moon was up, bathing the world in a soft blue light. I could see my way clearly and started walking.

I was lucky. The road into Nanaimo remained deserted. I didn't encounter any cougars or bad people. And Ronald was too far gone into his Gordon's gin to notice I'd decamped.

I found my way to the bus station and huddled, shivering, on an outside bench until early morning when I caught the first bus back to Victoria. The $20 Miss Whitton had slipped me paid for the ticket.

Back at boarding school, my true home, Mrs. Blake drew on the school's scholarship fund to pay my way through to the end of term. Later she helped me apply for the student loans that put me through university. Ronald did telephone the school a few times, raging, but in the end his burning desire to save money outweighed his thirst for control and he gave it up.

***

"You, OK?" Gordon asked at breakfast. "You seem, well, anxious. Maybe you shouldn't go to work today. Maybe I should stay home with you."

"I'm fine, I'm absolutely fine. It's the boy. Seeing him…I…the past feels crushing when I let it in. Like I'm drowning."

"Then don't think about it." Gordon poured us more coffee. "I never do. The past is gone, it's irrelevant."

"I don't understand how you can feel that way."

"Look at me. I'm a nerd. My life in school was awful until I got my revenge and became a highly paid tax accountant."

I had to laugh. The reason I loved Gordon, with his soft brown hair and mild hazel eyes, was that he was so funny and down-to-earth.

But I couldn't let the past go. "How old were you when you started remembering?"

Gordon frowned. "I don't know, four, maybe five."

"I don't remember anything before age eight. It's a blank, an empty space. I don't think that's normal."

"Everybody's different." He fiddled with the crumbs of his croissant. "Look, you're obviously upset about that kid. Why don't you ask your old roommate, Patricia, back at U. Vic? It's a long shot, I know, but it's worth a try, right?"

"I haven't talked or written to Patty for ages. We lost touch after she did the whole marriage-with-kids thing."

And in truth I felt guilty, because I owed Patty so much. Not only were we best friends all through university, she'd strong-armed her dad into giving me a job at his grocery store. Without that extra money, I wouldn't have finished my math degree.

"Just phone her already," Gordon said.

And so I did. Being a senior actuary at the insurance company, I had a fair amount of autonomy, so I worked at home that morning. Remembering that Victoria time was three hours behind Toronto's, I waited until noon before I dialed Patty's number.

She answered on the second ring; she sounded frazzled.

"Helen? Oh, my God, I don't believe it! How *are* you? Nobody died, I hope."

"All good here. Gordon and I are still together. And no, we're not married."

"And here's me hoping I'd have a wedding to go to."

Patty, ever the extrovert, launched into tales of feeding her three teenaged sons, their latest family sailing expedition and her part-time job as events coordinator at their yacht club.

I tried to stem the tide. "Look, I found this picture my mom kept of a little boy. I haven't a clue who he is. Could you look at it on the off-chance that you might recognize him?"

"Sure, fax it to my office at the club. I'll be there later this afternoon. Isn't it fun to be able to say 'my office?' About time we women did!"

She called me at home late that night. She had no idea who the boy was.

"He's so cute. Absolutely adorable," she said. "Maybe he's one of your English cousins."

"No, both my parents were only children."

"Like you, I know. Maybe he's the kid of one of their friends back in England. Look, if you're really bothered, you could, well, ask your dad."

"I haven't spoken to Ronald in 20 years."

"Sorry, I didn't know it was still an issue between you two."

"Honestly, Patty, I don't even know if he's alive." In fact, I hope he's not, I added silently.

I sensed her hesitation at the other end of the line. "You could always check out your parents' friends in Calgary."

"*Calgary*?"

"Yes, where you and your folks lived before you moved to Nanaimo. Don't you remember Ronald's funny story about you getting frostbite playing outside in Calgary and how he threatened to cut off your leg?"

"No, I don't."

And I had no memories of Calgary, none at all. After we hung up, I retrieved the blue aerogram letter from Mother's keepsake box. There, under the printed name "Mrs. Ronald Pierce" was the address, 1102 -18th Avenue SW, Calgary, Alberta.

How could I have missed that?

***

"I'm flying to Calgary tomorrow," I told Gordon when he got home. "I want to see that address for myself."

"What earthly good will that do? OK, so you lived in Calgary, what, 30 years ago? What if the house is gone and there's nothing there but a ten-story building? You'll have flown all that way for nothing."

"There's something else." I told him about my phone conversation with Patty. "*She* remembers that I lived in Calgary. Even some nasty story about Ronald threatening to cut off my leg when I got frostbite. I don't remember that story."

Gordon thought for a minute. "Did Ronald visit you and Patty at U. Vic.? Maybe that's when he told her that story about you. You said he could turn on the charm when he wanted."

Ronald had never visited us at university, I'd made sure of that. "It doesn't matter. I'm flying to Calgary."

"OK," Gordon said. "Then I'm coming with you."

"No, I need to do this alone."

***

The next morning Gordon drove me to the airport, not bothering to hide his misgivings. I promised to call him every night on my new Nokia cell phone, forget the cost. Weren't we DINKS—double income no kids? We could afford the long-distance charges.

Landing in Calgary four hours later, I took in the vast yellow grasslands fringed by the faraway Rocky Mountains. The March afternoon air felt as balmy as summer when I walked to the car rental office.

"I thought Calgary would be much colder than Toronto, especially this early in the year," I said to the man behind the counter.

"It's the chinook," he said. "Only happens on the prairies. The west wind blows down the slopes of the Rockies and pushes up the temperature 25 degrees."

"And what happens when the wind changes?"

"Well, then you got a problem," he laughed. "The temperature comes down hard. You don't want to get caught outside without a coat."

It felt surreal filling out the paperwork for my Honda Accord, but once I was sitting behind the steering wheel, I felt free.

I drove out of the airport and promptly got lost. Calgary, I soon discovered, sprawled over the prairie like a tattered quilt, pieces of city interspersed by tracts of wilderness or industrial wasteland. Each piece was its own entity. Downtown with its tall buildings could be any modern city. To the north lay a suburb of split-level, wood-frame houses with perfectly trimmed lawns, a time capsule from the 1950s. Heading south, I meandered through the hills and valleys where Calgary's well-to-do lived, passing houses of brick and stone surrounded by tall trees.

The street I wanted, 18th Avenue SW, branched off a busy road lined with shops. I completely missed the turn, so I drove on until I came to an elementary school built of mud-brown stone.

I pulled into the visitors' parking lot. Could I have gone to school here? I parked and climbed out into the sunshine, smiling at the playground and the separate boys' and girls' entrances.

But nothing, no memories at all.

I took my chances and left my winter coat in the car. It was a long walk back down the busy road. Stopping to catch my bearings, I spotted a retro diner with a red neon sign saying "Open" and when I looked up, there was the signpost for 18th Avenue SW.

I took a deep breath and stepped into the quiet of a residential street.

Low-rise apartment buildings lined both sides of the road. So Gordon, as usual, was right. The single-family homes had been torn down to make way for more compressed living. I searched in my purse for Mother's aerogram letter and checked the address: Number 1102 lay much farther down the street.

In the distance, the apartment buildings appeared to give way to single-family houses. My heart lifted.

The first residence I reached was a heritage home with gingerbread woodwork. Sadly, that was not Number 1102. Immediately past it lay an empty lot turned into a communal garden. A man, wearing a red-and-black checked shirt and soiled jeans, was hard at work tearing dead plants from the soil. He noticed me, set down his trowel and came over, knocking the dirt from his leather work gloves.

"Can I help you with something?" He was about 50, short and wiry, with straight dark hair combed back from his forehead.

"Sure," I said. "I'm looking for Number 1102."

"What for?"

"It's, well, personal."

He gave me a look without saying anything further.

"Well, um, thanks." What's your problem, I thought and carried on down the sidewalk, checking each house number as I went.

All the houses looked modern, built within the last ten years. Finally, I arrived at Number 1102. More stylish than its neighbors, it sported a yellow stucco façade, a closely trimmed front lawn and a low boxwood hedge bordering the sidewalk.

Boxwood…I reached out to touch it.

"What do you think you're doing?"

The man from the allotments stood so close behind me, I jumped.

"Why are you following me?" I shot back.

"Because that's my house you're looking at. What's your interest in it?"

"I think I lived here as a child." When he didn't reply, I said, "Obviously, not *your* house, but the house that stood here before. The one they tore down to build your place. Do you know what it looked like?"

His eyes narrowed, but he didn't say anything.

"I remember a garden with lilacs and a boxwood hedge like this one. And a wooden garage, all falling down. The house was covered in brown wood shingles."

He took a breath. "OK, wait here. Don't go away."

He went up the stone path to his house, bounded up the porch steps and disappeared inside.

I waited five minutes, then ten minutes, until it became clear he had no intention of reappearing or telling me anything.

Frustrated, I retraced my steps along the sidewalk. What a colossal waste of time, squandering money on an ephemeral childhood memory, a dream, a wishful fantasy!

I was losing it, I had to be.

A black-and-white police car pulled up next to the allotment garden. As I approached, a young patrolman climbed out.

"Ma'am, may I have a word?" Tall and well-built, he blocked my way forward.

"Is there a problem, Officer?"

"Mr. Doyle says you're taking an unusual interest in his home."

"Unusual interest?" Why that jerk Doyle! He'd called the cops while I stood waiting on the sidewalk.

"Could I see some ID?" the cop asked.

Wordlessly, I dug out my driver's license and gave it to him.

"So, you live in Toronto," he said. "Why were you checking out Mr. Doyle's house?"

"Checking out his house? Do I look like a burglar to you?"

He couldn't hide his smile. "We get female burglars in Calgary. Equal opportunity and all that."

"Your Mr. Doyle is a damn liar. I never set foot on his stupid property. I lived there when I was a kid, that's all. Now, am I under arrest or what?"

He held up his hands in a conciliatory gesture and let me by.

My heart was beating so rapidly by the time I reached the street corner, I was out of breath. I headed straight for the diner I'd spotted earlier, took refuge in a back booth and ordered a large Diet Coke with plenty of ice. What was I going to tell Gordon? That not only had I made a fool of myself, but I'd nearly been arrested?

I'd barely taken a sip of my drink when the cop materialized next to my booth.

"You're going to need this." He set my driver's license down on the table in front me.

I shoved it back into my wallet without a word.

"Do you mind if I join you?" he asked.

"What for?"

He slid onto the seat opposite me and took off his hat, revealing a headful of sandy hair. His eyes were a vivid blue; he couldn't have been more than 25 years old.

"I'm Constable Steve Novak," he said. "Look, we got off on the wrong foot back there. Mr. Doyle's a bit sensitive about people hanging around his place. Understandable on account of what happened, right?"

A chill ran through me. "What happened at Doyle's house?"

"You mean you don't know?"

"I live in Toronto. How would I know what happened in Calgary thousands of miles away?"

"It was all over the news."

"I'm not lying." I found Mother's secret envelope in my purse and showed him the blue aerogram letter. "See this? It's addressed to my mom. There's her name, Mrs. Ronald Pierce. The address is 1102-18th Avenue SW, the same as Doyle's house."

"May I see that?"

He frowned as he studied it. Suddenly he smiled. "This is written in Polish."

"My grandparents were Polish. Can *you* read what it says?"

He shook his head. "My dad can. If you bring this into the police department, I'll ask him to take a look."

"Your dad?" I said.

He nodded. "Superintendent Novak. He grew up speaking Polish as a kid." He handed the letter back to me. "And there's a detective, Sergeant Valerie Fox. I think you two should talk."

***

I checked into the Palliser, an old-fashioned CPR hotel in Calgary's downtown. I hadn't eaten since breakfast, so I made my way down to the Oak Room Bar where I ordered a club sandwich and a *Perfect Palliser*, the hotel's signature cocktail.

The ring of my cell phone startled me. But it wasn't Gordon, it was Patty.

"Hi there." She sounded disgustingly cheerful. "Gordon says you're in Calgary. Is that true?"

"I'm sitting in the bar of Calgary's grandest hotel even as we speak."

"Nice!" She hesitated, drew in a breath. "Were you joking when you said you didn't know if Ronald was alive?"

"No, I wasn't joking."

"OK, look, I never told you, because, well, you and your dad don't get along. Please don't take this the wrong way. Oh, this is so awkward!"

"Come on, Patty. Just tell me."

"All right, your dad belonged to our yacht club."

"What! How did that happen?"

"He moved to Victoria about 15 years ago, right after he retired. He was so keen to join. You know how much he missed the sea after the War. So, we, well, sponsored him."

So, Ronald had fooled Patty and her husband with his fairy tales about being a navigator on a destroyer during the Battle of the Atlantic. Lies, of course. He'd spent the war working as a clerk in a naval warehouse. In fact, that's where he and Mother met. After joining the Auxiliary Territorial Service, she was assigned to work for him. And Ronald had even lied about being a Lieutenant. Mother had shown me his discharge papers: he'd never risen above Petty Officer, Second Class.

"Helen, are you still there?"

Part of me wanted to rage at Patty for falling for Ronald's wiles, but then most people did.

"Is he…is he still living in Victoria?" I managed to say.

"No, I thought that's why you're in Calgary. He moved to the Peace River Veterans Hospital two years ago after he had that stroke."

***

So, Ronald was still alive. He'd be 80 now, a vulnerable age for strokes.

Back in my hotel room, I slumped down on the queen-sized bed, wondering what to tell Gordon. He was meeting his parents for dinner, so I left him a short voicemail at home, trying to sound cheerful and reassuring while telling him nothing.

I barely slept. My restless night was peopled with dreams: endless white corridors snaking into dead-ends, elderly men shouting, hard-faced nurses wielding sharp syringes…

The shrill cry of the hotel telephone woke me at 8 a.m.

"This is Detective Valerie Fox," a woman's voice said. "Am I speaking with Helen Pierce?"

I tried to rub the sleep from my eyes. "Yes, that's me."

"Could you come by police headquarters this morning?" she asked.

"Am I in trouble?"

She laughed. "Not yet. Ask the officer on the front desk to page me when you get here."

***

The police department occupied a tall gray municipal building less than a kilometer from the Palliser Hotel. The icy wind whipped through my winter coat, making me regret my decision to walk there. The chinook was over; the temperature had dropped to a wintry level.

Sergeant Fox looked nothing like a police detective. She was about my age, well-fed and a bit untidy. In her rumpled pink wool dress, she reminded me of a working mom dropping off her kids at school.

"Thanks for coming in. I'm Valerie Fox." She smiled. "I'm not what you were expecting, right?"

She led the way to her office on the third floor. The windowless room was so crammed with filing cabinets and loose files, there was barely enough room for the two of us.

"I head up our new department." She plonked herself down behind the desk and motioned me to take the single chair in front of it. "Do you know what a cold case is?"

I nodded. My mouth had gone dry. "Have you solved any?"

"A few thanks to new technologies like DNA testing." She leaned forward on her desk. "PC Novak says you have a letter proving that you lived at 1102 - 18th Avenue SW. May I see it?"

"It's in Polish," I said. "PC Novak said his father can read it."

"I'll make sure Superintendent Novak sees it."

I handed over the aerogram and watched her as she looked it over.

"May I ask how old you are?" she asked.

"I-I'm forty."

"So, you were born in 1950, right? That would make you seven when you lived here."

"How do you figure that?"

She pointed to the top of the letter. There was the date, April 13, 1957, written in English—unlike the rest of the letter.

"But I don't remember living there! I don't remember anything until we moved to Nanaimo when I was eight," I said.

She raised an eyebrow.

"That's why I'm here in Calgary. Because of the boy in the picture." I showed her the photo from Mother's envelope.

She breathed in sharply as she took it from me.

"Tell me what you remember." Her fingers trembled slightly as she held the photograph. "Every detail, no matter how trivial it seems."

Sun-bleached colors bombarded me: white, yellow, traces of red. The images had no form. I couldn't breathe. I was drowning in a river of paintings.

I told her about the boy's sunsuit, the lilacs, the boxwood hedge, the sun-warmed water in the wading pool. "The boy's blow-up toy had a really stupid name: Flub-a-dub."

I started to cry.

"It's okay, Helen." She held out a box of tissues. "What was the boy's name?"

"I don't know!"

The buzz of her desk telephone burst through the office. She answered it, listened intently.

"Superintendent Novak is asking for your letter." She slipped it into a folder. "I'll take it up to him. Just give me a quick minute."

I counted to ten after she left the office. Luck was with me. When I looked out the door, the hall was deserted.

I ran out of her office and down the stairs to the lobby almost before I thought about it. Oddly enough, the frigid air calmed me as I hurried back to the hotel and my car.

Let the police chase after me. There was something I had to do.

***

Macleod Trail, a major road that cuts through Calgary, wasn't busy. Last night, I'd studied the map from my rental car, memorizing the route to my destination. I headed there blindly, my mind on overdrive.

The Peace River Veterans Hospital turned out to be a red brick five-story building overlooking the foothills. The receptionist, a fiftyish woman with closely cropped auburn hair, sat perched behind the lone desk in the low-ceilinged lobby. Her name tag read Wanda Brown. Behind her, the hospital corridors branched out like the tentacles of an octopus.

I signed the guest register and asked to see Ronald.

"I don't recall meeting you before." Wanda gave me the evil eye and peered at my name in the registration book. "Are you a relative?"

"We're second cousins." A previously unknown daughter would only arouse suspicion, I decided. "I'm here in Calgary on business so I decided to drop by."

"I see," she said, though she plainly didn't.

"How *is* Ronald doing after his stroke?" I asked.

"Well, you can imagine how hard it is for Lieutenant Commander Pierce to have to rely on a walker. Especially after his thrilling life on the sea."

So, Ronald had promoted himself to an even loftier rank.

"I'll escort you upstairs. He's on the fifth floor. That's where our patients with, uh, special needs reside."

She set a sign saying "Back in 10" on her desk and hauled herself up from her chair. I followed her thickset form down the middle corridor to a set of elevators. What did she mean by "special needs?"

"So sad him losing his family like that," she said as the elevator arrived. "I suppose that explains things."

She was waiting for my reply.

"What? Oh, yes," I managed.

Stepping out of the elevator on the fifth floor, I was assailed by the sharp odor of cleaning fluid and whiffs of incontinence. Directly in front of us lay a small dining room where two orderlies in green cotton uniforms were clearing away the remains of the residents' breakfasts.

Wanda had a quick word with one of them. "Ronald's back in his room. He doesn't care for television. Thinks it's an American conspiracy," she confided.

Same bitter bias 23 years later, I thought.

She trudged down the dimly lit corridor. Halfway along, we passed a common room where several men in wheelchairs were parked in front of a TV set tuned to a game show. Some watched, others were lost in the fog of dementia.

At the end of the corridor, she threw open the door to a large ward. All the beds were empty except for the one closest to the door. In it lay a shriveled white-haired man, the flesh hanging loosely from his arms. I was about to tell Wanda that this man couldn't be Ronald when he turned his gaze on me. Those eyes, dark, implacable, had not changed.

"You," he said. "What are you doing here?"

"It's nice to see you, too, Ronald." I gave Wanda a pointed look. She shrugged and retreated partway down the hallway.

I shut the door to the ward and went closer to the bed.

Ronald folded his brown-spotted hands on top of his rumpled bedding. His fingernails had grown long. "What do you want?"

"We have unfinished business, you and I, Petty Officer Ronald Pierce." That got a reaction. "I paid a visit to 18th Avenue SW. The address where you, Mother and I lived."

"I have no idea what you're talking about." His mouth made a straight line. "I never wanted children. I always told your mother that raising you was a waste of time and money."

"Of course you did, even if it was *her* money."

My grandparents' gift from England had paid for my boarding school, but the money had run out by the time Mother died—or so he maintained.

A dark thought snaked through me. "What happened to Mother? Was it really an aneurysm? Or did you—did you do something to her?"

"Don't be ridiculous."

"Was she a burden to you after her money ran out? Don't lie to me. You hurt her, didn't you? That's why you became such a believer in cremation!"

"You, Madam, need to see a doctor."

He turned his head away from me to face the green curtain that separated his bed from the one next to him.

"Don't ignore me! Who is this boy?" I leaned over him and held the photograph in front of his face, forcing him to look at it.

His body went rigid. He rolled back to face me.

"How dare you!"

I recognized the burning rage in his eyes. His claw-like hand seized a fistful of my hair, dragging me down. I fought back, holding the photo out of his reach. It was mine, my answer to everything. He was not going to take it from me.

I felt a searing pain as his fingernails scraped down my cheek. He was astonishingly strong. I screamed in pain and fear.

The room exploded with light and noise. People were shouting. A warm body pressed against my side. The odor of male sweat and disinfectant filled my nostrils.

Suddenly I was free. I staggered, flailing my arms to keep my balance. And landed in the middle of the ward.

One of the orderlies from the dining room struggled to hold Ronald down. Ronald's whole body was writhing, his legs kicking.

"What did you do to him?" Wanda yelled. "I'm calling the police!"

"Do that! Call them right now. He attacked *me*!" Blood dripped from my cut cheek onto my suit collar.

"That's it, Ronnie," the orderly shouted. "You're going back in the locked ward."

"But it's her fault," Wanda cried. "He was OK before."

"For God's sake, don't just stand there, Wanda. Get the nurse! Get his meds!" The orderly dodged Ronald's fist.

The photo of the boy, torn almost in half, had fallen to the floor. I scooped it up. Shoved it into my pocket and fled.

I battled through a maelstrom of colors. Fractured images bombarded me: massive snow-covered mountains, a wooden garage all falling down, guns, dead ducks, a child's stroller…

Back in the safety of my rental car, a phone was ringing. Ten rings, then 20. My purse was vibrating.

The cell phone—I answered it.

"Helen, thank God!" Gordon said. "I'm at your hotel. Where the hell are you?"

"You're here? In Calgary?"

"Are you OK? You sound upset."

I gave him the address of the veterans' hospital.

Gordon arrived in a taxi 20 minutes later. I was in no condition to drive, so he took over. We headed to the nearest pharmacy where we bought a bandage for my cheek. On the way there, I told him what had happened with Ronald and the police.

"You have to go back and speak to that detective," Gordon said. "Tell her about Ronald."

"What if my mind is playing tricks on me?"

"You need to know the truth." He took my hand. "*We* need to know the truth, Helen, no matter what."

***

Detective Fox didn't berate me for running away earlier. This time she led the way to a large office with windows overlooking Calgary's cityscape. A tall, white-haired man in a dark suit was waiting for us at his desk, the file folder in front of him.

He rose as we walked in. His eyes were the same vivid blue as PC Novak's, the young constable who'd accosted me on 18th Avenue SW.

"I'm Superintendent Novak," he said. "Thanks for coming in." He motioned us over to a sofa and chairs by the windows.

Once we took our seats, I asked, "Is that my letter in the folder?"

He nodded. "We realize this is very difficult for you, Ms. Pierce."

"My memory comes in bits and pieces," I said.

"Take your time. Anything you can tell us would be helpful, anything at all."

I took a deep breath. "Ronald, my father, liked to go duck hunting. Plucking and cleaning the ducks made a mess in the house, so he'd leave them in the garage at the end of the garden. I'd sneak in after he'd gone to work. I'd spread their wings and will them back to life. I wanted them to fly again."

I felt a rush of fear. I saw steep gray cliffs, hanging glaciers, ice blue water…

"I remember the three of us driving in a blue car, Ronald's Austin, I think. We passed a mountain called Edith Cavell. Mother told me the Germans shot her in the war even though she was a nurse. That's how I learned that good people die—and that bad people win.

"We stopped at a lookout. The edge wasn't rock but smooth blonde sand, because we were beside a river. A pine tree, the size of a Christmas tree, had fallen next to the water. Ronald took out his camera and told me to go stand by the river. I didn't want to, because the current was strong and I couldn't swim.

"'Step back. Do as you're told,' he said.

"I was scared. I thought that maybe if I held onto the pine tree, I wouldn't fall in. He kept shouting, 'Step back, step back!' His eyebrows made a dark "V" as he stared at me through the lens. It made a dark circle, a void."

"He didn't hurt you," Detective Fox said after a minute. "Your mother stopped him."

"Yes, she must have."

Memory took me like the ice-blue waters of the river. "I remember my parents arguing. Ronald was shouting at Mother that he never wanted children. Mother was crying. She said Ronald shouldn't have taken the baby out in the stroller during the chinook. He felt cold on the way home. That's why he cried. Ronald shouldn't have hit him. She wanted to call the doctor, but Ronald wouldn't let her."

I could no longer hold back my tears. Gordon wrapped his arms around me. I pressed myself against him and cried.

"What happened to the boy?" Gordon said. "Helen has a right to know."

Superintendent Novak cleared his throat. "This case always stuck with me. It's why I set up our Cold Case Unit. And why I put Valerie, one of my best detectives, in charge of it.

"Fifteen years ago, in 1975, Mr. Doyle bought the property at 1102. When his contractors dug out the back garden, they found the remains of an old garage and under it, the skeleton of a little boy. The kid had been there a long time, probably since the late 1950s."

When I lived there…

"There were signs of trauma," Detective Fox said. "But we couldn't identify him."

"What about the property tax records?" Gordon asked. "I'm thinking like an accountant, I know, but wouldn't they tell you who owned the house?"

"The tax records proved to be a dead end," Fox said. "The old house at Number 1102 was a rental. The landlord had lost his records." She turned to me. "You are our first real lead."

Nobody spoke. I could hear the tick of the baseboard heating, human voices in the offices, phones ringing.

Carefully I placed the torn photo of the boy next to Novak's folder. "Would you read me the letter now?"

"Of course." Novak opened the folder, took out the aerogram and read:

> *"Dear Krystina,*
>
> *"Your father and I always taught you that a wife must obey her husband, but we were wrong. You have two beautiful children. You must think of them.*
>
> *"We have enough money to help you now. Please come home to us in England. We will send you the tickets.*
>
> *"Your loving Mother, Maria."*

None of us spoke.

"Mother couldn't face my grandparents after the boy died," I said at last. "She used their money to send me to boarding school. To protect me." I touched the bandage on my face. "Why can't I remember? Why can't I remember that I had a little brother?"

"It's traumatic amnesia." Detective Fox placed her warm hand on mine. "Many abused children experience it. You're not alone."

"Ronald needs to pay for what he did to Helen and her brother," Gordon said. "He's here in Calgary, living at the veterans' hospital."

That got Novak and Fox's interest.

"But he's too old now," I said. "He'll get away with it like he has all his life."

"No, believe me, he won't," Novak said. "His age won't save him from justice."

The setting sun streamed in through the windows of Novak's office. I could feel the prickle of grass under my feet, the warmth of the water in the boy's wading pool, the scent of lilacs everywhere. The boy was splashing me with water.

"I remember now," I said. "I remember the boy in the picture. He was my little brother and I loved him.

"His name was Michael."

The 13th Letter
M
The End

Meet the Mesdames and Messieurs of Mayhem

Catherine Astolfo is an award-winning writer of short stories and the author of seven novels and two novellas. Catherine won the Arthur Ellis Award for Best Crime Short Story in 2012 for "What Kelly Did" and again in 2018 for "The Outlier," included in the Mesdames of Mayhem Anthology, *13 Claws*.

Catherine's most recent book is *Auntie Beers*. With an historical twist and quite different from her other novels, this one is a collection of connected short stories. Published by Carrick Publishing, *Auntie Beers* is available everywhere.

Rosemary Aubert is the author of the acclaimed *Ellis Portal mystery series*. Her research for crime fiction includes a 25-year career as a professional in the Canadian criminal justice system. She also published romance novels, poetry collections, and a book of short stories.

Rosemary has lectured across Canada and the United States. She presented writing workshops for private organizations, and taught at the School of Continuing Studies at the University of Toronto and at Loyalist College. She is a two-time winner of the Arthur Ellis Award for crime fiction.

Visit Rosemary at: http://www.rosemaryaubert.com/

Canadian author **J.E. Barnard** writes and edits award-winning fiction. Her first *Falls Mystery* novel brought home the CWC Award of Excellence and her second *Maddie Hatter Adventure* was named Alberta Book of the Year. She's been a finalist for the UK Debut Dagger and the Prix Aurora for Canadian SFF. She lives in a vine-covered cottage, keeping cats and secrets.

Find out more about Jayne's published works and her editing practice at https://linktr.ee/je_barnard .

Puzzles, people, and nefarious minds have attracted **Jane Burfield** since childhood. She enjoys reading and writing mysteries to explore crime, and to find satisfying revenge on crooks who harm the innocent.

A lifelong resident of Toronto, Jane has witnessed increasing urban violence and disgruntlement. She raised three wonderful daughters to treat all people with kindness and to be curious, but most of all to value justice.

After careers in journalism, teaching and finance, Jane used her experiences to begin writing crime. In 2001, she won the Boney Pete Award for her first short story, Slow Death and Taxes. Since then, she has been a finalist for the Arthur Ellis Short Story Award, and has had stories published in many anthologies. Crime is sweet. Justice is sweeter.

M.H. (Madeleine) Callway worked in science, business, and IT before returning to her childhood love of writing. She met Queen Elizabeth, toured working mines and helped solve a real-life murder case!

Her thriller, *Windigo Fire*, was a finalist for the CWC Best First Novel Award. She has more than 20 published works of short fiction, many of which won or were shortlisted for major awards, including the Crime Writers of Canada and the Derringer. Her two books of collected short stories are *Glow Grass and Other Tales* and *Snake Oil and Other Tales* (Carrick Publishing)

In 2013, Madeleine and Donna Carrick co-founded the Mesdames and Messieurs of Mayhem, now a national collective of 25 leading Canadian crime writers and artists.

https://mhcallway.com

www.mesdamesofmayhem.com

Called the "Queen of Comedy" by the *Toronto Sun*, **Melodie Campbell** was also named the "Canadian Literary heir to Donald Westlake" by *Ellery Queen Mystery Magazine.* Winner of ten awards, including the Derringer (US) and the Crime Writers of Canada Award of Excellence, she has multiple bestsellers and was featured in *USA Today.*

Her publications include over one hundred comedy credits, eighteen novels and sixty short stories, but she's best known for *The Goddaughter* mob caper series. *The Merry Widow Murders* has just been released by Cormorant Books. "The high society flair of *Death on the Nile* meets a 1920s ocean liner in this sensational mystery from Melodie Campbell." ~*Open Book*

Donna Carrick is a thriller author, host of the *Dead to Writes* podcast, an indie publisher (Carrick Publishing,) former treasurer of Crime Writers of Canada, and a longtime member of Sisters in Crime. Her novella *The Noon God* and novels *The First Excellence* and *Gold And Fishes* have all, at various times, topped Amazon's Bestselling Thriller charts. Her story "Watermelon Weekend" (*Thirteen*) was a finalist for the Crime Writers of Canada 2014 Best Short Story Award.

Visit Donna at donnacarrick.com and carrickpublishing.com.

Find *Dead To Writes* at YouTube or subscribe to *Dead to Writes* wherever you get your podcasts.

Originally from South Africa, **Lisa de Nikolits** is the award-winning author of eleven published novels (Inanna Publications). She has appeared on recommended reading lists for *Chatelaine, Canadian Living, Hello!, Quill & Quire,* and the *CBC. The Occult Persuasion and The Anarchist's Solution* was longlisted for a Sunburst Award for Excellence in Canadian Literature of The Fantastic and *The Rage Room* was a finalist in the International Book Awards, 2021.

No Fury Like That was published in Italian in 2019 by Edizione Le Assassine under the title *Una furia dell'altro mondo.* Her short fiction and poetry have been published in international anthologies and journals, including the Crime Writers of Canada's 40th Anniversary anthology (2022).

You can find her on Facebook and Instagram or at lisawriter.com.

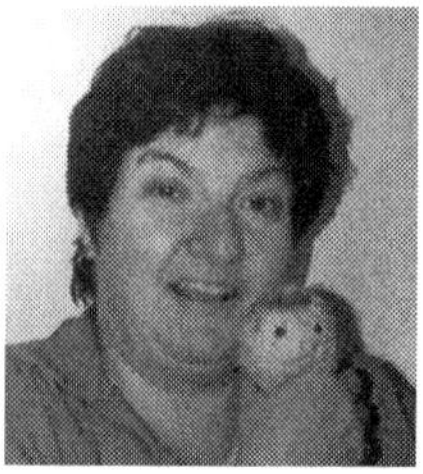

Cheryl Freedman is a long-time freelance editor who edits anything she finds interesting, including crime fiction, academic papers, Jewish mysticism books and articles, memoirs, and more. She was the executive director of Crime Writers of Canada for 10 years as well as the sometime-chair of the Bloody Words Mystery Conference and its successor, the Bony Blithe Light Mystery Award.

With her interest in ferrets, fairy tales, and folklore, she is currently writing a fairy tale mystery featuring a half-ogre/half-human PI and a bipedal talking, fedora-wearing ferret.

Therese Greenwood's short crime fiction has appeared across North America. She won the Spur Award from the Western Writers of America for best short story.

She is a three-time finalist for the Crime Writers of Canada's best short story prize. Her memoir of the Fort McMurray wildfire, *What You Take With You: Wildfire, Family and the Road Home*, was a Finalist for an Alberta Book Publishing Award.

Blair Keetch is a mystery writer based in Toronto.

His story "A Contrapuntal Duet" was selected for the emerging new mystery writer for *In the Key of Thirteen*, a crime anthology by the Mesdames and Messieurs of Mayhem.

Other stories include "Deadly Cargo" in *Heartbreaks & Half-Truths*, "Sleep, Perchance to Die" in *A Grave Diagnosis* (Carrick Publishing,) and "Killings4Sale" in *Asinine Assassins*. His story "Sex, Lies and Snowmobiles" is part of the 40th Anniversary Crime Writers of Canada anthology *Cold Canadian Crime*. "To Catch a Kumiho" is included in the anthology *In the Spirit of 13* and was nominated as 2022 Best Short Crime story for the CWC Awards of Excellence.

Stories can be found at www.darkstormybc.com and www.ShotgunHoney.

Keep in touch @ BlairKeetch.com.

Sylvia Maultash Warsh is the author of the Dr. Rebecca Temple novels, one of which won an Edgar. The other two were nominated for major awards. Her historical novel, *The Queen of Unforgetting*, was chosen by Project Bookmark Canada for a plaque installation on their literary map.

She has had a novella as well as many short stories published, six of which have been shortlisted for Derringers and Crime Writers of Canada awards. Her new novel, *The Orphan*, was published in spring, 2024. She teaches writing to seniors.

Rosemary McCracken is the author of the *Pat Tierney Mystery Series*, and a Derringer Award, Debut Dagger and Unhanged Arthur finalist. Her short stories have appeared in numerous collections and magazines. Rosemary lives and writes in Toronto.

Cat Mills is an award-winning documentary filmmaker based in Toronto. She has worked with *CBC*, *TVO* and *Al Jazeera* and her films have been screened at festivals around the world. Cat's writing debut appeared in *In The Spirit of 13* by the Mesdames and Messieurs of Mayhem. She's excited to join for another anthology.

Lynne Murphy has been a member of the Mesdames of Mayhem from the beginning. She is the author of a number of short stories—many of those appear in her book, *Potluck and Other Stories.* She lives in Toronto where she is also a member of Sisters in Crime and Crime Writers of Canada.

Ed Piwowarczyk is a retired journalist, who has worked for the *National Post*, the *Toronto Sun* and the *Sault Star*. He is currently a freelance fiction editor. A lifelong fan of crime fiction, Ed's short stories have been published in Mesdames of Mayhem and Toronto Sisters in Crime anthologies.

Rosalind Place has been writing since childhood; her first work was a 5-page book carefully printed on colored paper in grade school. After growing up, she first became a poet and went on to publish several literary stories in magazines. Her first foray into the mystery genre appeared in our third anthology and her work has appeared in all our subsequent anthologies. She ventured into the horror genre with a chilling tale accepted for publication in the upcoming collection "Dastardly Damsels."

Rosalind recently completed her first book, *White Cougar Farm*, a story of magic and discovery set in rural Ontario in the 1960s.

Lorna Poplak is a Toronto-based writer, editor, and researcher with a fascination for the dark side of history. She is a member of Crime Writers of Canada and Sisters in Crime.

Her two nonfiction books, both published by Dundurn Press, are *Drop Dead: A Horrible History of Hanging in Canada* (2017) and *The Don: The Story of Toronto's Infamous Jail* (2021). In 2022, *The Don* was shortlisted for both the Crime Writers of Canada Excellence Award and the Heritage Toronto Book Award. Lorna is currently working on a nonfiction book about great (and not so great!) prison escapes, to be published by Dundurn in 2025.

For more information, please visit: lornapoplak.com.

Madona Skaff is the author of the *Naya Investigates* series, about a woman disabled by multiple sclerosis, who turns sleuth to solve crimes. She's also written a stand-alone science fiction thriller called *Shifting Trust.* Most recently, she has an article in *Women Take the Conn: a collection of essays about the women of Star Trek*, written by women authors.

She has several mystery and science fiction short stories published. The story in this anthology, *The 13th Letter*, is the third installment of the continuing adventures of ex-conman Lennie, who solves murders—with the help of the victim.

Caro Soles' novels include mysteries, erotica, gay lit, the occasional bit of dark fantasy, and science fiction.

She received the Derrick Murdoch Award from the Crime Writers of Canada, and her work has been shortlisted for the Lambda Literary Award, the Aurora Award, and the Stoker Award.

After 25 years of teaching writing at George Brown College, Caro is now staying home to write about Merculians.

Kevin Thornton lives in Northern Canada, where the temperature often gets down below -40. Prior to that, he was a military contractor in Afghanistan, where the winters were only -20, but the summers reached +50. (These are SI units. In American, that translates to bloody cold and damn hot.)

He has been a newspaper columnist, a soldier and a forklift driver. On occasion he has been shortlisted for awards, seldom winning. He is a devoted cricket follower and he has been a member of many varied writing organizations. Over the years he quit most of them, but still retains his membership in the Keyswriters group, founded by Ronald Knox and G.K. Chesterton.

He writes short stories reasonably successfully. He has a perfectly lovely wife, two ambivalent sons, and a cross German Shepherd. He is mostly content.

Melissa Yi is an emergency physician and writer whose heroine, resident Dr. Hope Sze, leaps from fixing ingrown toenails to solving full-blown murders. Hope's life takes a supernatural turn as she battles the force of Cthulhu in the emergency room in Killing Me Sloth-LY. (https://www.kickstarter.com/projects/melissayi/weird).

Melissa won the 2023 Derringer Award for the best short mystery in the English language and the Prix Aurora Award for the best speculative poem in Canada. She also loves dogs, yummy food, and the sound of frogs at night.

Since Melissa wastes too much time on social media, you can find her on most platforms through: https://linktr.ee/melissayi. Win a free gift with a newsletter subscription at http://www.melissayuaninnes.com.

Made in the USA
Middletown, DE
14 October 2024

62607369R00239